P9-DNV-654

SECRET JUSTICE

ALSO BY JAMES W. HUSTON

Balance of Power

The Price of Power

Flash Point

Fallout

The Shadows of Power

JAMES W. HUSTON

SECRET JUSTICE

WILLIAM MORROW | *AN IMPRINT OF* HARPERCOLLINS*PUBLISHERS*

SECRET JUSTICE. Copyright © 2003 by James W. Huston.
All rights reserved. Printed in the United States of America.
No part of this book may be used or reproduced in any manner
whatsoever without written permission except in the case of brief
quotations embodied in critical articles and reviews.
For information address HarperCollins Publishers Inc.,
10 East 53rd Street, New York, NY 10022.

HarperCollins books may be purchased for educational,
business, or sales promotional use. For information please write:
Special Markets Department, HarperCollins Publishers Inc.,
10 East 53rd Street, New York, NY 10022.

FIRST EDITION

Printed on acid-free paper

Library of Congress Cataloging-in-Publication Data has been applied for.

ISBN 0-06-000837-7

03 04 05 06 07 JTC/QW 10 9 8 7 6 5 4 3 2 1

For Stephanie

SECRET JUSTICE

Pierre Lahoud stood and smiled. "At last, you have arrived," he said to Wahamed Duar, perhaps the most hated man in the world. They embraced in a cold, distrusting, automatic manner. They crossed warily to the single table sitting in the middle of the candlelit room. Duar took the far side of the table, the side facing the single door. He sat slowly, scrutinizing everyone. His men were dispersed throughout the room, their weapons at their sides.

Acacia controlled his expression of shocked disbelief. Where had Duar been? All the buildings had been searched carefully. They had been waiting for him in this abandoned building in the remote desert of Sudan for two hours—how could ten men show up out of nowhere?

He stood and moved slowly toward the exit. He had to transmit the signal to the American Special Forces circling overhead, waiting for this meeting, waiting to catch Duar.

Duar saw him. "*No one* leaves this room," he said in Arabic with unshakable authority. His light eyes were fixed on Acacia.

"I have to relieve myself," Acacia protested with a faint smile as sweat formed under his arms.

"I don't care if you piss on your feet. No one leaves this room."

Acacia nodded and shrugged as if it didn't matter, but he had to activate his pen. It would put everything else in motion. He took it out of his pocket and opened a small notebook as if preparing to take notes.

"No notes," Duar said, still looking at him, staring into his eyes.

Acacia looked at Lahoud, his boss, who nodded.

Acacia glanced up. His pen had to acquire GPS satellites to get a fix and transmit that fix in a burst transmission. Latitude and longitude. It was all they needed. The existence of the signal would tell them the meeting was under way, and the numbers in the signal would tell them where. But he had to get outside. The roof of the building had been destroyed in whatever action had caused this crossroads to be abandoned, but the thick stucco walls were high, perhaps three stories, with bare crossbeams. There was some chance he could acquire two satellites through the destroyed roof; he had no choice. He pressed the end of his ballpoint pen and moved it slowly to his pocket.

Lahoud's six other men sat on the floor in random places, much like Duar's, with their weapons next to them. Their faces were equally full of distrust. Others stood guard outside the building.

Acacia examined Duar, a man neither he nor Lahoud had ever met but knew by reputation. He was nearly six feet tall, thin, and good-looking. He was a native of Sudan and had worked with Usama bin Laden when he was based in Sudan. When bin Laden had been asked to leave by the government of Sudan, Duar had stayed behind to start his own organization to accomplish the same objectives independently. He had been shockingly successful in his grisly business. He was now the most sought-after terrorist in the world. The Americans wanted him badly, obsessively. The bombing of the American embassy in Cairo had been the final straw. It had caused the deaths of forty-six Americans including the ambassador. Fifty-five Egyptians had also been killed outside the embassy compound by the enormous blast. It had been seen for what it was—a simultaneous attack on America and Egypt's secular government.

Duar had finally agreed to the meeting with Lahoud, one of the world's leading arms merchants, because Lahoud could deliver what Duar wanted most—weapons grade plutonium. Lahoud claimed to have enough to make a nuclear weapon. Duar was buying. Today Lahoud had only a microscopic amount, just enough to prove he could bring more.

The instant Acacia triggered his pen it searched for the L band GPS transmissions from the twenty-four satellites. Two were high enough to be useful deep inside the dim room. The pen quickly calculated its position and fired its encrypted burst transmission. He hoped to God the transmission went out and was heard, but he knew if the Americans received his signal all hell would break loose.

High over Sudan, Lieutenant Kent Rathman, Rat as he was known, waited with the rest of his SAS team, a Special Operations group of the CIA, as they orbited in one of the Air Force C-17s. He stomped his feet on the hard deck against the cold and looked at his watch again. He paced back and forth in the belly of the noisy jet. The other team members watched him. They were accustomed to his boundless energy and intensity.

Rat leaned on one of the Toyota Land Cruisers painted as Sudanese Army vehicles. The Toyotas would be the first out the door if Rat's team was the lucky one, the closest team to the agent on the ground known to them only by his code name Acacia, a name selected by the CIA's random word generation software that had come to rest in the tree section.

The four C-17s were strategically placed. Each carried an American Special Forces team in a quadrant of Sudan. Each was ready, eager, to jump out of the large cargo planes as soon as the meeting was located. The meeting was expected to last only thirty minutes. No more. They knew they wouldn't have time to fly across the country to get to the meeting. They had to hope one of the teams was on top of the location when the signal was received.

They had waited the night before but never received the signal. This night they had launched again. Their hope had waned as they orbited past eleven, then past midnight. Rat squinted in frustration at Groomer in the low light. He didn't need to say anything. Groomer had worked with Rat for three years, first in Dev Group, the Navy's secret counterterrorism team, then in the SAS. In the Navy, Groomer was a lieutenant, junior grade, and in Rat's SAS team he was the executive officer, or number two. He knew exactly what Rat was thinking: if one of the other teams gets to go it will be wrong, unfair, and unjust. They'd prepared for this mission three times before. They had orbited all night twice before, all for nothing, because Duar was always suspicious and had spooked. But this time, they thought it would go. He was believed to have picked a location so remote that he would feel secure, confident that no one would sneak up on him unexpectedly, and certainly not in thirty minutes.

Groomer walked over to Rat. Rat looked at him quickly to see if he had new information or data that Rat could throw into the hopper that was turning furiously in his brain. He didn't, he just wanted to chat. "What do you think? We gonna go?"

"We deserve this."

" 'Cause it was your idea?"

"No." Rat smiled. "Because it's *us*. We always deserve to go."

Groomer smiled back and fingered the camouflage paint on the Land Cruiser. "Hell, Rat, if it were me, I'd just drop a bomb on these assholes and vaporize them. Why do we have to go in?"

"You heard Jacobs. They want Duar *alive*. Any cost. Otherwise you're right. One airplane off a carrier, one JDAM, these guys are gone. They think Duar will open the entire worldwide operation for them. They just need the right can opener. We're it."

Groomer shook his head. "I'd just vaporize them."

It was the Global Hawk that received the weak transmission, the pilotless drone flying sixty-five thousand feet above Sudan. The signal from Acacia's pen was fainter than expected but the reserved frequency was unmistakable. The drone instantly amplified the signal and relayed it to a hundred waiting receivers. The RIVET JOINT RC-135 received it as soon as the Global Hawk sent it off. The officer monitoring the frequency quickly relayed it to all the Special Operations teams, then examined the chart superimposed on the screen in front of him. The location was automatically marked in southwest Sudan, one of the remotest parts of the country. He sat back and waited.

"Bingo," Rat said as he stared at the small color screen on his Rugged Personal Digital Assistant, his RPDA-88. It was highly modified and included a GPS receiver and encrypted e-mail capability. "Here we go," he yelled. Groomer stood by the Land Cruiser to look over Rat's shoulder at the screen. Rat furiously manipulated the buttons on the side of the screen to call up the map of Sudan with Acacia's location automatically marked as a waypoint. "We're it," Rat exclaimed, seeing the fix in his sector.

The pilots knew it at the same instant. He felt the large C-17 bank toward the destination.

"Everybody up!" Rat yelled, motioning with his hands.

Rat pictured the jump in his mind. The moon would be behind them, but it was a waxing crescent and would be of only marginal help without their night-vision devices.

Rat looked at the Air Force sergeant, the jumpmaster, who was listening carefully on his intercom. He held up two hands. Ten minutes.

Rat nodded. Everyone on his team had seen the signal. He didn't have to repeat it. Many, like Rat and Groomer, were actually Navy SEALs operating on temporary assignment with the CIA.

His men checked their parachutes and weapons again and tightened their helmets. Rat had been one of the few in the CIA who had been allowed to see the information provided by Acacia. It was stunning. The man's infiltration of Pierre Lahoud's illegal arms sales organization had been bold and spectacularly successful. What Lahoud didn't know was that Acacia, his new finance man, was with the Jordanian GID, the General Intelligence Department, and was working with the CIA. Rat had worked with him before. The reason Acacia had gone to such trouble to work with Lahoud was to be there when Lahoud met with Duar. His only job was to send his single electronic signal when the two were in the same room. The American Special Forces knew he was there, and what he looked like. He was one of the two people the Special Forces were to bring out alive.

Rat opened the file box he had brought aboard the plane. He fingered the files until he found the one that corresponded to Acacia's location. It had been identified as one of the twenty or so possible meeting locations in his area. Rat tore through the intelligence information again. He had read through it before several times, but now he tried to memorize everything in it, the satellite photos, the infrared images, and the messages. He returned the file and called up the photographs of Duar, Lahoud, and Acacia on his RPDA. He studied Duar's face. There was only one known photo of Duar. It was a grainy blowup of a distant photo. He had dark long hair, a wispy beard, and light eyes.

Rat tried to imagine him without a beard, with a buzz haircut, anything that would make him more difficult to identify. Lahoud was easy; a big square face on a short square body.

The crew chief leaned down toward Rat. "Five minutes!" he yelled, holding up five fingers.

Rat nodded. "Radio check," he said on his microphone, attached to his helmet.

The eleven others gave him a thumbs-up.

Rat stood up, reattached his RPDA to his lanyard and stuck it into a pocket. He walked back to the ramp that was now almost completely down. The C-17 had descended to twenty-five thousand feet but the air was still bracingly cold. The jumpmaster pressed a button and the three pallets bearing the Land Cruisers inched toward the ramp.

They reached the drop point, got a green light, and the three Toyotas flew out the back of the C-17 into the blackness. Rat went to the back of the ramp, lowered his goggles, turned on his oxygen, and dived into the night.

Rat dropped toward the African desert and watched the illuminated altimeter on his wrist. He controlled the instinct to gasp for air from the shock of the coldness. He slowed his descent rate with his arms and pulled the ripcord at exactly ten thousand feet. The rectangular-shaped para-glider canopy opened over his head with a vicious jerk. He stabilized his descent and pulled the handles to turn toward his destination. He pulled his RPDA out of his chest pocket to check his position with the GPS imbedded in the RPDA. He verified his heading and distance to their destination and made a course correction. He looked ahead; he could see the roads and the intersection where they were to land ten miles away. Those behind him were also above him. All their para-gliders were dark green and invisible in the night. Rat's alone had a white arrow on the top of it pointing forward, invisible from below, but easy to see in the faint moonlight from above.

They glided silently, dropping steadily. The sand was a pale gray below them in the half moon. He looked down as the first Toyota slammed into the sand. He couldn't tell if it had landed upright. Rat checked his GPS again, then pulled out a ten-powered night rifle scope to see if he could find the buildings. He found them instantly, but saw more than he had expected. He could see at least four, maybe five, men walking between the buildings. His team had twelve. The sole support he could hope to get was from a Spooky gunship that was on its way. It would orbit ten miles away to be called in only in an emergency. To call the Spooky would be an admission of failure.

He checked the nightscope again and saw men standing guard around the biggest building. Rat turned down toward the south to approach the landing area into the wind that was from the northeast, slightly behind him into his right. The others followed. He placed the scope back in his pocket as well as his RPDA. He made sure everything was secure. He tugged on the strap of his H&K MP5N submachine gun to make sure it was attached tightly to his chest and prepared to hit the ground. He turned sharply into the wind, guiding his para-glider carefully.

He dropped far enough below the rise that even the top of his para-glider would be invisible to the small intersection where Duar sat just over the ridge. He touched down in the sand and ran quickly to arrest his ground speed. His feet slogged through the soft sand and he tumbled over. As the para-glider began to drag him across the sand, he quickly released one of the Koch fittings dumping the air out of the glider. He jumped up, released the other Koch fitting on his shoulder harness, and began rolling up the para-glider. He wrapped it into a tight ball and began digging in the sand. He placed the para-glider in the hole and poured sand on top of it. The others landed behind him, silent except for an occasional grunt or curse.

They buried their para-gliders and quickly made their way to Rat, who was kneeling in the sand. Groomer and three others hurried to the Land Cruisers and checked for damage. They were perfectly intact. They unstrapped the vehicles from their pallets, jumped in, and started the engines. The Toyotas responded instantly. Groomer and the others drove them off the pallets, across the loose sand, and onto the road. Groomer's Toyota was in front with the engine idling and the lights off. The markings of the Sudanese Army were clearly visible in the moonlight.

Rat spoke quietly to his men. "Everybody okay?" as they all climbed out of their harnesses and adjusted their Sudanese Army desert camouflage uniforms.

They all nodded as they removed their helmets and pulled desert brown headscarves over their heads. They put goggles over their eyes, giving them a Rat Patrol look that disguised light skin, red hair, or blue eyes. Rat got right to the point. "Three guard posts, one on each of the roads, and a third closer in, next to the buildings. Banger, you're going to have to get up on top when we're stopped and hit the guard by the building. I can't tell how far apart they are, but it's probably close to five hundred yards. You'll have to be quick about it. There are two of them. You up for that?"

Banger nodded. "I'll have to get the window out."

"Get it now," Rat said. To the others, "You all know the plan. Any questions?" There weren't any. "Let's go."

Banger hurried to the backseat of one of the Land Cruisers, removed the rear window, and tossed it into the sand.

The rest of Rat's SAS team loaded quickly into their assigned seats. Groomer turned on his lights and accelerated down the road. The three Land Cruisers drove at a leisurely pace, mimicking the pace of a Sudanese Army patrol with no particular concerns. They crested the hill and could clearly see the intersection and the buildings. Rat scanned the area quickly looking for any changes. The guards were right where he expected them to be. They were clearly alarmed to see three approaching vehicles. One of the guards reached for the large binoculars on his chest. *Good,* Rat thought. *Use those big lenses to read the Sudanese Army markings.*

The guard did. He pulled the binoculars over his head and handed them to the man next to him. Rat looked past them and saw the two men outside the main building, and the two men guarding the road on the other side of the cluster of buildings looking north for traffic. They too were now aware of the approaching vehicles.

Groomer drove on, now less than a half-mile from the guards.

Rat wanted to be able to get to the main building where the meeting was occurring without alerting those inside. "Up you go," he said to Banger. "Take out the other road guards before you hit the two by the building."

"Give it a try, sir. They're out there a bit. Can I hit them while we're still moving?"

"If you get a good shot. Use your sound suppressor."

Banger reached through the missing rear window, grabbed the back of the large roof rack, and pulled himself up onto the roof of the Land Cruiser. The other SAS team member handed him his M-25, a sniper rifle designed specially for the American Special Forces. He lay on top of the vehicle on a pad that had been lashed to the roof. He looked through his huge nightscope at the first group of guards to see if they were alerted and ready to do something about the approaching Toyotas. Their body language told him they were annoyed, confused, and not quite sure what to do about the Sudanese Army. Suddenly, the first guard, the one who had been wearing the large binoculars, said something to the second guard, who quickly nodded and broke into a jog toward the main building a hundred yards away.

"Shit," Rat said. He had wanted to preserve radio silence as long as he could. He transmitted quickly to Banger—but the entire team could hear—"*Don't let him report.*"

Directly over his head Banger had already formed the same conclusion and decided that the guards by the main building were going to have to go first. His sound-suppressed rifle coughed and the jogging guard pitched forward in the sand. The guards leaning against the wall of the main building laughed, thinking he had tripped. When he didn't move or get up, they were confused. They had heard nothing. They pushed away from the wall and began walking toward the guard lying face down in the sand.

Banger fired again and one of them went down in a heap. The other now realized what was happening and turned to warn those in the main building. Too late. Banger's third shot reached him before he could cry out. The bullet slammed into his back then expanded as it tore through his heart.

The guard with the binoculars was completely unaware of the bullets flying over his head. He was standing up tall, waiting for the Sudanese Army patrol to stop. He had prepared himself for such a moment, but hadn't expected it to happen. He put out his hand to stop the vehicles as Groomer did what he was told, stopping a good ten paces from the guard, with his bright lights still on. He wanted the guard to come to him.

Banger's rifle jerked again, and one of the guards on the other side of the compound spun around and fell to the sand. As his partner bent over to determine what had happened, Banger fired again. The bullet hit him in the side, knocking him away from the first guard and tearing him open. He fell to the ground in agony, unable to speak.

The guard with the binoculars approached the Land Cruiser. Rat wasn't going to give him a chance to guess what was happening. Rat threw open his door and jumped out. He could see that the man was taken aback by the major's insignia Rat was wearing on his Sudanese uniform. Rat took advantage of the surprise and yelled at him in his unaccented Arabic, "What is the meaning of this? Who the hell are you? What authority do you have to stop the Army? And why do you have an automatic weapon that you dare to show to the Army?"

The guard didn't know what to say. Rat lowered his MP5N with sound suppressor and fired a three-round burst into the guard's chest. He fell to the ground, killed instantly.

Rat looked around quickly. They were within a hundred yards of the main building and still had a chance of approaching without being discovered. He gave the "hold" sign and Groomer and Robby, another SEAL, put the Land Cruisers in park and climbed out. Rat wanted them to leave the engines running—it would now be more likely that someone would notice the new silence than a distant engine.

Banger rolled off the top of the Land Cruiser as the others poured out. Rat began a steady jog toward the main building as the others spread out and followed him. Rat had given clear instructions—two men were to be taken alive at any cost: Acacia and Wahamed Duar. If they could capture others, like Lahoud, fine. But those two had to come out alive.

Rat reached the outside wall of the main building. The others ran to cover the exits and the other buildings. Groomer stood by the door into the main building. Rat looked at the wall to determine its thickness. Robby knew what he wanted. He too had worked with Rat in Dev Group and was a communications and electronics specialist. He reached into his backpack and handed Rat a device slightly bigger than his hand. Rat nodded and placed the Ultra Wide Band Through-Wall Radar Transceiver against the wall. He activated it and waited as the electronic waves coursed their way through the wall and the room behind it and returned, generating a picture of the room and everything in it, including people. Almost every man in the room was holding a weapon, but in a nonthreatening position. Most had them at their sides, stocks resting on the concrete floor.

The glint patch in Acacia's pen identified him. Rat pointed at the shiny spot, which Groomer acknowledged. It was Groomer's job to get Acacia out unscathed. Rat studied how the people were sitting and standing. He knew everyone would be facing and deferring to Duar.

Rat motioned for the three squad leaders and watched the images for a few more seconds with them. They all knew where Acacia was in the room, and they knew to avoid the two at the table. Duar had to be one of the men sitting at the table, and the other almost certainly was Lahoud. Rat turned off the device and handed it back to Robby.

Rat spoke softly into his microphone. "Ten seconds. Groomer's second in."

The CIA team ensured their weapons were ready. Most carried H&K MP5Ns like Rat, a small submachine gun that weighed only six and a half pounds. Favored by the SEALs, they were reliable and accurate, and their 9-mm round was subsonic—they could use silencers. But this time Rat's team was going in without silencers. Noise was a weapon against those who weren't ready for it.

Rat raised his hand. The others lined up behind him. He lifted the lever to the door and walked in slowly with his submachine gun on his hip and began speaking loudly in Arabic. "I am Major Wassoud of the Sudanese Army. Who is in charge here? Who told those men to stop our Army patrol?" Rat's heart was pounding as he looked around the room. He immediately recognized Duar.

Rat's Sudanese desert camouflage uniform was perfect. He wore the shoulder badge of an officer of the southern security detail. The two men at the table looked at him in fury. Duar immediately suspected something. But Rat's boldness gave him just enough time to get ten SAS team members into the room. They picked their targets quickly and pointed their weapons directly at them. The men in the room with Duar and Lahoud were reluctant to reach for their own weapons. Rat paused, then pointed his weapon at Duar and yelled in Arabic, "American Special Forces! Lay down your weapons!"

Three of the men behind Duar quickly raised their AK-47s toward Rat and were immediately gunned down. The room erupted in pandemonium. Duar's men tried to stand up and bring their automatic weapons to bear on the intruders. Several began shooting but were hit by American fire before they could even get their assault rifles to their shoulders. The sound of automatic weapons fire was deafening as muzzle flashes illuminated every corner of the room. The Americans trained for just such an event every day. Duar's and Lahoud's men were up trying to aim, looking for cover, falling to the floor to fire, and falling to the floor dead; blood was flying, bullets chipped the floor and walls, and men screamed in fear and agony.

Groomer ran to Acacia and pulled him away from the wall. Lahoud saw the look in Acacia's eye. He knew he had been betrayed. He stood and pulled a handgun out of the folds of his robe to shoot Acacia. Groomer fired quickly and the short square man dropped in a heap.

Duar bolted toward the back of the room with two of his men covering his move. Rat saw him go through the door, but knew it led outside through a small hallway. Two of his men were waiting at the other end of that hallway. "Banger, coming your way."

"Roger."

Suddenly bullets zipped by Rat's head as he moved left. The American next to him was hit twice in the face and spun to the floor, dead. Rat turned to the assailant, furious. He raised his weapon to kill the man who had just shot the American. The man threw down his AK-47 and held up his hands. He had a slight wound on his shoulder, but was otherwise fine. As Rat hesitated another man fired at him. Rat turned slightly and blew open his belly. Bullets flew wildly into the wall and out the top of the building as the man fell to the floor still clutching the trigger of his weapon.

Rat glanced at the downed American. *"Damn it!"* he yelled. The firing died down, the clicky sounds of the AKs vanished, replaced by the deeper chop of the American weapons. The fight was over in less than a minute. Some men lay dead and others writhed on the floor, dying. The one he had spared sat in the corner with his superficial wounds.

Three of the Americans rushed around the room disarming everyone and ensuring that there was no additional threat.

"Everyone okay?" Rat asked.

The others responded by number, through twelve, with number nine silent.

"Somebody get over here and keep an eye on this son of a bitch. He shot Nubs in the face then threw his gun down. Banger, you get Duar? He charged out the back of the room."

"Didn't come out this way, sir, " Banger replied.

Rat frowned and looked at Groomer, who had put Acacia on the floor near the door. Groomer grabbed one of the other members of the team. "Stay with him. Nobody touches him at all."

He nodded.

Groomer followed Rat toward the door. Rat approached cautiously, confused by where Duar could have gone. He kept his weapon trained in front of him. Groomer was right behind him and to his left. "What we got here, Groomer? Where'd he go?"

"Must be between us and the door, right?"

"Must be a soft wall here somewhere."

"Or floor." Rat stopped. "I don't like this. They can hear us. Might shoot through a wall. Robby!"

Robby ran to where they were.

"Give me the Ultra Wide Band."

He took the device out of his backpack and Rat held it to the walls, then the floor. There was some ambiguity about what was behind them, some space, or odd construction, but no people. No stairways, no ladders, no obvious escapes. "What the hell," he muttered to no one in particular. He turned the device off and handed it back to Robby. "I think I'll ask that mother who shot Nubs where he is."

Groomer stopped and started backing out of the hallway. "And what if he doesn't want to tell us?"

"Post somebody here by the hallway entrance in case he or someone else comes back. If he left in a tunnel, he may have more men there."

"Will do," Groomer replied.

Rat reentered the main hall with its stucco walls and exposed beams. It was a well-constructed building. Rat wondered what it had been, and why it was abandoned. He looked at the dead men on the floor. He was completely unmoved. He had no sympathy for terrorists. They were subhuman to him. The bodies lay all over, bright red blood pooling around each of their bodies and going dark when exposed to the air for a few seconds. Each man had fallen in his own haphazard way. Several still had open-eyed surprised looks on their faces. The Americans stepped around them, making sure they were dead. Robby, one of the two black team members, was videotaping the entire scene with a miniature digital video camera. His radioman's rating only scratched the surface of his vast capabilities—he was a technological wizard.

Rat saw Robby videotaping. "You call in the helos?"

Robby nodded. "Fifteen minutes."

Rat checked his watch and considered whether he had time. "Toad, take six men and check every inch within a hundred yards of this build- ing. That asshole has an escape tunnel or some way out of here. Find out where he came out. If you find anything, any sign of life, let me know."

Toad nodded, grabbed five men, and hurried outside.

"All right, where's that live one?" Rat asked, stepping over a dead terrorist. "And where's Acacia?" He came upon Nubs. "*Damn* it," he said, stooping to examine his wounds. He pulled the desert scarf up. Nubs's face was ruined. The two AK-47 bullets had entered just above the lower jaw on the left side of his face. The exit wounds in the back of his head were massive. Death had been instantaneous. "I'm going to rip somebody's head off," Rat said, marching to the only living terror- ist in the room. He fought the building fury he felt, the white anger that occasionally got him in trouble.

Acacia stood and followed Rat to the corner.

Rat stared at the man on the floor. He waited for the man to look up at him.

Rat glanced at the wooden table strewn with papers. "Somebody get all these papers. We'll let intel take a look at those out on the ship." He turned to Acacia and spoke in Arabic. "You okay?"

Acacia looked him in the eyes. "Speak English. I don't want him—"

he said, indicating the surviving terrorist, "—to understand." He went on in English. "What are you going to do with him?"

"I came to get Duar. You know where he is?"

"No."

"He was here, wasn't he?"

Acacia flared angrily. "I wouldn't have sent the signal if he wasn't. I am not *stupid*."

"Then where is he now?"

"I don't know." He looked around the room at the dead men. "If he is not dead, *you* must have let him escape. But he cannot have gone far."

Rat regarded the prisoner. "I'm not leaving without Duar, even if we have to burn this building down. I think I'll ask this one a few questions."

"And after you ask him questions?"

"I'll take him out to the ship with us so the pros can interrogate him. Robby, find me a bucket of liquid. Water, anything, coffee, goat's milk, whatever. And two good-sized cups. Must be a kitchen around somewhere."

"You gonna water-board this guy, sir?" Robby asked, his eyes getting bigger.

"If he makes me," Rat replied.

Robby left the room.

Rat turned back to Acacia. "We've only got a few minutes."

"I was told everyone would probably be killed except Duar."

"This man surrendered. Can't shoot him in cold blood."

"*I* can," Acacia said, looking at the man.

Rat stared at him, then understood. "He'll be put away for so long he'll forget all about you."

"He will get the word out that I betrayed them."

Rat didn't reply.

Acacia spoke quietly. "After you're done, just turn your back for ten seconds. You can be furious with me afterward." He paused.

"Sorry," Rat replied. "Can't do that."

"Then you may have to stop me."

"I probably can do that."

The Jordanian's anger was starting to show on his face. "You are more interested in protecting him than me?"

"No, I'm not. But I'm not going to let you murder him."

Acacia turned his back and walked away.

"Bring him over here," Rat said loudly.

The terrorist was brought to him.

Rat spoke to him in Arabic. "What's your name?" he asked.

The man said nothing.

Rat slapped him in the face with his open hand. He yelled, "What's your name?"

The man's eyes flamed with anger. He spat, "Mazmin."

Rat looked at him intently and spoke softly. "I'm going to ask you some questions, and you are going to answer. Do you understand?"

Mazmin was emboldened. "I will not answer any questions."

Rat replied quickly, "You may *think* you're not going to answer, but I guarantee you that you will."

Mazmin shook his head.

Rat asked, "Where is Wahamed Duar? Your boss?"

Mazmin shook his head again, growing firmer with every passing second that he wasn't shot.

Acacia stood two steps behind Rat, fuming, fingering the trigger on the 9-mm semiautomatic handgun in his pocket.

Rat stared at Mazmin.

Robby came back into the room carrying a large, heavy animal trough full of water. He set it down carefully as some sloshed over the side and darkened the concrete floor.

"Robby, help me with this table. We've got to make a water board out of it. Turn it over and rip the legs off."

They flipped the table over, laying it on the floor with the legs sticking up. Each gave a few sharp blows with the heels of their hands to two legs, splintering the legs off quickly.

"Turn the table back over and put the legs under one end. I need some incline." He looked up. "Groomer. I need you to hold his head. Get a shirt or something off one of the dead guys."

Groomer threw the sling of his weapon over his head to free his hands and rushed to help. They slid the four table legs under one end of the table, pointing the shattered ends toward the center of the table. It raised one end of the table higher than the other end by the thickness of the square legs—about four inches.

"Think that's enough?" Rat asked.

"Beats the hell out of me," Groomer said.

"Put him on the table."

Two other SAS men grabbed Mazmin and threw him down on the table on his back. They held his arms while another came and held his legs. Mazmin's eyes showed fear. He began yelling in Arabic, "You can't do this to me!"

"Shut up," Groomer said, "whatever the hell you're saying." He grabbed Mazmin's head and pulled him down to the lower end of the table. Groomer kneeled on the floor and folded up a shirt lengthwise. He placed it across Mazmin's eyes and forehead. He rolled up the excess on the sides of his head so the shirt stretched tight. Groomer leaned down with all his weight, pinning Mazmin's head to the table. His mouth and nose were still exposed. He struggled to get free, but it was hopeless.

Rat dragged the water closer to the table and took the two cups in his hands. Mazmin's chest was heaving from his heavy breathing. He knew something bad was about to happen.

Rat leaned over so his mouth was right next to Mazmin's ear. "Where is Duar?"

"I don't know any Duar."

Rat lifted the dripping cup of water four inches above Mazmin's face and poured a quick stream into his nose. Mazmin blew it out, afraid of more.

"Where is Duar?" Rat asked, with the image of Nubs's shattered face vivid in his mind and the white anger fighting to return.

"Don't know—"

Rat poured quickly while Mazmin's mouth was open. Water went into his mouth and nose, but he was ready for it. He closed his mouth and stopped breathing.

Rat continued to pour water from the cup into his nose in a constant stream. As he poured, he filled the other cup. As soon as the first cup was nearly empty, he began pouring from the second cup, one continuous stream of water. As the second cup emptied, the first was refilled and ready to be poured behind the second. Again and again, one cup, then the other, an endless stream of water. "You have to breathe some-time, and when you do, all you're going to get into your lungs is water. And unless you tell me what I want to know, you're never going to get another breath of air. Think about that," he said as he continued to pour.

Over a minute passed, but Mazmin couldn't stand his burning lungs anymore. He gasped for breath but there wasn't any air; he sucked the water deep into his lungs. Rat kept pouring.

Mazmin tried desperately to breathe, but all he got was water, in and out, and again, nothing but water. He tried to cry out, but the water wouldn't even let him form a scream. There was no air to pass through his vocal cords. Rat poured one cup after another. No break. No air. Mazmin's body strained against the men holding his arms and legs as he fought for breath. He was drowning and he knew it.

Mazmin tried to beg for mercy. Rat stopped the water flow. "Where is Duar?"

Mazmin's chest heaved as he breathed deeply again and again, grateful for the air. "I don't know."

"Bullshit!" Rat said as he dipped his cups back into the water. He began pouring and Mazmin began yelling then snapped his mouth again and held his breath.

Groomer tightened his grip on the fabric, putting extra weight on Mazmin's head, driving it into the hard wooden table.

Mazmin's lungs were burning from not having enough air. He wouldn't be able to hold his breath for long. He tried to get a quick breath through his nose, but choked on it. The water went into his lungs and stomach. His stomach fought the intrusion and he began to throw up, sending food up against the water. Rat didn't stop. He knew Mazmin was within a minute of breaking. He had seen many men on the water board. They all broke.

The water washed away the vomit and ran back down into his lungs. Mazmin couldn't stand any more. He was on the verge of passing out. If he was about to die, he couldn't even tell Rat. He tried to nod his head. Rat knew if he didn't stop Mazmin would be dead in thirty sec-onds. He stopped the water. "Where is Duar?"

Mazmin spit the water out and blew it out of his nose, furious and fearful. He began crying. "If I tell you, you stop this!"

"If I believe you."

"In a well! Perhaps three hundred meters to the south."

Rat turned on his encrypted UHF radio. *"Banger, check for a well three hundred meters to the south. Duar may be there."*

"Roger. Copy. On our way."

Rat dipped his cups back into the water and filled them. He looked down at Mazmin. He knew he had heard the cups. He was confident that the sound alone was too horrible for him to handle right now. "Who does Duar report to?"

"Nobody. He ran everything."

"How did he communicate with others?"

"I don't know."

Rat poured a small stream of water onto Mazmin's face.

The man screamed. "I don't know! I did things for him. I was not with him. I don't know how he communicated with anybody."

Rat wasn't buying it. He began pouring water into the man's nose and mouth again. Mazmin tried to scream, but again it was muffled by the constant presence of water. He fought it, but it was no use. He inhaled again and sucked water into his lungs, completely filling them with what felt like an ocean of water.

Mazmin suddenly went unconscious and sagged as his mouth hung open. Rat stopped pouring. He looked at Groomer.

Rat stood up. "That's enough for him. Turn him over."

They rolled him over on his stomach. Rat pressed Mazmin's back between his shoulder blades. The water gushed out of his lungs, running down the table and onto the floor. He raised the man's arms behind him and nearly touched his elbows. He repeated the motion two or three times until he heard Mazmin gasp for air.

Rat looked at the SAS men who had been holding Mazmin's arms and legs. "Hold him here. I'm going to go find that well. Groomer, come with me." Then loudly in Arabic, "And if I don't find Duar, I'm going to come back here and stab *him* in the eye."

He was interrupted by the receiver in his ear. *"We've got what may be a well. Small building. Nobody in there."*

Rat lowered his night-vision device and walked carefully through the room and into the darkness. Groomer was right behind him. *"Maybe he's in the well itself. I'm on my way."* He broke into a trot. *"Robby, you up?"*

"Robby."

"Check in with the helos. Get an updated ETA."

"Wilco."

He found the small building. The others were watching for him outside, waiting for his instructions. He looked at Groomer.

Toad said, "Two flat doors on top folded closed. The well is probably underneath those doors."

Rat walked directly inside the building. His men covered the entrance and all sides from the outside. Rat stooped down and studied the two doors over the well opening. They had handles. He was tempted to just grab one of the doors and fling it open. He said to Groomer, "Could be booby-trapped."

"ETA five minutes," Robby transmitted.

"Roger," Rat replied. He glanced at his watch. Rat could hear himself breathing. "Give me some line, or wire. He stuck out his hand and felt nylon cord being placed in his open palm. He carefully wrapped the line around one of the handles that was attached to the door over the well and retreated back to the outside.

He handed the line to Groomer. "When I say, pull on this and get on the ground."

Groomer took it and nodded.

Rat kneeled down next to Groomer with his submachine gun pointed at the well. He took a breath and nodded to Groomer.

Groomer gave a huge pull and lay flat on the ground. The door flapped opened immediately and slammed over. Suddenly, bullets rang out in the well house. At first, Rat couldn't tell where they were coming from, then he realized the bullets were flying into the roof of the well house. They were coming from inside the well. Someone was definitely in the well, and he had been surprised.

"He's got to be standing on something, or suspended by something," Groomer said.

Rat crawled back into the well house on his belly as the bullets continued out of the well. He examined the top of the well from the side; a rope was tied to the hinge of the opposite door. He slid back outside as the harmless firing stopped.

Rat turned to Groomer. "He's on a rope. How the hell do we get this guy out of there without killing him?"

Groomer nodded. "We need to get our rope underneath his—but he'll see it." He thought as he surveyed the room. "We need to distract him. I'll pull open the other door. Give me one second. That's all I need. Let me blacken this rope. When I'm ready, fire some bursts right over the mouth of the well. I'll slip our rope under his. Then I'll just pull his ass up out of there."

"First I'll drop something heavy into the well. He doesn't know we want him alive. He'll think it's a grenade. He'll try to look down before he looks up and tries to get out. That's when I'll fire. He'll feel trapped." Rat transmitted, "*Everybody away from the south side of the well house. I'll be firing directly across the mouth of the well. Anybody see a rock, or piece of building anywhere? I need something that weighs a couple of pounds that will sound like a grenade hitting the water.*"

Robby answered. "*Drop a real grenade. Just don't arm it.*"

"*Good idea,*" Rat replied. He took one of the grenades out of the pocket of his vest. He nodded at Groomer.

Groomer tied the rope to the second handle, backed away slightly, and pulled the second door wide open. The firing started again, slamming harmlessly into the ceiling. Duar was in too far to aim with any angle out of the well.

Rat lay directly next to the opening. Groomer moved up with his now blackened rope and nodded at Rat. Rat tossed the grenade into the opening. He heard it click against the wall of the well, then clunk into something. He heard the man curse. He had hit him in the head with the grenade, which then tumbled past him into the water below with a loud splash. Rat started firing.

With amazing speed Groomer slid his hand underneath the rope down in the well. He pulled it around and walked back out of the well house. The line was perhaps twenty feet long. He held both ends. "You, and you," he said, pointing to two team members, "give me a hand here. We've got to pull this asshole out of this well like he's been shot out of a cannon. Heave on this line when I say." He moved the rope over his shoulder and the other two got behind him and did likewise.

Rat moved into the well house and gave Groomer the sign.

"Go!" Groomer yelled as he started pulling with all his might. They ran away from the well house. The man in the well rapidly rose from his hidden position. Rat watched as his head and the barrel of an AK-47 reached the top of the opening. Rat moved in behind him.

As soon as the terrorist's head broke the surface he started shooting. Rat waited until the barrel of his weapon began to clear the well's edge. Rat grabbed the barrel of the assault rifle. Duar tried to turn around, but had nothing to push off from. He was standing on a loop of rope that was unstable.

Rat pulled the rifle back hard, making sure it didn't point at him. He struck the man's wrist sharply, causing the man to cry out and release the rifle. Rat tossed it away and grabbed the man by the throat, pulling him backward out of the well.

The man was as big as Rat and struggled. Rat put him in a choke hold, cutting off his air. The man grabbed at Rat's arm, but had no hope of breaking the grip.

Groomer felt the rope go slack and ran back into the well house. He took the man's legs and forced him out of the well. As the man tried to kick him, Groomer reached up and punched him in the groin. Rat released his grip and the man moaned in pain.

Groomer grabbed his legs again and turned him over on the floor. He whipped plastic hand ties out of his pocket and bound the man's hands together. He took out a flashlight and shone it in the man's face. "It's him. Sure as hell." Groomer smiled.

Rat and Groomer stood up and jerked Duar to his feet. Rat could hear the approaching CH-53s. "Let's get him out to the carrier."

Mr. President, we got Duar!" Sarah St. James, the National Security Adviser, announced with barely contained pleasure.

President Kendrick sat back in his chair in the oval office. He was surprised but very pleased. "Alive?" he asked.

"Alive. There was quite a fight; all the terrorists except Duar—and one of his men—were killed. Those two we got out alive. Unharmed."

"Are they going out to the carrier?"

"Yes, sir. The *Belleau Wood.*"

"How many people know this?"

"I'm not sure. The message I saw was addressed to the usual people. I assume the people on the *Belleau Wood* know, or will know. Other than that—"

"We need to keep a lid on the fact that we got him. If the press hears about it, they'll melt down."

Sarah couldn't imagine how they could keep this from the press for long. Duar was the most wanted terrorist in the world. Why wouldn't the President want to broadcast that to everyone?

"Does Secretary Stuntz know?" the President asked.

"I suspect so, but I didn't talk to him."

"You just came straight here because you wanted to be the one to tell me about it," he said, smiling.

"Probably true," she admitted. "I was excited."

"How did you hear about it?"

She said sheepishly, "Lieutenant Rathman." She gave President Kendrick the best security advice she could give him. The standard government information and intelligence was helpful, but not enough as she saw it. She had carefully and quietly groomed people in several departments of the government who reported information she might find of interest directly to her by encrypted e-mail. She often knew about important things before the Director of the CIA learned of them. And in some cases, she was directly in touch with the operators themselves. The people who did things, like Rat, not the people who wrote reports. She had much more faith in people low on the chain of command. Those high up, especially those who were in Washington, were too often sycophants, telling her what she wanted to hear instead of what they really thought. When she was doing graduate work in international relations she had become fascinated with Franklin D. Roosevelt. He was the one she emulated in bypassing those with stars on their shoulders or ambition in their eyes.

"And how did your boy get this to you so fast?"

"He's not." She decided not to argue. "He has some new communication device. It's the latest thing—a PDA with GPS, and he can hook up to the SIPRNET and send classified, encrypted e-mails. He has my e-mail address. Works anywhere in the world."

"I'll bet he didn't send a courtesy copy to the Secretary of Defense, or the Director of Central Intelligence, his bosses."

"I'll bet he would if they asked. You know how it works, Mr. President. You even told me to keep you informed of things he sent me if they were particularly interesting."

"Where was he when he sent you this e-mail?"

"On the helicopter flying from Sudan out to the carrier."

"Amazing." His thoughts went back to her response. "It's funny, all I have to do is mention Secretary Stuntz and your face looks like you just drank vinegar."

"Sorry."

"Why do you dislike him so much?"

"It's not that. It's . . . nothing."

Kendrick knew what was bothering her. "You think I promised you Defense, don't you?"

"No, I understand."

"You think I promised, and I've gone back on my word."

"No, sir."

"I didn't promise. I said if the opportunity ever arose, would you be interested? Isn't that what I asked you?"

"I don't really remember, sir. But it doesn't—"

He saw her disappointment. "Maybe it will happen one day. Don't let your ambition run away with you."

She nodded. She remembered his assurance as much more direct than he remembered. But he could do whatever he wanted. "Yes, sir," she said finally. "I'm happy to work with you in whatever capacity—"

"Don't patronize me," he said, his face turning pink. "You may get your chance one day." He pushed back his sandy hair, then started. He felt guilty for not asking the obvious question earlier. "Any American casualties?"

"One, sir. One man got shot in the face. Killed instantly. They got the Jordanian spy out unharmed too."

"We need to decide what to do with this Duar. We need to know everything he knows, above everything else. I'd like to have some time with him before the whole world knows we have him and they start telling us what to do. We need to interrogate him. Too bad we can't 'encourage' him to talk."

"Oh, I think the people who do this have certain ways to make it happen."

"Good. We need to get his entire operation and roll it up."

◆ ◆ ◆

The helicopter touched down on the USS *Belleau Wood,* LHA-3, a twenty-eight-year-old helicopter attack carrier full of Marines. Rat had stared at Duar and Mazmin for the entire flight. The terrorists had tried to look mean yet apathetic, as if their capture was a mere setback that would be set right soon. Mazmin had coughed uncontrollably throughout the flight. Rat had begun to wonder if he was contagious.

As the helicopter blades slowed, the top of the sun broke over the horizon, giving the sky a golden glow. Few on the ship knew who was in the helicopter. To the other sailors and Marines onboard this helicopter looked just like many others that flew off the *Belleau Wood* every day. They knew it wasn't a Marine helicopter; the dark gray paint and extremely subtle, almost invisible, markings were different. But there wasn't enough difference to make them particularly curious. Those who did know waited anxiously for the helicopter to unload—they had been awakened when the excitement spread of the dazzling success of the mission.

The jet engines continued to turn as the sailors on the flight deck ran to place chocks around its wheels to keep it from rolling on the moving deck.

Two members of Rat's team grabbed Duar's arms tightly and walked him down the ramp. His face expressed shock and dismay when he realized he was on an American warship at sea. His head spun, searching in vain for some sign of land. Several Masters at Arms—the ship's police force—walked to the helicopter to escort Duar and Mazmin. Duar's legs stiffened as he resisted and struggled. Two SAS members lifted him up so only his toes were in contact with the ship's deck as they hustled him toward the island of the carrier.

Rat stepped off the ramp of the helicopter and watched Duar fight his way toward the island. As the second helicopter was settling onto the fantail at the other end of the *Belleau Wood,* Rat followed Duar.

Mazmin fought his escorts even more than Duar had. He tried to spit on Rat as he walked by. Rat told the MAAs to stop. They quickly looked at him and noticed the Sudanese Army uniform and hat. The chief petty officer in charge of the group wasn't about to stop for some African major. He looked at the major again. He noticed Rat's dark skin but thought it was probably from a tan. Rat didn't have the look of an African, or Middle Easterner. And his bright blue eyes were a dead giveaway. He noticed Rat's arms, the highly defined taut muscles that showed great strength without bulk, and the carriage of someone who knew how to handle himself. The chief was very confused. He started to push Mazmin on, but Rat said, "I'm Lieutenant Rathman. Navy SEAL."

"Sorry, sir," the chief said. "The uniform threw me."

"Threw him too," Rat said, smiling. The smile vanished as he looked into Mazmin's hostile eyes. He spoke to Mazmin in Arabic. "I'm going to visit you tonight, asshole. You think almost drowning in the desert was bad? Tonight it's the real thing. Swim call. I'm going to drag you out of the brig and throw you over the side when nobody's looking. You'll fall into the black ocean yelling for help and nobody will hear you." Rat smiled at him and walked a good distance behind him to the island.

"You cannot."

"Just remember, my name is Rat. R-A-T. I'll let you know it's me before I get you out of the brig. I don't want you to have any doubt in your mind about what's happening. But remember, it will be very late tonight, when you're asleep. I'll expect you to get up well. No sleeping in. Make sure you set your alarm."

"You are a whore," Mazmin said.

Rat looked at him with a cold glare. He wanted Mazmin to think he was crazy, that he might do anything, like facing a pitcher that threw incredibly hard and was so wild you never knew where the ball was going. He wanted Mazmin to think of going to sleep as an act of courage. He gave the chief a nod to take Mazmin and they pushed him toward the island.

Groomer loved Rat and the games he played with bad people. "What the hell did you say to him? He looks like he saw a ghost."

"Told him tonight he might get a chance to see what drowning was really like."

"You're cruel."

"Just like to give them something to think about."

"You doin' the interrogation?"

"I'm going to ask to sit in. I don't know who they've got aboard to do it. If they've got an Arabic speaker who knows his ass from his elbow maybe they'll be okay."

"Uh-oh," Groomer said as they stepped through the hatch into the island. Several people were obviously waiting for them, including the captain of the ship.

"Are you Kent Rathman?"

"Yes, sir."

"Yes. I'm Captain Larry Hogan."

"What can I do for you, sir?"

"You got Duar?"

"Yes, sir. We did."

"We'd like to hear the details of the operation."

"Yes, sir. I have to send a message to my boss first, then I'd be glad to give you all a debrief."

Hogan frowned. He wasn't used to being put off. "How long will it take you to complete your message?"

"Not more than twenty minutes, sir."

"Fine. Come to my wardroom when you're done, and we can talk about it. Have some breakfast."

"Very well, sir."

"You know where it is?"

"I'm sure I can find it, sir."

"Good. I've asked Petty Officer Brady to escort you and make sure you're taken care of. See you at breakfast," Hogan said, returning the way he'd come.

Rat turned to a sailor standing nearby. "Can you direct me to the comm center?"

"It's kind of hard, sir. I'd be glad to escort you there."

"Let's go," Rat said.

He and Groomer finished the message to Don Jacobs—the head of the CIA Counterterrorism Center, the CTC—in fifteen minutes. Rat noticed the sailor had not only escorted them there, he had waited for them. "You still here? You spying on us?" Rat asked, pulling his chain.

"Not at all, sir," the sailor said, his face reddening.

"We've got to go to the captain's wardroom. Can you get us there?"

"Yes, sir." He hurried out of the comm center. "Right this way."

They were there in less than three minutes. Brady opened the door for Rat, and he and Groomer, the only other officer on the team, stepped into the beautiful, carpeted room where the captain ate his meals and had staff meetings. It could comfortably seat twenty. There were five mess specialists in crisp white jackets serving breakfast to the officers around the table.

As soon as Rat smelled the bacon his mouth began to water. He re-

SECRET JUSTICE | 29

alized how hungry he was. He hadn't eaten anything since boarding the C-17 the night before. The Air Force had offered some mysterious packaged food while they were circling over the desert, but Rat had passed. He didn't want stomach cramps as he dived out of a jet at twenty-five thousand feet.

Rat saw the captain sitting at the head of the table. He was directly under one of the many spotlights in the overhead that gave the room its special look. His bald head reflected the spotlight like a mirror. Rat tried not to laugh.

"Rathman! Come in!" Hogan yelled. "Sit right up here at my table. What's the name of your other man?"

"Ted Groome," Rat said.

"Both of you, sit here. You must be starving. What'll it be? They'll fix you anything you want."

Rat took a deep breath as he let his imagination run away with him. He looked at the mess specialist who waited expectantly for this oddly dressed American to decide. "Can you fix a waffle? A big, fat, Belgian waffle with maple syrup?"

"No problem, sir. Want some bacon and scrambled eggs on the side?"

"Absolutely," Rat replied. "Thanks."

"You, sir?" he asked Groomer.

"Same," Groomer said.

"Coffee?" the captain asked as he passed the silver coffeepot down the table.

Rat nodded and extended his cup.

Hogan spoke loudly over the din. "Attention, everyone. I'd like everyone to keep quiet, while Mr. Rathman here tells us how the mission went, and how he got the famous Wahamed Duar." It was the first many had heard that Duar had been captured. Their eyes showed their surprise and excitement. Hogan lowered his voice. "I predict right now that we will be asked to conduct the first major tribunal right here aboard this ship. It is imperative that we keep it confidential for now. If it leaks out, it could be catastrophic. No e-mails to your wives or husbands explaining to them that we have Duar and are going to put him on trial. Just keep that knowledge in your own little heads. Now, I want to give Mr. Rathman here a chance to tell us all what happened. So," he said, turning to his left where Rat was sitting. "The floor's yours."

Rat nodded. "It went as briefed. We happened to be the closest when the signal went out. We jumped—"

The door to the wardroom flew open. A red-faced captain stormed in. Rat noticed the medical insignia on one of his collars. The ship's surgeon no doubt, and *pissed*. He had a light complexion and blondish hair, what there was of it. It was mostly combed over to cover a growing bald spot, and some of the longer hairs had fallen down on the wrong side, tickling his ear. The fact he didn't notice was a bad sign to Rat.

Hogan looked irritated. "This is our ship's surgeon, Dr. Tim Satterly. What is it doctor?"

Satterly could barely speak. "Sir, one of those men that was just brought on board isn't *doing* too well," he announced with an air pregnant with implication.

"What do you mean?" Hogan asked.

"This man described how some *maniac* had tried to kill him. Had, in fact, *tortured* him." The doctor looked around the room, wondering if the maniac was in the room. His cheeks were blotchy.

"He looked okay to me," Hogan said, smiling.

Satterly didn't see the humor. His outrage was growing. "Sir, he was tortured with water. It was poured into his nose and mouth until he almost drowned. He lost consciousness. They had to revive him."

Hogan shook his head. "He's delusional."

"He just collapsed in sick bay, Captain. He has a temperature, sir. I ordered a chest X ray. He has pneumonia that has been brought on by something very intrusive. What he described could do it."

"That fast?"

"Yes, sir."

The wardroom grew deathly quiet. The mess specialists, unaware of the tension in the air, came rushing out of the kitchen and placed the two large plates of food in front of Rat and Groomer. Rat stared at it. He wanted the doctor to leave so he could eat.

Having finally noticed the two odd uniforms in the room, Satterly directed his gaze at Rat. Captain Hogan waited until the messmen had withdrawn. Everyone had stopped eating. No one even reached for a coffee cup. They all wanted to avoid whatever was going to happen next. The hum of the ship, the general noise that had been mere background until then suddenly dominated the room. Captain Hogan turned his head and looked at Rat. "You want to explain this to me?"

The Marine guard nodded at Rat, who opened the steel door and stepped through. Rat was one of the few people allowed automatic access to the prisoner. The door closed behind Rat and was locked again by the Marine from the outside.

Rat had changed to his American desert camouflage uniform with no insignia or indication of service. The other man in the room wore the standard Navy officer's uniform, the short-sleeve khaki uniform that was ubiquitous on the ship. He wore the rank of a commander, with two rows of ribbons and no name tag. He had come onto the ship to do the interrogation, and was thought to be with naval intelligence.

Only Rat knew that Ken Barone, the man in the uniform, had never served a day in the Navy. His full name was Kendall Pierce Barone, which he sometimes used, but just as often he was called KP. He was legendary for being able to speak perfect Arabic, even regional dialects. He could speak Jordanian Arabic, or Egyptian, or Syrian, with the appropriate minor differences in pronunciation and usage. He was from the DO, the Directorate of Operations of the CIA, and was their best Arabic-speaking interrogator. He had been waiting on the *Belleau Wood* in the hope someone of significance would be captured. He knew Rat and agreed to let him come and go during the interrogation. There were two other American interrogators and the promise of a fourth, a man from Sudan.

Rat looked at Duar for the first time since loading him aboard the helicopter. He was sitting on the other side of a standard Navy metal table with his hands on the table. Rough hands that knew manual labor. Duar's skin was dark from the sun and his eyes shone from the deep sockets where they were buried in his face. His eyes were set so deep they looked considerably darker than in the photograph. Rat spoke to Barone in English. "Any progress?"

Barone looked at Rat cautiously. "You sure he doesn't speak English?"

"No. How long you been going?"

"Just getting started. He's not giving us much yet." Barone watched Duar out of the corner of his eye. "Maybe if you give him the same treatment you gave that other guy . . ."

Rat thought of the red-faced doctor. He knew he hadn't heard the last about it. Rat watched Duar, who showed no recognition. "Keep going. I just want to listen."

Barone turned back toward Duar and spoke in a resonant Arabic. "Where do you live?"

Duar shook his head.

"What is your name?"

"Mohammed el-Mahdi."

"You were meeting with Pierre Lahoud in Sudan. Why?"

"I was meeting with no one."

"To purchase nuclear material."

"No."

"Lahoud brought nuclear material with him. We have it."

Duar turned away from Barone.

"Do you deny that you were there to buy nuclear material? To see if it was of sufficiently high quality to make a nuclear weapon?"

No answer.

"Who were you going to get to build the bomb? Where were you going to use it? Did you have a plan?"

Rat watched the back of Duar's head as Barone's questions bounced off. He was listening carefully. There was something funny about Duar's approach. He seemed to be trying to learn, not protect information. He was alert and careful, but not afraid.

Rat stood quietly and reached across the table. He slapped Duar in the back of the head sharply. "You're not answering the questions."

Duar spun around angrily. "You cannot attack me!"

"I can do whatever I want," Rat said.

"You cannot violate the Geneva Convention!"

"Never heard of it."

Duar breathed heavily.

Barone looked at Rat. "Can I talk to you outside?"

Rat nodded. They walked to the door and knocked on it. The Marine opened the door and let them out into the passageway. He closed and locked the door behind them.

"I don't know about this guy," Barone said. "He's a strange one."

"Only the most wanted terrorist in the world."

Barone nodded. "He's sure not going to tell us anything voluntarily."

"Give me a few minutes with him."

"We need more tools. We ask questions, they refuse to answer them. Same old story."

"Just wear him down. Stay on him."

"Oh, I will. Sleep deprivation, lights on all night, the usual stuff. But I'm not getting a good feeling about this one. I've done a lot of the interrogation at Gitmo: same story. Bad attitudes, not helpful, lying to us, telling us a bunch of scary stuff that they just make up, basically flipping us off, and our hands are tied." He considered the information they had gotten from others. "Why is it they can murder us, and we can't even *touch* them?"

"Let me have him to myself for a while. I don't think he responds well to getting smacked in the back of the head. Make him angry. Don't show him the respect he's used to getting. Tell you what, just tell him I'm a maniac and you're going to let me do the interrogation if you can't get anything out of him."

Barone kept a serious face. "I just might."

"Tell him I told you I'm going to throw him over the side tonight, and you believe me. If he doesn't start talking, you're going to let me."

"I never tell them anything that isn't true. Have to keep my credibility."

"Right." Rat smiled. "Look, I've got to get a message off. I'll catch up with you later. Let me know if he starts talking."

◆　◆　◆

The excitement aboard the *Belleau Wood* was nothing compared to the elation in Washington. Sarah St. James sat in the situation room of the White House looking smug as the Secretary of Defense, the Chief of Staff, the Director of the CIA, the Attorney General, and the Chairman of the Joint Chiefs took their seats.

President Kendrick was pleased. He took his seat at the head of the table and opened a manila file that had been placed in front of him. It contained photographs of the two terrorists who had been captured, as well as clips from the digital video Robby had taken of the raid. Kendrick was one who liked to see the final result in pictures, not read a cold report from some agency that tried to take the life out of what happened. He knew that they were involved in a deadly business, and he was willing to look that deadly business in the eye. He required the rest of the cabinet and his staff to be equally ready to deal with reality and not see the War on Terrorism as some sterile event fought by drones and satellites against faceless adversaries.

"Good morning, everyone," President Kendrick said. "I have to say, kudos go out to both the Agency and the Department of Defense. This was an amazing coordinated operation that worked to perfection," he said enthusiastically. He wondered how he could publicize it properly, to give his administration a much needed boost. "When I first heard of the plan to have Special Operations teams in the air over Sudan I have to say I was skeptical. Some of you were more enthusiastic about it than I was. But based on your advice, we authorized it, and it worked. So thanks to all of you and especially to the Agency and the Department of Defense." President Kendrick looked around the room. "So now what do we do with them?"

Howard Stuntz, the pompous Secretary of Defense, spoke first. "Sir, I have to say that this operation was magnificent. It showed a tremendous coordination between the Air Force, the Agency, the Navy and Marine Corps team, and in fact shows we can—"

"What do we do with Duar?" Kendrick interrupted.

Stewart Woods, the Director of the CIA, spoke. His frown foreshadowed his concerns. "Part of the idea certainly was the chance to interrogate him. However, preliminary reports from the interrogators say they're not getting much. He refuses even to acknowledge who he is. He claims to be someone else entirely, from Khartoum. We can't really force him to talk. I'm not sure we're *going* to get much from him."

Kendrick was annoyed. "We go to all this trouble to capture him alive, and for what? So he can spit in our faces? We can't get anything out of him? None of his plans, his support structure, his finances, nothing?"

The DCI nodded reluctantly. "I'm afraid that's right, sir. Our hands are pretty much tied. We don't torture people. Short of that, there's really no way to get them to talk, at least not these kinds of men. With a common criminal you can negotiate a shorter sentence, or get them to turn state's evidence, but a terrorist? He's not afraid of a sentence. Not even afraid to die. He won't disclose anything without *strong* encouragement."

"Then why try to capture them at all? Why not just drop a bomb on this meeting and be done with it?"

Stuntz nodded. "Just say the word."

Kendrick shook his head. "Seriously. Why can't we squeeze them a little?"

Woods replied, "We signed the Convention against Torture in 1994. Promised all the civilized countries in the world not to do that."

"I can see that you don't want political torture, death squads, people out of control, but it seems to me that professional interrogators ought to have some more tools in their box to find out what people like Duar are planning." He paused and was acutely aware of the silence. "Am I way off base here?"

St. James was uncomfortable. "Sir, it's one of the things that sets us apart. We don't execute prisoners, we don't torture people to get information from them. It makes us *different*. If we stoop to that level, we've taken the first step of becoming like them, where human life doesn't matter. They may not value our lives, but we value theirs. I think we need to resist the temptation. What else would make us different?"

"A *lot*," Kendrick said, growing more annoyed. "What *can* we do? Can we take away his food? Can we yell at him? Can we threaten him?"

Woods spoke. "We have some things we can do, but they're very limited. Some sleep deprivation, some harassment, those sorts of things, but if you actually read the Geneva Convention, even those things are probably across the line."

"Do what you can. We need to know what he knows," Kendrick said. He sat back and thought. "But then what? A tribunal, right? Where?"

St. James interjected, "Couldn't we bring him back and try him here? Why go through the difficulty of a tribunal?"

Stuntz almost laughed. "And give him one of our patented American circus trials? You can't be serious."

"I am very serious. The tribunal sounds like a short cut. Like a Kangaroo court. Why not just do it the usual way? I mean we tried Ramsey Yousef for trying to blow up the World Trade Center. I didn't hear any complaints about a circus trial."

"I sure did," the Attorney General said.

"Well, in any case, he wasn't successful, and we were. He was convicted and sits in prison forever. Why can't we do that again?"

Stuntz leaned forward. "Because we don't *have* to. We captured this guy outside of the United States. He doesn't get the protections of the Constitution. He can't get some wise-ass lawyer to stand up and start making a bunch of noise on his behalf at the expense of the U.S. taxpayers. And if we use the tribunal, more evidence is admissible. Some hearsay comes in. We don't have to get a unanimous verdict. We don't have to expose the case, the result, the vote, whatever, to much of an appeal. Hell, when they did a tribunal back in World War II they even did it here on U.S. soil when they captured those six German spies— two of whom were *U.S. citizens*. And they were *executed*. Like this guy ought to be."

President Kendrick spoke. "It seems to me the tribunal is the path of least resistance and most likely success. Mr. Attorney General, am I right?"

"That's all true, sir. That's how the DOD wrote the rules. I'm sure those rules will be tested someday, but that's how they stand—"

Stuntz interrupted. "Your question, Mr. President, was what do we do now? Notwithstanding what the Director has said about the value of interrogation, I see great value in trying this terrorist, and, if the evidence supports it, executing him—"

"We don't have the balls to execute him," the Attorney General said, then catching himself and wishing he hadn't said it.

The President looked at him bemusedly.

"Whether we have the—courage—is certainly something that we want to consider," the Attorney General continued. "But the real issue, Mr. President, is whether to keep this tribunal secret. We have rules on the conduct of these tribunals, and we've had test runs with low-level terrorists. But this one is the big one. So do we tell people we're doing it? Or do we keep it completely secret?"

"We can't keep it secret," Stuntz said with the great authority he always thought his statements carried. "The rules have been published for months—we told everyone they wouldn't be conducted in secret, and the ones we've done were public. We can't very well go back on that. Well, I guess we could, but it would look very suspicious."

Woods shook his head. "Secrecy would be a bad idea anyway. All it takes is one person to think something's wrong, or unfair, and you'd be unable to stop the publicity. Just one sailor could mention the trial in an e-mail to his family, or the *Washington Post*, that the world's number-one terrorist happens to be on the *Belleau Wood* and was being tried. I can guarantee you that that will happen. Then the newspapers start calling and accusing us of bad faith. What are we trying to hide? We didn't even tell them that he had been captured? Why not reassure the American people of our competence by showing them that we can and in fact *did* capture the world's leading terrorist?"

"Sarah?"

"I think the Director is right, Mr. President. It's going to be difficult, if not impossible, to keep the lid on the fact that we have Duar. And once the press gets wind of it, they will absolutely go berserk. Some of that may go our way, but a lot of it will be accusatory if we try to keep it secret. I'm afraid if word gets out that we're going to try Duar aboard the *Belleau Wood,* and not bring him back to the States, somebody is going to think that's unfair. We've seen it already in some previous cases. But for this one, people are going to go all out. Maybe Duar will get American lawyers involved. I think we should take control of this right away. Hold a press conference. Announce the capture of Duar today, before it gets stale, and tell them he's going to be tried in a tribunal."

"You agree, Mr. Attorney General?"

"I do. We'd be happy to try him here in the United States, but I frankly don't want to give him a platform. I don't want him to hold press conferences every day talking about how evil America is, and how we don't appreciate his objectives, and how we need to pull out of the Middle East and abandon Israel. I'm sick of hearing that crap. I say put him on trial aboard the *Belleau Wood* under the rules developed by the Department of Defense."

Kendrick rubbed his chin. "Mr. Stuntz, you have your military prosecutors ready to go?"

"Yes, sir."

"Get them out there. Let's get this thing under way as soon as possible."

Stuntz hesitated. "Are we going to go for a capital charge? Do we have the nerve to execute this murderer?"

"Capital charge? Absolutely. Does everybody agree?" Kendrick asked, implying only one correct answer.

Those around the table nodded.

They were about to leave when St. James spoke. "We'd better have a damage-control plan too."

Stuntz replied, "Damage to what?"

"When this thing hits the press, which it will do, we'd better be ready to respond."

Kendrick frowned, not following her at all. "We won't need damage control, Sarah," Kendrick said decisively. "We're not getting anything out of this guy. So I'm going public with this today. We'll tell them we've captured Duar. Big kudos all around. He's being held in an 'undisclosed location'—I love that—and that we are evaluating whether to put him on trial in a tribunal or simply hold him as a combatant until the cessation of hostilities. The cessation of hostilities, of course, is up to us to define." He smiled. "Since we're fighting terrorists, that could be when there's no more terrorism. We could put him on trial *then*, at the end of hostilities. We could just put the evidence in a box, wait as long as we want, then pull it out when we felt like it, years from now. But of course we have no intention of doing that. I kind of like where we are on this one, frankly. We're going to push it as hard and as fast as we can. String him up."

♦   ♦   ♦

Rat stepped out of the shower in his condo in Washington, D.C. Unlike many of those who worked for him in his cover as the CEO of a security company, he lived in Washington itself, not in one of the suburbs. He loved the energy of the city. He dried off and picked up the portable phone on the cradle next to his bed. As he toweled off his legs he speed-dialed and put the phone against a shoulder.

"Hello?"

"Hey. I'm back."

"Yeah. Where you been?" Andrea Ash asked, knowing she wouldn't get an answer.

"Right here in my apartment. I was just watching television here for the last few days."

"To think you were there the whole time and I never thought to call."

"What are you up to?"

"You know, same old stuff. Practicing medicine in a Navy hospital. It's like practicing law in jail."

"Come on, Bethesda's a good hospital."

"It is. I just like making fun of it."

"You doing anything tonight?"

"Not really."

He glanced at the clock. It was seven o'clock. "Did you eat yet?"

"Only once."

"Perfect. How about I pick you up in twenty minutes and we go out for dinner?"

"Sounds great. See you then."

Rat dressed and drove to Maryland. He had met Andrea on his first assignment for the CIA. Intelligence had learned of an Algerian who intended to shoot down the Blue Angels. It had fallen to him to stop it. She was the flight surgeon for the Blue Angels, the second woman to hold that position. When she moved to Maryland to work at Bethesda they had started dating seriously. He hadn't dated anyone seriously for almost three years. Andrea though had gotten deep inside him. She confounded him and drove him crazy, and he loved it.

He ran up to her door and banged on it loudly. The door opened and Andrea smiled at him. She kissed him gently. "I missed you."

"Likewise," he said. "Come on. I'm starved."

They drove to a nearby seafood restaurant that Andrea loved. Rat thought it was below average because most of their fish was frozen, but the atmosphere was perfect. They had mastered the nautical decor and every room was walled off by enormous salt water aquariums with Chesapeake and Atlantic fish swimming around.

They ordered and sipped their iced tea as they waited for their food. "So, really," Andrea pressed. "Where have you been?"

"You know I can't talk about it."

"I don't want to know exactly where you have been or exactly what you have been doing, just tell me basically where in the world you have been. What continent?"

"Sorry."

"You're not much fun."

"No doubt. But at least I'm back."

"How long are you going to be here?"

"I never know."

"No, you never do. I'm getting used to it, but not completely."

Their food arrived and they began eating the steaming seafood off the oversized plates.

"I talked to my detailer today," she said.

Rat was surprised. Detailers were in charge of job assignments. They were the people you talked with when you were ready to rotate to your next job in the Navy. "You've only been at this job for six months."

"They have a burning need for a flight surgeon on one of the carriers. Since going to sea is career enhancing they wanted to know if I wanted the job."

"It's easy. The answer is no."

"Just like that?"

"Yep. Just like that."

"Easy for you to say. Everything you do is golden. Everything you think about or say is automatically career enhancing. But what about for me?"

Rat looked at her curiously. "Where is this coming from? Last time we talked, you didn't even want a Navy career. You wanted to get out and earn some money as a real doctor."

"Well, maybe I do and maybe I don't. I talked to a few doctors out there in the real world, and they're not all that happy. And the demand for flight surgeons isn't all that intense. In fact the position doesn't really exist. It's only in the Navy they pay you to hang around airplanes, get a few flight hours, give pilots physicals, and call yourself a flight surgeon. It's a great job, and if you want to keep doing it they'll make you a captain. If you want to do that, you have to go to sea at some point. This is my chance."

"Which carrier?" Rat asked.

"The USS *Belleau Wood*. Have you ever been aboard it?"

Rat suppressed a smile. "Yeah, couple of times. Kind of old, but in really good shape."

"What do you think?"

"I told you. I wouldn't do it unless you really want to stay in the Navy for a career. Decide that first."

Andrea nodded silently as her mind wandered away from Rat and to the question of whether to stay in the Navy for twenty or more years.

♦   ♦   ♦

Captain Tim Satterly, the surgeon of the *Belleau Wood*, bent over the unconscious man in his sick bay. Ever since reporting Mazmin's condition to Captain Hogan and confronting the American wearing a Sudanese Army uniform—probably illegal under the laws of war, Satterly thought—his concern had grown. The man had been mostly unconscious for the better part of two days. The IV antibiotics were having no effect. His fever continued to rage. The chest X rays showed the fluid in the top third of both lungs, and the amount increasing with every hour. Satterly had seen numerous cases of pneumonia. He couldn't recall one that started in the upper lobes, and he had never seen a case he couldn't stop. He knew people died from pneumonia every day, but never in his hands. He had also never seen a case get so bad so quickly.

Mazmin was the only one in sick bay. He lay in the middle bed in the middle room, with unoccupied beds to his left and right over immaculate waxed green tile. Dr. Satterly wore his khaki uniform under his white medical coat. He put the electronic ear-thermometer in the man's ear canal and received an instantaneous reading—105 degrees. Satterly shook his head. He listened to the man's labored breathing through his stethoscope. He looked once again at the oxygen number from the clip attached to Mazmin's forefinger. Sixty percent, and going down. They were fighting a losing battle.

Satterly was haunted by what this prisoner had said. Tortured, nearly drowned. On a table in a room surrounded by blood and death. The pneumonia he was battling could easily have been caused by the trauma he had described, depending on what was in the water that went into his lungs. He was aware of the risk of believing a prisoner. He had dealt with enough brig rats on the ship and criminals on their way to Leavenworth to realize they could be very creative in their accusations—always close enough to reality to be difficult to disprove. But Satterly found it hard to believe that this prisoner would come to the ship a few hours after his capture with a cohesive story supported by medical evidence that he couldn't control.

Satterly's face reddened again as he thought of the cowboy Special Forces operative torturing a prisoner, violating the Geneva Convention and probably ten other things. *Just like the terrorists.* The War on Terrorism was a moral war; from his perspective it would be lost when the moral high ground was abandoned. The man lying in front of him showed that either it had been abandoned, or those responsible for preserving the moral high ground didn't care. Ends were fast becoming more important than means.

He took the latest chest X ray and jammed it up onto the light box hanging on the bulkhead. It showed faint indications of what might be foreign substances in the lungs, which could account for the aggressiveness of the infection.

Lieutenant Chris Murphy, his assistant surgeon, was equally puzzled. They both knew, without saying, that Mazmin was beyond saving.

They felt helpless. No one had ever died in sick bay from a sickness since either of them reported to the *Belleau Wood*. Others had died from trauma, but never from sickness. "What do you think, Captain?"

"I think if he doesn't start responding to the antibiotics immediately we're going to lose him." He looked at the ice packs surrounding the man's neck and head and under his arms.

"What's making him go so *fast*?"

Satterly pointed to the X rays. "Foreign bodies in his lungs. He sucked something into his lungs."

Murphy couldn't believe it. "How?"

Satterly gave him a knowing, disapproving look. "Is there any doubt?" He watched Mazmin labor in his attempts to breathe. "If he dies, I'm not going to let it rest. I'm going to make sure whoever is responsible for this will pay for it."

"How?"

Satterly didn't respond.

"So our guy here," Murphy said. "If he got tortured like he said, would that cause him to get an infection like this? And how would he get foreign substances if all they were doing was pouring water down his throat?"

"I don't know. I can't figure it out. I guess we should consider he has some rare African disease we're not familiar with. But it sure looks like regular old pneumonia to me."

"What should we do?"

Satterly pulled the X ray off the light box, and turned it off. "We're doing everything we can. We've got him on our strongest antibiotic, we've given him shots, we're cooling him down, and we're making no progress. We just have to keep monitoring him and hope he turns around soon, or he's not going to be with us long."

Chapter 4.

Rat walked straight to the Counterterrorism Center, the CTC, that consumed acres of space on the ground floor of CIA headquarters in Langley, Virginia. He walked across the crowded, humming area full of cubicles where most of the people worked in a frenetic environment. He had never been to the CTC before the War on Terrorism; the Navy's counterterrorism unit didn't work with the CIA except in extraordinary circumstances—circumstances that Rat had never encountered.

He had heard that before September 11 there had been about five hundred analysts in the CTC. Now there were more than eleven hundred. Twenty-five hundred cables a day poured in from sources as diverse as those interrogating prisoners in Guantánamo Bay, Cuba, to foreign intelligence services passing on tips on terrorist organizations. Instead of trucking pizzas in all night as had occurred regularly after 9/11, the CIA cafeteria had agreed to stay open on nights and weekends to accommodate the increased activity.

The CTC ground out five hundred terrorism intelligence reports a month, which were distributed to eighty different government agencies. A video conference was held three times a day with the National Security Council. And every day at five in the afternoon, Stewart Woods, the Director of the Central Intelligence Agency, summoned the forty senior officers from the CTC, the Agency's Directorate of Intelligence, and the clandestine Directorate of Operations, to the conference room just off his seventh-floor office for a grilling on the day's terrorism intelligence. And it all swirled around Don Jacobs.

Rat looked for Jacobs, the Director of Counterterrorism, the man for whom Rat worked during his current temporary assignment from the Navy to the CIA's SAS. Jacobs was unrelenting. He didn't eat or sleep, or not so anyone else could tell, and thought of nothing except how to kill or capture those in the world who were sworn to destroy the United States. He wanted to find the barns they were hiding in and burn them down. Rat couldn't agree more. He loved Jacobs's vision and attitude. It was Jacobs who had made his new assignment exciting, who got his juices flowing. It was the promise of action, not just endless training for future missions that never happened. And Jacobs promised creative, one-off missions, not searching for lost al Qaeda in caves in Pakistan that much of the Special Forces community had been relegated to. It was a picture Rat couldn't resist.

Jacobs had been right, too. Rat had been on numerous missions that had been creative, bold, and successful. There had been a twinge of Washington that Rat didn't care for, like an unwanted spice in an otherwise delicious meal, but given everything else he liked about his temporary position at the CIA, it was worth it. Or at least so far.

Rat headed to Jacobs's office. As he walked across the large CTC area he was reminded of how different it was after years of being a naval officer and working with the SEALs. There was much more of a sense of working in an office, being a bureaucrat. That was part of what he was supposed to remedy in his time at the Agency. A large task, he noted. The Agency reduced everything to the lowest common denominator. The intelligence that got passed on, the analysis that made it into the reports, was the analysis they could get everyone to sign off on. The truly bold, insightful, or creative analysts were sandpapered down to commonality by those around them and especially those above them. Rat had seen enough intelligence reports to know they weren't usually helpful. Not only were they watered down by analysts trying to please every boss, but they relied almost exclusively on satellite intelligence. They were excellent in saying that a certain number of tanks had moved from A to B, but virtually worthless in predicting what a person or regime might do with those tanks. It was the result of the American obsession with satellites and technology. Easy to raise a billion dollars for another satellite, but there was no money to raise the salaries of the analysts, who made less than plumbers.

But Rat didn't expect to solve any of that. He just kept it in mind. He had been brought to the Agency to put a little kick in their Special Forces. He had been doing just that. Don Jacobs appreciated the skill he had brought to the SAS, the Special Activities Staff, as it was euphemistically called.

Rat reached Jacobs's office and was surprised to find him there. The door was open. He knocked.

Jacobs looked up. "Well, look what the cat drug in." He smiled. He stood and shook Rat's hand. "Good work. Brilliant, even. I'll bet you were about to wet your pants to see who got to drop in on Duar."

Rat smiled. "You always wonder how big a hornet's nest you're jumping into. If he had thirty guys spread out, we'd have had our hands full. But it worked out."

"How long you been in town?"

"Night before last."

Jacobs raised his eyebrows as he sat back down, wondering why Rat hadn't checked in before now. "What's her name?"

"Andrea."

"Right. You told me about her before."

"Yes, sir. Former Blue Angels flight surgeon."

"Right. When do I get to meet her?"

"Whenever you want. But I thought you liked being the mysterious boss who was heard about but never seen."

"Always like to meet the pretty women."

"Did I say she was pretty?"

Jacobs smiled. He looked at Rat's tan face and intense eyes. He was striking. Very unlikely he would date a homely woman. "I've read your draft report. Sounds like it went by the numbers. All because of your plan. I must say it was pretty ingenious. Good report too, by the way."

"Thanks."

Jacobs gave him a knowing look. "I'm going to put you in for some special recognition for this one. It was yours."

Rat looked away, embarrassed. "You don't need to do anything—"

"I want to."

"I was thinking of taking some leave."

"What for?"

"Just some time off. Would that be a problem?"

"We've been talking about that training that you were going to do."

Rat frowned.

"Small-boat training. You're the expert in maritime activities. Right?"

"And?"

"And you're supposed to spread your wisdom to others. Teach them how to drive boats, go fast, I don't know. All that boat shit."

"Right."

"Set for next week."

"Oh," Rat said, disappointed.

"Down at The Point."

"When?"

"Monday. First thing."

Rat nodded unenthusiastically as he stood to leave Jacobs's office.

"One other thing," Jacobs said. "That surgeon aboard the *Belleau Wood* could be a problem. He's screaming hard and loud. He has a hard-on about one of the captured terrorists. Claims you tortured him."

Rat didn't respond.

"So?"

"What?"

"Did you?"

"Did I what?"

"Torture him?"

"I interrogated him. He's the one who told us where Duar was. Without him, we wouldn't have found Duar. He'd still be out there plotting to kill a few hundred thousand Americans."

"I'm not accusing you of anything, but if this is going to get ugly, I need to know now how big a fight we're going to have." He looked at Rat's face. "I'm on your side."

"I appreciate it," Rat said. "I've got to get going."

"That's it?" Jacobs stood in amazement as Rat walked out of his office and closed the door behind him. "Rat!"

♦ ♦ ♦

John Johnson twirled a pencil in his left hand as he moved the laser mouse deftly with his right. He had wasted enough time already looking at news sites. He spent the first half hour of work every day in his job at the NSA, the National Security Agency, reading the latest news on-line. He read the *New York Times,* the *Washington Post, USA Today,* CNN.com, the *London Times,* even his hometown newspaper, the *Albuquerque Journal,* and the student newspaper at his alma mater, the New Mexico Military Institute, where he had completed his two-year degree. He kept track of everything he wanted to on the Internet. He was a master of the Internet in part because it was now his job. He spent most of every day on-line, looking for one thing—terrorists.

He closed the window for the *New York Times,* took a deep breath and a deep gulp of coffee as he prepared to descend into the pits, into the seedy side of his job. Much to his dismay, he had discovered that one of the favorite places for terrorists to communicate with anonymity was in chat rooms on pornography sites. He closed his eyes momentarily and logged on to one of the many pornography sites to which he subscribed. He generally liked his job, but having to search pornography sites every day disgusted him. It was corrosive, debasing. The first images quickly came onto his screen. He gritted his teeth. He could be as moved as the next man by the sight of a beautiful woman scantily clothed. But this stuff was horrendous. Terrorists used these sites because they apparently didn't expect governments to look for them there.

Two years ago Johnson had been asked to participate in a newly formed group to decide how best to capitalize on the Internet, how to best use it to their advantage. The Internet had made the NSA's work much more difficult. The volume of electronic traffic had gone up exponentially every year since the Internet had become commonplace. It enabled people to communicate in ways that were difficult to discover.

He tried to focus on the side of the screen as he clicked through the pages to the chat room. He had almost gotten to the point where he didn't notice the images anymore but some of them were so jarring that he couldn't ignore them. It seemed to him that the more perverse, the more disgusting the site, the more likely it was that the people he was looking for were there. They seemed to think that the government wouldn't go to places where child pornography or bestiality was featured. They were almost right.

He finally made it to the chat room. There were pages of comments, some trying to be humorous, some by those for whom English was clearly not their first language. He adjusted his glasses as he read. He had come to recognize people, even those who tried to disguise themselves with several different names or identities. They misspelled or misused the same words or jammed hints or clues into their messages for their intended readers that were obvious to a cryptologist like Johnson, trained for years in the caverns of Navy cryptology. He was sure he could recognize a large number of the participants, much like a third grade teacher might recognize a student's work.

Johnson read quickly. Nothing interesting or suspicious. He directed a recording device that copied the chat room's writing onto a separate hard drive and went to Pornography Site Number Five on his list, his list of fifty. He recalled this site clearly as it was here he had found evidence of Wahamed Duar's operation. Two people communicated repeatedly with different screen names, and hinted at dates that started lining up with other things he knew about Duar's operation. It made him sufficiently suspicious that he passed his tentative beliefs uphill where his superiors had agreed with him. They had been impressed and told him so. It had given him a renewed sense of mission that was now starting to wane.

He leaned forward and rested his head on his hand as he looked at the comments in the chat room. He tried to envision the people on the other side of the screen typing these words. Probably mostly single men sitting in dark rooms desperate for affection, recognition, or companionship, who had twisted their idea of a relationship into what was before them. Johnson read on, his eyes drifting from one obscene comment to another when he noticed a couple of remarks that seemed out of keeping with the rest.

He concentrated on two who seemed to be having their own implicit subconversation. He quickly captured the usernames and began working backward to find their Internet addresses and the ISP—the Internet Service Provider—through which they were working.

The NSA's ability to work with ISPs in other countries was little known. In fact the NSA had created a list of every single ISP in the world by country or area, four hundred eighty of them around the globe. No one knew the NSA could target an ISP by country. Many people believed e-mail to be anonymous, not so much in content, which they suspected might be intercepted, but anonymous in location. But the NSA had been busy. Pakistan, for example, only had fifty-five ISP address ranges registered to the country. The smaller the country, the smaller the pond he had to explore compared to the giant ocean of the Internet. If they wanted to know exactly how the routing worked, they would send someone to one of the numerous Internet cafés in, say, Pakistan, who would send an e-mail that could be easily traced. From then on, the NSA could track any e-mail coming from that block in Islamabad, or Karachi. And that wasn't their only tool.

Johnson began his most recent exploration with a frown. He had heard that Rat, a good friend of his, had captured Wahamed Duar. Everyone had assumed Duar's organization must be crippled. Yet from his recollection, the traffic he was now seeing on Pornography Site Number Five was strikingly similar to that he had seen from Duar's organization before the attack in Sudan. Johnson began making electronic notes in a file on a pop-up window on his computer.

He dumped them into an electronic folder that was part of the NSA's top-secret system for tracking Internet traffic, CARNIVORE, an electronic monitoring system that straddled virtually all the important ISP servers in the world and allowed the United States to monitor Internet traffic. When it was in the TCP full mode, it collected every word of every communication that passed through the server. The NSA could then use its supercomputers to monitor the words themselves for patterns, particular words such as "bomb," or anything else they were looking for. They could even store the data and come back to analyze it later. They could track where it came from, and where it went. But they never acknowledged the ability to do either, even though CARNIVORE itself was being replaced by an upgraded system called DCS 1000, or as it was fondly known, ENHANCED CARNI-VORE.

Johnson watched as CARNIVORE went to work. He drank his cooling coffee and wrinkled his nose at the staleness. He put the cup down. Shit, he thought. Duar's organization was still kicking, still planning, and hadn't missed a beat. It even looked like the same people.

♦　♦　♦

Lieutenant Murphy dozed in the office just off the main treatment room of the sick bay on the second deck of the *Belleau Wood*. There was a rap on the door.

"Dr. Murphy, I think you'd better come look at our patient."

Murphy looked up at the woman whose voice he didn't recognize. It was a corpsman who had joined the ship the week before. "Huh?" he said as he tried to shake the cobwebs from his head. It was the tone of the corpsman's voice that alarmed him, a tone of urgency. "What is it?"

"His vitals are off the charts. His temperature is a hundred and six, his breathing is extremely labored, and, frankly, I think he's about to code on us."

Murphy raced to the bedside of their lone patient. He was clearly struggling. He was flushed and seemed to be sagging into the bed. Murphy looked at the corpsman. "Get Dr. Satterly down here right away." The corpsman ran out of the sick bay heading for the office to dial Satterly.

Murphy leaned toward the patient. "Mazmin!" he said loudly. "Mazmin, pull out of it!" Mazmin didn't respond. His eyes were rolled up very high. Murphy could feel the heat of his skin without even touching it. He turned to another corpsman. "Get me some more ice packs. We may be nearing the end here."

♦　♦　♦

Rat turned his old Porsche 911 convertible into the underground garage at his Washington office, where he maintained his company, International Security Consultants, Inc. It allowed him and his team to operate anywhere and do whatever they wanted with complete deniability from whatever arm of the government was using their services at the moment. Officially he was still active duty Navy; a lieutenant in Dev Group, or DEVGRU as it was known in the Navy, when it was spoken of at all, usually with a quiet tone and a glance over the shoulder. But Rat was also with the CIA and carried other IDs that no one could refute or challenge because they were completely authentic. He was whatever he needed to be.

The meeting was scheduled for 0630, the same time Rat liked to start everything in the day. He liked to get meetings and discussions out of the way early to allow time for more important things. By the time he got to the conference room—a room certified for discussing top-secret intelligence—the rest of the team was already in place. Six of the eleven were former members of Dev Group. The other five were SAS members who had been placed in Rat's group prior to Sudan, one of whom was new. Nubs's replacement.

He was ten minutes early, as were they. They knew what happened to those who were late. Rat said if you couldn't be on time for a stupid meeting in Washington, he had no confidence you could be on time for something important. He had thrown one man off the team for being five minutes late. The others had been speechless. They regarded Rat as friendly, fair, and even thought he had a good sense of humor. But when it came to operations, the preparation for which began long before the actual event, he was incredibly intense and serious. It was at least part of what accounted for his success and reputation. Nothing got in the way of results.

"Morning," Rat said as he tossed his thin leather briefcase on the conference room table.

"Morning," they replied. The atmosphere was one of self-congratulation. Most smiled and drank from paper coffee cups.

"Everyone read the report?"

They all nodded.

"Jacobs has the draft, but he's waiting for the final. This is it. I know this is putting the cart before the horse, but Jacobs is in a hurry. So comments?"

Robby smiled. His dreadlocks hung down beside his dark black face. It was a wig he wore. He had closely cut hair, but when he wore his dreads he looked completely authentic. He could incorporate numerous accents if needed. "I noticed there's no mention of our Jordanian friend wanting to slot the guy we captured."

Rat smiled back, amused at the image of the Jordanian being turned loose on Mazmin, who was now complaining about his medical care and his treatment at the hands of the Americans. "I thought we'd let him off easy. In fact I left him out of the report entirely. We had to hint about the guy who gave us a signal that we used to jump in. But I don't know who's going to get this report. His existence is above the clearance level of about ninety-eight percent of the Agency."

Robby flipped to another page of the report. "You didn't mention the use of the Ultra Wide Band. That was its first tactical and combat use, unless I'm mistaken. That wall was pretty damned thick. Seems to me we ought to tell everyone how effective it was. Maybe they'll fund it a little more."

Rat nodded and made a note to himself. "Think you could do a paragraph on that?"

Robby nodded. "But I'm thinking we ought to do a separate report. Maybe an addendum, or technical report that could be attached . . ."

"No, they'll ask for more if they want it," Rat replied. "Groomer? Anything?"

"No, sir. Pretty much a textbook operation. We got Duar, we got another guy from his organization, we got the Jordanian, we got in and out of there with only one casualty—which is pretty amazing considering all the bullets flying around—and accomplished the mission. Frankly, we looked pretty good. Although I feel pretty shitty about Nubs."

Rat nodded and looked at those around the table. "We need to have a farewell party for Nubs."

There were immediate grunts of agreement.

"A wake. We've got to honor him. One of the finest men I've ever known. Just tears me up that he got hit. Unlucky. We've got to invite Carrie, and have a really ripping party. Who knows her the best?"

"I do," Robby said. "I went to his house at least once a week."

"You want to talk to Carrie and see if she's up for it?"

"Sure. I'll take care of the whole—"

Suddenly Rat's small encrypted digital cell phone rang. He was annoyed but looked at the number on the readout. "Rat," he said, quickly putting the phone to his ear. He listened carefully. "When?" He listened again. He nodded. "Okay. Thanks for calling." He pushed the top of the phone down onto the rest of the shaft and tossed the phone onto his briefcase.

The others in the room waited. They knew only a few people had the number to that phone. "The guy we captured in Sudan who was in sick bay just died," Rat reported.

Several of the men in the conference room looked away. They were the ones who thought his treatment of Mazmin had crossed the line. They had known better than to say anything in the middle of Sudan, but now that it was over, they showed their disapproval.

Groomer was the first to speak. "I'm pretty broken up about that," he said, thinking instead of what Mazmin had done to Nubs. "I was thinking he and I could become close friends one day. But what got him?"

Rat picked up the phone and slid the top up and down nervously. "Pneumonia."

"How the hell did he get pneumonia?" Groomer asked.

"Probably from the water and shit in his lungs," Rat said.

"What difference does it make?" Banger asked. "I don't give a shit about him, frankly. If I had the chance I'd have shot him right in the face."

"That captain on the ship seems to care a lot. The ship's surgeon."

"Meaning what?" Banger asked. "What's he going to do?"

"The same thing we all did," Rat said. "Write a report."

"Saying what?"

"He did an autopsy. He's going to say the guy died from pneumonia caused by water and foreign objects in his lungs that got infected."

"What foreign substances?"

"Vomit," Rat said reluctantly.

"So what?" Groomer said, growing annoyed.

"The cause of the vomit's the problem. Doctor's going to put in his report that he died from torture."

No one in the room said a word. They all understood the implications. Torture, as in intentionally hurting someone to get information from them, or just to hurt them, was illegal. Forbidden.

Sellers, one of the newer members of the team and one who was not from Dev Group, said, "So maybe we ought to just tell everybody exactly what happened. We don't say shit about it in the official report," he said, indicating.

"Why would we do that?" Rat asked.

"Because the truth is always the right thing."

Rat opened his briefcase. "Starting Monday we're all going to The Point. Jacobs wants us to get smart on small-boat operations. Some of you don't have any experience in that at all, and there will be other SAS teams down there. We'll rendezvous at Quantico. We're going to helo down. We'll be there the rest of the week. Any questions?"

Robby waved his hand. "We need to do anything about this report the surgeon's going to do?"

Rat shook his head. "We'll deal with it when it happens, if anything happens. We've got work to do."

"May be too late then," Robby said.

"I'll take that chance," Rat said. "Okay. So let's talk about the Sudan op. Good, bad, and other. Except the interrogation part. We'll leave that alone for now."

John Johnson of the NSA, freed for a while from the pornography sites, pulled his old Cherokee to the end of the rutted road by the small pier on a base Johnson had never been to. In fact he had never heard of it, until he e-mailed Rat and said he had to talk to him. Rat had directed him to the secure Web site that detailed the base's location. Johnson had jumped at the chance to get out of his cubicle and away from the pornography sites and drove down past the Great Dismal Swamp near Elizabeth City, North Carolina. He was to see Rat at the Harvey Point Defense Testing Activity, or The Point, as it was called. It was built during World War II to serve as a base for antisubmarine blimps. Now it was used as an advanced training center for the CIA. Most thought all high-level CIA training occurred at Camp Peary near Williamsburg, Virginia. The Basic Operations Course for the CIA was taught at the ten-thousand-acre Camp Peary, or The Farm, as it was called. The Farm was used extensively by the DO, the Directorate of Operations. But advanced paramilitary operations were all conducted at The Point in North Carolina.

Rat stood near the group of fast inflatable boats idling at the end of the pier, yelling instructions over the loud engines. The men were anxious to get underway. Rat wore a sleeveless wetsuit top. The spring day was crisp and the inland water was choppy. It was blocked from the full Atlantic swell and wave action by the outer banks of North Carolina, the long islands that stretched all along the northeast corner of the state that acted like breakwaters, or hurricane magnets, depending on the season. Rat was ready to get on the water and show his men what the high-speed boats could do; he would control one boat, Groomer and Robby would each be at the helm of a boat, and Rat was going to let Sellers control the fourth boat. He had seen a certain look in Sellers's eyes at the meeting on Saturday. He hadn't liked it; it was a look of distrust. Rat didn't believe everyone had to agree with him all the time. But what he couldn't stand was disloyalty, or being undercut. If someone had something against him, or thought he was wrong, fine. But he wasn't about to be sabotaged.

Johnson stared at the scene with his arms crossed. He didn't want to interfere. He was happy to spend the entire day there, even if it meant just watching people race around in boats. Rat saw him and stopped in mid-sentence. Rat liked Johnson. He had met him years ago in the Navy. As a cryptologist Johnson had worked intimately with the SEALs.

When Johnson had joined the NSA, Rat had talked to him on occasion. Nothing very regular, or organized; they would get together every few months just to get caught up. Rat had recruited Johnson to be one of the people to whom Sarah St. James, the National Security Adviser, looked for raw intelligence information. She didn't even want classified information. She wanted opinions, thoughts, direction, wisdom. Johnson had been thrilled to become part of her shadow intelligence organization.

Rat waved. He could read Johnson's body language. He had something big to say. "Give me a second," Rat yelled at the rest of the team as he jogged up the pier to Johnson. He extended his hand and Johnson shook it. Rat removed his Oakley sunglasses. "Hey. You made it."

"How you doin'?"

"Fine. Doing some boat training. I can't take much time. Will this take long? You want to talk tonight? You can share my room at the BOQ."

Johnson shook his head. "I found something you should know about. It may be kind of premature, but if I'm right, you might be able to start looking for other things, supporting information. Or somebody could," Johnson said. "It's sort of about Sudan."

Rat frowned. "What about Sudan?"

"Duar. His organization."

"What about it?" Rat said, impatience growing.

"As I understand it, you guys got Duar in Sudan. Am I right? I mean that's what the President said in his press conference. That is right, isn't it, not some smoke we're blowing to try to get him later or something . . ."

Rat nodded. "Yeah, we got him. What of it?"

"I was pretty much on top of Duar's communication network. The Internet traffic that was coming out of Sudan from their ISPs, well, we had made a lot of progress. It's what led the Agency to put a man on the arms merchant's staff . . . you know all that. We were in good shape there."

"And?"

He glanced around. "You know CARNIVORE?"

Rat nodded.

"Well, just for fun, I continued to monitor the same sites Duar and his friends were using before you got him. They're still operating. Somebody out there is still communicating. And it's not just close, it's . . . well, at least I . . ." Johnson hesitated. "I can't be sure yet." He looked up at Rat. "But I think it's the same people. Not just people working for him, but the very same people who were communicating before your Sudan operation."

Rat watched the men continue to hold the boats for him. He looked at Johnson, then out at the Albemarle Sound. The chop was increasing. It was going to be quite a banging once they got their boats going at high speed. The longer he waited, the worse it was going to get. "What are you saying?"

"I don't know what it means. I'm just here to tell you that somehow Duar's organization is intact. You guys got all of them, or a good number of them, and captured the head guy. But they're still out there doing business. I just wanted to tell you. I thought you'd want to know. You can tell our mutual friend if you want." He kicked a rock. "Plus, I just wanted an excuse to get out of my cubicle."

Rat was concerned. What did the Internet traffic mean? How could Duar's group still be a threat? Maybe it was bigger than they had initially thought. "Can you tell what they're talking about?"

"I think they're planning another strike. The failure of the purchase in Sudan may be a hiccup, but they're not too concerned."

"You think they've got another source for plutonium?" he asked.

"Can't tell. But there's a lot of planning going on."

Rat nodded, his mind spinning. He looked back at Johnson. "You're welcome to stay if you want. You can even come out in one of the boats. My treat."

Johnson put up a hand. "No thanks, Rat. I'd get seasick."

"Nah," Rat replied. "You'd be bouncing *way* too hard to notice any seasickness."

"Pass."

Rat smiled and headed down to the pier. "These guys never quit, do they?"

Johnson shook his head.

Rat shot him a look. "Neither do we."

◆　◆　◆

Sharon Rakoff walked into Secretary of Defense Stuntz's office for the second time that day. She took advantage of her special access perhaps once a month, but twice in a day was unheard of. Stuntz clearly didn't like it. "Excuse me, Mr. Secretary."

He looked up from a report he was reading and removed his reading glasses. "What?" he said.

"There's a man here to see you."

"I don't have any appointments. I cleared my calendar to go through this budget."

"Yes, sir. He's rather insistent. He's from Europe."

"So *what?*"

"He's Belgian. A lawyer of some kind. He's with the ICC," she said.

"What the hell does he want?" Stuntz asked.

"He wouldn't tell me. He said he'd only tell you, and you would definitely want to hear what he has to say."

"No diplomatic contact? No communication through regular channels? No notice he's coming from Belgium? Sounds like a bunch of bullshit to me," he said, his voice rising.

"Yes, sir. It did to me too, but he said he was doing all he could to avoid raising this to a level of formal contact. He said that would take it out of his hands and he wouldn't be able to stop it."

Stuntz frowned. "Stop what?"

"He wouldn't say. Here's his card."

Stuntz sighed deeply and took the card: Didier Picque, the International Criminal Court. He examined it, and tossed it on his desk. He closed the notebook with the draft budget and pushed it to the corner of his immaculate desk. "Where is he?"

"In the sitting area."

"Show him in. Get Leslie in here. I want someone else to hear whatever he has to say."

"Yes, sir." She turned and left the office, closing the door silently behind her.

She returned a few moments later. "Mr. Secretary?" Rakoff said. "May I present Mr.—Monsieur—Didier Picque."

"Good afternoon," he said to Picque.

"Good afternoon," Picque replied. He was wearing an expensive double-breasted suit and Italian shoes. His dark brown hair was rather long and wavy. He carried a worn soft-sided black briefcase. "Thank you for seeing me. I know it was unorthodox, but once you hear what I have to say, I think you'll understand." He had a noticeable French accent and was soft-spoken.

"Sure," Stuntz said skeptically. He looked at Rakoff. "Where's Ms. Slater?"

"She's coming."

"Would you like some coffee or something?"

"No thank you," Picque said.

"Have a seat."

Leslie Slater, an attorney from the General Counsel's Office of the Department of Defense, hurried in, carrying a flat notebook that had a legal pad inside. "Sorry, sir."

"No problem," he said, then introduced her to Picque.

"I don't have much time," Stuntz said. "Why are you here?"

Picque smiled. "I understand. I came unannounced. Frankly, I'm here at my own insistence. I thought you should know about a . . . development right away, so you could take whatever steps you thought necessary." He paused and saw that Stuntz was waiting for him. "You recently conducted an operation in Sudan."

"Sure."

"Very well done, I must say. It is the talk of military communities throughout Europe. Daring, creative, bold, efficient, and quick. You can't ask for much better than that—"

"Go on."

"During this operation, many people were killed—"

"That happens when you're going after terrorists who aren't real interested in being captured."

"No doubt. And you captured Duar, which is amazing. Congratulations."

"Thanks."

"Apparently there was another man who was captured. He was taken out to one of your ships, where I understand he was to be tried by one of your tribunals."

"Don't tell me you're here to complain about our tribunals. Feel free to write a letter to the editor, telling them all your brilliant thoughts. I'm sure—"

Picque was shaking his head. "No, no, not at all. I have some issues with those tribunals, but that's for another day, if at all. I'm here about something else entirely."

"What?"

"The second man captured has died."

Stuntz was surprised. "How do you know that?"

"That doesn't matter."

"It does to me, especially if you have access to classified information."

"His death is classified?"

"I don't know. I asked you how you know."

"That too is for another time."

"What the hell is your point?"

"The man who died, Mazmin is his name, died of pneumonia because he was tortured by one of your Special Operations men. He was nearly drowned, threw up, and ingested his own vomit into his lungs."

"What makes you think he was tortured?"

"I'm quite sure. And the reason I'm here is that in spite of the brilliance of your operation, this death has gotten Europe's attention, and in particular the International Criminal Court. This is a war crime." His French accent was beginning to annoy Stuntz. Picque sat forward slightly. "To make a long discussion short, the ICC is investigating. If it turns out to be as I know it is, either you will prosecute whoever did this, or we will."

"You don't have jurisdiction."

"Yes, sir, we do."

"We never signed that stupid treaty."

"That doesn't matter. It was given global effect by those who did sign it. We can prosecute a war crime that occurred anywhere, even against people from countries who are not signatories."

He knew Picque was right. Stuntz glanced at Slater, who was taking notes and trying to control her expressions of surprise and outrage. "We got an exemption."

Picque nodded in a patronizing way. "Yes, but the exemption for the United States was for one year, and it was for peacekeeping missions. That year has long passed, and this wasn't a peacekeeping mission. I'm afraid what happened is right in the heart of what the new court was created for."

Stuntz wanted to stick a pencil in Picque's eye. He hated being cornered, especially when he was unprepared. "I don't know about any of this. What do you want?"

"I want your assurance that he will be prosecuted. If he is, then the ICC will have no role. As you know, we only prosecute when the home country of the criminal is unable or, um, unwilling to prosecute."

Stuntz didn't want to give him an answer. "Thank you for coming. Now if—"

Picque wasn't about to be pushed aside. "I need to know today what your intentions are. If we don't get some assurance that you personally will deal with it, and pursue it, then we will go public. We have a press conference scheduled for tomorrow in The Hague."

Stuntz said. "Why me? Why aren't you sitting in the Attorney General's office?"

"Because this man was a member of the Department of Defense. You have jurisdiction to court-martial him."

Stuntz breathed in deeply as he stalled for time. Then something struck him. "What did you say the man's name was again?"

"Rathman. Kent Rathman. He goes by a nickname—Rat, I believe."

◆　◆　◆

The large gray CH-46D Sea Knight helicopter settled onto the deck of the *Belleau Wood*. The six huge blades, three forward and three aft, sagged as the weight came off the helicopter. The motorized ramp gently touched the deck. Several people walked out of the helicopter still wearing their cranial helmets and flotation vests. They proceeded carefully, getting their bearings from the long vibration-filled helicopter ride. They felt numb.

They walked to the island and went down to the captain's wardroom. Leading the group was Commander Barry Little, a prosecutor from the Fifth Fleet judge advocate's staff. He had brought two other attorneys with him to make up the prosecution team for the tribunal. When the message had been received at Fifth Fleet headquarters, Little had seen it before anyone else in the chain of command above him. He had immediately drafted a proposal for the admiral appointing himself as the prosecutor. He wasn't about to let someone else take this plum. He wanted to try Duar himself and obtain the death penalty. Anything short of capital punishment would be a failure.

Right behind Little was Commander Elizabeth Watson, the attorney who had been selected to defend Duar. She had tried many cases on the opposite side of Little. Years ago they had served as prosecuting attorneys at the San Diego Naval Base, where they had been friends; but since then she had found herself mostly on the other side, defending accused criminals in courts-martial.

Inside the wardroom, Captain Hogan motioned for the attorneys to sit down. "Welcome to the *Belleau Wood*. I'm Captain Hogan. All your bags are being placed in your staterooms. We have rooms available for each of you that correspond to your rank. I'll get your keys and frame numbers to you shortly. It's my job to ensure that you get whatever you need to conduct this trial. If you need something and you can't get it, let me know and I'll fix it. I don't know when the trial is supposed to start. Do any of you?"

Little spoke. "Commander Barry Little, Captain. I'll be the chief prosecutor." He said it with a little more pride than called for. "The date hasn't been set yet, but it won't be long. We're trying to move as fast as we can. We're here to get it set up, gather the evidence together, and get underway. When we are ready, they'll send the court members and the military judge who is going to preside over the trial."

"Do you know the name of the judge yet?"

"No, sir. As of this morning it hadn't been decided."

"Fine," Hogan said. "The interrogation is ongoing. Will you be involved? I must say it hasn't been very productive."

"All of which was done outside the presence of counsel, I assume?" Watson said with a sharp tone.

Hogan looked at her with disapproval. "And you are?"

"Sorry. I'm Commander Elizabeth Watson. I'll be heading up the defense team."

"Lucky you." Hogan smiled, trying to break some of the tension he had just created. "You get to defend the most wanted terrorist in the world."

"Yes, sir. I do. Either we do a trial and he gets someone to represent him, or we just tie him to a post and shoot him. Which would you prefer?"

Hogan's eyes narrowed. "I don't need any of that, Commander. You might do better to hold your tongue a little."

"Yes, sir, *sorry*," she said, not meaning it.

"In answer to your question, yes, I think the interrogation was done outside the presence of counsel. Is there a problem with that?"

"That may depend on whether anyone intends on using any of it in this tribunal."

"I don't know anything about evidence, or who's going to use it. I just know that the men who were here to do the interrogation have left and will be back. I get the sense they're going to keep going."

"When can I see him?" Watson asked.

"In due time. I thought first we would go over the procedures, the location for the trial, the instructions we have received from the Secretary of Defense, and other matters."

Little spoke. "Thank you for allowing us to do this aboard your ship, sir."

"Frankly, I wish this were aboard a naval station somewhere—perhaps in Italy, or Spain, or Guantánamo Bay, which seems to me ideal. But in any case, it is to be here, so we'll need to make accommodations."

"Where are we going to hold this tribunal?" Watson asked.

"Right here," the captain replied, looking around the wardroom. "It's big enough, private, and secure enough. Is it okay with you?"

She looked around. "Yes. It looks fine. Is there an office that I can use to prepare his defense?"

Captain Hogan fought not to say what he wanted to say. He paused just long enough to let her know he could do as he wished. "Of course. We will provide you with whatever you need."

◆　◆　◆

"So, Pat, what do you think?" Stuntz asked

Patrick Cleveland, the general counsel to the Department of Defense, breathed in deeply. He wasn't ready to have the discussion yet. His staff hadn't completed the research. But the Secretary of Defense, his boss, had insisted. He loved his job, but Stuntz was a very hard man to work for. He didn't care much about the subtleties of the law; he saw it mostly as an impediment. "I don't have final answers but do have some idea of where we're going to end up, so if you'd like—"

Stuntz looked like a hunter who had spotted a buck. "So can we?"

"Prosecute him?"

Stuntz nodded.

Cleveland nodded reluctantly. "Yes. Have you seen the report from that doctor on board the *Belleau Wood*?"

"The autopsy?"

"Well, it's more than an autopsy. It contains information in it about the raid itself, about the Navy officer's conduct—he tortured the man, and it resulted in the man's death. It would be manslaughter, almost certainly. And a violation of the Geneva Convention, because the man was in custody and no longer resisting. We could definitely court-martial him."

Stuntz leaned back in his squeaky leather chair and pondered the implications. "I don't want to court-martial him."

Cleveland was confused. "I thought that was the whole idea."

"*Prosecuting* him is the idea. Not court-martialing him."

"But he's a naval officer. He would need to be court-martialed."

"Couldn't Justice do it?"

Cleveland hadn't thought about it, nor had he asked any of his staff to research it. "I'm not sure," he said cautiously. "There may be concurrent jurisdiction . . ."

"Well, make it so they do. That's why I brought you here. You're the big smart New York trial lawyer. Let's see some of that magic."

Cleveland was unimpressed. "I don't have the ability to make the law something that it isn't. I can't just confer jurisdiction on a court that hasn't been granted that juris—"

"Don't give me a bunch of legal bullshit. Get over to Justice and *tell* them to prosecute him. The last thing we need is for the ICC to stick their noses into this."

"I'll see what I can do. If we send it to Justice, if Rathman has a lawyer that has any brains at all, he'll move for a dismissal. My guess is that it should be granted."

"And what lawyer will he get? If it's in federal court, he won't be entitled to an attorney, will he?"

"He's probably not poor enough."

"Exactly. So he'll hire some second-rate lawyer from Washington—he'll have a lot to choose from—and the guy will be overworked and miss half the things he's supposed to do. Don't worry about it."

Cleveland rose and prepared to leave. "I'm not confident this will work."

Stuntz didn't say anything.

Cleveland looked into Stuntz's eyes for the political reason behind what he had been told. He was sure it was there somewhere. "Why do you care where he gets tried? What difference does it make?"

"I don't want to look vindictive."

"Because he works for Sarah St. James?"

"He doesn't *work* for her, but he talks to her. Gives her information. He and others give her sort of a leg up in the intelligence world. Aggravates the hell out of me."

"So you actually are being vindictive, aren't you?"

"Yeah. I am. I'd love to string him up by his little neck. But this is just as good. Anything to maker her holiness look worse is okay by me."

◆　◆　◆

Elizabeth Watson walked down the passageway behind two sailors. The hard heels of her shoes were loud on the shiny tile. She sort of liked that, having an audible presence just by walking. She also happened to be the senior woman on board. There were two lieutenant commanders, but she was the only commander. She always checked when she was at a command.

The lead sailor, a burly first class petty officer who was a Master at Arms opened a hatch and led her down two ladders to the brig. Before he opened the last hatch, he turned to Watson and said, "This isn't the friendliest guy you've ever met, ma'am. I'd use some caution with him."

They went to the window outside the brig where a senior chief petty officer was waiting for them. He stood taller when he saw Commander Watson approaching. The first class petty officer tried to give him a look, a caution, but he didn't see it. "Good morning, ma'am. You're here to see the prisoner?"

"Yes. Mr. Duar. Where is he?"

"He's in a private cell. I'll be happy to take you there." He stepped around the thin bulkhead and brought the keys with him. He unlocked the main door to the brig and stepped through. "Right this way," he said. The two petty officers stayed back and only Watson and the chief stepped through. They stopped in front of a thick steel hatch that was dogged and padlocked. The chief inserted a key, noisily took off the heavy padlock, and looked at Watson. "If you need anything, please just let me know. I'll be right outside. If I hear anything I don't like, I'll come in immediately, whether I'm interrupting something or not. Okay, ma'am?"

"Fine. Open it."

"Yes, ma'am," he said, turning the key.

Watson stepped through and the chief closed the door behind her. Her bravery seemed to fall away from her and land outside the room. She was exposed. She felt a cold chill on the back of her neck as she stood face-to-face with Duar. She was surprised by the depth of anger in his dark eyes. It suddenly struck Elizabeth that she had forgotten something very important. "Chief!" she yelled.

He opened the door immediately. "Yes?"

"We need the interpreter."

"Yes, ma'am. He was waiting at the office. I should have brought him along. Sorry."

Watson took the time to evaluate Duar. He leaned against the far bulkhead eerily motionless. His hair was longer than it appeared in the grainy black-and-white photo she had seen, and his complexion was darker than she had expected. He was almost handsome. She was five six, and he was much taller, perhaps six feet.

The hatch opened again and the interpreter stepped into the small room. "Sorry," he said. "I'm ready whenever you are."

"Good. Let's do this." She spoke to Duar in English, looking at him the entire time. The interpreter quickly converted her words to Arabic.

"Good morning. My name is Elizabeth Watson. I have been assigned to be your attorney. I'll do my best to defend you—"

"My what?" Duar asked, frowning.

"Your attorney. Your advocate. You're going to be put on trial, and I'm going to defend you."

"What am I being charged with?"

"Murder of Americans, conspiracy to murder Americans. Conspiracy to commit terrorist acts. Did you not receive the charges against you?"

"I've seen nothing."

"I'll bring them today—a written copy of charges. But that is the heart of the matter. In any case, I'll be defending it."

"You will be my attorney?"

Elizabeth warmed. "Yes—"

Duar said loudly, "And who pays you?"

"The United States Government."

"A *woman,* paid for by the United States, defending me in a trial? This is an insult. It is against Islam, it is against my tradition and my culture."

"Why?" Watson asked, unable to control the redness climbing up into her face.

"You are a woman. You're not qualified to defend me from anything. I would rather go without an attorney than be defended by you."

"I'm afraid you don't have a lot of choice. I've been assigned to you by the American government—"

Duar clenched his jaw. "I will *never* speak with you, I will *never* tell you anything, and if you are there to defend me I will not participate in the trial. Get me someone else."

The translator completed his translation and looked at her sheepishly.

"Fine," she replied. "Then I will ensure you get a different attorney. You're also entitled to a civilian attorney. I do not know how you would pay for a civilian attorney, nor do I know how you would contact one. But if you want a civilian attorney, you're entitled to one. I would also, if I were you, contact the press. That's going to be your best bet for a fair trial in this setting. Good-bye." She turned and banged her flat hand on the heavy hatch. The chief opened it immediately and she and the interpreter stepped through.

She was furious. It would have been the biggest case of her life. She had looked forward to defending Duar, to bleeding for him. He had no idea how much she would have sacrificed for him, how hard she would have worked for him. But he didn't care a bit. To him it was impossible because she was a woman.

But if she were honest with herself, she knew, she would have to admit it was as much about her as it was him. Defending him in the first big tribunal in the War on Terrorism would have made her a household name. It would have been her chance at fame and notoriety. When she retired in two years, this case alone would have made her marketable as an attorney. She could get a good, high-paying job in the private sector. But Duar had changed all that.

She stepped over one knee-knocker after another as she hurried down the passageway toward the ladder. She headed directly to her stateroom. She would pack her things, get the next helo off the ship, and get back to her office at Fifth Fleet. The hell with Duar anyway. What an *asshole,* she thought. She would love the opportunity to stick it to him; but vengeance wasn't a praiseworthy instinct. She was ashamed she felt as she did, but only slightly.

Rat walked into Jacobs's office. He had been paged and had no idea what it was about. Jacobs sat at his desk talking on the telephone. He glanced up and saw Rat. He motioned for him to sit down. "I'd like to be with him—I don't care. I understand." He looked at Rat as he listened angrily to the person on the other end of the line. "I'll tell them what I would do, and he can do what he wants. Okay, fine. Five minutes." Jacobs hung up the phone. He was drained. "Rat, how you doing?"

"Fine. What's up? I got your page."

Jacobs sat silently. He seemed lost for words. "Rat," he said in a tone and with a look that Rat didn't like at all, "there are times in our lives where things happen beyond our control. In my experience, it's those times that determine our character. Maybe it's better said our character determines how those times come out. I think this is going to be one of yours."

Rat stared at Jacobs, wondering what he was talking about. "I'm not following you, sir."

"The FBI is here."

Rat hesitated. "For what?"

"To see you. To interview you."

"About what?"

"About that terrorist who died. The one with the vomit in his lungs.

The one who started screaming he'd been tortured as soon as he got aboard the ship."

"Why would the FBI want to talk to me about him?"

Jacobs scowled at him. "Why do you think?"

"I don't know."

"Because somebody thinks you dicked up. Somebody thinks you may need to be charged because somebody thinks that torturing prisoners—or whatever one calls them—is a bad thing. Shit, Rat, what were you thinking? You can't throw someone like that on the water board . . . and let him survive to talk about it."

"Just trying to find Duar, sir. And we did."

"Roomful of witnesses? They'll all have to testify against you."

"They won't testify against me, sir."

"You cannot be that naive. Have you never heard of a subpoena? Do you not understand that if they don't testify against you they can go to prison too?"

"What happens now?" He felt exposed.

"Talk to the FBI. They're upstairs right now waiting for you. You decide whether you want to say anything or not, or whether you are going to ask for an attorney."

"If I ask for an attorney and start playing the defendant, my career here with the SAS is over. Is that about right?"

Jacobs considered. "I know what the implications are, Rat. You're the best operator we've got. I'll do anything to help you, but I can't change the facts."

Rat had known this might happen. Even while in Sudan, he had known it might come back to bite him. He had decided it was worth it. He had been willing to risk his life to get Duar, so risking his career, even a little jail time, was well worth it. And now the people who sat behind desks and read books were going to tell him what he should have done. "You coming with me?"

"Sure."

They walked to the conference room where the FBI was waiting. Jacobs spoke quietly to Rat as they walked down the marble hallway. "General counsel for the Agency will be there."

"Good."

Jacobs walked into the conference room like he owned it. There were three FBI agents, and Christopher Vithoulkas, the CIA's general counsel. They stood up quickly, surprised by Jacobs.

One of the FBI agents extended his hand and introduced himself. "Morning. I'm special agent David Dominoff, and this is special agent Lauren Reynolds, and Brent Harvey."

"Don Jacobs. This is Kent Rathman," he said, pointing.

Rat stood on the other side of the table from the FBI. He made no move to be friendly or shake anyone's hand.

"What did you want to see me about?" Rat asked.

Dominoff looked at Rat, surprised. "Well, I assumed you knew that we're here to talk about the man that was captured, the one who died aboard the *Belleau Wood*."

Rat said nothing.

"Before going further I must advise you that this is a criminal investigation. We're here to investigate whether a crime has been committed, and whether any charges should be brought. You are the focus of the criminal investigation. As such, you are a suspect of a crime, although we have not yet decided whether a crime has in fact been committed. This is the investigation phase. Even though it is only the investigation phase, we want to ensure that you understand that you're entitled to the presence of counsel to represent you even in this investigation phase. You do not have to answer any questions you do not want to. If you'd like to consult with an attorney, then let us know. If you say anything at all, it can and will be used against you. Do you want to have an attorney present at these questions?"

Rat never thought anyone would ask him that question. He was numb. "No."

"Very well. As we were saying, you are aware that one of the men you captured in Sudan died aboard the *Belleau Wood*."

"I heard that. Last time I saw him, he was walking around and looked fine. Maybe it's medical malpractice."

"Are you aware he died from pneumonia, caused by the ingestion of foreign objects—mostly vomit—into his lungs, which led to infection and death?"

"I've heard that."

"Do you know how he happened to have vomit in his lungs?" Dominoff stared at Rat with eyes that would intimidate most witnesses. Rat was not intimidated but he was acutely aware of the implications of what was happening.

"No comment."

"The man—whose name is Mazmin—said you had tortured him. Did you?"

"Define torture."

Dominoff was expecting another "no comment." He looked at Reynolds, who was taking notes furiously. She looked up. Some kind of understanding passed between them based on a look he gave her. Dominoff spoke slowly, "Well, I'm not sure I can give you an exhaustive definition, but let's just say it is the use of force or other means of persuasion to get someone to talk against their will. Do you agree with that definition?"

"I don't know."

"Did you do anything like that to this man who is now dead?"

"Other means of persuasion so they'll talk against their will? Like asking a question twice?"

"I wouldn't think that would be torture."

"What about yelling at him?"

"I wouldn't think so. Let's exclude those things from this inquiry," Dominoff said. "Did you do anything else to Mazmin to get him to tell you things against his will?"

"No comment." Rat was annoyed. "Let me ask you something, Special Agent Dominoff. Have you ever interrogated a suspect that wouldn't talk? Someone who had critical information? Did you ever work anybody over? Ever hit anybody?"

Dominoff wasn't biting. "What I may or may not have done is not at issue here, Mr. Rathman. What *is* at issue is what you may or may not have done in Sudan. If you don't want to answer my questions, just say so. But if I'm going to spend my time here with you I hope that you will answer my questions directly. Are you willing to do that?"

"Maybe. Let me ask you something else."

"Sure," Dominoff said, perturbed.

"Is it illegal, as in a violation of U.S. law, to torture a terrorist in a foreign country?"

"It is a violation of the Geneva Convention. If the person dies, it is also a violation of the U.S. criminal code. Since you are active duty military as well, it is also a violation of the UCMJ."

Rat was startled. "Are you serious? You're thinking of charging me with a violation of the Geneva Convention?"

"I am simply conducting an investigation. I would not be the one making a decision about who is charged with what."

"A terrorist is entitled to the protection of the Geneva Convention when *none* of the countries where he has ever lived have even *signed* the damned thing?"

"You can talk to the U.S. Attorney's Office about that if they indeed bring charges. I'm sure they will look into all of that."

"So you're investigating me for violating the Geneva Convention?"

"Yes, among other things."

"This interview is over." Rat stood up, pushed his chair back, and walked out the door.

◆　◆　◆

"Talk to your detailer?" Rat asked as he kissed Andrea and took off his leather jacket.

"Yeah. I was on hold for twenty minutes, but I finally got to talk to him. He says it's up to me."

"So what are you going to do?"

"I thought we were going out."

"Nah, we're staying here."

She frowned. "You said we were going to Occoquan, some seafood restaurant right on the water. I was really looking forward to it. What's changed?"

Rat was quiet. He sat on the couch and put his head back. "Just don't feel like it."

"You don't feel like seafood? Since when? You live on seafood. And you *always* like going out. You don't even have dishes in your condo."

"Right."

"You suddenly start living on a budget? You don't even know what a budget is." She stood over him looking down at his face. His eyes avoided hers. She grew concerned. "What's going on?"

"Just don't feel like going out. That's all."

"Well, I do. You've been gone all week, you finally get back and you want to sit around? Get your jacket on," she insisted.

He stood slowly and grabbed his jacket. "You drive."

They drove in nearly total silence all the way to Occoquan, Virginia. She stole glances at the side of his face as she drove.

He could tell she was beginning to worry about his demeanor. He was worried about it too. He felt surrounded by an enemy he couldn't fight. No fancy night operation was going to make this go away.

"I have no idea where this restaurant is," Andrea said.

"Turn right when you get to the river," he said.

She complied and he directed her to a large seafood restaurant that had electric signs advertising the fact that they served only fresh fish, nothing frozen ever. His spirits lifted as they got out of the car and he could smell the water. They made their way into the crowded waiting area. The hostess was taking names and handing out vibrating pagers rimmed with flashing red lights when activated. Rat slipped the pager into his pocket.

"Let's wait outside," he said.

"Isn't it too chilly?"

"Never," he said. "Got to breathe the fresh air."

They walked onto a large wooden deck overlooking the river. It was a cool night with low-hanging clouds that completely blocked the stars and moon. It made for a closed-in, damp feeling. Rat put his arm around Andrea as they walked slowly.

"So, do you have an opinion on what I should do?"

Rat frowned. "About what?"

Andrea was unimpressed. "About going to sea. About taking a job on a ship. I'm not even due to rotate, and the detailer called me to give me the first shot at this job. He said it would be good for my career. So what do you think?"

"Go for it."

"Just like that?"

He glanced away from the river toward her. "Sure. Why not? Why wouldn't you?"

"How about 'I'd sure miss you, it would be hard to not see you every week, but we could look forward to when you got off sea duty' —something like that?"

"That's what I should have said. Brief me next time—"

His pocket started vibrating. He pulled out the flashing pager. "We're up." They walked quickly back toward the restaurant.

The hostess seated them in the back by a window overlooking the swollen river. They gave their orders to the waiter.

Andrea didn't wait. "So what's going on? What's eating you? You having second thoughts about me?"

Rat looked into her eyes and smiled. "It's got nothing to do with you." He wanted to tell her all about it. But he couldn't tell her about the things that would make it all make sense. He was sure to look evasive or stupid. "I got a visit from the FBI today."

Andrea's face clouded. "What for?"

"A mission. I can't really go into it. It isn't public."

"A recent mission?"

He nodded.

Her sharp mind scanned recent information, news, anything that would give her any hints. It hit her. "You're the one who captured Wahamed Duar?"

"Maybe."

"Of course," she said, seeing several loose pieces suddenly fall into place. "Something happened?"

"One guy died after the fact."

"From what?"

"From pneumonia."

"What would that have to do with you?"

"I may—they think maybe some things I did contributed to his problems. Maybe caused them."

"How?"

"I was asking him some questions. He didn't want to answer."

"Did you do anything wrong?"

"I guess that's the question."

"So what happened? What did they say? Did you give them what they wanted?"

"I don't think so. I didn't really give them anything."

Andrea glanced up over Rat's shoulder, toward the hostess station. She saw three men in suits. No one else in the restaurant was wearing a tie, let alone a suit. "Why would three men be here in suits?"

"It's them."

"Who?"

"The FBI. They're here for me."

"You know they're here?"

"I saw their reflection in the window. They've been watching us."

"Do you want to go to the rest room or something?"

"I'm not going to run if that's what you're saying. If they came to get me, then they'll get me. I'm not going to become some fugitive. They followed us all the way here from Maryland."

"You knew they were here?"

He nodded. "Sure."

"Why didn't you say something?"

"I thought they might just be following me. No problem with that. It's like having your own bodyguards."

She looked at them again, then pulled her eyes away when they saw her. "They're coming."

Rat was annoyed. "They wanted to pick a time to achieve maximum embarrassment. Couldn't possibly have approached me when I was standing outside on the walkway. No, has to be in here, while eating dinner. *Ass*holes."

The three FBI agents walked quickly toward Rat from the back. They stood around the table facing the window. "Kent Rathman?"

Rat looked up at them. "Care to join us?"

"Are you Kent Rathman?"

"You know who I am. Don't be stupid."

"Sir, you're under arrest. Would you come with us please?"

"Do I have a choice?"

"No, sir. I'm afraid you don't."

Rat stood up and one of the special agents grabbed his arms from behind him. The others in the restaurant had now picked up on what was happening. The room full of people stared as the FBI agent put metal handcuffs on Rat and locked his arms behind him.

Andrea was beside herself. She was on her feet. "What is the charge?"

The FBI didn't respond. They maneuvered Rat between the tables toward the door.

◆ ◆ ◆

Rat never thought he'd find himself in a federal correctional building. At least not as a prisoner wearing a blue jumpsuit. He'd made a phone call to Andrea to encourage her to get a lawyer for him. He had no idea where he'd find the money for a decent lawyer. At least if he had gotten court-martialed he would be entitled to a military lawyer he would have some respect for. But here, who? A federal defender? Although he would qualify as broke compared to anyone with real money, he was quite sure he wouldn't be poor enough to qualify to get a free federal defender.

But Andrea had come through, or at least claimed to have. She assured him that his lawyer was on his way over to see him. He hadn't even been there for four hours. She must have really jumped on it. He couldn't imagine how she would find a decent lawyer who would be willing to come out on Saturday night and see him in custody.

Rat waited as the guard pulled the metal door back and motioned for Rat to step into the room. It was an ordinary, small conference room. Not the kind of room in movies, where prisoners are separated by bulletproof glass from those there to visit them.

He sat in a green folding chair with his hands on the table, still in handcuffs. The metal door slid open. An old man stepped through the door carefully. He sat in the chair across from Rat. Rat was speechless. The man had to be seventy years old. His thick hair was combed straight back from his forehead and was so white it had a tint of yellow to it. "Richard Skyles," the man said gruffly, extending his hand.

"Kent Rathman," Rat said.

As they shook hands Rat noticed that there was a catheter hanging out of the back of the man's right hand. He was horrified. "What is *that*?" Rat asked before he could stop himself.

"I was getting some medical treatment today. Ignore it."

Rat's eyes raced over the man he was supposed to rely on to keep him out of prison. His tie was slightly crooked, and although Rat didn't know one tie from another, this tie had seen better days. Tiny strings hung from it as if the cheap silk had been snagged a few dozen times. The white shirt seemed not quite as white as it should be. "So Andrea called you?"

"Yeah. She told me you needed my help."

"I need somebody's help." He looked at Skyles hard. "But why should it be you?"

Skyles returned his penetrating gaze. "You're concerned about my age. Don't worry about it. I can kick the ass of any U.S. Attorney in Washington."

Rat wasn't impressed. He'd heard a lot of big talk. "Really."

"Yes. Really."

"How'd Andrea find you?"

"I assume she got a reference from somebody. What the hell difference does it make?"

"I guess I need to make sure you're the right guy. I'm in deep trouble."

"I am the right guy."

"How do I know that?"

He leaned forward. "I've tried more cases against the government, against U.S. Attorneys, than anyone in D.C."

"That means you've been doing it a long time. That's all."

"And I've gotten more people off than anyone else. No doubt about it."

Rat asked, "How much do you charge?"

"I'll try to get myself appointed by the federal defender's office and paid by the government. They pay more than I might get if I worked at McDonald's—not a lot, but a little more—but it's a hell of a lot more fun, especially when I get to go against the federal government."

"You don't mind going against the federal government?"

"No. It's the thing I like to do. I hate the government, and every chance I get to oppose it in whatever they're doing, it's pure joy to me. Representing you will be a great joy."

"You know what the charges are?"

"Yes."

"You think you can fight these guys?"

Skyles eyes narrowed. "I am going to be a shit-stick for the U.S. Attorney. Every time they rub up against me, they're going to get *shit* all over them. They will be so annoyed they'll spend half their time just trying to get rid of me. I'll fight them every single step on every single issue. I'll make their lives miserable. I'll call them twenty-four hours a day. I'll file motions they've never even seen. I'll defend you to the death." He sat back. "And we will prevail."

"You're not talking about doing things that are across the line, are you?"

"Never. Just annoying as hell, as obnoxious as hell, and as effective as hell."

Rat was unconvinced. "I'm a pretty straight shooter. I don't like angles and agendas. I don't mind a good fight, even when the odds aren't very good. But I like going straight at it."

Skyles shook his head. "No such thing as a straight fight in criminal court. No such thing as a fair fight at all. Do you really think you can bring to bear the assets necessary to fight the United States Government? Seriously? You think you can put together an army of attorneys to fight whatever army they can put on the other side? You can't get a fair fight when you go against the U.S. Attorney's Office or the Department of Justice. When these guys turn their sights on you, you're dead. They will get you. You'll be convicted of one thing or another. And unless I'm here to protect you, you'll go to prison for many years. But they hate me, and I hate them. When I come around the fight is as close to fair as you're going to get. I've faced almost all of them. I've beaten every one of them. I've tried cases against the United States Government for forty years." Skyles tried to force himself to stand up quickly but he didn't have the strength. He got up slowly and stood behind his chair. Rat noticed that his suit was wrinkled. "I am a little off the wall, I admit. But that's what makes me so *damned* effective."

"So assuming that I do ask you to defend me, what's your plan? I'd like to keep this quiet. I don't want it to get out that I've been arrested and am in jail, about to go on trial for some horrible crime."

"Keep it quiet?" Skyles asked, rubbing the back of his hand around the catheter. "Are you out of your mind? That's *exactly* what the government will want to do. My guess is they're schizophrenic about whether they should have even brought these charges. Somebody somewhere sure wants to bring them, but I'll bet there are just as many people that said they shouldn't pursue it. And for every U.S. Attorney who will charge ahead enthusiastically, there'll be five or ten who would shy away from this case. The last thing they want to do is put some American hero on trial for doing something everybody in the country would say you should have done." Skyles put his hands in his pockets. "They have to convince a jury, see." He paused. "Did you really torture the guy?"

Rat took in a deep breath. "Are we free to talk?"

"They might be listening, but if they do it's a violation of the attorney-client privilege and I can get them in a shitload of trouble."

"Well," Rat began, "it depends on your definition. I did use some water, a little technique that's been around for a long time, to . . . encourage him to answer a few questions. I'm sure he thought it was unpleasant, but there wasn't supposed to be any long-term harm. I guess he got pneumonia."

"Too bad for him. Too bad the American public doesn't know what you did, because you captured Wahamed Duar, right?"

"Yes."

"I'm prepared to bet that the average American would torture one terrorist to capture the most wanted terrorist in the world. I think they would make that deal. And that's what's going to be hard on the DOJ. When they drag you before a jury, the jury's going to identify with you and not be sympathetic to the terrorist asshole who died."

"So now what?"

"Say the magic words, that you want me to represent you."

Rat stared at Skyles. "You sure you're up for this? You sure you're not too old?"

"I'm up for this." Skyles looked down at the table. He spoke slowly. "I will not let you down."

"Can I think about it?"

"Sure. But at least say you want me as part of your team. I have to jump in the U.S. Attorney's shit right away. I have to get them on their heels. You can always fire me, tell them that I was a loose cannon, but let me start the fight for you. Let me chew on them a little."

Rat couldn't believe Skyles. He was the opposite of what Rat had expected, especially from Andrea. She had good judgment, and good taste. She wouldn't send him some loser. Rat had envisioned having a sophisticated, soft-spoken but effective attorney who would somehow find some magic way to get him off. Skyles was a maniac. But maybe a maniac was what he needed.

Skyles grabbed his briefcase. "What do you say?"

Rat stood. "Let me think about it. Do you have a card?"

Skyles gave him his card. "Don't think too long. You need to get the prosecutors playing defense right away. They're not used to it. Give me a call and let me know what you decide." He walked slowly to the door with a hint of a limp.

"I'll be in touch."

Chapter

7

Elizabeth Watson stood silently in the wardroom, watching Commander Barry Little prepare his prosecution case. She was waiting for a helicopter to begin her long return flight to the Fifth Fleet. She considered helping Commander Little prepare his prosecution case, out of spite as much as anything, but that felt wrong. Still, she didn't understand Duar's animosity toward women. The world had seen the results of such fear, or animosity or whatever it should be called, with the fall of the Taliban in Afghanistan. But seeing it on television, hearing about the attitudes, was very different from personally experiencing it. She hadn't been ready for it.

She drank from a cup of hot tea and watched Little prepare outlines on his laptop. The wardroom door opened and a sailor came in from the communications center. "Commander Watson?" he said, walking toward her, a message in hand.

She nodded to him and took the message. "Thank you." She unfolded it and scanned for the location of her next assignment. When her eyes fell to the bottom of the message she felt a sense of panic. She couldn't believe what she was reading. She crossed over to Commander Little. "Barry, you're not going to believe this."

"Believe what?"

She handed him the message without saying another word.

He took it from her, recognized it as a Navy text message, and began reading. When he had gotten halfway, he glanced up at her in stunned disbelief. His eyes returned to the message and he read on. He examined the DTG, the Date Time Group of the message, which showed exactly when it was sent. He checked to see if it was April 1. It was not. He checked for the transmission authentication and the message number. All in order. "That's their solution to your getting fired by Duar?"

"That's what it says. You're now Duar's defense attorney, and I'm the prosecutor."

"That's nuts! We can't do that," Little said.

"They say they don't have anyone else they can spare. We're here. I didn't obtain any confidential information or establish any meaningful attorney-client relationship, so I'm free to prosecute him." The idea had begun to settle in. She found it exciting.

"Did you even interview him?"

"As soon as I said I was defending him he looked like he wanted to cut my throat. I am a woman, and by definition, not qualified."

Little's face was a sea of confusion. "The only thing I've been thinking about since I got here was how I was going to hang this sonofabitch from the highest yardarm. In fact, on my list of things to do was to check to see whether ships like this still *have* yardarms. I'm not even sure what a yardarm is, but I wanted to hang him from the highest one we could find—by his thumbs, then by his neck. Until dead." Little paused. "I've got real bad feelings about this guy, and I'm not sure I can really give him a proper defense." He closed his computer and stood up. He put his hands on his hips and his mouth formed a small, ironic smile. "But maybe my duty is to ensure he has a real shitty defense so he gets convicted and we can do our yardarm search. Maybe I'm just the right guy."

Watson frowned. "You will do your duty like any good attorney. I'm sure you will provide him with a good defense."

"You seem to be handling this pretty well."

Elizabeth smiled. "After meeting Mr. Duar, I can think of nothing I would rather do than prosecute his ass. See you in court."

♦　♦　♦

Sarah St. James sat alone in the back of the black government sedan as her driver skillfully weaved through traffic on the way to the Pentagon. She could not recall having been so angry. She prided herself on being calm, logical, analytical. It was one of her greatest weapons. When others got red and heated, she got calmer.

She had not called ahead. She knew Stuntz was there and she was just going to walk in on him. She didn't want to give him time to prepare his response. She got out in the underground entrance to the Pentagon and was quickly recognized and escorted into the building.

"Good morning, Ms. St. James. Can we be of some assistance to you?" a Marine asked.

"You can escort me, but that's all," she said without even slowing down. She knew how to get to Stuntz's office.

She reached the office and turned in. The receptionist was taken aback by the sudden appearance of the National Security Adviser. She stood up. "Good morning, Ms. St. James. May I help you?"

"Where is he?"

"Um . . . he's in his office . . . in a meeting. He's asked not to be disturbed. Is there something I can help you with?"

"No." She pushed her way into Stuntz's office. He was surrounded by members of his staff. "Mr. Secretary, may I have a word with you?"

Stuntz looked up at her. He was unsuccessful in his attempt to hide the shock on his face, shock mixed with concern. "Sarah! What in the world brings you to the Pentagon at this time today? Did we have a meeting that I've forgotten about?"

"No. We're going to have an unscheduled meeting."

"Could you give us a few minutes?" he asked his staff.

When the last staffer had closed the door behind him, St. James sat down across from Stuntz. She leaned her fists on the top of Stuntz's desk and looked into his eyes. "What did you mean by arresting Rathman?"

"What? What are you talking about?"

"The FBI arrested Kent Rathman, the very man that seems to make you feel so threatened. You had a tantrum when you found out he was sending me information. When he went after the man who wanted to shoot down the Blue Angels."

"Arrested him for what?"

"Torturing a terrorist. Geneva Convention violation, manslaughter, I don't know all of it."

"Who is charging him?"

"Justice."

"Then why are you talking to me? Why aren't you leaning on Dirks's desk and asking him what the hell *he* is doing?"

"Because Dirks doesn't have anything against Rathman. Or me. This is your work. I can smell it."

Stuntz frowned. "I don't like the sound of that."

Her voice grew softer and lower. "If this is your way to try and get to me it's not going to work."

Stuntz leaned back in his chair, separating himself from St. James. "I have heard something about this—your boy tortured that terrorist. Killed him, they say. Are you saying he shouldn't have to answer for it?"

"I don't know what happened. I'll find out. If something went wrong, or he did something he shouldn't have, I'll do what I think is appropriate. All I'm saying is I want to know whether you had a hand in this. Did you start this? Did you make sure that he was arrested and charged?"

"Sarah," he said in a patronizing tone that he knew would penetrate whatever reserve of civility remained. "I'm in the Department of Defense. I have no control over the Department of Justice or the U.S. Attorney. If you want to find out why they did what they did, ask *them*. Now please, I have to get on with my meeting."

"You deny it."

"Deny what?"

"You deny it was your idea to have Rathman arrested and charged?"

"I had nothing to do with it, Sarah. You can take my word for it."

She leaned back, considered, then sat forward again. "I don't believe you."

His eyes grew large. "You think I'd *lie* to you? You can't be serious."

"Come on, Howard. I'm not stupid. You resent me and always have. You don't think I belong here."

"You *don't*. You're way out of your league, playing secret government with all your little friends."

"Maybe you're the one who doesn't belong."

"Yes, well," he said. "You've even told the President that *you* would make a better Secretary of Defense than me. Haven't you?"

She felt betrayed. "I don't think I've ever said that. I have offered to take the position if it ever became available, true. But not at your expense. I haven't ever said I'm better than you."

Stuntz laughed. "Don't bullshit me, Sarah. I know you're damned ambitious. We all are. But you don't need to go to the President and stab me in the back when I'm not around."

"I didn't stab—"

"The hell you didn't. And I'll bet you were really pissed when the President didn't do what he had hinted he would do. Weren't you?"

"It's completely up to him."

"That's why he came to me and told me all about it. He asked me how long I wanted to be SEC DEF. I told him at least through his first term. After that, we'd see. He said that was good enough for him. So, Miss Security Adviser, you're just going to have to wait to see your little Machiavellian plan play out."

St. James hadn't expected the President to tell Stuntz about their private conversation. "I want you to stop the prosecution of Rathman."

"Stop it yourself. They've already issued the indictment. And if we don't prosecute him, the Europeans will. He's now a war criminal, and they know *all* about it."

◆　◆　◆

The U.S. marshals led Rat out of the dark blue van and into the underground passageway of the Department of Justice building in downtown Washington, D.C. They moved to the elevator and stepped inside. As the door closed, one of the marshals took out a key and inserted it into the elevator panel where a button might have been for the top floor. He turned the key, the elevator lurched upward, and the marshal returned the key to his pocket. Rat didn't even know where he was.

The marshals were as surprised as Rat at their destination. In all the years these marshals had worked for the government they had never seen a defendant taken to trial in the secret courtroom they all knew was there. The DOJ did not acknowledge the courtroom even existed. It was the courtroom for the FISA Court. The court that heard applications for secret wiretaps under the Foreign Intelligence Surveillance Act on people suspected of committing espionage against the United States.

The elevator stopped with a jerk and the marshals led Rat out into the area just outside the courtroom. There were no windows. To the right of the door was a small metal frame protruding from the wall. The marshal put his hand inside the frame and manipulated the rocker switches to release the cipher locks on the door. A solenoid snapped the steel bolt lock out of the way and the marshal pulled on the handle of the heavy door.

Rat was surprised by the room's opulence, its warmth. There were several large black leather chairs behind the massive bench in the front of the courtroom, and large tables for the attorneys. There was even room for perhaps twenty people to observe the court.

Skyles was waiting for him at the defense table. He stood as Rat approached. Skyles grinned. "Got your call."

"I can see that. Don't screw this up."

"You won't regret letting me represent you. We'll get these guys."

"Can I sit down?"

"Sure. Until the judge gets here."

Rat sat in the hardwood chair. "Do I have to have my hands bound all the time?"

"No. They should take those off." Skyles motioned for the marshal, who unlocked Rat's cuffs.

Rat rubbed his wrists. "A judge is going to hear this?"

"Right. Our trial judge."

"Know anything about him?"

"Lots." Skyles pulled a manila folder from his briefcase. It had been used before and Skyles had crossed out whatever had been written on the tabs and had written "U.S. v. Rathman" on the left, and "Judge Royce Wiggins" on the right. He opened the folder and brought out a report on Wiggins, including his picture. Rat looked at it quickly. Skyles turned toward Rat.

"Our judge is a member of the Foreign Intelligence Surveillance

Act Court, or FISA court, the court that meets in this room. Eleven judges from district courts around the country, three from the D.C. area. They meet in secret and hear requests for surveillance and searches. Intel stuff, spy stuff. They all feel real important, and nobody ever gets to see what they do here. There are three other judges, appellate judges that hear any appeals from their rulings, but in the twenty-five years that this court has existed, only one or two of their decisions have ever been appealed. Anyway, they've got a lot of power. They give the FBI and the NSA—the National—"

"I know who the NSA is."

"Right. In this court they don't even demand probable cause. Suspicion is good enough. They authorize electronic eavesdropping on people they believe are involved in espionage, terrorism, that sort of thing. Recently, after 9/11, more of this stuff was going on. The ACLU got wind of it and started going bat-shit, and lots of suits have followed. But so far it's all intact. This judge is one of the ones that hears that kind of thing, and has a clearance. The DOJ picked him to try this case."

"That's kind of like one team picking the umpire."

Skyles nodded. "Kind of is. If we want to challenge him, we can."

"Does he know what he's doing?"

Skyles put the file back in his briefcase. "Don't know. I spoke to some lawyers who tried cases in front of him in South Dakota, where he came from, and they sort of clammed up. Didn't want to talk about him. I finally got one guy to talk, and he said the judge is very decisive and stupid."

Rat clenched his jaw. "Stupid? And that's okay?"

"Just one guy's opinion. May just mean he lost a case. Hard to tell from one report. But for now, we're stuck with him."

"This morning is just about bail, right?"

"Just bail. We'll try to keep the judge from setting some huge bail amount. I'm sure the U.S. Attorney will ask for a lot of bail and claim that you're some sort of a flight risk. It will be total bullshit, but they're going to try to rub your nose in this thing every step of the way."

"That's comforting."

"They're not here to make us comfortable. They're here to make sure you stay locked up. You don't have any friends here except me—" He stopped as the judge entered the courtroom. "Stand up. Here we go."

The U.S. Attorney hurried through the cipher-locked door in the back and rushed to his table as the judge entered.

"All rise," the bailiff said as the judge took the bench.

The clerk spoke. "The United States District Court for the District of Columbia is now in session, the Honorable Royce Wiggins presiding. Please be seated."

There were eleven chairs. The judge simply took the middle chair. He sat heavily, placed a file in front of him, and combed back the thin hair on his head. He looked over his reading glasses. "Call the case," he ordered his clerk.

Rat tried to evaluate the judge as the clerk rose to read something. The tops of his reading glasses ran through his sight lines causing him to move his head dramatically whenever he wanted to see something. His face was blotchy and unhealthy-looking. There was no humor in the judge's demeanor whatsoever.

The clerk read, "Case number one on calendar, *United States* vs. *Kent Rathman*. State your appearances."

"Good morning, Your Honor," said the attorney who had rushed in at the last moment. "Assistant United States Attorney John Wolff on behalf of the United States."

Skyles stood after Wolff. "Good morning, Your Honor. Richard Skyles on behalf of Lieutenant Kent Rathman, the defendant."

Judge Wiggins looked toward the U.S. Attorney's table. "We're here for a bail hearing. I've read the papers. Mr. Wolff, anything to add?"

Rat watched Wolff closely. He didn't like what he saw. Wolff looked very competent and comfortable. He made Skyles look like a rube. Wolff was perhaps thirty-five, with closely cropped blond hair.

"This is a very serious case, Your Honor. It has national and even international implications. Not only is it serious in terms of the charges—manslaughter and a violation of the Geneva Convention—but it is serious in terms of the implications for the defendant involved. This is the kind of case that would ruin his career, and could cause him great personal embarrassment and humiliation. Rather than have such humiliation rest on his shoulders at the conclusion of this case, it is the belief of the United States that he would flee, and take his chances on not being brought back to trial."

"How much bail are you requesting?"

"One million dollars, Your Honor."

"Mr. Skyles?"

Skyles stood slowly, looking at the U.S. Attorney in disbelief before returning his attention to Judge Wiggins. "I frankly am shocked at the request of United States for bail, Your Honor. It is very clear that United States is the one that is embarrassed and humiliated by the existence of this trial. They're doing everything they can to keep this trial away from the scrutiny that it deserves. To make the claim that this all-American hero, this Naval Academy graduate, who is considered by everyone to be the best special forces operative in the country, is likely to flee the country he loves because of this ridiculous charge is outrageous. Kent Rathman isn't going anywhere. His job is here—which still requires his constant attention—his home is here, his girlfriend lives here, all his obligations are here. He's not going anywhere."

"Do you have a recommendation for the court?" the judge asked.

"Yes, Your Honor. Forgive me. Mr. Rathman respectfully requests that he be released on his own recognizance. As I said, he's not going anywhere."

"I'm going to set bail at fifty thousand dollars. Anything else for today?"

Wolff barked, "Your Honor, I request that Lieutenant Rathman be restricted to the D.C. area."

Skyles put out his hands. "On what grounds? His job may require him to travel with little or no notice. This is just another way for the government to take away his profession, to punish him before they have a conviction. He'll be here for trial, Your Honor, or anything else you want him to be at."

"He's a flight risk, Your Honor—"

"No, he's not, Mr. Wolff. Mr. Rathman's bail will be without travel restriction." He looked at Rat. "Mr. Rathman, you will not flee before your trial, will you?"

"No, sir," Rat said.

"And you will be here for your trial, won't you?"

"Yes, sir, I will."

"You give me your word as an officer?"

"Yes, sir, I do."

"Will there be anything else?"

"Yes, Your Honor," Skyles said. He looked around at the courtroom, as if in surprise. "Why are we in this secret courtroom with cipher door locks? Why are we not in an ordinary federal courtroom in the large federal courthouse the taxpayers have paid for that sits just a few blocks from here?"

Judge Wiggins frowned. "You know very well, Mr. Skyles, that this is a case which may involve secret and even top-secret evidence. I assume it is that concern that has led to the selection of this courtroom."

"I heard that might be the case, sir. But then what is this secret evidence? It has certainly not been provided to me by the U.S. Attorney."

"I'm sure you'll be informed at the earliest opportunity. Am I right, Mr. Wolff?"

"Considering we received word that Mr. Skyles was retained approximately two hours ago, we have not had the opportunity to provide him with the evidence that he is entitled to at this point. He will receive everything . . . to which he is entitled, Your Honor."

Skyles smiled. "Thank you, Mr. Wolff. I'll be over this afternoon."

The judge nodded. "Court is adjourned." He banged his gavel down and stood to leave the courtroom.

Skyles turned toward Rat. "Do you have fifty thousand dollars? Actually for bail, you'll only need about ten percent of that. Can you put it together?"

"I'll figure something out."

"I'm going to leave that in your hands. Call me if you get stuck. I'm going to go start rubbing against the U.S. Attorney. I've only seen this Wolff fellow once before. Never tried a case against him. Unfortunately, he is supposed to be one of the sharpest in the D.C. office. I guess we'll find out just how sharp he is. I'll see you later," Skyles said as he followed Wolff out the door.

The marshals took Rat by the arms and led him back to jail.

◆　◆　◆

Even though it was April, the day dawned cold and hard. The slate-gray sky warned of a building storm and likely snow. The three woodsmen stomped the night's cold out of their legs as they prepared to leave their camp just as they had done every day for the last four weeks. What had at first sounded like a lucrative easy job had turned into drudgery. They were there to find certain trees of certain diameters and single-cut them. It was tedious work, and only after accepting it had they realized that the trees they sought were hard to find. Only after arriving were they told their pay was based on *finding* and cutting the large trees, not just looking. They were to be paid by the piece.

One week to go and then they could go back to Tbilisi for a two-week break. They looked forward to returning to the city, the capital of the Republic of Georgia, to taste some high-quality vodka instead of the swill they had brought with them in their flasks. They wanted to see families and girlfriends, and get paid. Then when they renegotiated their pay and returned back to the woods of Georgia, the remote thankless woods of Abkhazia, they would be farther away from winter and the cold would have receded a few degrees.

They picked up their chain saws and hooks, and headed off to the trees they had found at the end of the day yesterday. Their feet were already cold as they shuffled through the beaten-down snow on the path left by them the night before. Thankfully there had been no new snow; it would be easy to find yesterday's trees by their footprints.

Giorgi, the biggest woodsman and the one clearly in charge of the group, began his usual grumbling as they left the camp. He, like the other two, had been born and raised in Georgia, and knew nothing other than working in the woods. Giorgi had brought an insulated coffee cup with him. He drank from it slowly as they walked, being careful not to burn his lip. "I say we start with the biggest tree that we marked yesterday. The one in the middle of that clearing. We can get the others to drag it out as we take on the other smaller trees around."

The two behind him, Shota and Tamar, nodded. They knew that to disagree with him was pointless; he simply talked to himself. They would do exactly what he said, whether he explained things to them on the way or just pointed and said, "Do this," or "Do that."

They had four kilometers to walk before they reached their destination. Giorgi finished his coffee and slipped the handle through a loop on his belt. "Let's walk faster. I'm freezing my balls off."

They picked up the pace along the path. As they walked they looked around for any other indication of life, or animals, or danger. They rarely saw anything that threatened them, but they kept their eyes open.

"Giorgi," Tamar called, pointing. "What is that?"

The others stopped and looked. The virgin snow, uniform and smooth, was two feet deep everywhere they looked, except where Tamar was pointing. It was as if the snow had a hole not even a hundred yards off their path. It was an odd spot, a place where the snow had melted, or just vanished. Dead grass and dirt were clearly visible.

Giorgi looked at the other two. "What is it?"

Shota shivered against the cold. "No idea. Something warm. Maybe a dead animal."

"I don't see a dead animal. And there's no blood." Giorgi looked around, looked at the sky to see how late it was getting. "Let's take a look."

They walked carefully toward the melted opening. They crouched as they neared it, as if they were sneaking up on something that they didn't know enough about. Giorgi's cup clanked against his knife. They slowed as they approached the clearing. They got to within ten feet before Giorgi put out his arms to stop the other two. They looked into the melted spot and saw a silver cylinder lying on the dead grass.

Tamar spoke. "What is it? And how did it get there?"

Giorgi said, "Must have been warm, like a thermos."

"You think someone else is out here and left their thermos?"

"There's nobody but our camp within a hundred kilometers. And I've never seen a thermos—"

"Then who left it there?" Tamar asked, growing annoyed.

Giorgi ignored him. "Let's see if it's still warm." Giorgi walked directly toward the cylinder. He knew he should be cautious but wasn't sure why. It didn't look dangerous, yet something was telling him to use extreme caution. Giorgi crouched down next to the cylinder and looked at it from as many angles as he could. The other two stood back slightly. "Looks harmless enough." He removed his hand from his glove and touched the cylinder with one finger. "It's warm."

"How?"

"I don't know. It's not boiling hot." He put his entire hand on it and felt the steady heat from the smooth metal cylinder. "We can use this to keep our tent warm." He picked it up and felt its heft. "It's not that heavy. Maybe five kilos. Here, warm your hands on it." The other two took their gloves off and touched it. Giorgi handed the cylinder to Shota. "Take this back and put it in our tent. Then come back and we'll go get that big tree. If that thing is still warm tonight, we'll use it for some extra heat, huh? We can always use some extra heat."

Shota smiled and headed back to their tent. "Always can use some extra heat. A lucky day for the best woodsmen! The others will be jealous of our new heater!"

Groomer had never been in Don Jacobs's office. He had been in the Counterterrorism Center several times but had never crossed the threshold of the office of the man in charge. It wasn't that he was afraid of Jacobs, or anyone else for that matter. It was that Rat was the one who dealt with people at this level. Groomer just went along. But now it was time for him to take things into his hands, just a little.

Jacobs was not expecting him and looked up in surprise when Groomer cleared his throat.

"You're with Rat," Jacobs said.

"Yes, sir. Lieutenant Junior Grade Ted Groome."

"What brings you here? Everything okay?" Jacobs asked, annoyed, not impressed by military rank, especially when it was the second-lowest rank in the Navy.

"No, everything is not okay. We've heard about what happened to Rat and don't quite understand how this has happened."

"I was surprised myself," Jacobs admitted. He tossed his pen on the desk. "Frankly, I was blind-sided."

"How?" Groomer asked, watching Jacobs's face for lies. "I thought you had your hand in everything."

Jacobs frowned slightly. "Meaning?"

"Nothing in particular, sir. I just figured it would be hard for anyone to pull anything like this without you knowing about it. Who's behind this? Because someone is."

"That's what I don't quite get. The Attorney General seems to be going after Rat, but I don't get his motivation. Whatever it is, I don't like it. This could give Rat, and the Agency, a black eye, and whoever else stands up for Rat. Even the Navy."

Groomer said, "I'll stand up for Rat. As will the other guys."

Jacobs shook his head. "I'm not talking about standing up like that. I'm talking about taking the fall. Washington-speak. Which agency, which politician, which appointee, is going to get his head cut off."

"Well, sir, I guess a question that I have is what are you going to do about this?"

"I don't know. I will say one thing though, I'll do what I can for Rat." Jacobs paused. "But if in fact he tortured this guy and the man died because of it, and they can prove it, we've got problems. So did he?"

Groomer hesitated.

Jacobs put up his hand. "Don't answer that question. Next thing you know they'll subpoena me and ask me what you said. If you don't say anything right now, it won't go against you. Keep your ears open as well. If you hear anything that you think I need to know, you can tell me about it. We're going to have to work this problem smart. But I don't think it's going to be that easy."

"No, sir. We've got to get him off though."

"Who's running the team?"

"I'm second in charge so until he gets out on bail, I am."

"Keep me posted."

Groomer stepped to the door, then turned around. "So as of right now, you have no plan to get him off." He waited, but Jacobs didn't reply. "Do you have any plans to do anything for Rat? Anything at all? I mean you approved this mission. You and Rat did all the planning."

Jacobs began working on a memo he was reviewing, then looked up. "Call me if you hear anything I need to know."

◆   ◆   ◆

"Where'd you find this Skyles guy, in a bus terminal?" Rat asked Andrea as they walked into her apartment in Maryland.

"I asked around Washington and found a guy who used to be a U.S. Attorney in D.C. I asked him who the U.S. Attorney feared the most. His name came up."

"I don't know about him, Andrea. He's a loose cannon. Undisciplined."

"Maybe. But maybe that's what you have to do as a defense attorney. I don't know. You want to take a shower?"

Rat sat down heavily on the couch. "Maybe three or four. Being in jail . . . what a stinking, filthy place. I've been a lot of dirty places, but jail . . . it's just so nasty. Makes you feel dirty inside."

Andrea could tell he had been affected. "So now what?"

"So now we'd better start getting our strategy together, or I'm going to end in a stinking filthy *prison*—although I'll tell you what, I will *never* go to prison. I would kill my—"

"Kent!"

"It's just not happening. You should know that. And it's kind of scary to think my life is in the hands of this Skyles lunatic, whose lifetime goal is to offend every U.S. Attorney in Washington." He looked at her. "Did I tell you that when he met with me he had a friggin' *catheter* hanging out of his hand? This guy said he wants to be a 'shit-stick' for every U.S. Attorney he runs into. So when they rub up against him they get shit all over them. How about that for a great strategy?"

"I'm sure he knows what he's doing."

He looked surprised. "How can you say that? He may have no idea. Maybe the U.S. Attorneys don't like to face him because he's incompetent. I've heard attorneys—"

"Then get another attorney!" she said, exasperated. "It's not like he's my brother. He's the only one whose name came up that you had *any* chance of affording without going completely bankrupt. If you don't like him, get one of those fancy five-hundred-dollar-an-hour lawyers and just sign over everything you own. Feel free!"

"We'll see how Skyles does," Rat replied.

Andrea sat down next to him. "I've got to tell you, since they came and got you at the restaurant, I've been a wreck. I need to know what's going on. Why are they going after you? What can I do? Do you want me to go to the press? Does Skyles want us to go to the press?"

"He said something about it. I just don't know if now is the right time."

"So what do we do now?"

"The trial's in Skyles's hands. I'm going back to work."

"You going to put your head in the sand? Pretend like there isn't anything happening? That you're not the focus of some tornado here in Washington that you can't even see? Don't you get that?"

"Oh, I get it, Andrea. I understand exactly what's happening. And I know who I need to talk to. It's time to call in some chips. I'm going to work on this problem from some angles other people will not expect."

"That's more like it," Andrea said, starting to relax for the first time in two days.

"I think I'll take a few showers now."

◆　◆　◆

"Good morning. I'm Commander Little. I've been appointed to defend you."

Duar looked up at him skeptically. He had seen the first person selected by the United States Government to defend him. He was equally unimpressed with Little. He said nothing.

"Do you mind if I sit down?"

The translator conveyed the message, and Duar pointed to the seat.

"Thank you." Little opened his briefcase and took out some papers. His khaki uniform was clean and crisp. His reddish hair was closely cut and he had a very serious look.

Duar examined the ribbons on his left breast, wondering what they meant. Once Duar realized he was not going to be killed or beaten he had grown comfortable with his surroundings.

"Have you had a chance to examine the charges being brought against you?"

"I know of no charges. I know that I have been taken against my will from my country."

"Well, perhaps you'll be able to return to your country if you get off."

"Is it possible to avoid these charges? Are you serious?"

"Yes. If you're innocent."

"But I am innocent."

Little smiled. "Well then maybe you will return to your country." He opened a file and began reading through it. "Can I ask you a few questions so we can start preparing your defense?"

Duar shrugged.

"They say they found you in a well with an AK-47, shooting at the American Special Forces when they came to arrest you. What were you doing in a well with a rifle?"

"Hiding. I was simply there. Can they ask me these questions in this trial?"

"That depends on whether we decide you should testify. We haven't decided yet. Everything you tell me is secret between us. It's called the attorney-client privilege."

"You work for the United States Government, and you'll keep secret what I tell you?" Duar asked, not believing Little would keep anything secret. He knew Little would have to report to someone and would surely report on what was said between them.

"Exactly. That is my obligation to you. You have my word."

"Your word doesn't mean *anything* to me."

Little rubbed the palm of his hand on his polyester khaki pants, trying to avoid saying something he would regret. "It may not now, but maybe as we learn to trust each other, it will. You need to confide in me so I can prepare your defense. It's to your advantage."

"In what way?" Duar demanded. "I want an attorney who is not an employee of the government who kidnapped me."

"You're entitled to any attorney you want. Even a civilian attorney."

Duar jumped to his feet, thrusting the metal chair behind him. "And how is it I am to contact any such person? I'm a captive, against my will! I'm not allowed to leave, or communicate. I have done nothing wrong and I'm being charged with horrible crimes. What are you going to do about this?"

"Who would you like to contact? I can make sure that your word reaches whoever you want to contact."

"I will let you know. I have done nothing."

"You keep saying that. Why do you say that? Do you deny that you were at the meeting in Sudan to purchase nuclear material?"

"I deny it. I had nothing to do with it."

"So even though you are Wahamed Duar, the most sought-after terrorist in the world, your intentions in meeting a well-known arms merchant who had plutonium with him in the middle of the Sudan were innocent."

Duar looked at Little with ferocious intensity. He leaned on the table. "I am not Wahamed Duar."

"Then who are you?"

"I am Mohammed el-Mahdi of Khartoum."

Little had seen the "It wasn't me! You've got the wrong guy!" defense so many times he had lost count. A lot of criminal defendants thought it was very clever. They didn't think anyone could actually identify them, or they thought they could create enough smoke about their identity to make a jury have a reasonable doubt. It rarely worked, and here, aboard the *Belleau Wood* in a tribunal, such a defense was even less likely to work. The jury was going to be a panel of military officers who wouldn't be thrown off by subterfuge. And they didn't need to convince the entire panel as they would in a criminal trial, just two-thirds. "What were you doing at that meeting?"

"Something I cannot discuss."

Little rolled his eyes, and closed the file.

◆　◆　◆

The Pankisi gorge of Georgia was notorious for its illegal residents, rough men from Chechnya and Afghanistan, from all over the world, who shared in the dream of Islamic rule. Most had fled from areas where they were being hunted. They knew they could hide in the Pankisi gorge. The government of the Republic of Georgia knew they were there, but they also knew that without using huge force they could never clear out the gorge. So Georgia left them alone, for now.

The night had grown bitterly cold, and several of the men gathered around a raging fire, telling stories and regaling each other with tales of hair-raising fights in Chechnya, Afghanistan, and other remote parts of South Central Asia. One man, obviously not Chechen or Georgian, sat on a large rock listening. He was reserved and careful. Always listening, rarely talking. All the others knew about him was that he was from somewhere in Africa.

Two of the Georgians were laughing uproariously, when one threw up his hands to silence the others. "Did you hear about those woodsmen?" He laughed, barely able to control himself. "They were cutting down trees, and found a cylinder in the snow. Did you hear about it?"

The man from Africa leaned in carefully. A man next to him continued to translate from Georgian to Arabic.

The Georgian pulled on his beard. His eyes were glazed over from vodka and his nose was running from the cold. He wiped his nose and continued. "They find a cylinder lying on the ground—it had melted the snow around it for about five meters. So what would you or I do? Something is wrong with that cylinder, right? We would go the other way. Right? What is in the cylinder? What is making the snow melt? Not these jackasses. They go right over and pick up the cylinder. It's warm, even hot—"

"Where did you hear all this?" a man asked, skeptical.

"On short wave radio. There was a report."

"So what happened?"

"So they decided this cylinder will help them stay warm. They take it back to their camp and put it in their tent, like some woman from Tbilisi, to keep them warm," the man said, choking on his laughter. "The next day they're so sick they have to call for a medical evacuation!"

The others looked at each other, not getting the significance of the comments. The man sitting on the rock understood the implications immediately. He stared at the bearded man. Another man asked what they all wanted to know, "Sick from what?"

"They had found a core of a small nuclear power generator! You know, the ones all over this damn country by the hundreds, weather stations, light stations. They got radiation sickness, and are now on their way to Moscow and Paris."

The man on the rock rose and walked toward the bearded man. "Where did this happen?"

He pointed west with his thumb. "Abkhazia."

"Do you know where there are others of these nuclear power generators?"

The bearded man was surprised by the interest. "Who the hell are you?"

He hesitated. "Hotary. Tayseer Hotary. From Sudan."

The bearded man spoke. "Humph," he said, unimpressed. "Yes, most are down there by the Black Sea. There are others elsewhere, all over southern Georgia."

"With nuclear cores?"

"Yes, of course."

"Could you find them?"

The man fought to regain sobriety. "Why are you so interested?"

"I came here to find them. I need someone to show me where they are. I have a use for these cores, these power generators."

The bearded man smiled, showing his crooked teeth in the firelight. "For the right price, yes, we can help you find one. At least one."

"I need more than one. Can you lead me to several? You will come with my men."

"Maybe. Maybe I'll bring a couple of my men too. You never know who you're going to run into. When do you want to leave?"

♦ ♦ ♦

Brad Walker, St. James's assistant on the National Security Council, stood in the front of the situation room and looked out over the group. As often as he had given the security briefings first thing in the morning, he'd never gotten used to looking into the eyes of the President of the United States, the Director of Central Intelligence, the Secretary of Defense, the Chairman of the National Security Council, and others who knew ten times more than he did about everything. The only thing he brought to the table was information that he had derived from reading messages and other intelligence during the evening and very early morning. He had the details but they had the strategic understanding that he was only beginning to grasp.

"Good morning, Mr. President. This is the security brief for Monday. Since it is the first Monday of the month, I would like to start with the military status of forces of various countries." He proceeded to summarize the military positions of all major countries, their locations of forces, the locations of submarines, aircraft carrier battle groups, and others that could pose a threat to American forces or interests.

"Next, sir, I'd like to start in East Asia. Overnight there was an attack on the Spanish embassy in Thailand. The cause of the attack was unclear but seemed to be indirectly related to a Basque group that has heretofore been unidentified. This is a new move by Basque separatists to take some of their terrorism outside of Spanish territory. Could signal a scaling up of separatist activity that has not been seen for a couple of years. Moving on to Vietnam . . ." Walker continued to summarize intelligence developments around the world that had come up since the last brief.

"In an update to the report we got yesterday of those Georgian woodsmen who found that nuclear core, the two who were taken to Moscow have died. The one taken to Paris is very sick, but may survive—"

President Kendrick interrupted. "What else do we know about these power generators?"

"They are called RTGs—Radiothermal Generators. Very small nuclear generators, Mr. President. The nuclear core is about the size of a loaf of bread. They were used to power weather stations, communications relay stations, navigation lights, and other devices in extremely remote parts of the Soviet Union. They required no power cables or power lines, and could work in any weather. They were supposed to be monitored and checked frequently. With the fall of the Soviet Union, they haven't been checked in years. Nobody is responsible for them anymore. Many of the countries in which these generators are found don't even know they're there."

"What's in the nuclear cores?" the President asked, frowning.

Walker hesitated. "I am afraid I don't know, Mr. President, I'll find—"

"Strontium," Stewart Woods interjected. "Strontium and cesium."

"Remind me of whether those materials are problematic," the President said.

Walker was silent. Woods continued. "Definitely problematic. This is one of those little problems from the former Soviet Union. We've talked about warheads from the Russian nuclear arsenal that may have disappeared, and of course we're working that problem. But this problem is of a different breed entirely. There are several hundred of these RTGs out there. They can be deadly."

President Kendrick tapped his fingers lightly on the table. "Is this something we need to worry about?"

Stuntz jumped in. "We have given this a lot of thought. This is a new kind of threat, and it's something that we have to evaluate on a regular basis. This story about these woodsmen is something that has caused great concern. We're analyzing it very carefully."

Kendrick looked at Stuntz. "Meaning what exactly, Howard?"

"Well, sir, to be frank, I think it now shows that there are several hundred possible sources for a dirty bomb."

"Explain," Kendrick said.

"The cores of these remote power generators are highly radioactive, and deadly. The strontium or cesium can kill easily. And these cores, maybe ten pounds or so, are full of this stuff. Already in powder form. Easy to spread. If someone wanted to be ugly about it, all they would have to do is take that ten-pound core, strap it to some ordinary explosives, drive into a city, and detonate it. The resulting radiation would make a lot of people sick, kill a few, but worse, contaminate a very large area for a very long period of time. It would cost billions to clean it up. It would leave radioactivity all over the place. If they did five or ten of these at once, on the same day, say, they could shut down the ten major cities in the U.S. for decades."

Kendrick shook his head. "I don't like what I'm hearing. This sounds like just the kind of thing some low-grade terrorists could put together. We need to jump on this." He looked at the Secretary of State and the Secretary of Defense. I want you two guys to put together a joint team to contact Russia, and all the members of the former Soviet states, to find how many of these things there are, where they are, and what level of safety exists. I want a plan to take care of this. Either they monitor them or disable them, or we'll do it for them, with their permission, of course."

Stuntz and Richard Moore, the Secretary of State, nodded. "Will do, sir."

hanks for coming," Rat said to the members of the team, glancing at those he trusted the most, Groomer, Robby, and Banger. They were in the conference room of International Security Consultants, Inc.

"Nice to see that you're out of jail," Robby replied.

"If they hadn't let me out I'd have broken out. I was ready to kill somebody as it was. The question was who."

"So now what?" Groomer asked, cutting to the chase. He fingered a menacing Spyderco knife with amazing dexterity, opening the blade with one hand, then closing it again. "How do we get you out of these charges?"

"If the trial goes forward, they can make you guys testify. There were a bunch of people who were there who are going to be able to say that I caused this guy some sort of 'distress,'" Rat said, glancing quickly at Sellers, who looked away.

Robby shook his head vigorously, his dreadlocks moving rhythmically. "I'm not going to testify."

"I'm not going to testify," Groomer said, echoing Robby exactly.

"They'll subpoena you."

"I'll plead the Fifth."

"I asked my lawyer. They'll give you immunity. You can't plead the Fifth if they can't prosecute you."

Groomer's face showed determination. "Then I'll sit there like a stone. All of us will, right?" he said, looking around the table, getting mostly nods, but not from everyone. "They can put me in jail forever."

Rat nodded. "I appreciate that. We may very well be in jail forever together then. We can break out together. I may have to take the Fifth too."

"But what's the plan?" Robby asked, knowing the Rat always had a plan.

"I'm thinking about a plan for the team, for us, not the trial. We can't stand still. Jacobs wants us back in the fight."

"I think you need multiple plans," Banger said. "I think you have multiple targets and you'd better be ready to hit them all at once or you're going to get blind-sided. And don't forget, we're in Washington. Sometimes the biggest threat here is the government itself. These people shoot to kill. Not literally, but—"

"I hear you," Rat said. He stared out the large picture window at dawn over downtown Washington, D.C. "This is the most exposed I've ever felt. I need to get to the heart of this. This feels political. I need to get to the politicians."

"Now you're talking," Robby said. "You need me to drop a bug in somebody's office, let me know."

Rat replied, "I don't know if we should be stepping across those lines. I don't need another felony charge. I want to keep this clean. It just *pisses* me off that we go and capture the biggest terrorist in the world and *I'm* on trial for my life."

"It pisses us all off. Just let us know what to do."

Rat's mind was spinning. "We're going to have to think outside the norm. I'll share my Washington plan with you once I've figured out what to do. But first, we need to talk about what Johnson said." He saw confusion on the faces of two of the men. "The NSA guy, the guy who came down to The Point. It's gotten worse. The activity has picked up, especially in the last twenty-four hours. He thinks he intercepted a notice message. Where one side of the organization notifies the other side with a code word. Or even a generic word. The message he sent yesterday says Duar's organization has 'located' something. Not sure what. But there's a location indicator. Everybody see it?"

They nodded.

"So somebody is running Duar's operation in his absence. The snake has grown another head. We need to find that snake, and kill it once and for all. And whatever they've found, or located, we need to figure out what that is, and take care of it. That's what Jacobs wants us working on."

♦   ♦   ♦

"Hello?" David Stern said hurriedly, not wanting to answer the phone. But he had drawn cold-call duty at the ACLU office in Washington for the afternoon. It was a nuisance and kept him from working on his cases, which needed attention. Most of his office time was taken up doing capital punishment appeals, and trial time was spent on First Amendment cases. He hated capital punishment; it was barbaric and disgraceful. He loved doing whatever he could to stop it, or delay it, or confound it. Whatever it took. But he didn't love the rest of the work. The First Amendment cases were his true love.

"Is this Mr. Stern?"

Stern was surprised the man had his name. He heard the accent but couldn't place it.

"The receptionist said you were there."

"She was right."

"I would like to talk to you. I would like to retain you for a . . . friend."

"What sort of case?" Stern asked.

"It is not safe to talk about it over the phone."

Stern frowned and put his pen down. "And why would that be?"

"Because this is very important, and high profile, and the government is on the other side."

"Other side of what?"

"Of the . . . matter. We should meet."

Stern tried to determine how important this was without hearing any detail. He didn't have any free time to waste listening to wild accusations. The thing that both intrigued him and put him off was that this was for a "friend." That meant either the friend was unwilling to call, or, as was probably the case, unable. "Would you like to come here?"

"No. Meet me in an hour."

"Where?"

"I'll call you. I am not in Washington right now. It will be close to where you are right now."

"What's your name?"

"That doesn't matter. I'll call you in an hour."

The hour passed slowly. Stern had looked at the same motion papers several times during the hour he waited for the call. For reasons he couldn't articulate, he was intrigued. He hoped it wasn't a hoax. The man's voice was intense. That could mean a big case, or it could mean nothing. Stern's imagination was starting to run away with him. More than an hour had passed. He realized he had turned through three pages without really reading any of them. The phone rang again. He let it ring three times. "Yes?"

"Mr. Stern?"

It was him. He was on a cell phone. "Yes."

"Meet me at the coffee shop down the street from you. I'm already there."

"Stanley's?"

"Yes."

"What do you look like?"

"Don't worry. I know what you look like."

"I'll be right there."

Stern was annoyed by the games, but found himself hurrying to the coffee shop. He pushed the door open, walked in, and looked around. No one looked like the voice on the phone. He felt a tug at his elbow and turned. A man stood looking into his face.

"Mr. Stern?"

"Yes."

"I have a table," the man said, indicating a small table in the back of the coffee shop.

Stern followed the man back to the table and sat in the chair with a wicker seat. The man sat with his back to the door facing the wall, to Stern's left. "You want some coffee, something to drink?"

Stern nodded and got up. "Let me get a cup of coffee." He went to the counter and purchased a cup of black coffee in a clear glass cup.

He returned to the table and studied the man who had called. Short, dark, and clearly foreign, his eyes were so dark they were very nearly black. He had a day's growth of beard but otherwise looked well groomed. Probably an Arab, Stern thought, although he wasn't sure. Could be Egyptian, Turkish, Iranian, or even Israeli. "So what's this about?" he asked.

"My friend would like you to represent him."

"How did you hear about me?"

"From attorneys I asked. They said you were one of the smartest attorneys in Washington."

"Well, I wouldn't know about that. What kind of help does your friend need?"

"He is being charged with great crimes."

Stern asked, "What does that mean?"

"He is being held by the American military in a jail, a brig, I think they call it, and they are going to put him on trial."

"Where?"

"At sea."

"Why?" Stern asked, confused. "Is he in the Navy?"

"No. He is being held by the Navy, and interrogated, and is about to be put on trial with a Navy lawyer as his only representative."

"Who is your friend and what are they charging him with?"

The man sat back and unfolded the newspaper that was on top of the pile so that the front page of the *Washington Post* was face up. He put his finger on the photograph of Wahamed Duar that stared up from the *Post*.

Stern couldn't breathe. Thoughts were crashing into each other. "You want me to represent Wahamed *Duar*?"

"In the tribunal."

Stern didn't know where to start. There was so much to say, so many questions to ask. "They haven't disclosed where he is being kept."

"He is on the *Belleau Wood*, a Navy ship."

"How do you know that?"

"I know. They already have lawyers out there to prosecute him and defend him. Navy lawyers. You must get out to the ship right away."

"Does he know I'm Jewish?" Stern said.

"It doesn't matter. He needs the best defense he can get. The government wants to execute him. They are asking for the death penalty."

Stern sipped his coffee. "Why doesn't the press know about all this?"

"Because no one has told them."

"If I took on his defense, that's the first place I would go. They are a very valuable weapon. You have any problem with that?"

"Not at all. It is important to do that."

Stern nodded. Something made him hesitate. "I'll have to think about it."

"You have until tomorrow."

"What's the hurry?"

"If you are not going to help, I need to get someone who will."

Stern stood and finished his coffee. He set the glass cup on the table. "Fair enough."

The man stood, frustrated. "I will call you tomorrow." He stormed out of the coffee shop, clearly displeased with Stern's equivocation.

Stern picked up the *Post* and tucked it under his arm. He hadn't even read the articles about Duar. He so disliked the current administration he studiously avoided reading articles in which they crowed about their successes and patted themselves on the back. But now he had to find out exactly what had happened to Duar. How he had been captured, and exactly what he had supposedly done, and how they knew about it. He had to learn everything he could about Duar in one day.

♦   ♦   ♦

Wolff sat in the small conference room at the U.S. Attorney's office for the District of Columbia. He stared with a perplexed look at the other two Assistant U.S. Attorneys who were helping him prepare the case. He didn't look perplexed very often. He was always on top of whatever case he was preparing. He had never lost a case, and his success was due in part to his preparation. Wolff humbled them with his thoroughness and tirelessness. "How are we going to hang this guy?"

One of the young U.S. Attorneys, Jacob Rentz, fresh from three years of practice in a private litigation firm, answered reluctantly. "Well, we could just drag in the other Special Operations guys and have them testify."

Wolff shook his head. "Did you read the interview sheets? Every one of them said he wouldn't testify. They wanted to take the Fifth. They're afraid of getting charged as an accessory, or coconspirator. Reasonable concerns, I might add."

"Give them immunity."

Wolff paused. "How many cases have you tried?"

"Five."

"Drugs?"

"Mostly."

"You ever try to force anyone to testify?"

"Sure."

"Anybody ever refuse?"

"Not after we made deals, or gave immunity."

"This is a conspiracy of silence. These guys are like brothers. And we're going after their leader. This guy is considered the best Special Ops guy in the country. He single-handedly—have you read his file?"

"Some of it," Rentz fibbed.

"He's done it all. Every continent you can name, just about every kind of operation you can imagine, many of which aren't even in his file because they're still too highly classified. Even with clearances we can't get into them without a 'need to know.' Unfortunately it's essentially irrelevant to this case, so we don't have a need to know. We just need to appreciate that the men who work with Rathman worship the ground he walks on. They will go down for him. They will do anything for him. You get that?"

Rentz shrugged, undeterred. "So it's like the mafia. Big deal. We'll just subpoena their asses. They can't refuse in the face of an offer of immunity—they'll be put in jail for contempt."

"That's what I'm trying to tell you. They don't *care*. And if they don't testify, how can we prove Rat tortured this terrorist to death? We don't have any other eyewitnesses."

Barbara Lloyd jumped in. "I know I'm new to this, but when I read the operation report, there's someone in the report who is referred to only in passing. The report doesn't say, probably because whoever got it would know, but there was someone in the room who survived who wasn't with the Americans."

"Right. Duar."

Lloyd shook her head. "No. The one referred to only by his code name. Acacia. Can't we get him to testify?"

Wolff liked the idea. "I don't know. We'll have to go through the State Department, or the CIA, but I like it. Follow up with that."

Rentz said, "But how are we going to keep this case? We don't really have jurisdiction, do we?"

Wolff shook his head. "At first I didn't think so. But 18 U.S.C.A. §3261 does the trick. If Skyles wants to move for a dismissal and go to a court-martial instead, the judge might let him. But that requires an attorney who knows his ass from his elbow."

"Bad attorney?"

"He's a real piece of work. I don't know where Rathman found him, but he's borderline incompetent. Everyone else here who has tried a case against him said he's the biggest asshole they have ever had to deal with. He wins in spite of himself."

"He won't think of jurisdiction?"

"He's too busy trying to figure out where all the money went in his client trust account." They snickered at the image of Skyles staring at a bank statement wondering what had happened.

"Don't we need to bring it to the court's attention if we don't think there's jurisdiction?"

"We've taken the position we have jurisdiction by filing the indictment. If Skyles wants to argue we don't, that's his problem. And he's not smart enough to do it, so I think we're fine."

"So we start getting ready for trial."

"Exactly." He looked directly at Lloyd. "Our good doctor friend may be enough all by himself, but if you can find Acacia, and get him here, we'll be home free."

Chapter

10

Rat had been surprised by the late night summons. Jacobs never called at night, and never told him just to meet him. Rat drove his Porsche to Langley quickly. He had the top down and wore a lined windbreaker against the frigid air. He darted in and out of traffic far in excess of what was a safe speed. He stopped at the gate of CIA headquarters in Langley and showed his identification. The parking lot was almost empty except for a few government sedans. Rat came to a screeching, angled stop at the intersection of four parking spots and hurried to Jacobs's office. When he arrived he was surprised to find KP Barone there, the same man who had been interrogating Duar on-board the *Belleau Wood*. Rat greeted him in Arabic.

Jacobs spoke to Rat, "So they let you out of the hoosegow, huh?"

"Fifty thou. And I really appreciate your putting up the money."

Jacobs's face turned pink. "I couldn't very well use government money . . . You remember Ken Barone?"

"Sure," Rat said, extending his hand.

"Sit down," Jacobs said.

The three men sat.

"There are two things we have to talk about. First, we're having a hell of a time getting anything out of Duar."

"Nothing?"

Barone shook his head. "He's playing with us. We're getting nothing. He's making like he's stupid. Like he'd consider talking, except he doesn't know anything. Claims not to be Duar. You've seen that kind."

Rat nodded.

"Makes it harder now that he's represented by an attorney," Barone lamented. "And not just one attorney. There's a second one on the way. He sends this fax to the captain of the ship telling him to make sure nobody asks his client any questions without him being present—"

Jacobs interjected, "Some pinhead ACLU lawyer. We need to get information from Duar about his network, his support structure, finances, everything that we kept him alive to get. We haven't gotten shit so far."

Rat looked at Barone. "You run through your entire bag of tricks?"

Barone nodded, hating to acknowledge his failure.

Rat looked at Jacobs. "What do you want me to do?"

"I'm thinking we need to get more creative."

"I've tried that. It didn't work out so well."

"Different."

"Like what?"

"Maybe we can have him meet some other people."

"You want to render him?"

"That's what I'm thinking about."

"Let me take him. Where are you thinking about?"

"I don't know. Where do you think?"

"I'm thinking the country where he blew up our embassy. Where he killed a bunch of civilians that weren't even Americans, who are ready to charge him with capital crimes as soon as we're done executing him."

"Egypt."

"Exactly. And I know just the guy."

Barone nodded vigorously.

"Duar's awfully high profile. Everybody's watching him. I'm not sure we can pull it off."

"What if I can get the National Security Adviser to sign off on it?"

Jacobs looked surprised. "Think you could?"

"Maybe."

"We can't be complicit in torture."

"We wouldn't be. Tell them they have to play by the rules. Duar won't know their hands are tied at all. And we'll tell him—I'll tell him—that he's pissed away his chance to tell *us,* so now it's out of our hands. He's going to have to face some really bad men who don't give a shit about the Geneva Convention."

◆   ◆   ◆

The seven men walked through the deep forest on the southern coast of Georgia. The snow was mostly gone, with some remnants in the shadows of the hills. Tayseer Hotary, the man who had been sitting on the rock when the cores were discussed in the Pankisi gorge, was in the back.

Hotary caught his breath as they headed up the next hill. One of the Georgians asked, "Why do you care so much about these generators?"

Hotary looked at him with annoyance. He considered ignoring him, but he realized the man was stupid. "I've told others. Did you not hear? We have been looking for a way to have power where we operate. Remote power, without the need for fuel, or power lines. This can solve the problem. We need to get the cores to do it."

The Georgian nodded.

Hotary asked him, "What is his name?" pointing at the large, bearded Georgian whom he had met at the fire.

"Him? That is Nino. Nino Jorbenadze. He is famous. A leader of Georgians in support of the Chechens. The government hates him."

Hotary nodded. "Why did he come here himself if he is so important?"

"Because he is the only one who knows where these things are. He used to work on them. And he wants your money," the man said, smiling through his gray teeth. "He doesn't trust us with money."

They crested the hill and could now see the Black Sea in the distance. Hotary could smell the salt in the air.

Nino walked faster down the hill. Hotary followed. Nino pointed to a small gray generator at the bottom of the hill. "There. This is the first."

Hotary controlled his pace as he descended toward the machine. He scanned the hills and trees for signs of life. He was wary of a trap, but saw nothing that gave him concern. The men rushed to the RTG and surrounded it. The device was completely silent. Hotary could tell it wasn't operating, and from the looks of it, it hadn't in some time.

It was four feet tall and perhaps three feet wide. It sat on a concrete slab that had cracked and was sagging in the middle. The generator was made of steel but was showing its age. Long exposure to the elements had caused rust to form at the corners. Hotary turned to Nino. "You remember how to take out the core?"

"We had to do it dozens of times."

Hotary studied the rusted steel. "Is there any danger?"

"If it's cracked, or broken, it'll kill you."

"How do we know if it's cracked or broken?"

"You get someone to do it who you don't like," Nino said, laughing. "Like you!" He took off his backpack and removed several tools. "Here," he said, handing a wrench to Hotary. "You go first. You're the one who wants these things so bad. All I have to do is show you where they are, and take the money you promised me. And if you don't show me the money now, you'll never see the core."

Hotary considered killing Nino now, but Nino knew where the other nine generators were.

Nino's face grew serious. His beard blew in the wind as he looked down at Hotary. "This is as far as I go without getting paid. You said you had to see the generator first. This is it."

Hotary reached inside his cloak. "Here," he said, handing him a stack of U.S. one-hundred-dollar bills.

The Georgian counted them, then looked up. "Where's the rest?"

"You get it when we've taken the core out of the tenth generator."

"Then we'd better hurry," Nino laughed as he put the bills in his own grimy pocket. "Move," he said as he went to the back of the RTG and expertly began loosening the bolts on the access door.

◆ ◆ ◆

Andrea put her carry-on bag down by the gate at Dulles airport and readjusted her jacket. She put the strap back on her shoulder and walked slowly toward the gate.

Rat said, "You'd better get on board."

Andrea turned to him and held his hand. "You aren't upset enough. You should be despondent that I'm leaving. Crushed. Overwhelmed. Unable to control—"

"I am," Rat said. "Can't you tell?"

"No, I really can't. That's why I brought it up." She got a frisky look on her face. "I'm going out into the storm, Rat. Into harm's way, the War on Terrorism. Something that *you* have never experienced. I'll be in danger and you will probably be up all night every night watching sports and worrying about me. So how can you be so calm?" she smiled.

Rat loved her sense of humor. "I need you to do something for me." He had wanted to talk to her about it earlier. Each day after he'd thought of it he planned on bringing it up, but each day it was harder. He knew she would think he was using her. He just needed her help. She had offered to do anything, but this had a different feel.

Andrea glanced over her shoulder at the bus that would carry the passengers out to the airplane.

Rat knew what she was thinking. "There's another bus. And probably one after that. We have a couple of minutes."

She put her bag down and ran her hand through her hair. "Okay. What is it?"

"When you get to the *Belleau Wood*—well, you're going to be the flight surgeon, but there are some things going on out there that are important."

Andrea frowned. "It's just a bunch of Marines. I'll just be doing flight physicals, and grounding people who have colds."

Rat shook his head quickly and looked around the airport terminal for anyone who might be trying to eavesdrop. He moved slightly to stand directly in front of Andrea. He leaned his head slightly down so that anyone trying to listen would have trouble reading his lips. He could also see the entire terminal as the bus was now to his back. "Remember what the President said, that Wahamed Duar was being held in an 'undisclosed location'? He's on the *Belleau Wood*."

"How can that be?"

"That's where the tribunal is going to be."

"Wow," she considered. "What could I do about him?"

"What I want you to do is about me, not him."

"Your trial?"

"My crucifixion."

"You want me to stay and help? I really feel like I can be more use to you here. The timing is horrible."

"No. You have to go. They told you if you didn't accept now, they were going to fill the job with someone else."

"The job isn't that important, Kent. I would much rather be with you."

"The only reason I'm in trouble is because of a doctor on your ship. He—"

"A doctor? The surgeon? Dr. Satterly?"

"The very guy."

"How could he have anything to do with you?" she asked.

"He was treating one of the terrorists. The guy who died. Satterly got pissed and decided to make me his personal crusade."

Andrea shook her head in disbelief. "He has a good reputation in the medical community. He's supposed to be a good guy."

"I just know he's got it in for me. See if there's anything out there that I can use in my defense."

Andrea hesitated. She was suddenly feeling a slight pinch she had not felt before. "You want me to spy for you?"

"Just listen carefully. Tell me if you hear anything."

"I don't know. The medical community is kind of close—"

"This guy is trying to send me to prison, Andrea. I'm not asking you to go through his underwear drawer. Just pay attention."

Andrea smiled awkwardly. "I don't know . . ."

The last bus was preparing to leave the gate for her airplane to Rome. Rat walked toward it with Andrea's carry-on bag. "You need to go."

Andrea was silent.

"See if you can figure out why that doctor has it in for me. And if you get a chance to meet Duar, see what you think of him."

Andrea took her carry-on bag and hesitated. After a moment, a long moment for each of them, she walked through the door of the bus without any farewell, without a kiss or even a reassuring look.

Rat watched to see if she would at least turn around, at least wave. She entered the bus and never looked back.

◆ ◆ ◆

Rat had only met Sarah St. James once. He had corresponded with her several times by the encrypted e-mails that had probably given rise to the difficulties that he now found himself in. As much as he hated calling in political chips, or asking people to do *anything* for him, it was time.

He assumed Brad Walker, St. James's assistant, would get to work early. He had been waiting for him for fifteen minutes, since five forty-five. Rat watched each car pull up to the gate of the White House. He recognized Walker in his car, fourth car in line waiting to get into the gate. Rat crossed the sidewalk to Walker's American sedan and rapped on the window. Walker looked up startled. He didn't recognize Rat. Walker wasn't sure what to do. His car was trapped between others waiting to enter the White House grounds. He reached his left hand to lower the electronic window and hesitated.

Rat tapped on the window again. He didn't look like a homeless man, or some psycho serial-killer, but still . . . Walker glanced at the gate where the security guards were now carefully watching Rat. He lowered the window three inches. "Yes?"

"Mr. Walker, Kent Rathman." Rat could almost hear Walker searching for that name to generate some recognition.

"What can I do for you?"

"I need a ride through the gate. I need you to take me to see Ms. St. James."

"I can't do that—"

"Sure you can. I'm Rat."

"Of course, sorry. I wasn't . . . expecting you. I'm still not sure I can just take you in. You have to have an appointment. And then the National Security Adviser doesn't just have people drop in to see her—"

"Open the door," Rat said.

The door locks sounded and Rat's door opened. He climbed into the front seat of the sedan and closed the door behind him. "Thanks. I've left a couple of messages for her, but she's awfully busy. I probably could've done this a different way, but I wanted to meet you anyway."

Walker was clearly uncomfortable. He felt threatened, but knew he shouldn't be. He knew of Rat's magical reputation in the special forces and how loyal he had been to Sarah St. James in spite of his reluctance to become entangled in politics. "I wanted to meet you too. You're sort of legendary," Walker offered.

"How do you like your job?"

"Great. Tough to get, but very exciting."

They pulled up to the gate at the White House and Walker showed the guard his identification. "This is Mr. Kent Rathman. He's with me."

The guard leaned over and looked through the window at Rathman. "You have any identification, sir?"

Rathman pulled out his active duty military identification and handed it to the guard.

The guard went to the guardhouse and entered Rat's name into the database. He returned the ID and waved them through.

Rat had never been in the White House parking lot. He got out of Walker's car and followed him toward the white building that seemed bigger close up. They walked around to the special entrance and went directly in. Secret Service greeted them at the door and checked their IDs again. Walker greeted them by name and went directly through the hallway toward the National Security Adviser's office. Walker said quietly, "She's not going to be too happy about your unscheduled appearance. She's pretty organized and doesn't like her schedule to be disrupted."

"This shouldn't take that long."

Walker turned into Sarah St. James's office. "Morning, Millie. Is Ms. St. James at her desk?"

"As always."

"This is Kent Rathman. Millie Grossman."

Rat nodded and extended his hand. "Morning."

"Morning," Millie said as she studied him with deep curiosity.

"Can we go in?" Walker asked.

Millie nodded.

Walker opened the door and went right into Sarah St. James's plush office. She glanced up from her desk, expecting to see Walker, but then recognized Rat. "Mr. Rathman. What a surprise," she said with a tone of annoyance. "Do you know Brad? Is that how you got in here?"

Rathman entered the office and looked around. "We just met. I came here to see you."

"I'm afraid we have a morning brief in just a few minutes. We don't really have time for a meeting that was not on our calendar."

"That's okay. I have time."

St. James could tell that he was intent on seeing her, and resistance was going to get her nowhere. "Sit down."

"No, I need to get going. I just wanted to ask you a couple of quick questions."

"Do you and I need privacy? Is it okay if Mr. Walker stays?"

"Sure. . . . You have any idea how this happened? Any idea what's going on—the behind-the-scenes stuff? How did I end up in somebody's crosshairs?"

St. James glanced at the clock and replied, "What do you think?"

"They think I work for you, and it's a way to get to you—to short-circuit your little private intelligence network."

"And who do you think it is?" she asked as she gathered up several documents and placed them in her thin briefcase. She turned to Brad Walker. "Are you ready for the brief? We haven't even gone over what you're going to say."

"I was kind of hoping we could grab a couple of minutes to go over a few things," Walker replied.

Rat realized his clever idea of seeing Sarah St. James had been misguided. He was irritating her, his only friend in the administration, the only one who might actually do something for him. "I should have called and gotten an appointment. I'm sorry. I may have to go out of town soon. I just wanted to talk to you for a second."

She walked around the desk without replying, heading for the door and her brief.

"I've heard it's the Secretary of Defense."

She stopped. "I think so too, but I can't prove it."

"Any way you can make this trial stop?" There. He had asked the question he had come to ask. He had done what he hated to do, asked for help.

She put the long leather strap from her briefcase over her shoulder. "Did you have to torture that guy?" St. James asked.

"I wasn't leaving without Duar. We knew he was there."

"How did you know?"

"The agent. He would only signal if he saw Duar with his own eyes."

"So why did you have to almost drown that man?"

He hesitated. "Do you really want me to go into it?"

"Yes."

He knew better. "Field interrogation. Why such interest in this guy?"

"Because he died! People care when other people die. We try to live by higher standards than the run-of-the-mill terrorist, Rat. Do you not *get* that?"

"How many people were killed in the raid?" he asked.

St. James hesitated. "I don't know. Ten or twelve."

"Sixteen terrorists. How many Americans killed or wounded?"

"I don't know. What difference does that make?"

"Because everybody knows a lot more about this one guy who died of pneumonia than about others who died, or were wounded. Even Americans."

"You're missing the point. They have charged you with something. Either you did it, or you didn't. Pointing out other things that make people look stupid won't help you advance your cause at all."

"Are we supposed to be real nice to these guys? We can kill them, but at some point, we can't even touch them. I want to know when that is."

"When they stop fighting. When they lay down their arms."

Rat smiled. "These guys *never* quit fighting. They don't surrender, like POWs. They just try to find a new way to cut your throat. You ever read about Guadalcanal?"

"Some," she replied defensively.

"After the first real battle with the Marines when the Japanese had their asses handed to them, the injured Japanese lay on the battlefield moaning. The Marines ran out to help them. We wanted to take them prisoner, give them medical attention, and treat them properly under the Geneva Convention—even though Japan never *signed* the Geneva

Convention. When the Marines got there to help, the Japanese soldiers rolled over and handed the Marines live hand grenades killing the Marines and themselves. You aware of that?"

"Not really."

"So what do you do when you're a Marine after the next battle and a Japanese soldier is moaning on the next battlefield?"

St. James shook her head subtly. She didn't want to answer.

"You *shoot* him, that's what you do. We tried to give them quarter, and they wouldn't take it. So you shoot them. That could be considered shooting a wounded soldier, or a POW, which is 'illegal.' Would you be okay with that?"

"What does that have to do with what you did?"

"I just want to see if there's any ambiguity in your mind. Any room for discussion. Or if everything is crystal clear. Because I find when things are crystal clear, I'm usually dealing with someone who has never been in combat."

"This is different. This man—"

"And when he knows the location of the most wanted terrorist in the world, you can't ask him in a way that might make him un*comfortable*? Seriously? Is that what you want? I ask him, he flips me off, and I say oh, okay, you win, and we come home without Duar? *That's* what you want?"

St. James had heard enough. "I have to go brief."

"One other thing. Do you really think we'll get anything out of Duar by interrogating him with no threat of harm behind it?"

"I would expect our interrogators to be very effective."

"You expect wrong. We're more hamstrung than a cop. We don't have anything to give. What lesser sentence do we have to offer? Better conditions? More food? A call home? Money? New identity? We're not dealing with the mafia here. These murderers spit in our faces. What do you have to offer Duar that will persuade him to talk?"

"We've had our best interrogators on it—"

"I was *there*. I saw him in action."

"And?" she asked.

"He didn't get anything, nor will he. You know what we did in Guantánamo?"

"Vaguely."

"They called it stress and duress. They'd make them kneel for hours, or make them wear hoods, or spray-paint goggles and make them wear them."

"We got some good information."

He nodded. "Some. But you'll never crack a really hard case like that. You know what they tell us?"

She stared at him.

"If you don't violate someone's human rights some of the time you probably aren't doing your job. Believe that? Of course when you do, theoretically, they charge you like a criminal and claim they don't know anything about it."

"All we can do is try. I need to go." She paused. "So how do we get anything out of him?"

"Render him."

"What?"

"Send him to a friend. Like Egypt. They're dying to interrogate him. He blew up our damned embassy in Cairo—a bunch of Egyptians were killed. They aren't happy about that, and Sudan borders Egypt to the south. They're scared to death he's going to export his poison across the border more, and even hook up with the Islamic Jihad. We give him to them, and who knows, maybe they'll have more luck."

"They'll torture him."

Rat shook his head. "We make them promise not to. But Duar won't know that. He'll think they have a free hand and may sing just to avoid the unknown."

St. James considered. "We couldn't let them have a free hand."

"If we give them limits, they'll . . . probably go along."

She didn't like it.

"Don Jacobs is already trying to get authority to get Duar to Egypt. If you back it, it will happen."

"I'll think about it. I'm not very comfortable with it."

Rat shook his head as she prepared to hurry to the brief.

She stopped. "What?"

"Why send me—send the team—into Sudan to capture him?"

"So we could learn about his plans, his network."

"How? Exactly *how* did you plan to learn all that?"

"Interrogation."

Rat fell silent, then changed the subject. "The Secretary of Defense isn't my direct boss right now, but he can definitely ruin me. He got the DOJ to do the work for him, but you're the only one I know who might be able to stop this."

She walked by him and out the door.

He followed her into the hallway. "Couldn't you talk to Stuntz? Or the Attorney General?"

She stopped. "I already have."

Rat was caught off guard. "And nothing?"

"I can't stop it. You're on your own."

Chapter 11

Right this way, ma'am," the petty officer said to Andrea as he led her down the ladder toward her stateroom. She had just landed aboard the *Belleau Wood* on a CH-53 helicopter from Kenya. It had been a jarring flight, full of vibrations and misgivings. She looked forward to her new position, but the closer she got to the ship, the more she wondered whether she had made the right decision.

She had left Washington angry. She had wanted Rat to know it too. His request had confirmed a deep suspicion she had had about him, that to him, his job was more important than almost anything else, like he had some special privileged position. The idea of him torturing a man to death had changed how she saw him. She selfishly prayed he would get off, but wasn't sure that was the right result ethically. Maybe he deserved to be convicted. He sure hadn't denied what had happened; he believed it was justified somehow because of who the man was. She couldn't get herself to look at it that way. She had tried. She loved Rat and wanted to give him the benefit of the doubt in every way. She trusted him, but this had cast him in a new light. It was troubling.

Being on the *Belleau Wood* would be a good break for her. She would have time to think, and time to practice medicine as a professional. She'd have time to be herself and see how she really felt about Rat. Maybe it would change things. If that was the result, so be it.

"This is it, ma'am," the petty officer said as he stopped in front of her stateroom door and ran the magnetic key through the reader. The idea of having her own private stateroom aboard a huge warship was exciting to her. She truly felt part of the Navy. It was one thing to wear the uniform, to live on Navy bases and work at Navy hospitals, even to be the flight surgeon for the Blue Angels as she had been before Bethesda, but going to sea on a warship was the real Navy.

She followed him into the room, impressed by its size. It was obviously a commander's stateroom, probably reserved for the commanding officer of a helicopter squadron, a lieutenant colonel or a Navy commander. But since there were few other female officers with whom she could share, she had a room to herself.

The petty officer explained the calendar for laundry pickup, the phone number to the stateroom, and showed her how to fold down the bed and the desk. She fought back a smile as he closed the door behind him. Suddenly the door opened again and he stepped back through. "Sorry," he said, knocking on the door even though he was already inside. "I forgot to tell you something. Dr. Satterly asked if he could meet you for dinner tonight. He said he would stop by your stateroom about 1730 and pick you up, show you where the wardroom was. Would that be okay?"

Andrea was surprised. "Is that customary?"

The petty officer avoided her gaze. "Not that I've heard, ma'am, but I wouldn't really know."

"Let me guess," Andrea said. "He's single."

"I believe he was recently divorced," the petty officer said, not quite grinning.

"And he's willing to take a chance that I'm not ugly. Or fat." She was very far from both.

"I wouldn't know anything about that, ma'am."

"Which doctor is it you said?"

"The ship's surgeon. Dr. Satterly."

"Tell him I'll be here at 1730."

◆　◆　◆

Andrea had saved organizing her fold-down desk as the last thing she would do to set herself up in her stateroom. She loved the room. It was austere, but it was so . . . nautical. She had been on Navy ships before, but only for a night or two, and never had her own stateroom assigned to her for the next several months, even years.

She heard a confident rap on her door and checked her watch. Exactly 1730. She had made a special effort not to look good. She wore no makeup and had done nothing in particular to her hair. She waited for a moment, stood, and opened the door.

"Dr. Ash?" the man said.

"Yes. I'm Andrea Ash. And you are?"

"Dr. Tim Satterly. The ship's surgeon. Welcome aboard, and welcome to the *Belleau Wood* medical team. We are thrilled to have you."

Andrea extended her hand. She was surprised by Satterly. She had intended to hate him the moment she met him. She had heard good things about him in the medical community, but Rat had made her think ill of him. He seemed truly happy to see her, and his smile looked genuine. He had an intensely curious way about him, as if he was always trying to learn. He wasn't at all what she was expecting.

"Shall we go grab some dinner?"

"Sure. Lead the way."

Satterly stepped back and allowed her to exit her stateroom. She closed the door behind her and slid the magnetic key into the pocket of her khaki trousers. He walked down the passageway and spoke to her over his shoulder. "I've heard a lot about you. Your reputation precedes you."

"What have you heard?"

"We don't get too many Blue Angel flight surgeons out here. Weren't you the first female Blue Angel flight surgeon?"

"Second."

"That's still pretty impressive." He pointed to his left as they walked. "That's my stateroom right there."

She looked at the door as she passed by. There was a large bumper sticker at an angle across the middle of the door. She read it out loud. "*Médecins sans Frontières?*" she groped, not doing well with the French.

He stopped. "Yeah. Doctors Without Borders."

"Of course, right."

"You heard of them?"

"Sure. I get their literature all the time."

"We try to get medical care to where it's needed around the world regardless of poverty, politics, difficulty, or danger. Great group of people. Won the Nobel Peace Prize in 1999."

"You work with them?"

"I spend three of my four weeks of leave each year with them doing surgeries in a tent somewhere or other. It's really rewarding. I do more surgeries in three weeks there than in six months here." He walked on.

"Anyone ever say anything to you about them? Criticize you about it?"

"No, why would they?" He frowned.

"I don't know. They're kind of liberal, aren't they?"

"What's wrong with that?"

"They're pretty critical of the United States sometimes."

"Sometimes we deserve it."

"You a member of any other organizations?"

He looked at her curiously. "What difference does it make?"

"Just wondered if anyone ever gave you any grief, that's all. I mean you didn't have to put a sticker on your door. You must be trying to make some kind of point."

He shook his head. "Only statement I'm making is for human rights. Amnesty International, Human Rights Watch, those sorts of things. I support what they're doing. How can anybody be against human rights?"

"I know what you mean."

"Here we are," he said. He pushed open the door and stepped into the large, spacious wardroom. There were several officers sitting at the cloth-covered tables. "Over here. We tend to sit in the same place every time." She stood near the table until it was clear where she was supposed to sit. She pulled the chair back and sat down.

Satterly introduced her to the other officers at the table. He watched their reactions when they realized that she had been permanently assigned to the *Belleau Wood*. They knew a female flight surgeon was coming, but were still surprised by her, especially because she wasn't homely or cold.

She sat next to Lieutenant Murphy.

Satterly asked her, "What inspired you to come out to the *Belleau Wood*? Wanted to be where the action is?"

"Basically because the detailer said I should. He said it would be good for my career. But what action are you talking about?" Andrea asked, feigning ignorance.

Satterly lowered his voice. "They've been able to keep the lid on it so far, but I'm sure it's going to blow up pretty soon. There's a hell of a lot that has happened here, and a hell of a lot more that's going to happen. Could be a very exciting place to be over the next thirty days."

"What happened?" The mess specialists placed their food in front of them. Andrea picked up her silverware, looked at Satterly, and waited.

"Have you ever heard of Wahamed Duar?" His eyes lit up with excitement.

"Sure. The terrorist. The guy who was just captured."

"He's here."

"Where?"

"On the ship."

"How did he get here?"

"We captured him. We went into Sudan, busted up a meeting he was having, captured him, and brought him back to the ship for trial."

Andrea couldn't resist. "Were you with the Special Forces? Sort of like a medic?"

Satterly sat back a little bit, but rode it. "I wasn't actually with the team that captured them, but I was here when they brought him in. I was one of the first to see him—I had to give him some minor medical attention. I was there when they started interviewing him, and was with him for several hours."

"Who captured him?"

"A group of our Special Forces. I'm not actually sure who they were working for. Might have been the Navy, might be the CIA. They were wearing Sudanese uniforms—probably illegal under the rules of war, knowing them."

"Pretty impressive work."

Satterly's face clouded and his smile vanished. "Except they *tortured* one of the terrorists to death."

"Here?"

"In Sudan. Out in the field. I'm not really sure where. The guy died from it."

"I thought you said you weren't there," Andrea said glancing at Murphy, who looked away.

"He died *here*. We tried to save him but couldn't. I talked to him. He said the head guy had tortured him."

"Was he bleeding? Broken fingers, bones?"

"No, no," Satterly said. "He used water. Something I *now* know is called the water board. It's not supposed to permanently damage anyone, but this guy threw up and aspirated the vomit. He died of pneumonia."

"How do you know it was from being tortured?"

"We did an autopsy. His lungs were full of food and infection. There was also an indication of drowning in his lungs. Water damage."

"Who is this American?" she asked.

"I never heard his name. I just heard people calling him Rat."

"Strange name."

Satterly swallowed and put his fork down. "I'll tell you what, Andrea, I'm going to do whatever I can to make sure he has to answer for that. He shouldn't get away with torturing prisoners. That's wrong. That's not what America is all about. We have to be a lot bigger than that."

She almost nodded. "What can you do about it? I mean it's sort of out of your reach."

He got a knowing, insider's look in his eyes. "I'm going to make sure he pays for it."

"How?"

"You'll see."

She ate in silence.

Satterly continued, "It's the very kind of thing I was talking about."

"What?"

"About when human rights organizations criticize the States. This is the very kind of thing, torturing a prisoner. If they criticized us for this, we'd deserve it. Don't you agree?"

"I guess I'd need to know more," she said, dodging.

"Like what?"

"I don't know."

"We have to hold on to what's good about us, Andrea. Otherwise we just become animals. Isn't that the definition of civilization? The ability to control base instincts and live together?"

"I guess so."

"That's what I'm about at the core, Andrea," he said, finishing his milk. "Preservation of humanity. The things that make us human. Killing is easy. Hurting is easy. Rising above those things, resisting temptation, that's much harder."

◆　◆　◆

"Josephine, how are you doing?" Skyles asked as he sat down heavily in a chair on the other side of her desk at the *Washington Post*. Her desk was one among many in an open area full of noise and activity.

Josephine Block looked up. "I got your message. I tried to be gone when you said you'd be here."

Skyles looked wounded. "This is a great story. I came right to you. You need to be in on this."

Josephine pushed her reading glasses up on top of her red hair, dyed from the cheapest bottle in the corner drugstore next to her condo. The gray roots were showing through on the left side where the part was. She had a wrinkled, dumpy look about her, but her eyes were bright and inquisitive. "I've had to listen to enough of your BS to know it's not worth the trouble. What do you have this time, a child molester? Rapist? Tax evader? All wanting their stories published to make them look better?"

"Come on. Are you willing to listen or not?"

"Not."

"You have to listen to this. This isn't the usual thing at all. This is huge." He could tell she was listening with one ear as she typed. He doubted she was actually typing anything. "Picture this," Skyles said. "American Special Forces hero arrested to protect terrorist."

She looked up. "Right. To protect terrorist. That's exactly what is happening, I'm sure."

"Are you familiar with the top-secret courtroom that exists on the top of the Department of Justice? Cipher locks? The foreign intelligence whatever stuff?"

She nodded. "Basically."

"Well, my all-American client—and I'm talking Captain America himself—is being tried in that courtroom. He's been charged with manslaughter—killing a terrorist, by torture. And he's been charged with violating the Geneva Convention. All because Stuntz is scared to death of Sarah St. James."

"Huh? Talk about a non sequitur."

"Because he is a suspicious, sneaky son of a bitch, and she wants his job. She has people all over the government, her shadow government, her spies, her operators, if you will. They're not very well known. But one of them is my client."

Josephine began typing lightly again on her keyboard. "And what about your client? What did he do to some poor terrorist?"

"If you read the charges you'll find that he's been charged with torturing a terrorist to death. But if you get into it you'll find something else equally interesting." Skyles slid forward on his chair and imposed himself into her space. She frowned. "There's also another big piece of this you haven't heard about. I'm talking front page. Guaranteed. Want to know what it is?"

"I'm dying," she said.

"He's the one who captured Wahamed Duar, the guy who is on the front page of your newspaper every day."

"The plot thickens."

"And I know where Duar is."

"The government says an undisclosed location."

"Right. And I know where that undisclosed location is."

"How do you know?"

"I just told you, my client is the one who captured him. He's the one who took him to that undisclosed location."

Josephine looked at Skyles. "Where?"

"Ask the government. Because you didn't hear any of this from me."

"Did they bring him to the United States?"

He shook his head. "On an American warship. They're going to try him in a tribunal."

"What ship?"

"The *Belleau Wood.*"

"I'll check into it. Who is doing the court-martial of your client?"

"It's not a court-martial. They threw it over to the U.S. Attorney's Office. Wolff. You know him?"

She nodded. "Let me have your card, because I'm sure you're not at the same number you were at two years ago when we last spoke."

"I am actually, but here's my card anyway. I'm counting on you."

"For what?"

"To expose those who want no exposure. Our only currency here in this great town of ours. You've got to help my client. He has quite a story."

"Did he kill the guy?"

"No comment."

Josephine tossed his card on her desk and returned her attention to her computer.

◆　◆　◆

The CH-46 helicopter's rotor blades slowed and stopped but the jet engines that pushed them continued to scream. Sailors placed chocks around its wheels on the deck of the *Belleau Wood* to keep it from rolling. Rat and Groomer walked down the ramp to the island. A sailor waited for them at the island and held the hatch open against the stiff wind. They stepped through and waited as the sailor pulled the steel hatch closed and dogged it down. He turned and hurried up a ladder. They followed him, up one ladder after another until they were on the ship's bridge. "Request permission to enter the bridge!" the sailor said loudly.

The Officer of the Deck looked at the group and gave the requested permission.

The sailor led Rat and Groomer through the starboard hatch to where the captain was standing.

Rat spoke quickly. "You asked to see us?"

Captain Logan looked at him and immediately recognized him. "Not *you*. Why'd they send you back out here?"

"It's great to be back on your ship, sir," Rat said, trying vainly to deflect the captain's hostility.

Logan reached into his green nylon jacket pocket and pulled out a Navy message. "I get a message like this, I'm supposed to just say 'okay'? Do whatever you want? I'm responsible for him. Most-wanted terrorist in the world, I'm told, he's in my brig, and now I'm supposed to just release him to you?"

"Yes, sir. That's exactly right."

"Why?"

Rat reached over and took the message from Logan. He read it carefully, although not for the first time. He had drafted it in Washington. "It doesn't say in the message what the reason is, just that it's official government business. But it is an official order, through official channels. You need to release him into our custody."

Logan knew Rat was right. "What are you going to do with him?"

"I'm not at liberty to discuss that, Captain."

Logan was frustrated. He looked at Rat. "What is it with you guys? No uniform markings, no name tags, no insignia, no nothing. Who are you?"

"I'm just a regular SEAL temporarily on loan to the SAS, part of the CIA, Captain." Rat wanted Logan to think he was being forthcoming, which he was, in part. "Same as my XO here."

"How many more of you guys are there on that helicopter?"

"Well, sir, there are twelve of us, and six or so should already be in the brig preparing Mr. Duar for his little trip. We don't want anyone seeing him or having any idea of what we're doing. You did see in the message that we expect to have him back in your brig within seventy-two hours? It could take longer, but I doubt it."

"Tell me this, at least. Where are you going with him?"

"Sorry, sir."

Logan clenched his hand around the message. "You going to take him somewhere where you can torture him? Like you did that other guy?"

Rat paused. "I'm not going to touch him."

"You'll have to sign a receipt for him," Logan said finally, weakly.

"Happy to, sir. Do you mind if we get down to the brig now?"

Logan shook his head and turned away. The sun had set thirty minutes before and the ship was just growing dark enough to suit Rat's purposes.

He and Groomer slid down the rails of the ladders and rushed to the brig. One of his men saw them coming and swung the door open instantly, then followed them in.

Three of his men had put a military flight suit on Duar and put a nylon bag over his head. The bag was tied at the neck and was impossible to remove without using both hands. Two of his own men had put on identical flight suits and had bags on their heads. All three of them had their hands and feet bound. The three "prisoners" were then hooked together.

Rat leaned toward Duar and spoke softly in Arabic. "If you make a false move I will personally cave in your head. It would be a pleasure. Do you understand me?"

Duar made no response.

"Let's go," Rat said. They moved all three out of the brig and forward to the ammunition elevator. They stood on the elevator as it lifted them to the flight deck and the waiting CH-46. Duar was quiet. Rat watched him carefully.

The group moved as one across the windy but quiet flight deck. The three prisoners shuffled against their restrictive bindings. The escorts pulled the three men up the ramp into the waiting helicopter as the engines started to whine. The ramp came up and the helicopter came alive. The blades bit into the moist air and lifted them into the air. As they cleared the flight deck below them and the black sea that was all around, Rat took the bindings and hoods off his two men, who sat on either side of Duar. They put their normal gear back on, and settled in for the long flight to Kenya, then Egypt.

Groomer stood over Duar. He looked at Rat. "What do you think they'll get out of him?"

Rat considered Groomer's question; it was the one *he* wanted an answer to.

Groomer asked before Rat could answer, "And how come you trust the Egyptians?"

Rat wasn't sure how much to say. Even Groomer didn't know much about what he had done in the past. "I've operated with them."

"That's it?"

"That's it. Now we see."

Groomer nodded, sat back down on the nylon seat, and settled in.

◆　◆　◆

Sadeq Satti walked confidently into the headquarters of the Liberian International Shipping Company in Monrovia, Liberia. He was dressed in a casual white open-collared shirt with expensive trousers and Italian loafers. He carried a burgundy briefcase tucked under his arm. He had the air of one accustomed to making business deals and discussing finances. He had an appointment with Thomas Lisbie, the director of shipping operations for the company, and had intentionally arrived fifteen minutes late. He was shown up the stairs to a tiled waiting room outside Lisbie's office. He sat in one of the cheap folding chairs and tried to make himself comfortable. He chain-smoked in the heat as rivulets of sweat ran down his chest and onto his thin belly. He hated Liberia. It had all the trappings of capitalism but none of the benefits. The nice buildings, clean streets, and jobs one might hope to see as the benefit of such free trade never seemed to make it to Monrovia. The money just changed hands between international operators without noticeably benefiting the country.

Satti tapped his ash onto the clean tile floor and studied the innumerable pictures of ships on the walls. Liberia was proud of its tradition of having the largest merchant fleet in the world. More ships in the world's ocean trade were registered in Liberia than anywhere else.

After a thirty-minute wait, which caused Satti great amusement, he was shown into Lisbie's office. "Good morning, sir. You must be Mr. Satti. Thank you for waiting. I'm Thomas Lisbie," he said as he walked around his desk and shook his hand. The office of the Liberian International Shipping Company overlooked the St. Paul River, which with the Mesulrado River formed the port of Monrovia, one of the best deep-water ports in Africa. It was quite busy, and Lisbie liked to be able to see his ships at a glance.

Satti sat across from Lisbie and placed his briefcase in the chair next to him. He lit another cigarette. "Good morning. Thank you for seeing me," he said in a deep, melodic voice. "Did you get my correspondence?"

Lisbie nodded. "Yes. You want to ship three containers and fifteen people." He scanned his desk to see if the fax was still lying there as it had been for two days. He couldn't find it. He looked at Satti and was surprised to see him staring at him. "The three containers are no problem. We have scheduled them on the ship which you requested. That is not a problem at all. But we do not carry passengers."

Satti nodded knowingly as he took an impossibly long drag on his cigarette. As he answered Lisbie, the smoke came through his vocal cords muffling his voice. "Make them crew."

"What?" Lisbie asked. "Did you say crew? Are they rated able-bodied seamen?"

"Yes," he lied.

The Liberian smiled. He found the entire idea amusing. "I'm not sure why I asked that, because it doesn't really matter. We have all the crew we need. We're happy to transport your cargo, especially at the premiums which you're willing to pay—and which we appreciate. But we don't transport passengers. It is against corporate policy."

Silence hung awkwardly in the air. Satti continued to smoke. He ignored the ashtray on the desk and dropped more ash on the floor. Satti was obviously not going to accept the answer Lisbie had given him. "What solution do you propose?"

"Solution to what problem? The passengers?" Lisbie asked. He was growing quite uncomfortable. Satti's calmness unsettled him. "I'm afraid if that's what you're referring to, I don't see a solution. If you'd like, I could make arrangements for them to fly to arrive at the port at the same time as the ship. But I can't do that for free. You would need to pay for the costs. Other than that, I don't really see much of a solution."

"Are you aware of how much we're prepared to pay you?"

"I am well aware, Mr. Satti. And as I said, it is very generous. We're happy to take it, and happy to accept your payment, but not your passengers. By the way, for the cargo manifests, we need to know what's in the containers."

"Machinery. Dye-making machinery for a manufacturing plant," Satti replied. "What is your company's concern with passengers?"

"We don't have room. We do not have bunk-rooms, or staterooms. We're not set up to carry additional people, other than the crew. Perhaps one or two, but not fifteen," he said, hinting at one possible solution. "And the one or two would usually be someone from the management of the shipping company. I'm sure you understand."

Satti understood all right. He said nothing. He let the silence do his work for him.

Lisbie shifted in his chair and became acutely aware for the first time that his chair squeaked when he moved. A ship behind him about to be towed from its mooring gave one long blast on its whistle—getting under way. "Maybe we could figure out a way for one or two of your people to make the trip."

Satti remained silent. "I need to have fifteen of my people aboard the ship."

"I told you. I cannot do that."

Satti nodded knowingly as he dropped his cigarette on the floor and smashed it with his shoe. "Forgive me for not seeing it before this," Satti said. "I did not realize the difficulty this job is for you and for your family. You have needs as well. I failed to mention to you that we expect to pay you as a consultant for your help in preparing the contract. It was my oversight." He opened the briefcase to pull out an envelope stuffed with cash. "Allow me—"

"No, no," Lisbie said, holding up a hand. "You misunderstand. I do not want anything."

Satti removed his hand from the briefcase slowly. "Thank you for your candor. Our three containers will be here on time. Our fifteen men will be here the day the ship sails."

Lisbie was growing angry. "I have told you now several times I cannot."

Satti froze him with a look. "I will be back in ten days. When I come back you will tell me how you are going to get my fifteen people on the ship for the journey eastward. Do you understand?"

Lisbie was outraged. "I will not, sir. We will ship your goods—although I am having doubts about that right now—but we will not take your people."

Satti went on as if Lisbie hadn't said a word. "And when I come back in ten days, I'll pay you for the cost of transporting our people. If on reflection, you realize how much work you have had to do to accommodate our difficult requests, I will be more than happy to renew the offer for the consultant's fee that I offered you. It is quite substantial." He waited.

Lisbie stood. He had to assert himself. "We are not making any progress. I will process the contract for shipping your three containers."

Satti also stood. He was three or four inches taller than Lisbie and in much better shape. He had a physical presence Lisbie could never hope to have. Lisbie's physical presence was fairly represented by his small potbelly and wispy mustache. "I will see you in ten days. Perhaps during that time you will have a chance to think about me, and about what I have said. Then when I return, I am very confident you will have changed your mind."

Chapter 12

David Stern waited to be connected to the captain at the Pentagon whose name he had just spent forty-five minutes trying to uncover. This captain almost certainly wasn't the right person either, but it was a name and could direct him where he needed to go. Finally the captain came on the line. "Captain Wilhelm, JAG office, how can I help you?"

"Good afternoon, Captain. My name is David Stern. I'm with the ACLU office here in Washington." He stopped. He knew the reaction of most government employees when the ACLU called. It meant trouble. "Do you have a minute?"

"What's this about?" Wilhelm asked, annoyed.

"I would like to see my client. I need to speak with him and begin preparing his defense."

"And who might your client be?"

"Wahamed Duar." The complete silence told Stern all he needed to know. Duar was being held, and this captain knew about it.

"How were you retained?"

"That's none of your concern. I want to see my client, and I want to know how you plan to make that happen. I've already sent a fax to the captain of the ship."

"I don't plan on making anything happen. I don't know anything about any of this. I'm just taking notes. I'll find out who you need to talk to and I'll have that person call you back. What's your number?"

Stern gave it to him. "I need to hear from whoever this is this afternoon. My client's interests and rights are being trampled every minute he is unrepresented."

"He is represented."

"You acknowledge he is in custody? And by representation, did you mean appointed military counsel? Who is representing him right now? What is his or her e-mail address?"

"I'll have someone call you."

"Today."

The line went dead. Stern transferred Wilhelm's address off the Internet to the address line in Word and completed the letter he had already drafted confirming their conversation, and informing the JAG office at the Pentagon that he had been retained to represent Duar. He signed it and fed it to the fax machine. As the number dialed and the fax connection was made, Stern picked up the telephone and called Josephine Block at the *Washington Post*. She answered the phone. Jo was a straight shooter. Stern loved her; she wasn't afraid to run a story that fired right at the government.

She answered. "Josephine Block."

"Jo, David Stern, ACLU. I need to meet with you right away. I have a very large story for you."

She breathed heavily on the line. "Don't have time. I'm working on something."

"This will be worth your time. I guarantee it."

She sighed. "Come."

◆　◆　◆

"Mr. Lisbie, Sadeq Satti calling. I know it has only been seven days since we met, but I wondered if you had given what I said any more thought." He sat in his rental parked on the street outside the largest bank in Monrovia. He had bought the cell phone the day before for this one use.

"I have, and I have not changed my mind. I cannot do what you ask. I'm sorry. And three more days won't make any difference —"

"You haven't checked your bank account recently, I take it."

"What do you mean?"

"Have you?"

"Not really, no."

"When you do, you will find that it has perhaps more in it than it used to. Consider it a payment for your additional consideration. And there is a lot more where that came from if you do as I have asked."

"I . . . I can't really accept any payment," Lisbie said with some difficulty. He yearned to be free of debt, free to go where he wanted, to do what he wanted. But he wasn't about to compromise his principles for a bribe. Never had, never would. "I will return it to you at the address on your fax."

"No, keep it. It is a gift."

"I cannot."

Satti waited for a few awkward seconds. "Are you sure of your position?"

"Quite sure."

"That is too bad. Perhaps you will reconsider soon. You really must check with the bank," Satti said as he hit the "end" button on the cell phone.

Satti watched Lisbie's mother, an elderly woman, stop her old car in front of the bank. She had been lucky to get one of the six parking spots angling into the curb directly in front of the door. She wore a loose-fitting cotton dress and sandals. She moved slowly. The arthritis in her hips was as bad as he had been told. She wasn't demonstrative about her pain; she wasn't looking for sympathy, or help. She was just dealing with it, and it caused her to move slowly. Satti had followed her all morning as she completed her errands: the post office, the power company, a second-hand clothing store, and now the bank.

He could see her car clearly, even though it was a block away. He looked around the area. A few pedestrians. Some bystanders but not too many. The bank was a solid building. There might be someone hurt inside, but again, not too many. This was the place.

The bomb had been placed in her car under the hood the night before. Military grade C4. Harmless until Satti activated it remotely with his electronic detonator. Then it would go off the next time the starter was engaged. He waited. He lit another cigarette and let it dangle from the fingers of his left hand as his elbow hung out the window of his car. The heat was stifling. The sweat ran down his chest again. He yearned for the desert heat of Sudan, not the humid heat of central Africa, or the coast.

Satti took out his signal radio, turned it on, and depressed the trigger button. He saw a small green light illuminated on the top of the device. The receiver attached to the detonator returned the signal that the explosives were engaged and ready. He turned the radio off, placed it on the seat, and started his car. He completed a U-turn and drove away from the bank.

Lisbie's mother pushed the bank's heavy door open with great difficulty and turned down the sidewalk. As she approached her car she reached inside her bag for her keys. She sat gingerly and breathed deeply. Her hips hurt more today than usual. She needed hip replacement surgery. Her doctor had told her that if she lived on another continent maybe she could get the surgery, but not here. Until something changed she was just going to have to bear it. She shifted her weight painfully and reached her left foot forward against the pain to depress the clutch. She put the key in the ignition and turned it.

The C4 had been placed in the engine cavity on the firewall behind the steering column and shaped in such a way that the force would go first through the firewall into the passenger compartment. The remainder of the force would explode outward, causing maximum damage to the car's surroundings.

As soon as she turned the ignition, the electronic circuit to the detonator was complete. In a thousandth of a second the C4 had blown through the firewall and taken Lisbie's mother apart. The speed and violence of the explosion were faster than her senses could convey pain to her brain, faster even than her eyes could recognize that something was happening and transmit it to her brain. Everything was gone before she even knew it.

The car exploded in a flash of white light and a thundering bang that was so loud and sudden it felt like a hammer blow for blocks around. The force tore the facade off the bank and ripped the doors off their hinges. The second-floor windows exploded into a shower of glass that fell to the sidewalk with a bright tinkling that filled the sound void created by the explosion, hitting the pavement before the car returned to earth from its brief flight.

Satti heard the explosion from two miles away as he drove along a residential street. He tossed his cigarette out the window and turned his car toward his hotel.

Chapter

13

avid Stern found Josephine's desk with some difficulty. She was in her usual state of hurry and disarray. She didn't even look up when he sat down in the chair across from her, watching her type furiously on her computer. He waited for her attention. She finally glanced up. "What?"

"David Stern. We spoke."

"What's all this about? Big story, front page. What could be so important?"

"You've heard of Wahamed Duar?"

"Of course."

"He's my client."

"And?"

"He's in custody on a ship in the Indian Ocean. I've been retained and I'm going to go out there and defend him. This so-called tribunal. I've notified the Pentagon that I'm representing him."

"I heard about it, but not about you."

"How?"

"Another lawyer was in here for *his* client—some Navy officer who has been charged with torturing a terrorist. While capturing your client, I think."

Stern was shocked. "The government tortured my client?"

"I don't know. I'm looking into the other thing right now. Sounds like it may all be tied together." She stood quickly and grabbed her purse. "And I'm about to find out. The Pentagon spokesperson is about to give the weekly, routine, boring press conference. I'm going to see if I can make it unroutine."

◆　◆　◆

Two bright young faces, Russell Edwards and Mary Rowland, appeared in Don Jacobs's doorway. He didn't even know their names. The Counterterrorism Center had expanded so rapidly he had no hope of knowing everyone's name. "What?"

"We've got a car bombing."

"Where?" he asked, automatically assuming the most likely places, Jerusalem, Haifa, Jakarta, Berlin, Moscow, Colombia.

"Monrovia."

"*Liberia*?" he asked, perplexed.

Rowland nodded. "In front of a bank. Killed some poor old woman. The bomb was in her car. Blew her sky high. Literally. Blew the facade off the bank. Very high explosive content."

Jacobs leaned back, puzzled. "Nothing the hell ever happens in Liberia."

They watched him.

"Who's on this?" he asked.

"We are."

Jacobs considered how much attention to give this. There were always things to run to ground, threats, attacks, bombs, investigations, murders, intrigue, intelligence, and most of it was worthless. The key was picking what to follow. But Liberia? "Any preliminary thoughts?"

Edwards nodded. "Seems like a local thing to us. There's no evidence of any terrorist cells in Liberia. Maybe someone got a bill for his checking account that he didn't like."

Jacobs didn't smile. "Lot of shipping goes through Liberia. Largest merchant fleet in the world. Maybe somebody's got something going in shipping."

They both shrugged. "Maybe," Rowland said.

"Let's get some field intel. Find out who the mort is."

"Mort?"

"The woman. The old lady."

"Okay."

"Find out who she is. Those kinds of bombs don't usually go off in the wrong car. And if she was somebody's target, we need to know why."

"Makes sense."

"If the real target was someone else, if she was a message, we need to intercept that message." He could see the skepticism on their faces. He stood. "You think these terrorist cells stand up and say, 'Here we are!' and we then put on our flak jackets and go after them? This is a game of *subtlety*. Of deceit, subterfuge, hidden agendas, and murder. They play in the dark, like cockroaches. They don't like being obvious until they're ready for their next big move. Then they want to be *real* obvious."

The two new intelligence officers felt chastised. "We'll get on it. Can we contact the embassy?"

He frowned instantly. "Who the hell else would you contact?"

◆　◆　◆

Sadeq Satti had stayed out of sight for three days after the bomb, but the ten-day window he had given Lisbie was up. He parked down the street from the Liberian International Shipping Company and walked into the office slowly, confidently. He walked directly up the stairs to the tiled waiting room outside the closed door leading to Lisbie's office. He could hear Lisbie talking. He lit a cigarette, crossed his legs, and waited.

He listened carefully to Lisbie through the door. He was clearly agitated. Since only one side of the conversation was audible it was clear Lisbie was on the phone and alone. Satti could hear him pacing. Finally Lisbie opened the door to call for someone and saw Satti. His face went red. "You bastard!" Lisbie shouted as he rushed across the reception room and grabbed for Satti's throat.

Satti had expected something like this, but not here, and not so suddenly. He waited until Lisbie had committed himself, a man who clearly had not been in a fistfight since boyhood, at which point Satti rose, flicked his cigarette into Lisbie's face, and rammed his fist into Lisbie's soft belly. Lisbie crumpled at his feet. He kneeled on the tile, moaning, "You bastard!"

Satti leaned over. "How *dare* you attack me! I came here to conclude our business. What has gotten into you?"

Lisbie got up on one knee and rested his elbow on it. He breathed deeply. His hair fell unattractively onto his forehead. "Why my mother? Why did you have to hurt *her*?" Lisbie sobbed softly.

Satti feigned recognition from the reports he had read in the newspaper. "That car bomb? That was your mother?"

Lisbie looked up at him. "I know who you are and what you're capable of."

Satti shook his head. "You don't know me at all. I am so sorry for the loss of your mother. Is there anything I can do?"

Lisbie gained his composure and stood. He smoothed his shirt and dusted the dirt off his knees. "You can get the hell away from me and my company."

Satti pointed to the door. "Into your office," he ordered, pushing Lisbie. Satti closed the door behind them. He walked behind Lisbie's desk and looked at the ships in the harbor. He watched the men loading two large cargo ships just below them. He turned to Lisbie, who was standing awkwardly on the other side of the desk like a visitor.

"I have come here to conclude our business."

"We don't have any business to conclude."

"I told you I'd give you ten days to consider. I even called you three days ago. Now I am back."

Lisbie stood silently. His anger and grief had consumed him for three days. To be standing in his office facing the man who was responsible was more than he could take. "I will *never* do anything for you."

"You have had ten days to think about it. I expect you have now changed your mind." He turned. "Am I right?"

Lisbie stood with his head down.

"Am I right?" Satti asked, crossing over to stand right next to Lisbie, so Lisbie could feel his presence, smell him. "Right?"

Lisbie nodded. He knew he was next if he said no.

"Excellent," Satti said, stepping back and taking his cigarettes and Zippo lighter out of his pocket. "My men will be here the night the ship is scheduled to sail."

Lisbie shuffled to his desk and sat down. "Not before. They will board just before the ship pulls out. No more than an hour before. They'll have to berth in a small room, all together, and pay for their food."

Satti smiled and nodded. "You'll not regret it."

"I already do."

◆　◆　◆

Captain Pat White stood behind the podium with the Department of Defense seal on it and waited for the reporters to sit. As the spokesperson for the Pentagon she had been holding weekly press conferences for two months since taking over the position. She had finally grown comfortable in front of the cameras and swarming journalists who probed incessantly, mostly looking for scandal and controversy. So far in her tenure there hadn't been either.

She saw Josephine Block in the front row of the room full of reporters. White spread her notes in front of her. "First, I'd like to welcome you to today's briefing. I'd like to make a short statement, then open it up for whatever questions you may have." She began, "The War on Terrorism continues in many corners of the globe, with United States and allied forces pursuing al Qaeda and other terrorist forces. The most recent development is the identification of a large al Qaeda cell in Indonesia that is known to have heavy weapons. The Indonesian forces are cooperating and the group is being pursued as we speak. There will be no escape, and if they do not surrender unequivocally we expect to engage those forces within the week.

"In the Philippines the guerrilla forces have been routed and only a remnant remains. We will continue to assist Philippine security forces in pursuing them."

She covered the other six areas she had been told to include in her brief, then opened the briefing for questions.

Josephine's hand flew up with enthusiasm. White was annoyed and ignored her, taking the first question from a young woman in the back that she didn't recognize. It was a question about the budget.

White looked at Josephine's upraised hand in the bright lights and realized she could not ignore her any longer without being obvious. "Josephine?"

"It's my understanding that the Navy officer, the Navy Special Forces officer who led the team to capture Duar, is under arrest and is being charged with killing one of the terrorists that worked for Wahamed Duar." Josephine pushed her reading glasses down from her forehead onto her nose and checked the document she was holding, a copy of the indictment given to her by Skyles. She held it up. "I have a copy of the indictment here. He is being charged with a violation of the Geneva Convention for torturing the terrorist, and for manslaughter because the terrorist died." She put the indictment down in her lap and returned her glasses to their resting place. "And Duar himself is being held on the *Belleau Wood* where he is to stand trial in a tribunal. So my question is," Josephine said, "is there any truth to this? Do you have an American officer and the terrorist he captured about to go on trial at the same time?"

White stared at her. She had known it would come out some time, but she had been told that the indictment of Rathman had been vague enough that no one would pick up on its significance. What really galled White was how a reporter had linked the two to make the government look stupid. "Let me look into those matters—"

"We know Duar is in custody. Can you confirm he's on the *Belleau Wood* and that he's going to be tried in a tribunal?"

"Well yes, of course he will be tried in a tribunal. The President announced that last week."

"Tribunals are supposed to be open. Is he being held in secret? Is he being allowed access to a lawyer of his choice? That is guaranteed under the tribunal rules issued by the DOD. And what about Lieu-

tenant Kent Rathman—is he being charged with war crimes for capturing a terrorist? Whose idea was that?"

White feigned making notes. "Again, I'll have to get back to you on
these things. I'm sorry. That's all I have time for right now," White said,
confounding the remainder of the reporters. She turned and left the
stage for her office.

Chapter

14

Nino Jorbenadze turned to Hotary with an expectant look on his face. "That's it. You said you wanted ten. That's ten. There are more though, if you need them."

Hotary looked around the hillside as if considering whether to buy more. His men had read his intention and positioned themselves accordingly. Hotary replied, "If we got more, say three more, how much would you charge us?"

Nino liked the idea of more money. "A lot. These were the easiest to get to. Others are more difficult. It would be many more thousands of dollars. But you have a lot of money, Mr. Hotary. How do you have so much cash on you?" he asked, taking a step closer to him.

"Ten is enough," Hotary said.

Nino nodded as he waited for his money.

Hotary handed his AK-47 to one of his men to free both his hands to dig deeply into his clothing. It put the Georgians at ease to see him transfer his weapon. He spoke to Nino. "Do you want me to pay you all of it and then you split it up with your men?"

Nino frowned, annoyed at Hotary's blatant attempt to get between him and his men. "I will take care of it."

Hotary buried his arm deeply in the folds of his cloak. He pulled out a handgun and shot Nino in the chest. He collapsed in a heap on the damp ground. Hotary's men fired their assault rifles at the other

Georgians, who only had time to show horror on their faces. They too fell to the ground as they bled to death.

Hotary shot Nino again as he lay at his feet. "Did they think we would allow witnesses?"

His men shook their heads at the stupidity of the Georgians.

Hotary surveyed the nearby woods. "Bury them in there," he ordered. "They will be found, but the longer it takes the better."

◆　◆　◆

Rat removed the hood from Duar and pushed him down onto one of the beds in the brig aboard the *Belleau Wood*. "Welcome home," Rat said.

Duar said nothing, not even raising his head.

As they closed the heavy steel door and locked it, Groomer said, "He seems spooked."

Rat nodded. "Getting your nuts roasted can do that," Rat said.

"Rat!" Andrea said from behind him, shocked to see him. "What are you doing here?"

"Andrea. Hey. Dropping off Duar."

"Who got his nuts roasted?" Andrea asked from behind them. "What did you mean by that?"

"What are you doing down here?" Rat asked.

"Dr. Satterly asked me to check on the prisoner as soon as he got back."

Rat looked at Groomer. "I'm not sure that's a good idea."

"Why's that?" Andrea asked.

"He's very tired. He's been up quite a while." Rat could just imagine Andrea inspecting Duar with his blackened earlobes and scrotum. She'd flip.

"Dr. Satterly insisted that I see the prisoner no matter what."

"Why's that?" Rat asked.

"To make sure he's okay."

Rat could see a different look in Andrea's eyes. A distance he hadn't seen before. "Satterly your pal now?"

"No. He just told me a little about the prisoner who died. He said you tortured him to death."

"That's the guy I'm on trial for, Andrea. You know all about that."

"I didn't know he had vomit in his lungs. Or that you supposedly poured water down his mouth and nose so he couldn't breathe until he threw up—"

"You want the whole story or just parts of it?"

"You're going to tell me the whole thing now?"

"I can't. I can't even tell good Dr. Satterly the whole story. So based on half information he's ready to string me up."

"Whatever," she said. "Now please excuse me. I need to see the prisoner."

Groomer stepped subtly into her path. "He's resting."

She looked at Rat to see if he was going to intervene on her behalf. He wasn't. "Dr. Satterly said you wouldn't let me see Duar when you brought him back. He said the reason would be that you have done something to him you don't want me to know about."

"And that's why he sent you. Because he's too much of a coward to say anything to my face."

"Apparently last time he wasn't. He told me he confronted you in the wardroom, in front of God and everybody."

"You're right. I forgot how courageous—or should I say self-righteous—he was."

She stepped around Rat and stood in front of Groomer. "I need to see him now. Please step aside, Lieutenant *Junior Grade* Groomer," she said, to point out she was senior to him, at least in the Navy.

"He's sleeping."

"How do you know?"

"I was just in there."

"What did you do to him? Where did you take him?"

Rat said, "You really think that while I'm on trial for torturing one guy I'm going to take some other guy out and torture him?"

"I have no idea. I just know I've been told to see Duar, and not to take 'no' for an answer."

"And what if you got 'no' as the answer?"

"I'm supposed to call Dr. Satterly, and he'll come take care of it."

"You'd better call him," Rat said.

Andrea tried to control her anger. "Do you know what you're doing?"

"I sure do. But the one who doesn't is *you*. You're being used, and it's a game you're not part of. Tell Dr. Satterly that you tried, but I was obstinate. If he's got a problem with that, he should come deal with it *himself*."

Andrea nodded slowly. "I'll do that. But you and I need to talk. Soon." She waited for Rat to say something. He just looked at her. "I need to hear your side of this, because I'm starting to have my doubts."

"When the time is right. If I tell you now, they'll subpoena you and force you to testify against me."

Andrea nodded. She wanted to trust him. She badly wanted to be able to trust him. But she didn't. She turned and headed for a telephone to call Dr. Satterly.

◆   ◆   ◆

Rat left Groomer in charge of Duar and went to find the prosecutor. He had been told it was a woman, a commander. He climbed the ladders and went straight to her office, knowing it was on the starboard side of the ship by the frame number he had been given. Those in her office hadn't seen her in some time. They offered to call her. Rat got the frame number of her stateroom instead and went there himself.

Rat knocked loudly on the thin steel door.

"Who is it?" Watson said, surprised by the knock.

"Lieutenant Rathman," Rat said.

She came to the door and opened the door part of the way. Rat could see she was damp and had a towel wrapped around her. "Sorry, I just got out of the shower. I was working out." She looked at Rat's camouflage uniform and noticed there was no name tag, no insignia, no rank. Rat's boots had desert sand dust all over them.

"No problem. I'll wait."

Watson was surprised. "Do I know you?"

"I'm with the group that captured Duar. We brought him back."

"You're Rat."

Rat nodded. "I have something to give you."

"Like what?"

"Not out here," Rat said. "How long before you're ready?"

"Twenty minutes."

"How about I meet you up at your office in twenty?"

"Sure. What's this about?"

Rat was already gone. He was running up the ladders to the communications office. He had to get a message off to Washington. On the way back to the ship he had read the Arabic notes of the Egyptian colonel. Even though Rat hadn't been there when the information was collected, Duar had revealed numerous planned attacks in the United States set to occur in the next month. Rat had read the notes with a mixture of disbelief and horror. It was critical intelligence information, if true. It was the very information they had wanted to get from Duar when they set their minds to capture him. Rat was skeptical about much of the information, but he'd leave it up to others in Washington to determine what was true and what wasn't. They could cross-reference a lot of other intelligence information he wasn't privy to.

He sent copies of the Egyptian officer's notes back to the CIA via secure fax, and a message summarizing Duar's confession and the contents of the notes to the Agency and to the National Security Council via Sarah St. James. He would make sure her message went out first. She would know about it a few minutes before anyone else in Washington.

He sent off the faxes and the messages in time to be at Watson's office in the allotted twenty minutes. Watson wasn't there. Rat sat in one of the chairs and took his first deep breath of the day. He was bone tired. He was worried about Duar. Not only because of what the Egyptians had done to him, but what he had said were his intentions for the United States. And now Andrea was lining up against him. He checked his watch again as Watson walked in. He looked at the confession that he had placed on Watson's desk. He wondered if it was the best thing to do, to use a confession against him that was extracted through torture. She might actually be able to use it—he wasn't involved in the confession and hadn't expected it. If they got the confession through the acts of somebody else, well, so what? They didn't force it out of him. Egypt did. It just fell into their hands. But it didn't feel right. He wanted to get Duar put away for life, or better yet, executed. But he was getting a bad feeling about the entire thing.

"You're here," Watson said.

"Twenty minutes," he said, standing up. Her uniform hung on her as if it were on a hanger. She had large, protruding eyes that had a sadness about them.

"What's this about?" she asked as he walked around the desk and sat down.

Rat hesitated, then handed her the confession.

"What's this?"

"Read it."

"It's in Arabic."

"A translation is attached."

"Who did the translation?"

"I did."

"Are you qualified?"

"Probably not for court, but it's right. You can have it done later by whoever you want."

Watson looked at him skeptically, then paged through the document until she saw English. She read straight through to the end. She looked up. "Where did you get this?"

"In Egypt."

"How?"

"We took him to Egypt to let them question him. When I went to pick him up, he had signed this. I took it from the Egyptians and brought it back."

"What did they do to him to get it?"

"I don't know. I wasn't there."

"You don't know?"

"No. But I can see it wasn't pretty."

"Did you have anything to do with it?"

"No. When I came back to pick him up I found this confession."

"How do you know it's his signature?"

"I asked him. He said it was."

"They tortured this out of him. I don't know if we can use it for much."

"I thought you could use something from a foreign country if we weren't . . . involved."

"Sometimes. It's very tricky. I'll think about it."

"You'll think about it."

"Yeah. I'll think about it."

The more he got to know Watson, the less impressed he was. To think that this was the attorney who was responsible for prosecuting Duar was distressing. Rat stood up. "I've got to go."

"I've go to go too," Watson said.

Rat moved as Watson hurried out of her office with the copy of the confession. He reached into his pocket and pulled out the message that had been waiting for him at the communications center. He read it again, still annoyed. He skipped over the addressee information and the classifications and read the body of the message, which had been sent to him personally:

1. 125 SPECIAL FORCES TEAM MEMBERS BEING SENT TO
   GEORGIAN REPUBLIC FOR TRAINING OF GEORGIAN ARMY.
   TERRORISTS FROM GEORGIA, CHECHNYA, AFGHANISTAN,
   PAKISTAN, SUDAN, AND ELSEWHERE ACCUMULATING IN
   PANKISI GORGE REGION NORTH OF TBILISI. GEORGIAN ARMY
   NEEDS TRAINING AND WEAPONS TO GO INTO VALLEY AFTER
   TERRORISTS.

2. GEORGIANS HAVE REQUESTED YOU BY NAME. AGENCY AND
   DOD HAVE APPROVED. YOU ARE TO TRAVEL TO GEORGIA TAD
   WITH THREE OTHERS FROM YOUR TEAM FOR SPECIAL
   FORCES INSTRUCTION. MORE DETAILED ORDERS AWAIT
   ARRIVAL IN GEORGIA. OFFICER IN CHARGE OF
   DETACHMENT IS LIEUTENANT COLONEL JAMES SWIFT, USA.

Rat studied the message, wondering why the Georgians would request him by name. He looked at his RPDA and the e-mail from Sarah St. James. He was starting to regard her e-mails with suspicion. Her encouragement to "cooperate" fully with the Egyptians had come on a recommendation, she said, from Jacobs. And she said Johnson had enough traffic to link Duar's organization straight to Georgia. He looked at his watch. He had to talk to Andrea, to see if he could calm her down a little, then get off on the earliest transportation to the nearest airport and get to Georgia. Groomer, Robby, and Banger were going to be thrilled.

♦ ♦ ♦

Dr. Satterly's red face lit the way for him as he stormed to the bridge to see the captain. He had forgotten his hat—his cover—which was required on the bridge, but he didn't care. He opened the door and stepped onto the bridge. "Request permission to come onto the bridge."

The Officer of the Deck looked at him, noticed he was without his cover and decided not to make too much of it because he wasn't unrestricted line—not a warfare officer—and he was a captain. "Permission granted."

"Captain here?" Satterly asked.

The OOD motioned to the captain's chair on the port side of the bridge.

Captain Hogan was intently studying something on the horizon through enormous binoculars.

"Captain, he's done it again."

Logan looked at the surgeon. He didn't really like Satterly, but he was supposed to be a good doctor. "Meaning?"

"That Special Forces man. The one they call Rat? Whoever he is, Navy, CIA, whatever, he took Duar off the ship—"

"I know."

"Well, they came back, and I sent the new flight surgeon to see Duar as soon as he came back, to make sure nothing had happened. Plus I figured it would be less . . . I don't know, confrontational. I don't think he likes me. He wouldn't let her see him. So I went down there myself. Captain, he has been tortured."

Logan put down the binoculars and yelled to the OOD, "You got that trawler?"

"Yes, sir."

Logan looked at Satterly. "How do you know?"

"I checked him out. There are burn marks on his ears and his . . . testicles. He's been electrocuted."

Logan frowned. "You sure?"

"Yes, sir. I'm sure. And he seems different. This has really affected him. He's almost in shock."

"Is he at risk of dying?"

"No, I don't think so. But he's not the same man they took out of here. At least not yet."

"OOD?"

"Yes, sir."

"Get the comm officer up here. I need to send off a message right away."

◆ ◆ ◆

President Kendrick hated being pushed faster than he wanted to go by the press. He had told them almost everything from the day Duar was captured. But it was never enough. "They just don't ever let go, do they? No matter what we do, they use it to make us look bad. If we'd gone completely public right away, they'd have yelled at us for not giving him a lawyer, or something, start right in on us about tribunals, and how unfair they are. And if we hold off a little, it's because we're ashamed, or trying to hide something. Always the same."

Stuntz drank deeply from the coffee cup in front of him. "Press," he muttered. "Their goal in life is dis*ruption*. They carry a stick around just in case they find a government wheel with spokes."

Kendrick ignored him. "Now we have to explain." He looked at Stuntz. "And I want you to do the explaining."

"Me?" Stuntz almost choked.

"You have a good understanding of everything, and you're good on your feet. Hold a press conference. Tell them about the tribunal. Then you'll be grilled about this Rathman trial. You can tell them it's DOJ, but you should also be ready to defend the charges. The manslaughter charges. Geneva Convention. After all, it was your idea, wasn't it?"

Stuntz frowned, but said nothing.

"This afternoon."

Stuntz nodded.

"Sarah, what happened in Egypt?"

She knew he would ask, but his timing and directness surprised her.
"In what way?"

"Duar was taken off the ship to Egypt, and on return appears to
have been tortured. And this Rathman was with him the entire time.
What the hell is going on? He's one of the ones you're in contact with,
right? And he's the one who's going on *trial* for doing this to another
terrorist? Who authorized this?"

"The Egyptians wanted to talk to him and we needed some help in
the interrogation. As I understand it, it was a CIA request that was ac-
ceded to by the DOD, to give Egypt a chance to interrogate him. As I
recall, sir, we all wanted to have him interrogated, and our interrogation wasn't very effective. We discussed giving a friendly country the
chance to interrogate him."

"Did you know this Rathman was going to take him to Egypt?"

"Yes. Where did you hear about this?" she asked.

"From the captain of the ship. Through Defense," he said.

She glanced quickly at Stuntz, who pretended to be reading a
memo in front of him.

"The captain said his ship's surgeon reported that Duar was tortured with electric current. To his *testicles*."

She grimaced.

"According to the message he has charred skin. He's in a state of
shock. Won't talk to anyone. And now, I hear, his American lawyer—
ACLU type, of course—is on his way to the ship, courtesy of the DOD.
We promised that those tried in these tribunals would have civilian
lawyers if they wanted. There's a great idea. You know what his new
lawyer is going to do when he finds out his client has been tortured in
Egypt, of all places, while he has been denied access to his client? He's
going to go ape-shit. And then he'll call the *Post,* and *they'll* go ape-shit—
what's the name of that woman?"

"Josephine Block."

"Right, then *she'll* go ape-shit and this will become her hobby until
she makes someone look stupid. And it won't be me."

"I'll take care of it," Stuntz said. "We haven't really done anything wrong. The Egypt thing is fine. We can allow others to interrogate him whenever we want any time we want. There are a lot of other countries who have been harmed or threatened by this man. Egypt sees him as a huge threat, with his operation in Sudan and ties to Islamic Jihad. No doubt they got some good stuff out of him too. But we can't be seen to have anything to do with it. I was aware it was going to happen, sir, and if in the future you'd rather know about these things ahead of time, I'll be glad—"

"No," Kendrick said, waving his hand dismissively. "I just hate giving critics ammunition."

Stewart Woods spoke up. "We got a lot of extraordinary intelligence out of this and a confession, sir."

Kendrick looked at him. "Is it useful?"

"We think so."

Kendrick nodded. "If it allows us to interfere with their plans, stop attacks . . . I don't know."

◆   ◆   ◆

David Stern, Duar's new lawyer, fresh from the Washington, D.C., office of the ACLU, stepped off the helicopter onto the deck of the *Belleau Wood*. His senses were completely overwhelmed by the noise of the turning aircraft, the brightness of the ocean reflecting the sun, the smell of jet fuel, and the feel of the hard steel deck under the leather soles of his dress shoes.

He wore a lightweight brown suit that hadn't fared well in traveling halfway around the world from Washington. It looked like he had slept in it, because he had, several times—in London, Kenya, and finally on the helicopter, with his head dangling like a lamp on a ship. He was completely exhausted. His skin was shiny and pale.

He followed the sailor who had gestured to him and headed toward the island of the enormous ship. They stepped through the steel hatch and the sailor dogged it closed behind him. "You're here to see Commander Little, right?"

"I don't know. Who is he?"

"He's the Navy lawyer defending the terrorist."

"Yes, I remember Mr. Little's name, now that you mention it. And he's only an *alleged* terrorist."

"Right," the sailor replied, smiling, "alleged. I'll take you right to him. I'll get your bag and get you checked into your stateroom, sir. Then later I'll come by and show you where it is."

Stern stretched his back. "I'd like to get cleaned up and change my clothes."

"You'd rather do that first, sir?"

"I think I would, actually."

"Okay, sir. Then why don't we go right down to the admin office."

Stern followed him down the confusing labyrinth of ladders and gray passageways to the admin office, where several sailors milled around in dungarees. Stern checked in and was given a key.

The sailor escorted him to his stateroom, showed him how to use the phone and lights, and said he'd be back in fifteen minutes to take him to Commander Little's office. When he returned Stern was cleaned up and ready to see Little. When Stern stepped into the small office he saw a commander reading *Naval Aviation News*.

Little looked up.

The sailor introduced them. "Commander Little, this is David Stern, Mr. Stern, Commander Little."

Little stood slowly and extended his hand. "Barry Little. I'm in charge of the defense team. Nice to meet you."

"David Stern. Nice to meet you."

Little didn't like him. "I guess I've never been on the same side of anything as an ACLU lawyer."

Stern held his smile inside. "I guess I'm not surprised."

"How exactly did Duar hire you?"

"I am not at liberty to disclose that."

"How do we really know he hired you at all? How do we know you're not one of those ACLU assholes who goes around making clients up just so you can make a big splash and sue someone, or make some grandstand play?"

"I guess you should ask Mr. Duar whether he hired me. I'm sure you meet with him every day to prepare the defense. Right?"

"Pretty much. But since he got back from Egypt, he hasn't felt much like talking."

Stern was confused. "Egypt?"

"Some of the Special Forces guys came and took him to Egypt for a little free-agent interrogation by our close Egyptian allies. I think the Egyptians aren't as gentle as we Americans are in interrogation. They don't put up with bullshit."

Stern was horrified. "They tortured him?"

"Seems to be the case."

"What have you done about it?"

"What would you like me to do about it?"

"Notify those who need to know. Tell the press."

"I suspect they'll learn about it, but you're right, we should tell them."

"Did they get any information out of him that they plan to use in the tribunal?"

"Not that I know of. Nothing they've told me about."

"If they do, they're going to have a fight on their hands."

Little nodded. "Want to meet him?"

"Absolutely," Stern said, controlling his excitement.

Little led Stern out of the office and down the passageway. Sailors passed them, walking quickly in both directions. Stern noticed they were all wearing bell-bottom blue jeans and light blue shirts with their names stenciled over the pocket and their rating stamped on the upper portion of the left sleeve. He had expected them to be wearing the Navy uniforms he had seen in all the recruiting posters. He was beginning to recognize how ignorant he was about the Navy. He had never been on a Navy ship before, not even for a tour in a port.

Little spoke over his shoulder to Stern. "You know, I *hate* the ACLU. If I ever wonder what I think about something? I find out what the ACLU thinks about it and then take the opposite position."

Stern had heard it all before. "Very impressive thinking," he said. "What exactly is it you hate about the ACLU?"

"We probably ought not go there. We're on the same team here, right? The same side?"

"That's my understanding."

"Let's keep it that way."

"You brought it up, I was just trying to find out what was behind it."

"Hell, you probably hate the Navy and everything about—"

"I don't hate the Navy."

"You ever serve?"

"No."

"Why not?"

"I decided to serve my country in a different way, by helping those accused of crimes, by participating in the judicial system."

Little tried not to choke. *Serve the country in a different way. What a crock.* "How sacrificial. Do you even *know* anyone who served in the military? Any of your friends? Acquaintances even?"

Stern thought, somewhat embarrassed. "Not really." He changed the subject. "When was the last time you saw our client?"

"This morning."

"How was he doing?"

"Not so good. He's trying to dodge the charge with the oldest trick in the book—'It ain't me, man.' You've heard it a million times."

"Maybe they do have the wrong guy. I don't automatically assume something my client tells me is wrong, just because someone else has said it before."

Little stopped. "Have you seen the picture of Duar that's been in every newspaper in the country every other day for the last six months?"

"Yes."

"Then when you see him, you tell me it isn't him."

"Okay. I'll take a look. But I believe my client until he gives me a reason not to. Don't you?"

"My client is usually the government."

"Right, so what's your answer?"

"Very funny."

Stern's shoulder hit one of the hatches and he slowed momentarily. "Seriously, do you always believe what you get from the government? You find what the FBI or the ATF says to always be true?"

"Not always. They make mistakes like anyone."

"I'm not talking about mistakes. I'm talking about lying. Are you saying you've never seen someone from the government lie to get some defendant convicted?"

"Not saying that."

"I didn't think so."

They turned down a passageway athwartships and descended a ladder. "Did you ask for this assignment?"

Little stopped. "Nope. I was sent out here to prosecute the mass murdering son of a bitch who is now our client. But he wouldn't accept Commander Watson as his defense attorney."

"Why not?"

"Because she's a woman."

"Oh."

"I can't wait to see what he does when he finds out you're Jewish. This ought to be rich."

"How do you know I'm Jewish?"

Little was surprised. "You're not?"

"I just wondered how you would know that?"

"I guess I assumed Stern is a Jewish name. Isn't it?"

"Could be German. But yes, it's Jewish. Did you check to find out? Why would it matter?"

"Doesn't make a bit of difference to me. But I'll bet our Arab mass murdering client cares. I guess we'll find out. Follow me."

Little made a sharp turn around a bulkhead and slid down the ladder to the brig.

♦　♦　♦

Rat was concerned he didn't have enough time before the helo left and they headed on to Georgia, but he had to see Andrea. He didn't like the way they had left it at the brig. It had been unfortunate that she had been there. Probably typical of Satterly though, send a woman to do your bidding for you. He looked at the frame number on the scrap of paper in his hand and at the bulkheads as he walked aft on the port side of the carrier. He passed a door that had a sticker on it— *"Médecins sans Frontières."* He knew enough French to know what it meant. *Doctors Without Borders. Probably Satterly's stateroom,* Rat thought. *Who else on a carrier would belong to that organization? And who else would advertise it by putting a sticker on his door? What a dick. Not content to be a member, he has to be an evangelist for his cause.* He looked at the frame number just around the corner, and there was Andrea's room.

He knocked loudly on the door.

"Who is it?" Andrea called from inside.

"Rat."

"Kent?"

"Yeah," he said, hoping no one was listening. No one in the entire Navy called him Kent except Andrea. He hated that name; it sounded like the name of a kid who might win a spelling bee.

The door opened and Andrea was standing before him in her uniform slacks, shoes, and a white bra. Her hair was dripping wet.

His eyebrows went up. "Nice of you to take off your shirt for me."

"I don't really want to talk to you," she said, with a look he had never seen before.

He frowned. "Why not?"

She started to close the door.

He stuck his foot in the way, keeping the door open a few inches. "What's going on?"

She opened it again and said loudly, "I've seen him, Kent. I've seen what you did! I saw the burn marks on his ears and his balls. How could you do that?"

"I didn't."

"Right. You took him off the ship and brought him back and have no idea how he might have gotten tortured in between. Give me a break." She went to slam the door closed but he pushed it first, throwing it open. He stepped into her room and closed it behind him.

"You know, Andrea, I'm willing to take my lumps if I did something wrong, but you of all people. You don't even give me a chance to explain? Did you get all this from Satterly? More of his Doctors sans Whatever? You don't even ask me?"

She went to the sink and picked up the hair dryer. She dried her hair vigorously for five minutes. Rat sat in her desk chair and waited. Finally she turned off the hair dryer and retrieved her blouse from the closet. She put it on hurriedly. "I just can't believe what you did to that man, Kent."

"I had nothing to do with it."

"*Nothing?*"

"Nothing."

"Then who did?"

"The Egyptians. I wasn't anywhere near it when it happened."

"You expect me to believe that?"

"Yeah, I do. I wouldn't lie to you. You know that. I've always told you there will be things I can't tell you, and you'll just have to deal with that. But I won't lie to you. Never have."

"I don't believe you."

Rat was stung. "Fine." He considered walking out.

"You think it's okay? You just torture someone if you feel like it?"

"No. It depends on the circumstances."

"On what?"

"On what you're trying to do. Why you're doing it."

"So sometimes it's okay?"

"Sometimes."

"The end justifies the means?"

"No, but it is relevant."

"Meaning what?"

"If you know some guy has a nuclear weapon set to go off in ten minutes, you wouldn't twist his arm to find out where the bomb was?"

She hesitated. "That would never happen."

"You sure? What if it did?"

"It wouldn't."

"You're just afraid of the conclusion."

"We never capture somebody who knows where a bomb is."

"What if we capture somebody who knows where the most wanted terrorist in the world is, the guy who has a nuclear bomb and is *going* to set it off? We can't apply some pressure to find out where that other guy is and stop him before he even plants the bomb? I've got no problem with that at all."

"So you would just torture him."

"In that case I would. I'd be all over his ass. But in a way to get the information, not to hurt him, or maim him. To get intelligence."

"That's real convenient."

He stood up to look into her eyes. "Otherwise what? I ask him, 'Where's the other guy?' and he tells me to eat shit, and I say, okay, sorry to ask you a question. What can I do? What are my choices? Yell at him? Threaten him? What?"

"I don't know."

Rat shook his head. "People just don't get what we're dealing with. No idea. These people are evil, Andrea. They would like nothing better than to *murder* you. Nothing. And if you had children, they'd like to murder them too. And me, well, we can't even go into what they'd want to do to me."

"But if we torture them, we're just like them."

"That's such bullshit! People say that all the time, but they don't really think about it. I don't say we should torture them for fun, or to punish, just to gain information. And nothing that's permanent, or just to inflict pain, or intimidate. That's why water is so good. Effective, and no long-lasting effects."

"Unless it *kills* him."

"Yeah, well, that doesn't happen much."

"But it can corrupt you, Kent. Make you calloused to where you don't care about people anymore."

"Who told you that? *Satterly*?"

"Well, wouldn't it? You're *good*, Kent. It would take away your goodness. You'd become hardened, and mean."

"No, Andrea, I'm not good. Neither are you. None of us is good, not one."

"What?"

"It's a quote."

"From who?"

"Paul."

"Paul who?"

"Paul in Romans."

She was shocked. "You're quoting the *Bible*? Are you *serious*?"

"Yeah, I'm serious. And I can quote Homer and Plato if you want. We aren't perfect, Andrea. Nobody is. But we have to get these guys. And we need to rethink how. If we play by the same old Geneva Convention rules in a war where they're not wearing uniforms, killing civilians as their *main target,* murdering whoever they want and hiding in the shadows, it's going to be a much longer road and a lot more people are going to get killed. We need to shorten it up a lot. This is one way."

"No, it's not. It's a steep, slippery slope and you won't be able to stop."

"I disagree. But don't think of me as some evil guy."

"I don't know, Kent. I don't want us to become like them."

"Then don't. Stay as you are. I sure plan to."

"You won't be able to."

He crossed to her and put his hands on her shoulders. She was cold and unyielding. She looked into his eyes angrily. "You holding this against me?"

"Today I am. I need to think about this."

"Even though I had nothing to do with it?"

"You were there!"

"No, I wasn't. You want to know what's really going on?"

"Yes."

"I take the guy there, then while we're with him, watching the Egyptians do a kid glove interrogation—he was scared shitless though, so it was sort of effective—then we leave, like we're supposed to. We go back to get Duar and he's all messed up and the Egyptians are done with him. We got our intel, but they used the wrong methods. And I was nearby. So the guy who supposedly tortured one of these guys is now responsible for both. That's how *somebody* in Washington wants it to look. And now they're sending me to Georgia."

She considered what he had said. "Who?"

"I don't know. But probably Stuntz. He thinks I'm the key to taking St. James out of the picture."

"What about the guy who died on this ship? Did you have anything to do with that?"

"That's how we captured Duar. Does that matter?"

"Yeah, it matters. And if you did that, it doesn't justify it just because you got Duar."

"Whatever," he said. He turned and walked out of her room, closing the door loudly behind him.

◆ ◆ ◆

William DeLong had long wondered what he had done wrong to get assigned as the CIA Station Chief in Liberia. His career had been going so well. But he had obviously pissed someone off and ended up in Liberia, where nothing happened and nothing was ever expected to happen. Monrovia had all the advantages of the usual third world city—bad food, unsanitary conditions, unpredictable electricity, and enough discouragement to make him consider extreme scenarios to get home. But DeLong had decided to endure, to be the good soldier, and somehow get his CIA career back on track.

He got along well enough with the ambassador, Maureen Lipscomb, who had been given the ambassadorship as a political plum for being the Rhode Island campaign chairman of President Kendrick's election campaign. She had absolutely no foreign policy experience, and no real interest in Liberia or Africa; she hoped to use her current position as a stepping-stone for a run for the governorship of her home state. DeLong thought it was a stupid strategy, but what did he know about politics?

He now had a mission, a charge from Washington to get to the bottom of the car bombing that had blown some poor old lady sky high in front of a bank.

He examined the photographs of the remains of the car. The Liberian police had done a good job photographing the scene, but they had rejected the American offer of help in the investigation. They said they could handle it, which DeLong knew to be completely untrue. They were in way over their heads, so the chances of finding whoever did it were small and fading. They had rejected help from the English and

French as well, trying, he guessed, to show the world how independent and competent they were.

"Ray," DeLong said to his field officer, Ray Winter, who passed as a member of the State Department, working with visas. "What do you make of it?" he asked.

"Assassination."

He agreed. "Why do you say that?"

"Placement. They intended to blow into her from the engine compartment. If they wanted the bank, they would have put the explosives in the trunk. And judging by the force involved, it was very high explosive. Either a lot of it, or very high-quality stuff. Since it was in the engine cavity, probably high quality. Not enough room for a lot of it. Which means someone had access to military grade explosives, and probably could have put in a lot more. He put in just enough to ensure the driver was killed—in a spectacular way—but not enough to actually take out the building. He was after the old lady."

"Why?"

"No idea. She wasn't political, not involved in anything anyone I have talked to knew anything about, and threatened no one."

"What about her family?"

"Lived alone. Only son works for a local shipping company."

DeLong thought about that. "One son?"

"Only child."

"Anything on him?"

"Haven't really looked yet."

"Any reason he'd whack her? Inheritance? Life insurance? Anything?"

"I doubt it. She was pretty poor, but I'll check into it. But could be that he's the target too. Someone wants something from him."

"That's what I was thinking too. Someone stands to gain from this."

"Doesn't have that random, anarchy sort of look, does it. Looks like a target."

"We aren't going to get much help, but we've got to tell Washington why this happened. Their antiterror antennae are up and alert. Anything they can't explain may be linked to something else they don't know about. Or something they do." He stuffed the photos back into the envelope and handed them to Ray. "This could be our ticket out of this shit-hole."

Ray nodded, took the envelope, and stood. "I'm going to convince the Monrovian police that they need the FBI even though they don't know it yet. It's really our only chance of finding out what the hell happened here."

Chapter 15

Rat's airplane flared late and landed hard on the cracked runway at Tbilisi, Georgia. Rat sighed. He hated flying in airlines from places like Georgia and the Ukraine. He didn't trust them. They didn't have the budget to keep their airplanes in the condition he had come to expect from American and European airlines. Every flight was an adventure. He felt more exposed and out of control than at almost any other time. Even in the middle of a mission he always felt as if he was in control. But every time he stepped onto an airliner he didn't trust, he envisioned some drunk pilot flying poorly maintained equipment with him in the back, unable to do anything about it. *All for the cause,* he thought. *What cause? Freedom? The eradication of evil from the face of the earth? The eradication of terrorism?* For today, just the cause of helping the Georgians rid themselves of the infection of terrorists who were setting up a Lebanese Bekáa Valley right in the middle of their country, a place where terrorists were welcome from all over the world to come and train, share information, share troops, share ideology, and go forth to commit murder and mayhem on the Western world.

The four Navy SEALs, on temporary assignment to the CIA's SAS, hustled down the steps to the tarmac at Tbilisi. Several men were waiting to escort them to one of the three waiting Russian-made MI-24 Hind helicopters. Rat immediately recognized one of them, Captain

Mick McSwain of the U.S. Army Green Berets. He had known Mc-
Swain for years and had the highest respect for him. "Mick!" he yelled
over the sound of the helicopter engines as he stepped onto the
ground. "What the hell are *you* doing here?"

McSwain smiled. "I could ask you the same thing! What's a squid
doing this far from an ocean? This is Army territory, boy."

They shook hands and smiled, each grateful to see an old friend, as
Rat scanned the airport and the waiting helicopters. He noticed numerous American Green Berets and Georgian Army men in the helicopters. A Georgian officer walked toward them slowly. McSwain
waited, then introduced him. "Rat, this is Colonel Zurab Beridze.
Colonel, Kent Rathman." Beridze extended his hand and pointed to a
helicopter. "You will be with me in this helicopter!" he yelled in heavily accented English.

Rat nodded and looked at Mick. "Have you established a camp?"

"Two days ago. This is the last group."

"Great. Let's go. Are we going directly to the camp?"

Beridze shook his head vigorously. "No. One stop first. We must
check a thing. A development."

Rat looked at McSwain. "What kind of development?"

McSwain replied as he watched the colonel struggling for the
words. "They found three Georgians murdered near the remains of
one of their small, remote power-generating stations."

"And?"

"They're very concerned. They want to find out what happened.
Who did it, and whether they were able to get into the generating station."

"How long ago did this happen?" Rat asked as they walked toward
the helicopters and the blades began to turn.

"Found them yesterday."

Rat stopped and frowned. "What am I missing?"

"The generators are *nuclear powered*. The cores can be removed.
They're radioactive and could be used to make a really nasty dirty
bomb."

Rat suddenly realized why Johnson's suspicions were correct, and
why they were so ominous. "They know who did it?"

"They think maybe one of your guys."

"My guys?"

"Your buddies from Sudan."

"Duar's men."

"Who else? Why did you think they wanted you?"

An airman pulled the helicopter door up behind him and directed him to one of the webbed seats of the old Russian beast. It was dirty and noisy. The combined smells of jet fuel, dirt, and stale men pervaded the air in the cramped belly of the ungainly ship. The blades increased in speed, changed pitch, and beat their way into the air, pulling the large helicopter off the ground.

Rat watched the occupants of the helicopter bounce in unison as they continued to climb and turn away from Tbilisi. McSwain's words began to haunt him. Nuclear cores that could be used to make a dirty bomb. But if Johnson was wrong and it wasn't Duar's people, then who? Chechens for an attack on Moscow? Georgians? Others? The reports he had received had placed Afghanis, Pakistanis, Sudanese, even Saudi terrorists in the Pankisi gorge. A worldwide assembly of evil. Any of them might want radioactive material. And other than the Chechens or Georgians, almost any of the others would have America as their target.

The helicopters flew across the lush countryside for two hours, vibrating the occupants to near numbness, then slowed as they approached the stop Colonel Beridze had promised. Rat glanced at him as he felt the helicopter slow, and Beridze nodded enthusiastically. He pointed down to the ground as the helicopter descended to a large clearing in the woods. The trees weren't a factor, but the clearing was far from level. The helicopters settled heavily into the knee-high grass as the pilots pushed the collective to the floor, taking all lift off the blades. They shut down the engines and all the men climbed out, grateful for the chance to stretch their legs. Several walked a few steps away and began urinating with groans of relief.

Beridze gathered Rat and McSwain. "Come. To the truck, there." He walked westward to where several men stood near a truck at the tree line. The men had dug up the shallow graves of Nino and his men.

Rat glanced at the three dead men. "How did you find these guys?"

Beridze looked at the dead men, then pointed. "Local farmer. He was afraid we would blame him. One of the men was shot from the front, the other two shot from behind by automatic weapons. Looks like an ambush by friends. We found no blood from any other men." He turned to the man next to him and spoke in Georgian. He returned his attention to Rat. "Yes. No evidence of other men being shot. Just the three. Perhaps they had argument—but kill three at once? Three Georgians? Probably armed? That is not so easy."

Groomer bent down to examine the bodies. His first tour of duty in the Navy had been as a corpsman. He denied it when asked because he didn't want to get pigeonholed. He had served as a corpsman with the Marine Corps, then decided he wanted to be a SEAL. He had tried to eradicate any reference to medical skill in his record; he wanted to carry weapons and hurt people that were out to get the United States, not carry water for others who did the fighting. But he remembered enough of his medical training for it to be helpful sometimes.

He pulled latex gloves out of a pocket and put them on his large hands like someone who had done it hundreds of times. Beridze watched in amazement as Groomer went to the large man with a beard who was lying on his back with two bullet holes in his chest and lifted his arm to check for rigor mortis. The arm was limp and fell softly back to the ground when he let it go. Groomer checked his eyes, his hair, his fingernails. He pulled several maggots off Nino's face around his eyes and examined them carefully as small red ants from Nino crawled on Groomer's gloved hands. He looked at the maggots' stage of development and the number on Nino. He pulled out a magnifying glass and looked at Nino's face to see how much damage had been done by the fly larvae. He put the glass back, stood up, and removed his gloves. He tossed the gloves on Nino's chest.

"What do you think?" Rat asked.

"Hard to say for sure, but I'd say about three days."

"Shit," Rat said, looking at the truck nearby, its tracks, then for evidence of other vehicles. "How did they get here?" He looked at Beridze. "How far is the Black Sea from here?"

Beridze looked off toward the south. "Maybe two hundred kilometers."

Rat was interested in the three Georgians, but he was more interested in the power-generating station. "Where is the power station?"

"It is over there. But the core is gone." The colonel began walking toward the small structure. They walked through the grass and bristly weeds for two hundred yards until they came to the RTG. It was obviously inoperative. The decaying steel device was cold to the touch. There was rust on the corners and around the access doors. The concrete slab on which it rested was cracked; the generator leaned downhill.

Rat felt the edges with his fingers and examined the access door that had been left open. Beridze crouched next to him and inspected it with him. Rat looked at him, only inches away. "Whoever opened this knew what he was doing. He didn't use force. It takes a special tool." Groomer walked up behind them and bent over to look.

Beridze agreed. "We think they used the Georgians for finding them. Maybe to show them how to open. Then they were killed."

"Who carries a tool like that around?" Groomer asked.

Rat nodded. "Someone who was thinking ahead. Stole the tool when he was working on one of these."

Beridze agreed. "Many Georgians didn't like the Russians. Easy to think of ways to hurt them. Maybe come back later and disable all these. You get more work and make them angry."

"Could be," Rat said. "Any other RTGs missing their cores?"

They stood. "Three others that we have found opened. We look for others but Russia has very bad records. They can't tell us where, so we look. There are many more, but we don't know."

"Any idea of how many of these generators are in Georgia?"

"We are not sure. We think maybe thirty."

Rat couldn't believe it. Thirty nuclear generators, and they didn't know where they were. "Do you know how many in other countries?"

Beridze shook his head. "No, but we have heard. We heard over one hundred fifty. But we don't know. Ask your good Russian friends." He stood. "I wanted to see if this one was like the others. It is just like. But now they have killed their guides. They must have gotten what they wanted. Now they will use the nuclear cores."

Rat agreed. "Without a doubt."

"We don't know anything about who. We believe it is related to those in our country who don't belong here. The ones you have come to help us with, hiding in the Pankisi gorge."

"How many men in the Pankisi gorge that don't belong there?" Rat asked.

"A growing number, probably over one thousand."

"And you think some of them are from Sudan," Rat said.

"Some people tell us things. Since Duar was captured, we have heard of new men from Sudan. That is why we asked for you."

Rat sighed. "Colonel, you need to check all the other RTGs you can find. Right now. We need to know how big a problem we're dealing with."

"Of course."

"We need to find the ones that have been taken already." Rat looked around. "But how did they get here? There aren't any tracks."

One of the men who had arrived in the truck saw them looking. He knew what they were looking for. He pointed to an area inside the tree line. Rat frowned skeptically. No truck could get through those trees without leaving broken branches behind them and deep scars in the soft grass. There was none of that. The man continued to point.

Rat was puzzled by the man's insistence. He didn't see any vehicle tracks at all—then he saw a muddy section of ground torn up twenty feet from him. He and Groomer walked to it and kneeled down. "Take a look at this," Rat said. "Animals. These guys were traveling on horses." He stood up and yelled, "Banger!"

"Who's he?" McSwain asked.

"One of my guys. Very talented. Kind of a loner. Grew up on a ranch in Texas. Maybe he can make some sense of this."

Banger came running, glad to be able to contribute for the first time since they crossed into Georgian airspace. "Yes, sir," he said.

"What do you make of this?" Rat asked.

Banger looked at the tracks, walked away from the mess beside them, and looked for outgoing marks in the mud. He found them quickly, walked another fifty yards following them, then stopped to examine them closely. He matched them in sets by weight, pattern, and number, and began nodding.

"What you got?" Rat asked.

"Six horses," Banger said. "No doubt. And three donkeys."

Rat was surprised. "Donkeys?"

"Yep. Probably to carry the load. But if they came from the Pankisi gorge area—that would be a long way from here." He stood and wiped his hands on his pants. "I don't think they rode horses all the way here."

"Not a chance," Rat agreed. "Maybe they just had horses to get to this one because they didn't have an all-wheel truck to get through this wet ground."

"Want me to follow these tracks? See where they go?"

"Let's get Beridze to do that. They're not going to be at the end of that trail, I guarantee you. Too easy. We need to get to the Pankisi gorge and find them."

"Then we'd better cowboy up," Banger said enthusiastically.

McSwain had been watching Beridze. "We need to get going."

"Horses," Rat said, pointing. "Horses. You've got to be kidding me."

"So much for being high tech. Look, we got to go. We're going to lose the sun."

"Let's go," Rat said. They turned back to the helicopters. McSwain signaled to Beridze, who told the helicopters to get ready to go. The American and Georgian soldiers put out their cigarettes and hurried back into the helicopters as the pilots cranked the deafening jet engines.

McSwain yelled at Rat as they approached the helos, "Sure glad you're here. This is going to be real interesting. Too bad the Green Berets couldn't do it without you."

"Hey," Rat said. "Send me home. *Hurt* me."

"Just in time for your trial?"

Rat's look lost its humor as he recalled the coming trial. "Actually yeah. That's exactly where I should be, getting ready to be crucified. Lots to prepare for." He glanced at McSwain. "What have you heard?"

"Sounds like you rang some guy up in Sudan. They say you used a technique developed by the famous Green Berets in Vietnam. Of course the Green Berets would never hurt anyone, let alone *torture* anyone in the field. That would be wrong. So if asked I would have to deny any knowledge of any such technique." McSwain stopped so they stayed far enough away from the helos to still converse in a loud voice. "Basically the word is that you're somebody's scapegoat for something that none of us can understand. Word is you're about to get knifed in the back."

That was exactly how Rat felt, and helpless to do much about it. "Trial's supposed to start pretty soon. They're actually going to put me on trial. 'Course they offered to just let me go to jail for five years to avoid the trial. Believe that?"

"What if you're not there?" McSwain asked, wondering how Rat could get out of this political trial.

"I'm only out on bail. I promised to be there for the trial. If I don't show, then I'll be in real trouble."

"You'll beat it," McSwain argued. "Truth will win out."

Rat smiled ironically. "That's what I'm afraid of."

◆　◆　◆

Andrea stared at the photographs of Duar. The close-up photographs of the ear lobes were horrifying, but nothing compared to the photographs of his testicles. She had certainly seen enough of them giving flight physicals to an almost exclusively male population for years and taking care of the all-male Blue Angels as their flight surgeon. But until she examined Duar after his return from Egypt she had never seen testicles that had been electrocuted; she had never seen a scrotum with holes in the skin due to arcing electricity between the skin and the testicle inside. It made her stomach turn.

Since she had seen Rat, since he had stormed out of her stateroom in frustration, she had felt bad. She hadn't handled it well. She had been mad at herself, not the least because she didn't want to lose him. He was the first man who intrigued her, who captured her imagination. He was smart yet physical. Not a bookworm, but not just some muscled creep. There was something mysterious, even dangerous, about him.

But now, after seeing the photographs, all she could think of was Rat being responsible. She had begun to wonder if she had been attracted to the part of him that might be a character defect. It scared her. She had no idea Rat had that much cruelty inside. Was it more cruel though than being willing to shoot somebody or kill someone with a knife?

She thought back to when she had met him when she was the Blue Angels' flight surgeon. Rat had been hanging around with Ed Stovic, one of the new pilots in the Blues. She later learned that Rat was there to protect Stovic from an Algerian who was trying to kill him. Rat had told her what he was doing, and while they were in El Centro, California, the Blue Angels winter training base, he had asked her out. Their first date had been to a deserted hill in the desert where they had gone to shoot cans one night, an idea she had suggested half in jest. He had jumped at the chance, enthusiastic about a woman who wanted to shoot guns. She had gone and pretended to want to be there, at least for a time. Rat had pulled out the biggest gun she had ever seen, a .50 caliber Barrett sniper rifle. It looked like a ten-foot-long cannon. She had been horrified. He had been enthusiastic, then embarrassed. He realized he had miscalculated. She had learned something that was slightly unpleasant, or off-putting, about Rat, but had concluded it was part of his job, part of what he was expected to know how to do. Navy SEALs weren't like intelligence officers who made their living behind computer screens and in briefing rooms. SEALs knew weapons and how to kill. She had ignored that as she got to know him better, probably because she never saw the details of his job.

But torture? Was that part of his job description too? Was that something all Special Forces members knew how to do? Was that one of their dirty little secrets? What kind of a man was it that could cause this kind of misery in another human being without being affected himself?

She put the pictures down and picked up Satterly's report of Duar's medical examination after his return from Egypt. A yellow sticky on the top of it said, "Read this. I want to make sure you agree. I want you to look at it *completely* objectively. Let me know if I've overstated anything."

She read it carefully. Toward the end of the report he had strayed from a strictly medical report. He noted that the *cause* of the injury to Duar was torture at the hand of one Lieutenant Kent Rathman, a Spe-

cial Forces operative who was currently on trial —or would be soon—
for torturing another prisoner. She pressed her lips together and
looked up. She dialed Satterly's number from memory. He answered.
"You're really out to get him, aren't you?" she said.

"Who?" he asked, feigning confusion.

"Lieutenant Rathman. I'm reading your report."

"He's dangerous. He is a maniac. He has no respect for human life."

"How do you know he did this to Duar?"

"It's his signature. Whenever he shows up with a prisoner, they get
tortured."

"The last guy told you it was him, didn't he?"

"Yes. Mazmin. He told me all about it."

"Well have you asked Duar who did this to him?"

Satterly nodded. "Yes."

"What did he say?"

"He sat there like a stone. He's afraid to say anything, because if he
tells, that person will come back and hurt him more. That's what I
think."

"So he didn't say?"

"Why would he be afraid? Who could get to him on this ship? *Think*
about it. Not an Egyptian, if they actually took him anywhere. Only
someone in the Navy or from the States could get to him here. He's
afraid of Rathman."

Andrea hung up and closed her eyes.

♦   ♦   ♦

The judge looked out of place sitting behind the large bench that was
made for the eleven judges of the Foreign Intelligence Surveillance
Act Court even though he had had ten of the chairs removed. The
large wooden bench behind which he sat was still so large that it
dwarfed his presence and made the entire room feel out of balance.
All those in the courtroom had entered through the metal cipher
locked doors. Specially cleared U.S. marshals were posted at each entrance, in the well between the judge and the attorneys, and by the
witness stand, even though there would be no witnesses at the hearing today.

Skyles was in his element. He had annoyed the U.S. Attorney enough to know that his tactics were working. He made it a point to go by Wolff's office at least once a day with some request or other, most of which could be responded to easily with the production of one document, or agreeing to one date. He rarely called Wolff. He loved to stop by instead, to disrupt him in person, to force him to look into Skyles's eyes and see his careless attitude and antigovernment mindset. Yesterday he had stopped by to see Wolff just to tell him that he had been thinking about the hearing scheduled for the next week, and he had brought something Wolff would surely appreciate, a stipulation and order that granted Skyles's motion to dismiss the charges against Rathman. He said Wolff wouldn't want to embarrass himself by arguing against a motion that was so sure to be granted, so perhaps he would like to just stipulate to the judge entering the order. He had handed the document to him with a pen.

That had finally gotten to Wolff. He lost his cool and even called Skyles a "dick" —strong words from the icy Mr. Wolff.

As the judge sat and the clerk stood to call the calendar, Skyles waved at Wolff, who completely ignored him.

The clerk said, "Number one on calendar, *United States* vs. *Kent Rathman*. Please state your appearances."

"John Wolff, Assistant United States Attorney, for the United States."

"Thomas Skyles, for the wrongfully accused defendant, Kent Rathman."

The judge removed his glasses and sighed heavily. He wasn't about to allow little games to start in this case. "Please refrain from editorializing in minor things like stating your appearance Mr. Skyles. If you can't control yourself, I'll control you. Believe me."

Skyles looked at the floor in mock humility. "I'm sorry, Your Honor. I couldn't resist. When justice is a mere memory and a hero is charged with an inappropriate crime—"

"We're here to set the date for trial, Mr. Skyles. If you continue to take shots at the prosecution or me, or whoever you're shooting at, I will hold you in contempt in a heartbeat. Do I make myself clear?"

"Yes, Your Honor. I am sorry."

"Your client has not waived his right to a speedy trial. We therefore must proceed with all due speed. Unless, of course, he is prepared to waive his right to a speedy trial now," Judge Wiggins said.

"No, sir. He figures since the government doesn't have a case now, why give them time to make one up?"

Wiggins almost came out of his chair. "If you think you're going to win this little word game you've decided to start playing, you're wrong."

Skyles loved it. "Lieutenant Rathman is not prepared to waive his right to a speedy trial. Let's get this trial under way."

"Counsel?" the judge asked, looking at Wolff.

The Assistant U.S. Attorney shrugged. "I can't force them to waive their rights, but we do have some witness issues. We're trying to get people here from around the world, Your Honor. It isn't easy—"

"That's ridiculous—" Skyles interrupted.

"No commentary," the judge declared.

"Yes, sir. Sorry, Your Honor. I just have a hard time listening to the government's sanctimonious commentary about how difficult their case is, when every witness they've listed—with two exceptions—is employed by the government, and can be flown here at taxpayer cost on very little notice. It just doesn't cause me to be real sympathetic. If they have proof problems, they should have figured that out before they issued the indictment."

"In any case," the judge went on, "Mr. Wolff, can you be ready next week?"

Wolff almost choked. Skyles saw it.

Wolff answered, "Yes, Your Honor."

"Mr. Skyles?"

"We're ready now, Your Honor. I just need to get my client back to D.C., and we'll be ready."

"Where is he now?"

"I'm not at liberty to disclose that."

The judge looked insulted. "Where is he?"

Skyles hesitated, looked around the secure courtroom and saw there were no visitors, and said, "Georgia."

The judge frowned. "That's not that far. He should be able to be here by next week, don't you think?"

Skyles nodded, enjoying the judge's misunderstanding. "Yes, sir. No problem."

The judge looked at his clerk. "Trial to commence next Friday."

Chapter 16

The three lawyers stood in front of the judge aboard the *Belleau Wood*. His face showed the fatigue he felt from having just arrived on a helicopter that morning. On the left side of the makeshift courtroom—a courtroom fashioned out of the admiral's wardroom—stood David Stern and Commander Barry Little, their relationship having now deteriorated to outright distrust. At the other counsel table stood the prosecutor, Commander Elizabeth Watson, the scarecrow who couldn't seem to keep her hands still.

Stern felt out of place between two military attorneys in their white uniforms. He was painfully aware that it was a club, and although he had been given a visitor's pass, he wasn't a member.

Stern appraised the judge, Captain Gerald Graham. Graham was a big man, burly and freckled. His thick hair was a dark brown with a reddish tint. His hairy forearms protruded from his immaculate uniform. He looked more like a wrestler than a military judge. His reputation as a judge had preceded him though, and it wasn't that far removed from that of a wrestler. He had been a judge at the Norfolk Naval Base, and his nickname among the attorneys who practiced in front of him—both JAG lawyers and civilian lawyers—was Granite. He was unmovable. When he decided something, no additional argument or evidence would change his mind. He was also not swayed by lawyerly pleas, complaints, or whining. No one considered him unfair, simply unbending, unmovable, and humorless.

Judge Graham addressed the attorneys. "We're going to conduct this like a regular, ordinary trial. We're operating under a different set of rules as you know. You will also behave in accordance with the rules of evidence and rules of professional conduct. Is that clear?"

"Yes, Your Honor," all three lawyers responded simultaneously.

Stern noticed that Graham's withering gaze was directed mostly at him. He had probably done some research on who the attorneys were. He wasn't afraid or intimidated. He just didn't want Graham to hold anything against his client. Duar had enough problems in this trial without the judge holding Stern's presence against him.

"We have been instructed to get this trial under way as soon as possible. I have been sent out here to do that. I want to start the trial on Monday. Anyone have any objection to that?"

Stern couldn't believe his ears. He felt like he was being set up. He rose and spoke. "Yes, Your Honor. I have to object. I just arrived. I haven't even had time to meet my client yet. For whatever reason my access has been denied. I also have very serious concerns about how he has been treated since he was on the ship. There was apparently a night in which he was secreted—"

Judge Graham put up his hand. "I don't want to hear anything about that. I asked whether anyone had any objection to us beginning on Monday. You have now said that you do have an objection. Right?"

"Yes, Your Honor."

"What is your name again?"

"David Stern."

"Mr. Stern, as I understand it, you are cocounsel in this case representing Mr. Duar in the charges that have been brought against him. Am I correct?"

"Yes, sir."

"Then that means that your client has been represented by counsel for a time much longer than the short time you have been aboard this ship. Is that correct?"

"Yes, sir. Commander Little—"

"Has been representing your client since his arrival on this ship, correct?"

"Yes, sir."

"Then the fact that another attorney representing Mr. Duar has not had unfettered access to his client for some unspecified time is not a sufficient reason to continue the trial which I want to start on Monday. Do you have any other objections?"

"No, sir. Just some time to prepare."

"I suggest you start preparing. We're going to start this trial on Monday. Commander Watson, will you be ready for the prosecution?"

"Yes, Your Honor. We're ready to go."

Judge Graham sat back and removed his reading glasses. "Has everyone read the rules on the conduct of a tribunal?"

"Yes, Your Honor."

"Good. I'm going to hold you to them. I'll see you on Monday. All motions will be heard Friday at 0800. Anything else we need to deal with before Friday?"

Stern spoke, "Yes, sir. There is a very large matter which needs to be dealt with as soon as possible. It is a matter of the utmost importance and urgency. Frankly, it shows the extent to which the government is willing to go to obtain a conviction of my client in the absence of evidence."

"And what might that be?"

"I have been informed by the prosecutor that the government is intending to offer into evidence a supposed confession that was extracted from my client."

Graham spoke loudly in his booming voice. "And, let me guess," he said, pointing with his glasses, "it is *your* position that the confession was extracted by means that violated your client's due process rights. Am I right?"

Stern didn't like Graham's sarcasm. "Only if you believe that having holes burned in your scrotum might be a violation of due process."

Graham was shocked. "Are you making a claim that your client was tortured and forced to sign a confession?"

"Exactly." Stern let that idea hover in the room for a moment. He knew that everyone there was picturing a scrotum with holes in it, wondering what that would look like, and how exactly that was accomplished—horrified yet fascinated at the same time. "My client was taken off this ship under the control of the American military—or an intelligence agency, I'm not sure which—and returned in a tortured state with burn marks on his ears and scrotum. I have been given a confession by Commander Watson and told she intended to use it in this case. It is obvious—"

"You want to bring a motion to exclude the confession, I take it."

"Yes, sir."

Graham nodded. "That will be our first motion on Friday morning. Anything else?"

"Nothing, sir."

"See you Friday."

♦ ♦ ♦

The American C-130 Hercules touched down on the enormous concrete runway at the airfield the Soviets had abandoned and that the Georgians had let fall into disrepair. The plane taxied to where two men waited and signaled with flashlights. One of the men placed large wooden chocks behind the wheels, and the pilot shut down the engines.

The side door opened and a single passenger stepped out carefully in the darkness. He was carrying two heavy bags. He looked for whoever he was supposed to report to, but only expected to recognize him by a uniform. He saw Rat standing next to Colonel Beridze, McSwain, and two other Green Berets. He began walking toward them.

Rat extended his hand to the man who set down his two heavy cases. "You must be Mark James. I'm Kent Rathman."

"You're the one who requested me."

"Yes. This is Mick McSwain, with the Green Berets, and this is Colonel Beridze of the Georgian Army. Is that your detection gear?"

"Pleased to meet you," James answered. Then to Rat, "Yeah."

"Who do you work for?" Beridze asked.

"For the United States," James answered.

"This way," Rat pointed, heading toward the waiting trucks. "Thanks for coming to Georgia. Sorry to drag you here on such short notice. Your gear make it through intact?"

"Sure, no problem. And I've been here before. Several times."

Rat looked at him with surprise. "Why?"

James looked over his shoulder to see that Beridze couldn't hear. "Ever heard of Gamma Kolos?"

Rat shook his head.

"Our good Russian friends had a great idea. They thought maybe plants—crops—would grow better if they were radioactive. So they buried cesium 137 in the ground on a bunch of farms trying to irradiate the plants and see if they'd grow. They sort of forgot about the cesium they left in the ground, and when the Soviet Union collapsed, they left about a thousand of these cesium canisters all over the damned place. They don't even know where they are, but a bunch of them were in Georgia. We helped them look for them."

"Are you serious? Find any?"

"I'm very serious, and yeah, we found a lot of them. But I'm sure there are a lot of them still out there, waiting for some farm kid to plow them up, open the canister, and die."

"Isn't cesium the very same stuff that's in some of these RTGs we're looking for?"

"The very same. Really bad shit. Gamma emitter. Can kill you very dead. Half-life of about thirty years. And in the Gamma Kolos program that this Russian brain surgeon came up with, it's in the form of pellets or even a fine powder, like talcum. Blow that shit up and it will float all over the place taking radiation, death, and contamination with it. Hell, you don't really have to even do that. Just open the can and people start dying."

They reached the truck.

"Did you read the reports?" Rat asked.

"Yeah," James said.

Rat waited. "So what do you think?"

James shook his head in disgust. The truck's headlights illuminated his frowning face. "Pretty damned predictable. Russians made about five hundred of these remote generators. Have to assume someone will get ahold of one of them when you leave them in the middle of goddamned nowhere. The cesium cores are the worst. The others use radioactive strontium."

"Strontium?" Rat asked.

"It's a beta-emitter with a half-life of twenty-eight point five years."

James carefully placed his heavy bags in the backseat of one of the trucks.

"Could they use strontium for a dirty bomb?" Rat asked.

"It's not as bad as cesium, but it would still be a really nasty, ugly, dirty bomb. Not that it would kill all that many people, but imagine a city that is radioactive. Imagine Manhattan deserted for years. Not one or two years, ten or twenty. A ghost town." He looked up. "How many of the cores did they get?"

"We think at least ten."

"Any idea where they are?"

"We think they're in the Pankisi gorge."

"What's the plan?"

"We're going into the gorge tomorrow. We've got to find the cores before they do something with them. The colonel here," Rat said indicating Beridze, "says there are a few places where you expect people holding these things to hide. We're going to check them out. What's the range on your gear?"

"Depends on how much radiation there is and how well shielded it is. Generally, it's very sensitive."

"What about just flying a helicopter down the gorge? Could that do it?"

"If they're well shielded, we'll need to be within a few feet."

Rat was disappointed. "This may be a waste of time."

"Depends on what your expectations are. You just want to find out whether somebody has these cores, right?"

"And where they are. We need to get to them. And I'm beginning to suspect who it is, which makes the need to find them all that much greater."

"Who?"

They climbed into the trucks. "Duar's people."

James was shocked. "I thought we captured him."

"We did. But we didn't shut down his organization. Can you tell us whether these radioactive cores are in the gorge?"

"I can probably find out if they're there, but if it's a negative report—if we find no signs of them—we still can't say with that much certainty that they're not there. How big is this gorge?"

"It's about twenty miles across and fifty miles long."

"And it's full of revolutionaries, terrorists, and rebels?"

"Not so many, but enough to make it difficult. That's why we're training the Georgian Army. But the worst of it is they're hiding among the general population and refugees. It's hard to pick them out."

"So maybe we should do a flyby in the helicopter tonight—see if we get any readings. If not, we'll have to go in on the ground," James said as he climbed into the truck and leaned his head back on the back of the seat. The exhaustion from the long trip was catching up with him.

◆　◆　◆

The three FBI forensic experts sat in DeLong's office with their roll-on luggage and equipment stacked behind them. The leader of the team, Peter Symmes, spoke. "So what exactly is our role here?" He had that federal look about him, dark blue pants, cheap polo shirt, and government-issue haircut.

DeLong was quite proud of himself that he had convinced the police chief of Monrovia to allow the FBI to assist in the investigation. What he didn't know was whether it was too late. "To assist the Liberian police in the investigation."

"What does that mean exactly? Do we have control of the scene?"

"No, you don't. But the police—"

"Has the car been moved?"

"No. It's in exactly the same place it was when it landed. It has rained several times though."

Symmes grimaced. "That's always helpful." Symmes thought about the investigation for a moment. The one thing he didn't want was to be involved in an investigation that was going to be a failure. He was positive that if he was given a free hand and control of the evidence he would find out what had happened. But in his experience, when he went to a third world stink hole, and all the people who thought they were smart were walking around booting evidence out of sight, the likelihood of a successful investigation fell off the table. Either he was in charge, or he was gone. "What do you want out of this?"

"Who did this, how they did it, and why. We'll be working with you. We have people running down the victim's family, friends, other possible motives. But we need your help on the bomb. One of the . . . people on my staff said he thought it was C4."

"On what basis did he make that statement?"

"He examined the photographs."

Symmes tried not to show his contempt for such opinions. There was nothing he liked better than an amateur telling him the exact type of explosive used in a car bomb from a photograph. Even *he* couldn't do that.

"Maybe *you* can tell us," DeLong said, reading Symmes's silence. "Tell us what it was, where it came from, whatever. Look, we need some help here. We may be on to something. They don't have much terrorism here. If that's what it was—but it probably wasn't some loan shark angry at a debtor, or someone who hates banks that blew up someone to make a point. It may be that some bad people are here and we need to know what they're doing and why. And at the end of the day, it's always about us."

Symmes nodded.

"I've arranged for a vehicle to take you guys over to the scene. Remember, no jackets, hats, or anything else that say FBI."

Symmes shook his head. "So the geniuses can take credit for our work."

"I don't really care who gets credit. What I care about is finding out who did this."

"I care about both. Because we want them to call us first the next time, and they're more likely to do that when they know that we can help them, and that we will."

"True enough, but you saw the same messages I did. Washington wants this done quietly. We don't want whoever is behind this to know we're even sniffing around."

"Don't you think it may be sort of obvious? I mean I'm not exactly five foot six and black like most of the men around here."

"Nothing we can do about that."

Symmes stood up. "I'll be in touch."

◆　◆　◆

Colonel Zurab Beridze placed the detailed topographical map of the Pankisi gorge on the hood of the Russian-made diesel truck. It had six wheels, two rows of seats in the front—enough for six men—and a large bed with benches in it capable of carrying ten more men in the back. The truck, like the other behind it, was old and worn with visible rust on the sides. The taut canvas top over the bed was equally tired and had innumerable small holes, as if it had been splattered with acid. Beridze motioned for Rat, McSwain, and a Georgian Army captain to look at the map with him. "This is Captain Eldar Kolbaia," he said, gesturing to a soldier. "He will be in charge of this mission." Rat nodded at him and the man returned his nod. He was tall and in good shape. Very confident.

Beridze put his hand on the map. "Here it is," he said in his heavily accented English, pointing to the dirt road that ran around a small mountain and entered the Pankisi gorge. "The only way in from here."

Rat looked at the map then at the colonel. "How often do you have someone drive through the gorge?"

Beridze thought for a moment as he rubbed his face. "Perhaps once a month."

"Any problems?"

"Yes, of course."

"What kind?"

"People shoot at us from the hills; usually a long way off. Not very accurate. Also sometimes groups of people in the camps cross the road at the same time to block the road. Others approach to see who's inside, probably trying to decide whether to kill us. Or kidnap us," Beridze said with complete seriousness. "It is very, how do you say, um, tense? Difficult?"

The colonel continued. "So you go into the gorge . . . here. Based on the infrared images from the helicopter last night, most people are here, here, and here," he said, pointing with his thick finger. "The road is very rough. To get to the last place, and to get out from there you have to climb up a steep hill. Then back here. It is about eight hours." He looked at his captain. "You have a radio. Call if you need any help, and call from each enclave to report entering and leaving."

"You're not coming with us?" Rat asked, surprised.

Beridze shook his head vigorously. "I would not contribute. And a colonel is a much more interesting person to kidnap than a captain."

"What about kidnapping Americans?"

"Yes. It is a risk. That is why we gave you Georgian uniforms. Don't speak where anyone can hear you. Does your man have to get out of the vehicle for his machine to work?"

"No."

"Good. Stay in, stay out of sight."

The colonel said to the captain, "You had better get going. I don't want you to be left trying to get out of the gorge at night."

Rat nodded as he rested his hand on his MP5N, his favorite weapon. He felt for the extra clips in his belt, his grenades, and his .45 caliber handgun, a Para-Ordnance 14.45 LDA. He had even brought his night-vision goggles for good measure. He had heard the colonel's speech before; he knew after dark the gorge would grow much more dangerous. But he liked to believe that he did too.

The reluctant Georgian soldiers split up and climbed into the trucks. Rat climbed into the middle seat in the front of the first truck, next to the captain and to the right of the Georgian driver. Mark James sat right behind Rat.

Rat glanced at the driver, who seemed extraordinarily young, thin, and small. He did everything tentatively, as if doing it for the first time even if he had just done it thirty seconds before.

The trucks started their noisy engines and rolled away from the colonel. They rumbled up the dirt road to the entrance to the gorge thirty kilometers away.

They drove without incident and started up the hill on the rutted dirt road that would take them down into the gorge. The truck climbed easily but slowly as it rocked back and forth in the ruts. Rat thought of how easy it would be for a sniper to hit the truck if so inclined. A good sniper could take out the engine with one shot from fifteen hundred yards away. The young driver seemed competent, but Rat had no confidence in his instincts if they came under fire. Rat studied the controls to ensure he could drive the truck if it came to that.

Rat had begun to doubt the need for this high-risk foray into the Pankisi gorge, one of the most dangerous places on earth. But he had to find the radioactive cores. It was really just a hunch that they were in the gorge. If the cores weren't there it would mean they had yet another day's head start to wherever they were headed.

The two trucks protested and creaked as they made their way over the mountain, finally cresting the top and heading down the steep narrowing road dense with trees and foliage on both sides. The road worsened as the descent grew steeper. The driver forced the manual transmission into its lowest gear, grinding the teeth of the gearing to slow their nearly vertical descent. As they approached the bottom of the hill the road improved and flattened into the valley. The road opened up on both sides and everyone in both trucks visibly relaxed.

Groomer, Robby, and Mark James were in the backseat behind Rat. McSwain sat in the middle of the front seat of the second truck, with a Georgian sergeant to his right and Banger behind him. Captain Kolbaia studied the map as they bounced along the now predictable dirt road and spoke to the driver in Georgian. They rounded a sharp curve, straightened out for a mile, and saw smoke from the settlement. The captain picked up the radio and transmitted to Beridze that they were approaching the first enclave.

Rat watched the trees on either side of them. He began to smell the distinctive scent of rotten food and burnt flesh, probably a goat being cooked over a campfire, or perhaps dog, something Rat hadn't smelled in quite a while. He thought he saw several men in the woods with rifles pointed at them. His fingers curled around the trigger of his MP5N as they came around a bend and entered the settlement. He noticed the sad, thrown-together housing, mostly lean-tos and tents with an occasional tin shack. Open fires smoldered all around surrounded by general squalor and filth.

Their young driver slowed the truck as they approached numerous pedestrians who regarded them with suspicion and contempt. What Rat saw mostly was unhappiness. The men were surly and well armed. They looked Georgian, or Chechen for the most part, not that he could tell the difference. Rat looked in every direction for signs of Middle Eastern men, or Sudanese. He watched the people crossing the road and saw no one other than what appeared to be Chechen refugees.

The driver slowed as more people crossed the road and were joined by more still. "Here we go," the captain said with disgust. "It is just to make us stop."

The driver stopped as the road was completely blocked. Several large men with Russian assault rifles stood in front of the truck, while others moved around the truck. One came to the side where the captain was sitting and spoke to him in Georgian. "What are *you* doing here?" he asked with anger and an implied threat.

"Someone has found the core of a generator. They have taken it away. But it is still full of electricity. If someone opens it, or cracks it, or even drops it in the wrong way, it will electrocute them and anyone else within a fifty-meter radius. We have come to warn them, and get the device back."

Rat couldn't understand a word, and knew better than to ask in English what was being said.

"That *is* bad," the man replied, concerned. "What does this thing look like?"

"It is silver, about this long, and round. It is fairly heavy, maybe ten kilos."

"We have seen nothing like that. If we had, I would know about it. So you may go back."

"No, we must warn all the villages. We must tell everyone."

"Is that why you flew over our homes last night with your helicopters? Waking our children and trying to intimidate us?"

"I know nothing of this. What time did this occur? It might have been yet another incursion into our airspace by the Russians," the captain replied, hitting the Chechen hot button. These rebel Chechens owed Georgia a debt of gratitude. They could avoid the endless war in Chechnya by hiding—staging, as the Russians asserted—in Georgia, and but for the sovereignty of Georgia, would certainly be pursued into the Pankisi gorge by the Russian Army. The Russians accused the Georgians of protecting the Chechens, of being effectively coconspirators with them. It was the only thing that kept the Chechens, and whoever else was in the gorge, from attacking the Georgians outright and trying to establish complete control over the gorge.

But lately, there had grown a new assertiveness among some in the gorge. They had begun exploring the idea of staying in the gorge permanently, free from the Russian Army, free from the outside world; able to do whatever they wanted. There had been some sniper attacks, denial of access, but thus far, no direct confrontation.

"You find out and tell me. Yes?" the large man said.

"Yes."

"But tell me this," the Chechen man insisted. "Why do you think this missing electrical canister would be here?"

The captain tried to think quickly. He hadn't anticipated the question. "Because we know you don't have electricity. Maybe someone who knows a lot about generators knew what it was, and wanted to try to use it to set up an electrical generator here."

"That's a good idea," the man said, nodding. "Maybe if we find this thing, that's what we'll do instead of telling you about it."

"I wouldn't recommend it. You may have someone who thinks he's smart enough to do that, but I promise you, he isn't. It will kill him and several others. And then who will the people hold responsible? You?"

The Chechen had heard enough. "You need to leave us. We are busy people."

"Whoever did this killed three Chechen guides. Including one named—he looked at a slip of paper—Nino Jorbenadze. One of the men who took them to the location of this generator."

"What?" the man asked angrily. "Nino? They killed Nino? You are lying!" he screamed, lowering his rifle.

The captain handed him a photo of Nino lying in the shallow grave with maggots on his face.

The Georgian looked at the photo and threw it back into the truck. "It is fake. One of those digital photograph fakes."

"No, it isn't. I saw them myself. They were shot by the men they were guiding. Nino was shot in the chest, the others in the back."

"It is impossible!"

"A farmer who heard the shooting came as soon as he could, and saw several men retreating. He said the shooters did not look Georgian." He paused again. "Do you know who Nino was helping?"

The Chechen's face was dark with fury. "We let certain people in because we share ideology. We have the same goals. But our means are different. And some of them treat their friends just like their enemies when it suits them. We have seen some men deep in the gorge, but they are in many different places. Near the border, elsewhere. I doubt you will see them though, unless you go on foot. They never go near the roads."

The captain nodded. "Remember what I said."

He nodded and began to move away, then hesitated. "Wait," the man said. "This man sitting next to you."

The captain tried not to show any concern.

"Why is he carrying a fancy machine gun? Why does he not get the Georgian AK-47 like everyone else?"

The captain looked at Rat's machine pistol for the first time. He didn't know what to say. "We bought some new equipment to go after the non-Georgians here, like the men who shot Nino. This sergeant is one of the first to get one."

"And not you?"

"No. I like Russian equipment. I don't need a fancy German gun."

"Let me see it," the man said as others gathered behind him.

"No," the captain said. He glanced up to see if the road was clear. It wasn't.

"Yes. You must give me that fancy German gun or you will not pass. It is the toll," the man said, smiling maliciously.

"No toll. This road belongs to Georgia. The Georgian Army pays no toll to drive on our roads."

"You do today," the man said, holding out his hand.

Captain Kolbaia was furious. "Either you move now, get out of the way and stop making ridiculous demands, or I will order my men out of the trucks and force you, even if we have to shoot you to do it."

"You would never get out of here alive," the man said, returning his hard gaze.

"Maybe not, but I'd certainly kill you, which would make it worthwhile."

The man laughed, stepped back, and yelled at the others to clear the path. "We will keep our eyes out for your electricity canister!"

The captain spoke to the driver who jammed the stick shift into first gear and began slowly releasing the clutch. Rat spoke quietly to Mark James in the backseat to turn on his detection instrument. It was the size of a briefcase and was leaning against the door right behind the captain. He would have preferred to use headphones, but was content now to just watch the dials for indication of cesium or strontium. They were detectable in minute amounts with the remarkably sensitive gear James had. If they came within several hundred feet of one of the cores, he would find it. They hadn't found anything in the flyover the previous night, so James wasn't optimistic.

The truck crept through the people surrounding it. They all looked toward the leader, the one who wanted Rat's weapon, who had been talking to the Georgian captain. He was content to let them pass.

They drove on, finally clear of the people and the overflow of the camp, into the hilly gorge.

"What was that about?"

"We should have given you a Georgian weapon."

Rat thought about it. "You're probably right." He slid his weapon under the seat, out of sight.

They went from one hill to another, some covered with dense foliage, others stark and bare, covered only with sad grass. They saw no one but were sure they were being watched. The rutted road made it impossible to travel any faster than twenty kilometers per hour. Rat felt vulnerable. They passed through the next enclave without incident and with Mark James's quiet equipment sniffing for gamma and beta rays, then the enclave after that. By mid-afternoon they had gone as deep into the gorge as they were going to go. They had found the camps they had wanted to visit. They hadn't seen anyone who looked Sudanese, nor had they seen any of signs of the Europeans who supposedly had come to join the Chechen-Islamic struggle.

The captain turned to speak to Rat. "This is as far as we go. What do you want to do?"

"Is there any other way out?"

"There is another road that runs along the western side of the gorge. It is worse, and touches none of the populations. But who knows?"

"Let's take that road. We'll keep our instrumentation on all the way. Maybe we'll pick something up."

"It will be dark before we leave if we do that."

"We've got to find these radioactive cores."

The captain shrugged and instructed the driver to take the western road. They kept the instruments on throughout the bone-jarring ride, but found no sign of any of the missing nuclear cores. By the time they turned back onto the road on which they had entered the gorge, it was pitch dark. The moon was not yet visible over the hills.

The truck groaned and protested as it climbed the steep hill. The dull yellow headlights bounced around the road and off the countless trees. The diesel engine was tired and strained under the load. The driver was even more tired, and his efforts to avoid the ruts and holes were less successful.

Rat stared into the darkness wondering where the nuclear cores had gone. He was sure it was Duar's men who had taken them. It was part of their obsessive, unending quest to make either a thermonuclear bomb, or short of that, a dirty nuclear bomb that would spread deadly nuclear radiation without the necessity of a nuclear explosion.

He saw something flash in the corner of his eye. He turned and saw a rocket-propelled grenade flying directly at them. "Incoming!" he yelled. The captain turned where Rat was pointing and saw the RPG-7 coming from the downhill side of the road. Rat yelled, "Ambush! Get out!"

The captain continued to stare a split second too long. Rat reached across him, opened his door, and pushed him out on the uphill side of the truck just as the grenade slammed into the truck behind them. Rat followed the captain, hit the ground, and rolled clear. The captain shouted to his men as they tried to scramble out of the truck before the next grenade hit.

Rat ran to the truck behind them. He approached the burning wreck from the uphill side as Banger ran to him and pulled the caps off the nightscope on his sniper rifle. "Shit, sir, that was close."

"You see anybody?"

Banger shook his head.

Rat returned his attention to the burning truck. The heat was too intense for him to approach any closer than ten feet. He looked for McSwain, then saw what remained of him burning inside the cab. The armor-piercing grenade had penetrated the driver's door, lodged itself in the cab, and blown up, instantly killing the driver, McSwain, and the other Georgian.

"Damn it!" Rat exclaimed. He and the Georgian captain ran to the back of the burning truck and helped the two survivors out. They looked like ghosts or zombies, with heavy gray smoke rolling up from their uniforms. They were unresponsive to their captain; they had been deafened by the explosion.

James stood beside Rat in stunned silence. Suddenly he turned. "I've got to get the instruments!" He ran back toward the front truck.

"No!" Rat yelled, nearly following him, but then turned back toward the burning truck. Rat helped the survivors away from the flames. Everyone huddled in a group down the road from the two trucks, leaning in toward the hill. "No way to tell how many are here, but you can be sure they think they have enough to take us. If we stay here we'll be killed. We have to go right at them. We've already wasted too much time."

The captain's eyes were huge. He looked confused.

Rat said to him, "You ever been in combat?"

Captain Kolbaia shook his head.

"Take your men and go right at the source of the RPG. Spread out. Five meters apart. Stay low and fast. Don't stop until you're on top of them or you're clear of them. After you start, I'll take my men into the woods to the left and get behind them. We have night vision. I doubt they do, but don't count on them not having it. Be careful."

The silence was interrupted by automatic gunfire that tore into the trucks behind them. Rat looked up the hill and saw Mark James running toward them with his briefcase detection device. James made it to them unharmed. Rat noticed none of the gunfire aimed at James had come from uphill. "Dumbasses," Rat said. "Don't even know how to set up an ambush." To the captain, "You ready?"

The captain nodded. His mouth hung open slightly. The bullets were now slamming into the dirt where the road had been cut out of the hill. "I should be in charge of our plan. I am a Georgian Army officer and we are in Georgia."

"You're right. No doubt about it. But I've seen a little of this before. So this time let's do it my way. Next time we'll do it your way. Okay?"

He nodded. "We will go now."

"When you get to the edge of the trees, turn right about ten degrees and head right for the shooting. They'll be shooting in the dark—it will be hard to find you once we get inside the trees. The first twenty meters will be the most dangerous. They should be advancing now if they have any idea of what they're doing. They won't be expecting you to go right at them. You should be ready to shoot anyone in front of you, just don't go left. We'll be around your left flank and up behind them. As soon as you hear us fire you hit the deck and stop. It will sound very different. They're shooting AK-47s. Ours will sound very different, but you have to listen! You ready? You got that?"

The captain nodded as he shouted instructions to his men, who made sure their clips were in their rifles and a round was in the chamber. Everyone was ready.

Rat moved away from the captain with the other Americans following, the SEALs and Green Berets who hadn't been killed. Rat wondered why they hadn't fired on the truck in front. Standard ambush procedure—fire from both sides, and disable the front vehicle to block the road. They were almost surely advancing up the woods to attack them at close range with automatic weapons. Rat hurried down the road in a crouch until he was a hundred meters down the hill. He stopped, put on his night-vision goggles, and waited for the other Americans to do likewise.

He had worked and trained with Green Berets before. They watched him expectantly. He looked up and down the road, then into the woods. He and Groomer were the only American officers alive. He nodded, and gave them hand signals—he would go across the road first, they were to follow in uneven succession and spread out in the woods in a line abreast, all to the left of him.

Rat dashed across the road and stopped low when he penetrated the tree line. He held his MP5N on his shoulder, ready to fire at anything that moved. He could see everything in green and white. He could see the Georgians spreading out nicely in the woods to his right, making their way slowly in the darkness. He could also see the tracer bullets from their attackers racing toward the truck and now generally toward the Georgians. Rat went deeper into the woods another hundred meters and turned right. He walked just under a trot, careful not to blunder into a trap. The other Americans followed him, watching him, and watching farther out to their left to make sure they wouldn't get flanked themselves. They were five meters apart, instantly forming into a squad, bringing all their Special Forces training to bear. They pointed their submachine guns directly ahead of them with their fingers on the trigger, careful not to shoot before it was time, before they were right on top of their enemy.

Rat led the way, watching the shooting that was now ahead of them. He threaded his way through the trees, stopping every fifty meters to do a complete three-hundred-sixty-degree survey. Rat knew this wasn't how to run a counterambush operation. It was far too dangerous. His fire would be brought against the attackers from behind; his allies, the Georgians, were just on the other side. Any misses could end up hitting the Georgians. But this had developed too quickly. He didn't have time for the perfect strategy. He just knew they were going to have to take care of this themselves.

Rat kept up his pace. His breathing was even and easy. His senses were on edge. He was sure the attackers didn't yet know they were coming. The terrain grew steeper. They had chosen their ambush location well, but had not thought it through. They had left themselves vulnerable.

Rat stopped. He saw three men ahead hiding behind trees and firing on the Georgians beyond. He raised his hand, crouched down, and the other Americans stopped. They made their line perfectly straight and waited for Rat. They could all see what he saw. Rat looked for more men. He waited several seconds, then saw four more men clustered slightly to his left. They were moving slowly, toward the Georgians, not firing at all. None had night-vision devices.

Rat glanced to his left and gave the signal to advance. He began a slow trot with his weapon at his shoulder. He waited until he was twenty yards from the attackers and still undetected. He placed the gunsight on the back of the closest man and pulled the trigger for a three-round burst. His gun belched. The man lurched forward and a dark green stain spread over his back. The other two had heard the sound from behind them and turned to meet the threat. The other four to the left had heard the new sound, but didn't know where it was coming from. Confusion descended on the attackers.

The Georgians heard the Americans' weapons and stopped firing. They lay down on the ground. Rat and the other Americans kept firing in short bursts, hitting with three and five rounds at a time. The second shooter fell backward and slammed into a tree. He slumped to the ground and hit the third man who tried to push him away. He was hit immediately by Groomer's burst in the face and jerked back grotesquely to the ground.

The Americans ran past the three dead attackers after the four who were still advancing toward the Georgians, now thirty meters ahead of them. They were lying on the ground, very vulnerable. The attackers assumed they had all been injured, and were hurrying to finish the job.

The Green Berets who were holding down the left side of the line saw what was happening and fired quickly after the four to turn them back toward them and away from the Georgians.

The four heard the bullets ripping through the leaves close by them. One of them fell screaming, holding his back. The other three turned to face their new threat, kneeling in the woods. One of the Green Berets stopped and fired at the attacker farthest to the left. Robby caught the other two from the right side and they fell twenty yards in front of the Americans, who all stopped firing at the same time. They walked steadily forward, looking like aliens in their Georgian camouflage uniforms and night-vision goggles. The man who had been shot in the back reached for his weapon and was immediately executed by one shot from Banger.

Rat scanned the woods quickly for any other men, any other threat, then moved quickly to where the dead men lay. "Captain!" he called, alerting the Georgians.

The Georgians stood and walked toward him. Rat continued to call out, "You okay?"

"I've lost two men. What of your men?"

Rat quickly surveyed those with him. They were all okay. The Americans had already set up a perimeter around the area. "We're okay." He removed his night-vision goggles and knelt down next to one of the attackers. He pulled a small mag-light out of his pocket and shone it on the face of one of the dead men.

The Georgian captain looked through the man's pockets. No identification, no wallet, no money, no insignia on the cobbled-together uniform, nothing. "This was a suicide mission."

"They look like Chechens to you?" Rat asked. "Or Georgians?"

The captain looked at the face. He shook his head slowly. "I don't know who they are, but they are not Chechen or Georgian."

"Robby, get their pictures."

Robby nodded and pulled a small flat digital camera out of his pocket. He moved the flash up to the top, crouched in front of each dead attacker and took a face shot. He then backed off and took a body shot of each one. When he was done he quickly cycled through the digital images on the back of his camera, saw that he had gotten them all, and pushed it back into his pocket. "All set."

Rat turned to Captain Kolbaia. "We need you to get on your radio and get them to meet us with a helicopter. We've got to walk—we'll stay on the downhill side of the road and in the woods until we crest the hill and head down out of the gorge."

"Our only radio is still in truck."

Rat considered. "What kind was it?"

"FM."

"Robby, your magic little radio do FM?"

"Sure," Robby nodded. "But the range isn't great."

"Can you reach them when we get to the top of the hill?"

"Probably."

Rat looked uphill through the woods toward the flickering wreckage still burning on the road. "How far to a clearing?" he asked the captain.

"About five kilometers."

"Let's go."

They started walking through the woods carefully, with Kolbaia leading the way. Rat quickly checked their position on his PDA with a GPS fix.

Rat looked over at James, who was walking beside him. James was visibly shaken. "Never seen anything like that before?" Rat asked.

"Not even close," James said, swallowing hard to stop the nausea that was welling up.

"What's your confidence level we would have found the nuclear cores if they were there?"

James moved his mind off the image of Robby taking a picture of a man who had just had his face shot off, whose features had been replaced by fresh red meat, oozing blood and bone chips. "Um, good question. Maybe thirty percent."

"Damn," Rat said. "That's not very good."

James couldn't have agreed more.

Rat thought out loud, "They've got to get them out of the gorge. Can't fly them out. No airplanes here. Can't really walk them out, nowhere to go. Can't go through Russia, they'd get their asses shot off. Could go to Chechnya and use them against the Russians, but they killed Georgians to find them and probably don't like the Chechens either. I think they're aimed at us. But how?" Rat stopped. He had a sudden thought. "Could you detect radioactivity on a ship?"

"Depends on the size of the source. The strontium would probably be blocked, but the cesium's a gamma-emitter. It should be detectable, but with the right shielding—like the core containers themselves, if they're not breached . . . I'd want to get pretty close."

Rat was thinking of their escape. "Only way a ship can take anything from Georgia is all the way across the Black Sea. That must be six, seven hundred miles. Even with a decent ship, say ten knots, that's three days of sailing. And that assumes they got on board right away. Once they get across the Black Sea, they've got to go through the Bosporus by Istanbul, across the Sea of Marmara and then through the Dardanelles. Sort of like sailing down a hallway to the Mediterranean." He paused as they walked. James was beginning to breathe hard as he struggled with his heavy bags. "You sure you're with the DO?"

"Yeah. Why?"

"You're out of shape. You're fighting those bags like there's a dead cow in there. I thought all their guys were ready to climb buildings."

"I just came over from NEST—the Nuclear Emergency Search Team—"

"I know all about it."

"Okay. Anyway, I just started. The agency wanted its own ability to find nukes. Overseas, near embassies, wherever. I'm just here to find nukes and these bags are heavy."

"Those NEST guys are supposed to be pretty good."

"Four-hour response time anywhere in the country. I would usually stroll around a city with a briefcase, and headphones that look like they're plugged into a CD player, listening for any radioactivity. I'm not really trained for this spy stuff, or military stuff. I'm basically a nuclear engineer."

"Well, I'm supposed to be training the Georgians to go after the guys in the gorge. But they're going to be disappointed. You and I have to go somewhere else."

"Where?"

Rat smiled. "Çanakkale. You never been there?"

The doors to the courtroom on top of the Department of Justice were closed tightly behind the participants. Judge Royce Wiggins scowled from the bench as he had practiced doing for many years. The fluorescent lighting was stark and unflattering. Judge Wiggins spoke to Skyles. "This is your motion. I've read the moving papers. Tell me, why should we dismiss the charge relating to the Geneva Convention?"

Wolff sat down.

"Thank you, Your Honor. That is the very thing I would like to address this morning—"

"Obviously. That's why you filed the motion."

"Yes, sir. The charge relating to the Geneva Convention is defective in two ways: first, the Geneva Convention is not a statute upon which a prosecution can be based. It is a treaty. A charge cannot be brought directly as a violation of the Geneva Convention. And second, the obvious contemplation of Congress when the Geneva Convention was adopted was that wars would be fought against other countries that were signatories. It seems that the only thing that the Geneva Convention is really good at is predicting who it is we're going to fight. If you want to know who we're going to war against, just read the list of signatories. Whoever *didn't* sign it is who our enemy will be. Japan, North Korea, Vietnam, terrorists . . . We've had a lot of skirmishes and even wars since 1945, but not one time have we fought a signatory to the Geneva Convention. Need I remind the court of the hay that was made by North Vietnam in using the Geneva Convention against us even though they did not sign it?

"It is an *outrage* to prosecute someone for violating the Geneva Convention when the alleged victim is a terrorist. Obviously no terrorist organization has ever signed the Geneva Convention, nor would they, because they violate it every day. Their reason for *existence* is one big violation of the concepts represented by the Geneva Convention. They are a disgrace to the entire concept of treaties and conventions and rules of law and war. To say that they are not bound by such rules, yet we are, and we must prosecute those who violate the Convention that they hold in contempt threatens our ability to fight the War on Terrorism. If we want to hold ourselves to that standard, fine, issue orders and charge people when they violate them—in a court-martial, I would suggest."

Wolff stood up, unable to contain himself anymore.

"You'll get your chance to respond, Mr. Wolff. Please have a seat," Wiggins said.

Wolff nodded knowingly, returning to his seat.

"May I continue?"

The judge nodded.

"But equally important is that there is no enforcement mechanism under the Geneva Convention by which my client can be prosecuted. There is no statute."

The judge looked confused. "I'm not following you."

"That last point, Your Honor, is simply that the government has chosen to hide this trial from the military, from the ones who should be reviewing the conduct in question. We are in no position to judge a military officer—or more specifically a CIA agent who is actually still on active duty with the Navy—in the heat of battle."

"I think we are in exactly the right place to judge someone's conduct in the heat of battle," the judge said. "What is difficult about it? Either he has violated statutes and conventions or he has not."

"My point, Your Honor, is that the UCMJ was set up to take care of these kinds of charges against a military defendant. Our Congress wisely set up a separate military justice system for a reason. I submit that it was because they wanted the conduct at issue to be reviewed by other military officers, not a civilian jury. Here, my client is being deprived of that right."

"Anything else?"

"No, sir. Everything else is in my papers."

"You said two points."

"Really just one."

"Mr. Wolff?"

"Thank you, Your Honor. I'm afraid that Mr. Skyles's motion is as misplaced as his client's conduct was. To the extent I was able to follow his argument, it seems to be that there is no statutory authority for a charge of the Geneva Convention. We have dealt with that argument exhaustively in our papers. If the court wants me—"

"No, that won't be necessary."

The judge was getting a little tired of the argument. "You have anything else, Mr. Wolff?"

"A lot sir, but . . ."

"It won't be necessary," Judge Wiggins said. He could tell Skyles was going to stand and try to argue in rebuttal. "The motion is denied, Mr. Skyles, without prejudice. If you can show me better authority that your position is correct, I'll reconsider my ruling; but for now, this trial is going to go forward on both counts—manslaughter and violation of the Geneva Convention. Trial starts as scheduled." He paused. "Mr. Skyles," he said, removing his glasses and giving Skyles a deeply knowing look, "do you have any other motions, perhaps something dealing with jurisdiction?"

Skyles understood perfectly and answered quickly. "No, sir, I don't."

"Are you sure?" the judge said, amazed that Skyles wasn't picking up on his overt hint.

"Yes, sir. In fact I am prepared to stipulate that this court *does* have jurisdiction." He turned to Wolff. "Is the government prepared to agree to such a stipulation?"

Wolff tried not to roll his eyes. "Sure. Happy to."

Wiggins nodded. "Very well. The stipulation is accepted. Is there anything else?"

Skyles stood. "Well, yes, sir. Since the court now has jurisdiction that cannot be questioned by the parties due to the stipulation just entered on the record, I would like to renew my motion to dismiss the charge of violating the Geneva Convention because civilians aren't bound by convention. If the government wants to charge Mr. Rathman in this court, if they want to try him as a civilian, they cannot pursue the charge of violating the Geneva Convention." Skyles stole a glance at Wolff. He was sitting forward with his mouth slightly open.

"Mr. Wolff?"

Wolff's mouth was dry. "Since this wasn't in his papers, I'd have to take a look at the law in this regard, and I'm confident we are able to bring this charge in this court."

"I have no such confidence," Wiggins said. "I had expected this motion and looked at the law myself. He is right. Except in certain circumstances—and this isn't one of them—you cannot charge a civilian with violating the Geneva Convention, and the government has chosen, for whatever reason, not to charge Mr. Rathman under the UCMJ. That's your choice. But in this court he cannot be charged with violating the Geneva Convention. That charge is dismissed. This case will proceed on the one charge of manslaughter. And as to the jurisdiction stipulation, since it is something that can never be waived, Mr. Skyles has simply preserved an argument for appeal that he can raise at another time. This court is adjourned." He banged his gavel and walked out of the courtroom leaving Wolff staring at his back in disbelief.

◆　◆　◆

Rat, Robby, and Groomer stepped carefully onto the small boat that had been procured for them by the CIA field officer in Istanbul. He had gone to Çanakkale, the small Turkish city in the province that straddled the Dardanelles, to find a boat, a mission he thought was nuts; but he had received very specific instructions to make it happen.

Some additional gear had been flown overnight to Istanbul for James and had been waiting for them. They had retrieved the gear and driven straight to Çanakkale. The Americans wore working clothes that any Turk might wear on a boat.

James picked up the next piece of equipment and handed it over to

Robby, who was looking forward to learning all about this sophisticated gear he knew nothing about. He placed the box that was labeled navigation equipment in the cabin that stood six feet above the deck; it was more like a wheelhouse and was made of wood. The boat was at least forty years old, perhaps fifty.

Rat's experienced eyes took in the lines, the paint, the rotting wood, and the bent warped rudder and quickly concluded that the boat wasn't very seaworthy. Rat had spent much of his life on boats of one sort or another, most of which could go fifty knots at the drop of a hat and stop in two boat lengths. Riding on this wooden tub, which probably had a maximum speed of six knots, was not what he had in mind when he went to sea. But it was all they could get, and it was certainly innocuous and inconspicuous enough to accomplish their objective.

The owner of the boat smiled as the three Americans finished loading their gear aboard. He had no idea what they wanted or were planning on doing with his boat, only that they had paid five times the market value for his boat for a three-day period. Rat turned to the captain. "Do you speak English?"

The captain shook his head. "No. No English."

Rat changed to Arabic. "Arabic?"

The captain was surprised to hear Arabic come out of an American's mouth. He spoke Turkish as his first language, but also spoke Arabic. "Yes."

Rat continued, "We need this boat for three days. You should have already been paid."

"Yes."

"You've been paid more than this boat is worth."

The Turk shrugged. "Who is to say?"

"I am," Rat said. "And I'm going to captain this boat for the next three days. We don't need you. You can go back your family. We'll meet you here at this pier in three days."

The Turk's face clouded. "I am the captain of the boat. I do not let it out of my sight. It is my living, it is how I make money to feed my family."

Rat leaned toward the man and lowered his voice. "We don't need your services. I'll return the boat to you."

The man was desperate; he was sure he would never see his boat again. As he stared into Rat's eyes he could feel fear rising inside of him. He didn't know what would happen if he forced the issue. "I was going to live on the boat that now you tell me I cannot. I therefore must have some money to eat."

Rat had anticipated such a demand. He reached into his pocket and brought out a hundred dollars in Turkish currency. He handed it to the man. "This should do it."

The Turk grabbed the money and counted. "This will only get me through today. I must take a bus, I must—"

"That's all there is. We're leaving. Get off the boat."

The Turk knew he had done his best and stepped off onto the pier. "If you are not here . . ."

Rat said nothing as he jumped on the pier. The man scampered back. Rat nodded to Robby, who started the diesel engine on the boat. Rat released the two lines holding the boat, gave the boat a push with his right foot, and jumped back onto the boat as Robby pulled away from the pier.

"So how exactly are we going to do this?" James asked, glancing back at the confused Turk on the pier as he got smaller.

"We're going to sail north and south through the Dardanelles for three days and check every ship that passes for a radioactive signature. How close do we have to get?"

"If the cores are still intact we'll need to be within fifty yards."

"That's the assumption we're going to have to make." He walked into the wheelhouse and took the wheel from Robby, who went forward. James followed Rat into the wheelhouse.

"Can I ask you something?"

"Sure," Rat said as he studied the minimal instruments in front of him. He listened carefully to the sound of the steady diesel engine as he advanced the throttle slightly.

"I'm all for finding these things, believe me . . . but what makes you so sure that the cores are on a ship?"

"I don't see them loading these things aboard an airplane at some airport where they can be observed and when security is as tight as it is here. I think they're trying to get them out in a merchant ship—to rendezvous later with some other ship or airplane in some port outside of the Black Sea. The busier the port, the better."

"How do you know they haven't already passed through the Dardanelles and are heading west in the Mediterranean?"

"I don't. If they're already through, we're screwed."

Groomer added, "You still think it's Duar's people?"

Rat clutched the wheel tighter as waves broke over the bow, causing a mist to hit the windshield. He looked knowingly at Groomer. "Remember what Johnson said?"

"But we got Duar, captured another one, and killed most of his top guys. Who else could put this kind of thing together? Especially from Georgia where they haven't operated before?"

"That's the question that keeps haunting me," Rat replied. Rat steered the boat to the right through the chop, cutting across the bow of a large freighter that was bearing down on them. He looked at James. "We're going to piss off these captains, but I'll get us within fifty yards of every ship heading south."

"Let's do it," James said stepping out of the wheelhouse.

♦   ♦   ♦

Judge Gerald Graham had heard every excuse, every reason that someone should not be convicted in a criminal case, military and civilian alike, and was very rarely impressed. Even when he was impressed, he was careful not to show it. He sat behind the table draped with green felt aboard the *Belleau Wood* and looked at the attorneys in front of him. "Since this is our first real opportunity to speak about this case, I wanted to make sure that we are all operating from the same play book. Since the play book is rather fluid, and we're guided by the directives and instructions promulgated by the Department of Defense, which apply to no other kind of trial in the country or out of it, we need to ensure that we are working together in that regard. Has each of you had a chance to review the notebooks on how to conduct the tribunal?"

The three attorneys, Stern and Little at one table, and Elizabeth Watson at the other, nodded. They had reviewed the notebooks.

The judge spoke again. "Good. If any of you have questions, speak up. There will be no claim of surprise, or lack of understanding, or some other excuse related to the procedures as to why you have screwed up after today. Am I clear?"

"Yes, Your Honor," they said.

"Good. We're here this morning because Mr. Stern has filed a motion to exclude a confession signed by the defendant. Do I have that right?" he said, looking at Stern.

"Yes, sir. That is exactly right, except that you have assumed into your description of the document that the defendant did in fact dictate and sign the so-called confession. I think both of those things remain to be proved, but in any case, we want it excluded on other grounds."

The judge nodded. "You claim it was obtained through duress and torture."

"Yes, sir."

"Everybody have a seat. Mr. Stern, will you be arguing?"

"Yes, sir."

"Fine. And while I have your attention, since you have two attorneys representing Mr. Duar in this case, I want it very clear that we will not be having a tag team defense. One attorney can speak to one issue or witness. Is that clear?"

"Yes, sir. That is our intention."

"You may proceed."

Stern stood up and walked to the lectern that had been placed between the two counsel tables. "May it please the court. The rulings of the Supreme Court and all other courts in the land have long held under what is known as the exclusionary rule that evidence obtained in violation of a defendant's rights is to be excluded from evidence—"

Graham interrupted. "A defendant's constitutional rights, Mr. Stern."

"Yes, sir. And—"

"Is it your position that your client is entitled to the protection of the Constitution?"

"Yes, sir."

"On what grounds? He's not an American citizen, he's not a resident of the United States, his crime—his alleged crime—did not occur in the United States, and he was not returned to the United States for trial."

"Yes, sir, but he was on a sovereign U.S. vessel in the custody of the American military, taken *off* that ship, and tortured under the direct supervision and participation of American servicemen or intelligence agents.

"The rules of evidence have long-established constitutional rights both of which are an issue in this motion. My client—our client—was tortured in order to get the confession that is now being offered."

Stern walked to the side of the courtroom, the wardroom, and stood by an easel that had been erected by the bulkhead. A large board was on the easel, covered by a cloth. "Just to show the court what kind of men we're dealing with, I would offer as evidence in support of my motion a series of photographs." Stern pulled the cloth away to reveal a three- by four-foot blowup of a close-up photograph of Duar's scrotum. The image was shocking. Everyone in the room stared in horror and fascination. The burned skin was clearly visible. The black holes were surrounded by skin that was charred and peeled back from the places where the skin had burned completely through.

"This is what was done to my client, Your Honor," he said, taking down the first board onto which the photograph was glued, showing the other six in succession, including close-up pictures of Duar's earlobes and a broken tooth. "This is how they got the so-called confession." Stern put the first photograph back on the easel and returned to the lectern. "Frankly, Your Honor, I think anyone, any of us, would sign that confession to avoid more of this kind of treatment. *I* would certainly sign it.

"It is understandable that our country must combat terrorism in new and different ways, but we cannot suspend the rules of law by which we operate. One such rule prohibits admitting evidence that is coerced out of a defendant. It violates that defendant's rights, and it is unreliable. In this case, my client was dragged from *this very ship* in the middle of the night and taken to Egypt, where he was tortured to obtain this confession. He was then returned to the ship a mere shell of his former person. It will be obvious to the court that Mr. Duar has been damaged physically, mentally, and emotionally. Such means to elicit a confession are unacceptable in a civilized society. Confessions are routinely excluded in police brutality cases. This case is no different. The fact that the authority in question—the Navy, or the CIA—dragged Duar off the ship and had a surrogate—Egypt, I have now learned—conduct the torture does not remove the United States from its obligations to treat prisoners fairly and well. We cannot torture them, and we cannot hold against them something extracted through torture by a surrogate. Such an approach to justice is incomprehensible. Did the government really believe that it would get away with torture simply by taking it ashore? Did the United States really believe that it could ask its ally to use electricity on Duar's testicles to get information from him and then attempt to use it in this tribunal? Such cannot be the case. The rule of law is just that." Stern was gaining confidence. He could tell that the reputedly tough Judge Gerald Graham had been sickened by the pictures. It wasn't just theory. Someone had been horribly damaged, and the decision whether that mattered was his.

"So may the United States Government use a confession extracted from a defendant through supervised torture conducted by a surrogate?" He paused. "To allow such conduct is not only a violation of the rules of evidence and the United States Constitution but a violation of common sense, goodwill, and the fundamental morality that backs up the rule of law to make it rational and merciful. Thank you."

Stern sat down at the table next to Little, who whispered, "Nice job. Nice photo. Glad you kept his dick out of it."

Elizabeth Watson stood up in her gleaming white uniform and strode to the lectern. Graham nodded at her. "May it please the court, Mr. Stern's speech was quite moving. It was even interesting, and I must say, well presented. What it lacked though was legal and factual authority. In order to be persuasive to the court, legal authority must be cited if any exists. I cited the legal authority that stands for the proposition that confessions extracted outside the control of the United States Government or a state government, and on foreign sovereign territory, are admissible. The answer to the question presented is yes, such confessions or other evidence are admissible. It may be that Mr. Stern does not like those cases, it may be that he wants to write a law review article on how those cases are wrong, but it does not change the fact that the confession comes in.

"Everything else Mr. Stern said is irrelevant. The rule of law, as he discussed, is clear—the confession is admissible as long as the U.S. Government was not complicit in the commission of the torture. If the court has any doubt about that, I would direct the court's attention to the classified declaration of Mr. Kent Rathman. As you can see, he was personally in charge of the detail that took Mr. Duar to Egypt. Egypt wanted to interrogate him and the United States was willing to accommodate that request. Mr. Rathman was assured that Mr. Duar would not be harmed. When he was ready to return, he found Duar being subjected to certain unacceptable interrogation techniques, the results of which we have seen graphically this morning. He immediately intervened on behalf of Duar, stopped the interrogation, and brought him back to this ship. As he was leaving he found this confession and took it against the will of the Egyptians. He asked Duar if he in fact signed it, and Duar admitted it was his signature. It is authentic, not tainted by the involvement of any U.S. agent in obtaining it, and therefore admissible."

"Thank you, Commander Watson. Mr. Stern, do you have any reply?"

"Yes, sir." Stern stood with an ironic smile on his face. "It is remarkable indeed, Your Honor, that the United States bases its position on the declaration of a man who is himself about to go on trial for manslaughter for torturing and killing a man who supposedly worked for Mr. Duar. Mr. Rathman is completely unreliable. He would be implicated in *another* illegal act if his declaration were found to be untrue. He isn't here; I am not able to cross-examine him about what actually happened in Egypt." Stern looked over at Commander Watson, who was looking down at the notepad on which she was taking notes. Stern waited until she looked up. "How can the United States *not* be complicit in the torture of my client when they are the ones who dragged him out of the brig in this ship in the middle of the night? It flies in the face of logic and common sense to assert that the Americans who accompanied my client were there only to feed him, keep him warm, and buy him chewing gum."

"Thank you for your argument," Judge Graham said. He looked at the photograph, then at the lawyers. "I find that there is no evidence that the United States participated in, condoned, or encouraged the torture alleged to have occurred at the hands of officers of the Egyptian government. The confession is admittedly authentic, and therefore admissible unless tainted by illegal means in its creation. I find that the exclusionary rule does not apply to these facts. The motion by the defendant is denied. The confession will be allowed into evidence. This court is adjourned."

Stern couldn't believe it. He wanted to jump up and protest. He looked at Little, who showed no surprise at all. "You expected that?"

"Sure," Little said. "I told you that. Unless we could tie Rathman to the actual torture, we'd lose."

"How the hell are we supposed to do that?"

"No idea. That's why I thought it would come in."

"This is funny to you?" Stern asked.

"Sort of. I just can't get over that photo. I think you should take it back to your ACLU office in D.C. and hang it on the wall. Give you something to talk about," Little said, chuckling as he picked up his briefcase.

"Do you want to resign from his defense? I'm just not sure you're adding much."

"Neither are you, so far," Little said. "It was a good motion, you did a good job. Had to bring it. I would have done the same thing. I've just never seen a scrotum blown up that big before."

Stern turned and walked out of the room.

Little smiled at Watson and followed Stern.

◆　◆　◆

"Where are you going?" Andrea asked Satterly. He was packing a medical bag in the sick bay.

"Washington."

"What for?"

"I've been subpoenaed to testify in a trial."

Andrea caught herself. "Rathman's trial?"

Satterly looked at her suspiciously. "Yes. You know about it?"

"Sure. I read the *Washington Post* on-line every day. They've been giving it a lot of coverage. I think they're trying to make him look bad."

Satterly put his bag down and looked at her. "He *should* look bad. He's a bloody murderer."

"Why do you say that?"

"He tortured that poor man to death. He didn't care about the man's life at all."

"How do you know that?"

"He was here, Andrea. He told me over and over again that he had been tortured. And I watched him die. I did the autopsy. It was all consistent with what he had said."

"So you're going to testify for the prosecution?"

"You bet I am. And happy to do it. That man should go to prison. I'm grateful for the chance to put him there. We can't have Americans running all over the world torturing people and violating international laws and treaties. Did you know we signed a treaty in 1994 promising not to use torture at *all*? An international treaty. You aware of that? *Everybody* signed it—including us, which is rare enough. But we promised we wouldn't do it. And here's this Rathman violating it left and right. He doesn't care. He thinks he operates in a different world. He thinks he's above the law." He jerked the zipper of his bag closed and looked into her eyes, the emotion plain for her to see. "It's when the pressure is on, when things get the toughest, that we need to hold tightest to our principles. It's easy when there's no pressure, when a shortcut won't matter." Satterly paused and took a breath. He realized he had been talking too fast. He had gotten carried away.

"Why is this so important to you? Why do you care so much?"

He took a deep breath and sighed. "This is about us as a country, Andrea. It's what we're about. If we're just another country trying to get and keep power, to dominate the world regardless of the cost, count me out. But if we stand for something different, something good, then we have to choose between the expedient and the right. And there's a difference. These kinds of moral fights aren't won in one big battle, they're won in a million little battles, and attitudes, and winks. I for one won't wink at this kind of thing." He picked up his bag and headed for the door. "Take care."

"Have a good trip," Andrea said.

"Thanks. I will."

"Taking it kind of personally, aren't you?"

"You bet I am. He killed my patient." Satterly studied her face to see if she was making a game of him. "Gotta go catch the helo," he said and turned to hurry out the door.

"Tim, can I use your computer while you're gone? Mine doesn't do e-mail yet."

"Sure, no problem."

As soon as he was gone she walked directly to the administrative offices on the second deck and asked for a chit to request leave.

Chapter

18

The admiral's wardroom was packed and hummed with anticipation. Forty-eight hours earlier the Department of Defense had notified the world that Wahamed Duar was to be put on trial in a military tribunal aboard the *Belleau Wood*. The scramble among journalists to get aboard to report on the tribunal had been astonishing. They all wanted to see the trial and report it. They had needs—satellite feeds from the Indian Ocean, dedicated fax lines, high-speed Internet access, staterooms for all their reporters and technical people and unfettered access to all the participants including Duar himself. Stuntz, though, had anticipated it. He had set *rules*—only a limited number of reporters would be allowed to go to the ship to observe the trial in person. He had established a "pool," much as they would have done if they were suddenly going to war and called reporters to go with them.

The journalists who had been selected sat in the converted wardroom, exhausted from the scramble to get to the trial in the middle of the ocean. They sat in metal armchairs three rows deep. Interspersed among the journalists were the few sailors and Marines who were allowed to watch the trial, selected every day by a lottery of those aboard the ship. They were required to wear their dress uniforms to preserve the integrity of the court.

One journalist who had been excluded from the select group had threatened to lease a helicopter, fly out to the carrier, and land on the flight deck. The captain of the ship thought it would be quite colorful to watch a leased helicopter fly three hundred miles out into the open ocean and try to find the carrier. It was hard enough for those trained to find ships. A pilot not trained in naval flying, who did not know what the carrier might look like on radar—if the helicopter even had radar—had no chance of finding the carrier, and very few helicopters would have the range to fly to the carrier and make it back without re-fueling.

Sitting to the AP artist's left was Josephine Block from the *Washington Post*. She had immediately decided to go to Duar's trial when it was announced. She debated with herself and her editors whether her time would be better spent at sea with Duar or in D.C. watching Rat's trial. She hoped to watch them both.

She had had no trouble being accepted as a pool representative and had flown immediately to Kenya to catch the first available Navy heli-copter to the ship. She looked worn and disheveled. She had gotten aboard the night before and had "settled in" to her stateroom. She had been up almost all night from the odd noises aboard the ship, and hadn't yet persuaded herself that she should walk down the too public passageway in her bathrobe and two-dollar flip-flops to the communal shower. So far she had confined her cleaning to the sink.

She waited for the trial to begin with her pencil poised over her notepad, the same kind she had used for decades. The judge had made it clear that laptops weren't welcome in the courtroom. He didn't want the distraction of clicking keys.

Josephine found it amusing that the judge was concerned about the noise of nearly silent keys on a computer when her ears were con-stantly assaulted aboard the ship by the deafening noise of helicopters and Harrier jets, innumerable announcements, bos'n's pipings and fire drills. The judge had ensured that the speakers in the wardroom had been silenced, but the speakers in the passageway were still clearly au-dible.

There had been a great deal of controversy when tribunals were first set up under President Bush. But after the first few trials in Cuba the novelty had worn off and the public stopped paying attention. But those trials, it was now realized, were dry runs, attempts to ensure the process would work, that the rules were acceptable, and that the tribunal would function. Each of the men tried was an underling, a foot soldier, no one anyone had heard of, no one who was part of the inner circle of people who planned the destruction of the United States and the rest of the Western world.

Josephine noted everything significant in the courtroom, everything interesting about the people involved, the hum of the ship, the judge, and the gallery. She was excited, truly energized about a story for the first time in perhaps five years. She detected the faint sweet smell of a Pulitzer. This might be her last chance at journalistic glory.

The attorneys were sitting at the counsel table. The judge was announced and everyone in the room stood enthusiastically except Duar, who had to be pulled to his feet by Stern. Josephine strained to see Duar's face but could see only the back of his head. He carried himself like a beaten man. His hair was cut roughly, as if he had done it himself with scissors and no mirror.

"This court is now in session, the honorable Captain Gerald Graham presiding. Please be seated and come to order."

Everyone sat.

The judge spoke. "This tribunal is now in session. We will begin proceedings immediately unless any of you has further pretrial motions." The attorneys shook their heads. "Very well. As has been outlined in the notebooks that you have been given each side will be given an opportunity to present an opening statement. We will then turn to the prosecution for its case. Are you ready to proceed?" he asked Commander Elizabeth Watson.

Elizabeth looked very proper in her white uniform with skirt. She had the mandatory gold ball post earrings and white pumps. She had cleaned her uniform—or rather had it cleaned—the week prior and kept it in her closet untouched to ensure that when the day came her uniform would be perfect.

She stood and paused for a moment. "The United States is ready, Your Honor."

"You may proceed with your opening statement."

Elizabeth pushed her chair back and walked slowly to the lectern between the two tables, trying to control her heart rate. She addressed the court of five military officers: three Navy captains, and two Marine colonels selected by the admiral in charge of the Fifth Fleet, of which the *Belleau Wood* was a part. They sat beside Judge Gerald Graham, two on his right, and three on his left. They wore their tropical dress uniforms with short-sleeve shirts, the Navy officers in their distinctive whites, and the Marines in olive trousers and khaki shirts, all with impressive arrays of ribbons and warfare specialty pins.

She began. "May it please the court, this is a case about the terrorist who has conspired to attack the United States." Her voice sounded to her like it was coming from across the room. It sounded thin and tentative. She forced more air from her lungs through her pinched throat. "Wahamed Duar is the most sought-after, most wanted terrorist in the world. Through his writings, through his declarations to people both within his circle and to the general public, Duar has repeatedly threatened to destroy the United States. While the destruction of the United States is clearly outside of his power, his intention is clear—to do as much harm to the United States as he is capable of doing. He has enlisted numerous followers to assist him in that goal, several of whom were killed in the attempt to capture Mr. Duar in the Sudan.

"So what exactly are the charges? Mr. Duar is being charged with murdering American citizens and conspiracy to commit terrorist acts. The evidence will show that Duar has conspired to attack the United States on several occasions. We will produce his own writings, audiotapes of his conversations, documents captured from his operation, and testimony about his attempt to purchase weapons grade plutonium on the night of his capture. He intended to use the plutonium to create nuclear weapons to use against the United States. We will bring witnesses who will so testify.

"The evidence we will bring to this court is conclusive and irrefutable. At the conclusion of the evidence, the only possible outcome will be a vote of guilty. Thank you."

"Thank you, Counselor," Graham said, his face showing his surprise at the brevity and inadequacy of her opening statement. He looked at Stern. "Would the defense like to make an opening statement at this time?"

232 I JAMES W. HUSTON

"We would, Your Honor," Stern said. The judge nodded and Stern stood. Stern looked at the officers who were studying him; he wondered what they thought of an ACLU attorney defending a hated terrorist on a Navy ship. He was sure they wondered why Barry Little wasn't good enough, what he brought to the case that Barry Little couldn't bring. They could understand Little defending Duar. It was the job to which he had been assigned. But to volunteer? Or at least accept the job of defending Duar? Why? Stern figured they thought it was for money. How wrong they were.

Stern began. "This case is actually quite simple. The prosecution claims to have irrefutable evidence against Wahamed Duar. They may be right. They may have all the evidence needed to convict Wahamed Duar of conspiracy to commit terrorist acts. We are anxious to hear that evidence; because that which has been cited in the opening statement is totally unpersuasive. They simply declared that they have such evidence, they did not tell us what that evidence will show. But let's take the prosecutor at her word. Let's assume that she has the irrefutable evidence to convict Wahamed Duar. The prosecution's case will still fail. It will fail miserably. It will crash to the ground in a heap."

Stern stopped. He looked at the skeptical faces of the court and the judge. He turned around and looked at the equally skeptical faces of the journalists and others in the gallery. "The man sitting at the defense table, the man that they are attempting to put in prison forever—or worse yet, execute—is not Wahamed Duar. Not only is he not the terrorist that they believe they are attempting to convict with this so-called irrefutable evidence, but he has been telling them so ever since he came aboard the ship. From the time he arrived until today, he has repeatedly and consistently told them that his name is Mohammed al-Wadhi. He is a taxi driver from Khartoum in Sudan. But the Americans, the United States Navy, even the CIA, refused to believe him. They insist that he is Wahamed Duar. Well, one of the many good things about the American system of justice is that the prosecution has the burden of proof. She must *prove* that the man sitting at the defense table is in fact Wahamed Duar. We're here to tell you that they cannot so prove, because he is *not* Wahamed Duar. If necessary, we will put on evidence to prove that. We will be asking the court to dismiss this case when it is appropriate to do so. Thank you."

"Thank you, Counselor," the judge said. He looked back at Elizabeth Watson, whose face was hard and showed concern. She had obviously not anticipated difficulty in identifying the defendant. She knew of course it was her burden of proof to show that the person being charged, the one who had committed the crime at issue, was the defendant. She had never had any difficulty proving identity before. They always knew who was before them. She quickly reviewed what identification evidence she had contemplated, and tried to think of ways she could buttress the evidence that to her now seemed thinner than tolerable.

The judge continued. "Call your first witness."

◆　◆　◆

"Good morning, chief. Is the XO in?" Andrea asked the surly chief petty officer in the ship's admin office.

"Yes, ma'am. He's got several appointments, though. Can I ask what this is about?"

"I need to submit a leave request."

"Yes, ma'am. Just put it right over there in the leave request box and I'll make sure he gets it."

"I want him to get it right away. This morning."

"That I can't guarantee, ma'am." The chief looked back down at the paperwork he had been working on before she interrupted him.

"Then I want to see him right now."

"I'm sorry, but like I said, he's busy all morning. Then he has to go do an inspection—"

"Then I'll just tell him myself." She walked past the chief and knocked loudly on the XO's door. She knew she was over the line, past where protocol ended, into the high-risk area of annoying a superior officer.

"What!" the XO yelled from behind the door.

Andrea opened the door and stepped into the XO's office. She quickly realized she had stepped into a meeting of the department heads of the ship. "Excuse me, XO. I'm sorry. The chief told me you were in a meeting, and I just didn't listen to him. I'm sorry. I have a leave request that I wanted to give you."

The XO frowned over his reading glasses. He had a hard face that betrayed his complete lack of sympathy. "Emergency leave? Somebody *die*?"

"No, sir, it's ordinary leave. A friend—my boyfriend, I guess . . . is going on trial. He's the one who was involved in that incident in Sudan? The terrorists who died?"

"The one who tortured that poor man to death?" the XO asked.

"I guess that's what they're trying to find out."

"Hell, we ought to give him a medal. We ought to torture every one of those assholes. Maybe that would get their attention. Nothing else seems to. I mean after all, it was just the water board. *I* had to go through that. Damned unpleasant, but it won't kill you—or at least not usually. So you just want to go back to hold your boyfriend's hand?"

"I—I just wanted to be with him. To be there during this very difficult time."

The department heads stared at her, annoyed at having been interrupted.

The XO replied, "It will be a difficult time around here too. We're putting a terrorist on trial ourselves in case you hadn't noticed, and our surgeon has been subpoenaed back to that same trial you want to go to. You're the second-highest-ranking medical person aboard the ship. We can't afford to let you go. Keep your leave application. It's denied."

Andrea couldn't believe it. She had gotten along well with the XO the few times she had been required to deal with him. "Is there any way you could reconsider, sir?"

"No. Now please leave, because we're in the middle of a department head meeting and you just took five minutes of our allotted time."

Andrea nodded and backed toward the door. "I'm sorry to have interrupted you, sir." She closed the door behind her.

The chief was standing right by the door, listening to the entire conversation. He was trying to control the smirk on his face. "Sorry about that. I tried to tell you he was in a meeting, ma'am."

Andrea looked at him with daggers in her eyes, and walked out of the administrative offices. She went straight to her stateroom, closed the door behind her, and folded down her desk. She opened one of the drawers, the one into which she dumped her junk, things that didn't have a home elsewhere in her stateroom: belt buckles, ribbons, officer pins, small notebooks, innumerable things, Brasso, shoe strings, and keys. She dug through the drawer, looking for Skyles's business card. She was sure she had kept his card. She continued to dig and then found it. As she expected, it had his e-mail address on it. One word Satterly had said, that the XO had mentioned, rang in her ears. Subpoena. It was what had gotten Satterly off the ship. She took Satterly's stateroom key from her pocket, and headed to his room to use his computer.

◆　◆　◆

The *Tbilisi* was one of the few cargo ships in the world that sailed under a Georgian flag. It was a rundown small merchant ship of ten thousand tons. In spite of its looks, the steam plant was in remarkably good condition. The *Tbilisi* was able to steam at twelve knots consistently. If pressed, it could maintain eighteen knots for several hours.

The rusty hull and peeling paint on the superstructure went unnoticed among the dozens of other ships of equally poor condition as the *Tbilisi* pulled into Monrovia, Liberia. The ship had made the voyage from Georgia to western Africa very quickly. The containers, which had been loaded at the last minute, and for which twice the usual rate had been paid, sat on deck.

With the help of two tugs, the *Tbilisi* inched up to a pier controlled by the Liberian Shipping Company. The ship had been expected; its arrival was completely unremarkable and barely noticed by even those in the shipyards. The captain knew very little, only that this stop in Monrovia was to off-load three containers, and fifteen "sailors." They didn't look much like able-bodied seamen to him, but who was he to say.

As the ship finally moored and the tugs pulled away, the gangplank came down from the aft third of the ship and the sailors began walking off to explore Monrovia in the short time they would be there; the *Tbi-*

lisi was scheduled to leave that night—the sailors only had twelve hours ashore.

Lisbie looked out his window and watched the crew go ashore. He didn't know why Satti had insisted on getting his fifteen men onto his ship, but he knew it wasn't to learn the finer points of seamanship. He could pick out the men that Satti had forced him to list. They were less sure-footed coming down the gangplank than the true sailors. They hadn't been at sea for years if at all. Their internal balance systems didn't adjust back and forth to walking on a ship's deck and then on shore. They had rubber legs. Lisbie was grateful that they had at least cut their hair and dressed to look like the sailors from the *Tbilisi*.

Lisbie looked at all the people in view, those standing, sitting, leaning against buildings, those in groups working or avoiding work, and those walking away from their docks. He searched them to see if Satti was there to ensure his men had arrived. He was nowhere to be seen. He looked at the rubber-legged group that had walked off the ship that was now gathering out of sight behind a low-slung warehouse. They deferred to one man who was the only one really speaking. Lisbie studied him. He was thin and unremarkable. He looked somehow familiar, but Lisbie was sure he had never met him.

The man Lisbie was looking at, Tayseer Hotary, felt exposed. He wasn't to take his men aboard the Liberian ship until dark, which wasn't for another hour. He didn't want to let his men disperse in the city for fear of trouble that he couldn't foresee. And he didn't want to walk around as a group—too conspicuous. Nor could he stay where he was. Equally conspicuous. Hotary looked around anxiously. He glanced up and caught Lisbie's eye.

Lisbie pulled back from the window with his heart pounding. The man's look had chilled him.

Hotary had seen enough. He had to get his men aboard the ship now. He told the rest of his men to stay put and headed for the decrepit three-story hotel that stood three blocks from where his men were gathered. The paint was peeling off the outside walls in large chunks. He walked into the lobby alone and headed straight for the rickety stairs. He walked up to the third floor without looking right or left, like someone who had walked up those stairs hundreds of times.

He went to the room number that he had memorized and rapped gently on the door. Satti opened the door and Hotary quickly stepped through.

"Is everything ready?" he asked quickly.

Satti replied, "Here are the papers."

"Did you have any trouble?"

Satti didn't want him to know the full details. But he might already know more than he would let on. "Some."

Hotary looked at Satti quickly. "What have you done."

Satti smiled cautiously. "A little C4 in the car of a relative."

Hotary's look hardened. "You have caused unwanted attention."

"I had no choice."

Hotary was furious. "Was there an investigation?" he asked, controlling his voice.

"Yes, a comedy of Liberian police with a few foreigners."

"What foreigners?" Hotary asked.

"Some Americans, I think. They did not wear identification, but my sources inside the police tell me they were FBI."

"Did you not anticipate that?"

Satti's smile faded. "I couldn't imagine anyone being interested in one small event in Monrovia, Liberia. And the director of shipping refused. He absolutely refused. We were not going to get on the ship. I had to take drastic action."

Hotary walked closer to him until their faces were inches apart. "You should have thought of something more creative. Something that would not have drawn attention. I sent you here because I thought you could do it quietly. And you set off a bomb drawing attention from the United States?"

Satti raised his voice, trying not to yell. "What would you have had me do? Beg? Pull out a gun and hold it to his head? What would you have done?"

"I would have been *smarter*."

Satti knew better than to respond anymore. He had already stepped across the line. He knew who "Tayseer Hotary" was. He knew very well. And he knew that no one else had any idea. He changed the subject. He pointed to the packet he had given Hotary. "Your papers will get you aboard the ship. The containers should already have been transferred by now." He checked his watch.

"What time do we sail?"

"High tide. Just before midnight."

"I need to get the men aboard now. They are too conspicuous."

"I'm sure I can arrange that."

Chapter

19

The attendees at the meeting were gathering up their papers and placing items in briefcases, ready to depart. President Kendrick asked casually, "Anything else for the good of the cause?"

St. James hesitated. She had to stop Rathman's trial. She had to stick her neck out for him as he had done so many times for her. In the political world of Washington it was stupid for her to even bring it up. She knew that. But she owed it to Rat to make one last try. "The trial of that Navy lieutenant is set to begin tomorrow, Mr. President."

President Kendrick gave her a tired look. "I know. It's been in the newspapers every day for two weeks. The press is foaming at the mouth. In fact," he chuckled, "did you see that political cartoon in the Washington *Times* yesterday? It showed a new drink at Starbucks; it's called the Journalist. It's nothing *but* foam."

St. James waited for the President to stop chuckling. She asked, "Do we really want to go forward with this trial? Do we really want to air our dirty laundry before the entire world?"

His face grew serious. The others in the room stood silently, wanting no part of the discussion. "Seems to me we already have. Everyone knows he's on trial for torturing a terrorist. What would you suggest we do now? Shut it down *right* before he's given a fair trial? Just dismiss it? What would that say to the world? Sure, he may have tortured somebody, but we don't care?"

St. James sat forward. "No, sir. I think what it would say is that there isn't sufficient evidence to convict him—there was a fight, people were killed and injured—including Americans—but putting someone from Special Operations on trial is inappropriate based on the evidence."

"How could I say that? I don't know what the evidence is. Sounds to me like they may have the evidence. He tortured that man, and he died. We can't be out there torturing people regardless of the reason. We have to maintain the moral high ground. If we're torturing people, what does that say about us?"

"But even if he did what they say he did, which I don't know, all he did was use water to encourage this man to talk—"

"Why are we even discussing this?" Kendrick asked. He glanced at Stuntz, then back at Sarah. "Why do you care? I don't understand why this is so important to you."

Stuntz was enjoying the exchange. "Because he's one of her secret little informants. I think she told you about her little network of people who give her straight—raw as I think she called it—information outside of the usual chains of command or informational routes for intelligence. It was rather successful in allowing her to have some information the rest of us didn't have, or at least more quickly, or at least untainted by experienced minds and senior intelligence operatives. Of course the fact that some of it was inaccurate or biased certainly didn't—"

"I never had any biased or inaccurate information, Mr. President. And I never misused any chain of command or anything else. I resent Secretary Stuntz's implication—"

President Kendrick put up his hand. "I don't want to hear anything more about that. But do you know him?"

"He is an acquaintance. He has risked his life, he has been very successful in numerous missions, and I'm not sure he's getting a fair shake. Perhaps Secretary Stuntz can tell us how he came to be charged in the first place. How it is he had the general counsel of the DOD visit the Attorney General and force him to put Mr. Rathman on trial because the secretary didn't want to court-martial him. Because it might have looked too vindictive of the DOD."

"That's ridiculous," Stuntz said, forcing a chuckle, furious that someone, probably the Attorney General himself, had told St. James about the meeting.

The President considered for a moment. He turned to the Attorney General. "You do have the evidence, I take it."

Carl Dirks, the Attorney General, avoided Stuntz's glare and answered the President. "Yes, sir, I believe so."

"You're not sure?"

"I believe we can prove the case, Mr. President." He wasn't sure which way the political currents were running. "But it will depend on witness cooperation, which is very iffy. This Rathman fellow is very popular. He is popular with the public—as you can see from the public opinion polls, which are behind him only about eighty-three percent. The Europeans of course want to string him up, and the ICC is waiting in the wings.

"But as to the witnesses, I am told that the cooperation of some of the critical witnesses is not assured. We may have to—" the Attorney General looked around the room—"we may have to use a witness who is from a foreign country and subject to code-word control."

"You believe you can get a conviction?"

"Yes, I believe so."

The President continued, "What if you dismissed the case? What would be the implications?"

"Perhaps if we had discussed this when we debated whether to prosecute it might have made some sense. But now, now that it has made it into the newspapers and everyone in the world knows about it, I think to dismiss it now would be disastrous." He saw St. James go red. "It would make us look like we were endorsing the conduct. Plus, if we dismiss it, the ICC will prosecute him."

Kendrick hated the idea of the ICC. "I love that." He smiled. "It might be worth dropping the charges just so we can watch them melt down when we refuse to cooperate." He looked at Sarah St. James. "Well, Sarah, I think your boy is on his own. I hope he has a good lawyer. And if he didn't do anything wrong, then he won't be convicted. Right?"

"That's the theory," she said with deep disappointment. She had tried.

"Anything else?"

No one said a word.

◆   ◆   ◆

The night in Monrovia had turned black and hostile. A mist had begun to fall over the town, dampening the unceasing sounds of the waterfront. It suited Hotary's purposes. Lisbie had balked at Hotary getting aboard early. Satti had yielded rather then force another confrontation. They had waited under the eaves at the warehouse until it was completely dark. Hotary stepped out into the mist and walked away by himself. Two others waited a minute and followed, with one more following them. They walked to their new ship in groups of twos and threes until they were all heading toward the pier.

Hotary wanted to be first aboard to make sure there was no problem with their coming aboard. As he walked down the pier, he noticed how large the ship was that they would be boarding—the M/V *Monrovian Prince*. It was an enormous container ship, a fairly new ship of a new class. Most container ships were large and slab-sided, and needed to load and unload at specific ports that had special cranes that could lift the containers off the ships easily and move them to nearby truck or train facilities. This ship though had its own cranes, two towering steel cranes, one forward and one aft. They could be used to load and unload the containers. This new style of container ship could go to any port in the world and unload its containers—large steel boxes uniform in size and shape.

Hotary studied the containers on the deck. He could see their three containers at the very top in the middle of the ship as their instructions had been. Their containers were indistinguishable from the other containers on the ship, and fit into the space that had been saved for them.

There were three other ships moored at the pier across from the ship they were boarding. Sailors were coming and going in the mist, covering their heads with parkas, newspapers, or nothing at all. No one took notice of Hotary. He went to the gangplank and walked up the slatted walkway quickly. A sailor waited at the top. He stepped out of his covered spot to get in Hotary's way. "What do you want?"

"My name is Tayseer Hotary. I am a new member of the crew."

"Right," the sailor replied bitterly. "One of the fifteen new crew we don't need."

Just then two more of Hotary's men walked up the gangplank and stepped off without incident.

Hotary said, "Show us to our quarters."

The sailor bristled. "You don't give orders on this ship. You don't even tell us what you want. We'll tell you. And if you're crew, you'll do what *I* say. That clear?"

"Quarters," Hotary said as three more of his men arrived.

"Did you hear what I said?"

"Send for the man to show us to our quarters. Now."

"I don't think you heard me. *You* don't give orders."

Hotary stared at him without replying.

The sailor looked down, then back. "Delgadillo will show you. I'll call him," the sailor said.

By the time Delgadillo arrived, all of Hotary's men stood on the quarterdeck. As Delgadillo pointed forward and beckoned them to follow, Hotary stopped and spoke to the sailor. "What is your name?"

"Why?"

"Because when I start issuing orders, I want you to be the first to receive them."

"I look forward to it," the sailor said with a mean smile.

♦　♦　♦

The three days Rat had allotted to race up and down the Dardanelles with James and his magic equipment had passed with no sleep and no results. Ship after ship yelled at them on the radio for approaching too close, and time after time James shook his head. No gamma rays coming from any ship. Beta rays would be harder to find, they both knew, and none were found. At the end of the third day the officer who had procured the boat drove them to Istanbul and Rat flew back to Washington with his jaw clenched to face his trial.

He sat on the couch in his apartment watching ESPN. He had his bare feet up on the coffee table. It was already late and he knew he should be in bed. He needed to be fresh for the trial that started in the morning. He dreaded it. He felt trapped. He had an attorney that he doubted, and had no real argument to get out of the charge, as ridiculous a charge as he thought it was. But the time had arrived, and there was no escape. He had decided to wear his white Navy uniform, his best opportunity to make a good impression on the judge and the jury. He knew if he went to the trial in a civilian suit he would look and feel awkward.

Suddenly there was a loud knock on the door. Rat jumped up from the couch and thought of grabbing the handgun he kept in his apartment. He had been jumpy ever since his name and picture had been in the newspaper as the "Special Forces operative" who was being charged with torturing a terrorist from the Duar network. Rat knew better than anyone that all the people affiliated with Duar were not dead. He was sure he had been on their trail in Georgia, and now they might be on his. Georgia had to be left to others, and Groomer promised to report to him when he returned to the Pankisi gorge once more.

Rat had replaced the cheap hollow door with a solid wooden door for security. He also had two dead-bolt locks on the door. He had gone to substantial effort to install something of a periscope-like peephole in the wall to allow him to see visitors from the side. Rat looked into the peephole and saw Andrea. He smiled. He grabbed the door handle and jerked the door open.

Andrea stood at the door. "You took off your shirt just for me?"

He smiled. "I sure didn't think I'd see you for a while. And not here. How'd you get here?"

"I flew."

He stepped back and motioned for her to come in. "How'd you get off? Take leave?"

"I tried that," she said, setting her purse on the floor and taking off her jacket. "I got subpoenaed."

"By that U.S. Attorney?" he asked, horrified.

"No, by Skyles."

"What for?"

"He said I'd be a good witness and I should come."

"I thought you hated me."

She frowned. "I had to think about it a lot. I still don't know if what you did is exactly the right thing, but I don't like the fact that you could go to jail for it. If the Navy wanted to send you a letter or something, fine. But the Justice Department? A U.S. Attorney? I think you're right. It's political."

He nodded, studying her face. "We're okay?"

She nodded back. "I'm here to help."

"They might actually convict me, you know. I took a look at the witness list. They're calling people who were there. People who saw what happened."

"We'll just have to see what they say."

"I'm not going to prison, Andrea. Not ever."

"Meaning what?" she asked, her face clouding at the thought of him actually being convicted of a crime.

"I would disappear. And believe me, I know how to do that."

She sat next to him on the couch. "Let's think more positively. You're going to get off."

Rat raised his eyebrows once quickly. He wasn't so sure. "I'm glad you're here."

"So am I," she said. "Now. What can I do to help you get ready?"

"What are you going to say when you testify?"

"I'll show you," she said. She bent down and pulled out a handful of pages that she had printed out and brought with her.

◆　◆　◆

Ray Winter, DeLong's fellow CIA officer and his assistant in Monrovia, was in his late twenties and questioned everything. He shook the rain off his poncho, hung it on a hook in the entryway, and headed straight to Bill DeLong's office. DeLong was burning the midnight oil as he did every night. Winter knew he would be there. He knocked smartly on DeLong's door.

DeLong had turned off the overhead light and was operating with only a small desk lamp. The ambassador's instructions to preserve electricity had been very clear. Not so much to save on their electric bill, but because power in Monrovia was often in short supply and they didn't want to be seen as sucking more than their share of electricity from the community grid. The embassy had its own power generators, but they didn't like to use them either as that was perceived as arrogant.

"What's up?" DeLong asked, always happy to see Ray Winter, especially at odd times, which usually meant he had discovered something or had some curiosity that he was pursuing, always worth talking about.

"That car bomb thing."

"What about it?"

"You told me to keep an eye on the dead woman's son—the guy who works at Liberian shipping."

"Right, so?"

"So I, or some of our friends, have been keeping an eye on him ever since." Winter began moving his hands expressively while he spoke. "His name is Thomas Lisbie. Solid guy. Community guy. Never been in trouble, not political, never crosses anybody. But he looks around a lot. It's like he suspects somebody is watching him. I can't imagine that he thinks we're watching him. He's concerned about somebody else. Maybe the same person that whacked his mother. Anyway, he's been very predictable. Never overworks, never stays late, rarely in his office after dark, goes right home, comes right to work, goes out to dinner now and then, but nothing really noteworthy at all. Until tonight."

DeLong nodded to encourage him.

"So tonight, there he is in his office, overlooking the harbor, with the lights burning in his office. One hour, two hours, three hours after sunset. So we're like, what the hell? We start looking around. The only thing significant that happened—this seems bizarre—is a ship came in from the Black Sea. The *Tbilisi*. Pulls in and off-loads three containers, which are immediately put aboard another ship. A large container ship. That in itself is not that unusual. Ships switch containers all the time. But the *really* strange thing, and at first we didn't even notice, but then one of our friends pointed it out to me, fifteen men who got off the *Tbilisi* got on board the other cargo ship, the one where the three containers got moved to. That to me is odd. They waited behind a warehouse until it was dark, then walked to the other ship in groups of two, like they were married. And there's Lisbie, looking over the whole thing, like he's making sure it comes off."

DeLong had been listening intently. "What's the second ship? Where is it going?"

"It's called the *Monrovian Prince*. It's a large container ship and it's headed for Jacksonville, Florida."

DeLong frowned and leaned back, thinking. "What do they want with a large container ship?"

"Depends on what's in the containers. What if there's a nuke in there? Or . . . smallpox or anthrax?"

"Possible, but where would they get those?" He sat forward quickly. "And who is doing this? Whose containers are they? If they came off the *Tbilisi* are they Georgian?" His mind was racing, trying to correlate everything he had seen over the last two weeks in secret message traffic, terrorist warnings, alerts, hunches, and opinions of those in Washington he respected. "Not up to us to know everything. That's Langley's job. Get this off to Washington right away. They may have some other pieces of this puzzle."

"You want to look at the message before I send it off?"

DeLong nodded. "Get it to me in fifteen minutes."

♦ ♦ ♦

The Navy officers aboard the *Belleau Wood* had spent countless hours in the officers' mess discussing the difficulty of proving the case against Duar and watching Elizabeth Watson sitting by herself reviewing documents or notebooks full of something or other. They watched as her face grew clouded from the crushing burden on her shoulders.

As she pulled the chair back and sat at the counsel table her face still showed the burden they perceived. That night, like several before it, she had lain awake terrified of losing the case and watching Wahamed Duar go free. She visualized him demanding a helicopter from the United States to take him back to his home in Sudan. He would return a conquering hero. And if the images of the trial—the Kangaroo Trial as many countries were calling it—were absent from television, the images of Duar stepping off an American helicopter in triumph would be everywhere.

The judge and the court were seated. The rest of the room followed.

Judge Graham looked at Elizabeth. "Call your first witness."

Elizabeth stood, looked to the back of the wardroom where a wooden door was closed, and said, "The United States calls Suzanne Parks."

A first-class petty officer in his dress white uniform opened the door and bellowed into the passageway, "Suzanne Parks!"

A short woman in a pantsuit walked briskly into the courtroom carrying a file. She walked between the counsel tables and to the witness chair, which sat on an elevated platform to the right of the judge.

Elizabeth stood at the lectern. She opened her notebook. "Would you please tell the court where you're employed?"

Parks had her hair bound behind her with a clip. She appeared intelligent and energetic. She exuded confidence. "My name is Suzanne Parks. I'm employed by the Central Intelligence Agency in counterterrorism."

The crowd muttered and the journalists scribbled. They were surprised that someone would admit to being employed by the CIA, a prohibition that had long since been abandoned by the Agency, and that a counterterrorism expert would come out of the shadows and actually testify in court. They all took it as a sign of how serious the United States was about this trial and the extent to which they would go to get a conviction.

"How long have you been employed by the Agency?"

"Approximately ten years."

"Would you summarize your educational background, please?"

She did.

"As part of your job, have you had an opportunity to study the operations of Wahamed Duar?"

"I have been studying his operations and his organization for years."

Elizabeth paused, then continued. "How does one study the operations of an organization of someone who doesn't want their operation and organization to be studied? I don't suppose that, for example, Mr. Duar published an annual report that describes his operations in a brochure with photographs."

Stern rose. "Objection, Your Honor. Counsel's question is argumentative and attempts to testify instead of asking the witness for testimony."

"Overruled," the judge said. "You may answer the question."

Parks nodded in response to the judge's instruction. "Sure, it's not easy. But it's not that difficult sometimes. Mr. Duar for example was rather easy to trace in some regards and rather difficult in others. We have been able to track many of his financial dealings for example, and have attached—frozen—some of his assets and bank accounts around the world. But tracking him personally was much more difficult."

"Apparently someone was able to track him, as he was captured in the country of Sudan."

Stern rose. "Objection, leading. Additionally, Your Honor, whether it was Wahamed Duar who was captured in Sudan is one of the fundamental issues in this trial. It cannot simply be asserted as fact by counsel, when there is currently *no* proof before this court that Wahamed Duar was captured anywhere, let alone Sudan."

"Sustained. Please rephrase, Counsel."

"Let's get down to the basics. How do you know that the person you have been following is Wahamed Duar?"

"We have a photograph."

"Did you bring a copy of that photograph with you?"

Parks opened the file she had brought and pulled out an eight by ten photograph. "Yes I did. Here it is."

Elizabeth nodded. "Your Honor, a copy of that photograph has been premarked as Exhibit One."

"Very well. Are you offering it into evidence?"

"Yes, Your Honor."

"Any objection?"

"Yes, Your Honor. There's no foundation for this photograph. I have no idea what it is a photograph of, or where it came from, or what it purports to represent. We don't know—yet, anyway—who took it, when, or where. Nor is there any testimony that it hasn't been modified or tampered with. Until then, I would ask that Counsel be instructed to refrain from calling that a photograph of Wahamed Duar, whoever he is."

"This photograph was taken—"

"Just a minute," the judge said. "Commander Watson, do you intend to lay the foundation for this photograph through this witness? If so, please do so before asking her any further questions about its content."

"Yes, Your Honor. Ms. Parks, can you identify this photograph?"

"Yes. It was taken by a CIA employee. It is of Wahamed Duar when he was last seen in public in Khartoum," Parks replied.

"Move to strike, Your Honor," Stern protested. "Her testimony is hearsay. She is simply repeating what she has been told. She cannot authenticate the photograph herself."

Watson asked, "Ms. Parks, were you present when this photograph was taken?"

Parks hesitated. Watson had told her she would avoid asking if at all possible. "Yes, I was."

Stern sat down, surprised. The gallery was equally surprised. They tried to envision this bubbly American in a pantsuit in Khartoum, taking a photograph of a terrorist who had never been photographed before or since.

"How did you come to be in Khartoum?"

"I'm afraid I can't go into it. It was on Agency business, and I cannot disclose the details."

"Did you take the photograph?"

"I did not."

"Does the photograph fairly and accurately represent what it purports to be?"

"It does."

"Did you personally see the man who was photographed?"

"Yes."

"Did you see the person take the photograph that is Exhibit One?"

"I did."

"Has it been modified or changed in any way since it was developed?"

"No."

"Why is it so grainy?"

"It was taken at night." She considered how much to reveal. "Without a flash. With very high-speed film."

"I offer Exhibit One into evidence, Your Honor."

"Exhibit One will be admitted," the judge said.

Watson lowered her voice. "Do you see the man in this courtroom who is in that photograph?"

"Objection," Stern said. "It's just her—"

"Overruled."

Parks looked at the judge, then said, "Yes. He is sitting at the defense table."

"In your work following the operation and organization of Duar, what did you find? What, in other words, were his operations and what was the nature of his organization?"

"Objection, compound."

"Overruled."

"Duar has been attacking American interests and threatening the United States for years. He apparently believes that we are responsible for everything evil in the world. He has declared repeatedly his intention to attack the United States, and has done so. We have attributed five terrorist attacks to his organization against Americans and American interests."

"Resulting in how many deaths?"

"One hundred twenty-three."

"How do you know it was his organization that was involved in those attacks?"

"He said so."

"Don't you find that sometimes certain organizations claim responsibility for a particular attack when in fact they had nothing to do with it?"

"Not anymore. They know that if they claim responsibility for an attack, we will come and get them. People are much less likely to do that for something they didn't do than they used to be."

"Would you summarize for us the terrorist attacks that Duar is being charged with perpetrating against the United States, and the evidence you have that he was responsible?"

She did, at great length. She showed photographs of the scenes, autopsy photographs, destruction, and death. She made sure everyone in the room, including the journalists, were horrified. She wanted to show Wahamed Duar for what he was—a brutal killer. She reluctantly produced transcripts of cell phone calls by Duar to members of his family, and to his lieutenants. She told of the attack on the U.S. embassy in Cairo in tremendous, conclusive detail.

"But how do you know it was Duar?"

"Here are the faxes that were sent claiming responsibility for those very attacks. They were sent to a newspaper in London, and I obtained copies. The newspaper will not publish claims unless it authenticates them from the source. That was true of bin Laden, and it is true of Duar. These were authenticated by the paper's private sources."

"Objection, hearsay!" Stern protested.

Graham looked at Stern. "Mr. Stern, you have read the rules of the tribunal. The rules of evidence are relaxed. Hearsay is admissible if it is otherwise reliable. You know that. Your objection is overruled."

"Your Honor, I'd like to offer these faxes as Exhibits Seventeen, Eighteen, and Nineteen," Watson requested.

"They will be admitted."

Stern shook his head and sat down.

Watson turned to look at Stern triumphantly. "Your witness."

Chapter 20

The South Atlantic was as gray as the sky. The whitecaps broke all around the M/V *Monrovian Prince* as a light rain began to fall, driven sideways by the steady wind. Tayseer Hotary stepped onto the bridge silently. The captain drank deeply from his oversized coffee mug and stared to the west through the thick bridge windows. The captain turned and frowned, seeing Hotary. "What do you want?" he asked angrily.

Hotary stood silently.

"I don't know how you convinced my company to list you and your men as crew. We don't need you; you're in the way."

Hotary walked closer to the captain in a menacing way. "Actually it is you that is in the way. Not me."

The helmsman and the others on the bridge watched carefully. They had never heard anyone speak to the captain like that.

Hotary said, "I notice our speed is eight knots."

The captain looked at the shaft RPM. "Approximately."

"Increase your speed to twelve knots."

The captain stared at him in disbelief. "We are to arrive in port on a specific date at a specific time. We calculate the time to get there based on the most efficient speed of the ship, to burn the least amount of oil. That speed, which will put us in port on time, is eight knots. Not twelve."

"Increase your speed to twelve knots."

"Why the hell should I?"

"Because I said so."

"That's not good enough for me. This ship will arrive on time. We will do so by transiting the Atlantic at eight knots."

Hotary stared out the window at the complete grayness. He stared for two minutes without speaking. The captain finally directed his attention elsewhere.

Hotary spoke. "Please get on your radio and speak with Mr. Lisbie, your director of operations. Ask him whether you should follow my directions or not."

"I don't need Mr. Lisbie to tell me how to run my ship."

"Ask him."

The captain considered. Reluctantly he crossed to the back of the bridge, and picked up the radio handset.

♦ ♦ ♦

Rat sat at the large table full of members of the counterterrorism team at Langley. They had all made it there by 0600, the time Jacobs wanted to start the meeting due to Rat's trial. Don Jacobs was at the head of the table and nodded at Rat as he sat down. It was the first such meeting he had been invited to. Rat's pursuit of the Duar organization into Georgia after Sudan had gotten a lot of attention, initially because it was thought he was freelancing too much, but then because it had become obvious that he was on to something and had identified a warm trail with the help of John Johnson of the NSA. Rat had kept Jacobs informed of every step, of every theory he had, and had found him receptive and impressed. Jacobs didn't care where the information or solution came from, he just cared about results.

People stared at Rat in his whites as he sat at the table. Very few of them had even had a conversation with a member of the military. They regarded him with curiosity. They all knew about his trial, and had seen his picture everywhere. But to see him in person was somehow more impressive and interesting. They couldn't take their eyes off him.

Rat was much less concerned about how he looked than how Jacobs looked. He looked as if he had lost weight; his skin had grown gray and pale. He usually punctuated meetings and conversations with humor and kidding, but that had been missing for about two weeks.

Rat noticed the bulge in Jacobs's shirt pocket. He thought he could read "Marlboro" through the fabric. Jacobs had smoked years before but no one in the room had ever seen him smoke. Some thought Jacobs had called this early morning meeting to announce his resignation. They all waited expectantly.

"Thank you all for coming in this early. I expect to have a full day. We have a situation developing that is frankly keeping me up all night. I think I've been missing something. It wasn't until I talked to Rat yesterday that I got that cold feeling in my stomach. I wanted you to hear what he has to say. He has a rather busy day ahead of him, as we all know, but I wanted him to tell you what he is thinking. Rat?"

Rat stood and went to the head of the table. Jacobs moved his chair around to the side so he could watch. "Thanks," Rat said. "Since we captured Duar in Sudan he has been in custody aboard the *Belleau Wood*. You all know that. He has taken one short vacation during that time—to Egypt—but otherwise has been in custody. Some people, myself included, think that while we may have gotten the head of the snake, the body is still intact. Somehow his organization is still operating. In the files in front of you are the intercepted e-mails that the NSA believes are from his organization. John Johnson gave them to us. He has tracked the servers to Sudan and Georgia. As you've probably heard, I was in Georgia at the request of the Georgians to supplement the Green Berets who have been sent there to train them to help them clean out the Pankisi gorge. But they asked for me because they had heard that Duar's people had fled to Georgia and were operating out of there.

"Then we learn that nuclear cores from old Russian RTGs had disappeared and you start to see Duar's fingerprints everywhere.

"I thought they would try to get the cores out of the country by ship, and went to the Dardanelles to try to intercept the ship or at least identify it. But we were probably too late. They had too much of a head start. Either they left by air, earlier by ship, or are still in Georgia. I think I just missed them. I think a ship made it out of the Black Sea and into the Mediterranean undetected."

"We know all that," Shauna Smiley said from the other end of the table.

Rat glanced at her. "I'm sorry. I don't think I know you."

"Shauna Smiley. Intelligence."

Intelligence, as in the Directorate of Intelligence, *not* the Directorate of Operations. An analyst, not an operator. But Rat never considered it a possibility that she was an operator. She continued to give him a look of disrespect or judgment. "I think they have several nuclear cores, probably put them on a ship, and are headed for the United States. The thing that put it together for me yesterday, and the reason I went to Don with this, was I got a look at the report on the car bombing in Monrovia. I mean why Liberia? But the FBI report confirmed the early CIA initial impressions that it was military grade C4 and was intended to kill the driver. It was brought off with tremendous precision probably above the skill level of any Liberian anarchist or revolutionary. Somebody else was at work, somebody who was well trained with explosives. And someone who was able to get military-quality C4. The woman was the mother of the director of shipping operations of the Liberian International Shipping Company.

"Russell told me about some new information," he said, glancing at Russell Edwards, who nodded. "Yesterday, a Georgian ship pulled in to Liberia and transferred three containers and fifteen men to a Liberian ship headed for the United States.

"The last piece of information was obtained just this morning. A radio call was intercepted from a ship in the South Atlantic to the Liberian International Shipping Company. It was in the clear and was from the captain to Lisbie. The captain asked a very strange question. He asked Lisbie if he had to follow the directions of the new crew."

Jacobs looked at the faces of those around the table. They were all coming to the same conclusion he had already drawn.

"What did Lisbie say?" Shauna asked.

"He said the captain was to do whatever they told him. The transcript is in your folders."

She opened the file for the first time and flipped through it. "What did the captain say?"

"'Roger, out.'"

"Did we get a position on this ship?"

"The latitude and longitude are in the message."

Everybody waited. Rat went on. "I think the nuclear cores are aboard that container ship. It's called the *Monrovian Prince.* Her scheduled port of call is Jacksonville. Mr. Jacobs thinks this needs to go up the flagpole right away. Today." He looked to his left at Jacobs. "He wanted all of you to hear about it before he sent this on. Anybody see any holes? Any stupid thinking?"

They sat in stunned silence.

Jacobs stood. "We're going to brief the President on this. The Director wants him to know today."

Rat nodded.

Jacobs continued. "I told him you were just the guy to do that."

Rat couldn't believe it. "Do what?"

"I want you to brief the President. At the White House."

"I'm kind of occupied today."

"That's why I set the brief up at the White House for twelve-thirty. A car will pick you up in front of Justice at noon."

"I won't have any time to prepare."

"We'll get you some help."

Rat considered how he was going to keep from making a fool of himself in front of the President of the United States. "Maybe Russell could help. He seems to be up on this."

"Great idea."

◆ ◆ ◆

Everyone was in place in the packed courtroom on the top floor of the Justice Department. The jury had been sworn in and was waiting outside the courtroom to be summoned by the judge. Witnesses were excluded until they testified. Judge Royce Wiggins entered the courtroom from the back door fuming. He had pushed his reading glasses so high up on his nose that he could barely see over them. His jaw was clenched as the bailiff called the court to order and he sat down in the black leather chair behind the elevated bench. He waited, looked at the attorneys, and then spoke to Skyles. "Mr. Skyles, stand up."

The gallery sat up straight and strained to see Skyles. They were enthusiastic about drama this early in the trial.

Skyles stood up with a questioning look on his face. He hadn't yet done anything in this trial that he thought deserved a lecture. He had some things in mind, but Wiggins didn't know that yet. "Yes, sir?"

The judge held up a single sheet of paper. He looked directly at Skyles, putting his head down at an awkward angle in order to look out over his reading glasses. "Is this your idea of how to undercut this court? Is this your idea of how to avoid putting your client before this court, to try this case?"

Skyles had no idea what the judge was talking about. "I'm sorry, Your Honor . . . I really don't know what you have there . . ." he said, probing, watching for holes in the ice. "Is it something that I have filed or submitted?"

"Do you claim to be ignorant of this?" the judge asked, holding up the piece of paper.

"If Your Honor might tell me what 'this' is, I might be able to say."

The judge looked disgusted. "I received a fax this morning from a woman, a commander, who claims to be the prosecutor in the tribunal aboard the *Belleau Wood*. They have suddenly determined that your client is an indispensable witness for that trial. The fax said that his testimony is needed to identify the defendant as he was the one who in fact captured him. Did they just learn this information today? And now they have to have him for their trial, which as we all know since we all read the newspapers, is going on at the same time as Mr. Rathman's trial. Are you aware of this?"

"Your Honor, I am not aware of that fax. I was notified this morning by my client that he had been served with a subpoena at his house at 5:00 A.M. I did not know that the attorney who subpoenaed him also wrote to Your Honor."

Judge Wiggins didn't believe him. "In the last paragraph of the letter she confirms that she knows that this trial is ongoing and Mr. Rathman is the defendant. She asks that we continue his trial until he can get out to the *Belleau Wood* and testify in the tribunal." He looked at Skyles. "This is classic Skyles, from what I hear. It feels to me like one of your tricks, sir."

Skyles's face reddened. "Your Honor, I think that's unfair. I resent the implication that I participate in trickery—"

"Please, Mr. Skyles. Do not deny what everyone in the Washington bar knows. You are notorious for gamesmanship and trickery during trial. Do you deny it?"

"I absolutely deny it. I represent my clients vigorously. I have never tried a case in front of you and I'm now very concerned that you have brought into this courtroom a prejudice against me that you will hold against my client."

"I'm not biased against anyone," the judge roared. "I just believe that a leopard never changes its spots. Attorneys that practice law by gamesmanship don't change, and you don't develop a reputation in Washington for practicing that way unless there's some truth to it."

Skyles couldn't believe it. "Your Honor, if in fact you have heard such rumors, I think you owe it to me and my client to not prejudge, and to make your own decision on whether I'm behaving properly or not. That is all I would ask of you."

"And that's what you'll get. So tell me directly, did you know this fax was coming, and did you have any part in its being sent to me?"

"I *did* tell you directly, Your Honor. I had no idea it was coming, I have never seen it, I did not get a copy of it, and I had no role whatsoever in its being written, sent, or received."

"Very well," the judge said with a sarcastic smile on his face. "Then you have no opposition to my ignoring the fax. I want you to know that I'm *not* continuing this trial under any circumstances. We're going forward. Do you understand that?"

"Yes, sir, I do understand that. My client has been subpoenaed though, and I believe it is a legitimate subpoena issued by the United States Government. I'm therefore not sure that *he* can simply ignore it as you intend to do with the fax."

"I'm not going to ignore the fax, Mr. Skyles. I resent the implication of that remark—"

"I apologize, Your Honor, I thought that's what you just said."

"It is *not* what I just said. Do you want me to have the court reporter read back what I just said?"

Skyles fought to control his facial expressions. "No, Your Honor, that won't be necessary. My mistake."

"Your client can do whatever he wants with his subpoena. But he had better be here for this trial."

"Yes, sir. He will be here as . . . appropriate."

Judge Wiggins stared at Skyles to see if there was evasion in his eyes. He turned to the prosecutor. "Mr. Wolff."

Wolff stood up slowly as Skyles sat down. Wolff was enjoying the morning so far. "Yes, sir."

"Are you ready to proceed?"

"Yes, Your Honor."

"Bring in the jury."

They filed in through the door and sat in the jury box that had never before been used. No case had ever been tried in the courtroom on top of the Justice Building, just the secret hearings on whether requested government surveillance was going to be allowed on unsuspecting people who were alleged to have ties to foreign intelligence or operations. They sat in the box and glanced at Rat. They had been anxious to see him. They had heard enough during the jury selection process and read enough in the newspapers to know the trial was going to be interesting and had to do with torture. They knew the defendant was something of a Special Operations legend, and thought he looked composed and intelligent.

They let their eyes linger on Rat. They wanted to know what made him tick. As Wolff rose to give his opening statement, they gave him their attention, but kept an eye on Lieutenant Rathman, watching for his reaction.

Wolff began his opening statement predictably: outrage and offense at the idea of American Armed Forces or intelligence special operatives being allowed to torture other human beings. He continued, "To allow such conduct would make us like those we were fighting. The law has been clear for as long as the United States has been in existence—prisoners are treated as human beings; prisoners are not to be killed, or tortured, or mistreated. Such an understanding had been confirmed in the treaty called the Geneva Convention that was ratified—"

"Objection," Skyles cried, holding his hands out in shocked disbelief. "The Geneva Convention has nothing to do with this case, Your Honor! This case is about manslaughter. That's all. I—"

"Sustained," Judge Wiggins said. "Mr. Wolff, please limit your comments to the case before the court."

"Yes, sir," he said. "Lieutenant Kent Rathman, an active duty naval officer and a cowboy of a Special Operations operative, has violated the letter and the spirit of the law, but is not being charged with a violation of the Geneva Convention." He paused. "His charge is manslaughter—the wrongful, or negligent, killing of another. He knew that torturing the man that died was wrong." He looked at the jurors. "And he did it anyway.

"The evidence will show that Rathman intentionally tortured a man by the name of Mazmin. He tortured him by pouring water into his mouth and nose until he couldn't breathe—until he sucked the water into his lungs and stomach, until he fought desperately for breath and ultimately vomited and sucked the vomit into his lungs." Wolff looked outraged. "Mr. Rathman saw it all. He was poised over Mazmin, who was being held down by other CIA operatives. The vomit caused a raging infection that the best medicine and a naval surgeon couldn't stop. At the conclusion of the evidence there will be no doubt that Kent Rathman is guilty as charged." He looked at each juror to convey his seriousness and assess theirs, then sat down. His dark suit hid the perspiration under his arms.

Judge Wiggins looked at the jury. "Counsel for the defendant has chosen to defer his opening statement." The jury looked confused. They couldn't imagine why it would be to the advantage of the defendant to wait to tell them his side of the story but they were willing to wait. "Mr. Wolff, call your first witness."

"Thank you, Your Honor. United States calls Captain Tim Satterly."

Satterly walked into the courtroom quickly, with authority. He tried to control the look of triumph and enthusiasm on his face.

Rat watched him walk to the front of the courtroom. He could tell Satterly was proud of the four stripes on his uniform, the uniform of a

Navy captain; much more impressive than the two stripes on Rat's shoulder boards. But Rat had little regard for restricted line officers, the lawyers, the doctors, the supply pukes that made up the support structure of the Navy. They weren't unrestricted line officers and didn't have warfare specialties; they couldn't command anything or anyone in combat. He wished he could explain the difference to the jury.

Dr. Tim Satterly looked around the courtroom, impressed by the security, the mahogany, and the integrity of the court that he knew would, with his help, convict Kent Rathman and sentence him to prison. He looked at Rathman and tried not to frown. He also did not look away. He could tell that Rathman wanted to rip his heart out, but he knew Rathman couldn't touch him. He was going to be held accountable for what he had done, and Satterly thought that was appropriate and necessary.

He climbed into the witness stand and sat down. He was sworn in. After asking him preliminary questions, Wolff got right to the point. "Dr. Satterly, you were the head surgeon on the *Belleau Wood* when Wahamed Duar was captured. Correct?"

"That's right," Satterly said proudly.

"The individuals who participated in the raid did not launch from the *Belleau Wood*, did they?"

"No, they did not."

"So you had never met Lieutenant Kent Rathman, also known as Rat, before their raid was concluded. Is that right?"

"That's correct."

"Had you formed any opinion about Kent Rathman in some way other than meeting him before the raid?"

"No. I had never heard of him."

"Do you remember the day the raid occurred?"

"Very well." Satterly was trying to look extremely serious. Rat thought he just looked mean and vindictive.

"Were you on the *Belleau Wood* when the raiding team came aboard after the raid with two prisoners?"

Skyles jumped in. "Prisoners? I object, Your Honor! They were *not* prisoners, and not entitled to any protection afforded a prisoner. That is one of the ultimate questions for the jury. They were captured terrorists."

"Overruled."

"Did you personally see and examine the two prisoners?"

"Yes, I did."

"Do you remember a gentleman by the name of Mazmin?"

Skyles leaped to his feet. "Your Honor, I object to a mass murdering terrorist being called a gentleman. That is argumentative. If he wants to ask a question like 'Do you remember the mass murderer named Mazmin—' "

The judge showed his teeth in a barely restrained attempt to control his anger. "Mr. Skyles, if you have an objection, make it. I don't want to hear any speeches and argument through objection."

Skyles replied, "Very well then. Objection, argumentative."

"Overruled."

Wolff looked at Satterly. "You may answer the question."

"Yes, I do remember the gentleman named Mr. Mazmin very well."

"How did you first encounter him?"

"He was one of the two men captured in the raid. They brought him down to sick bay because he was not feeling well."

"Did you treat him aboard the *Belleau Wood*?"

"Yes, we did. I was in charge of his treatment."

"I take it ultimately he died. Is that right?"

Satterly nodded. "I'm afraid so."

"What did he die from?"

"Pneumonia."

"Was that unusual?"

"You see pneumonia now and then, but it is unusual to have such a raging case that kills you so quickly, and from vomit in the upper lobes."

"How do you know he died from pneumonia?"

Satterly sat up straighter in the chair. "After his death I performed an autopsy. I found terribly infected lungs, with food particles in his lungs."

"What conclusion did you draw from the foreign objects in his lungs?"

"That the infection was probably caused by vomiting that was then aspirated, breathed into his lungs."

"Have you ever seen anything like that before?" Wolff asked.

"I've seen people aspirate vomit before, but never like this, never with a huge volume of water, and an immediate infection in the upper lobes. I think the food had been recently consumed and carried some aggressive bacteria directly into his lungs."

"Do you have an opinion as to how someone could have food in his lungs?"

Skyles rose quickly. "Objection, Your Honor! This calls for expert witness testimony. United States has not designated any experts for medical opinions on the cause of death of *Mr. Mazmin.*"

"Overruled."

"But—"

"Overruled!"

Skyles sat down in apparent frustration.

"What is your opinion?" Wolff asked.

"It would take just the right combination of vomiting and angle and desperate breathing to force the food down into the lungs. You might see it in someone who has consumed too much alcohol and drowns in his own vomit, although his breathing would probably be shallow, not the desperate breathing of someone who is being deprived of his life's breath. This food was throughout his lungs. He was gasping for breath. Other than that, I can't imagine how you would do it . . . other than how Mr. Rathman did it to Mr. Mazmin."

As Skyles rose the judge ruled without him. "Strike the last sentence of his testimony." Judge Graham turned to the jury. "You will ignore his last sentence."

"Did you have an opportunity to speak with Mr. Mazmin before he died?"

"I did," Satterly said quietly, to make sure everyone in the room knew they were now getting to the heart of his testimony. "Several times."

"What did he tell you?"

"Objection! Hearsay." Skyles said from his chair.

"Sustained."

Wolff looked up at the judge, surprised, as if every ruling was sup-posed to be in his favor. "These are dying declarations, Your Honor."

"Then lay a foundation that the witness was dying, and we'll see about the hearsay."

"When Mr. Mazmin said these things to you, what was his condi-tion?"

Satterly had picked up on the judge's hint. "He was in deep distress. He had a temperature of a hundred and four. His pneumonia was bad, and he was declining. When he confirmed these things to me, he was clearly dying, and knew it. He knew it because I told him so. The last time he told me these things was about two hours before his death."

"Would you say that he told you these things when he was dying?"

"Without a doubt."

"What did he tell you?"

Satterly looked at Rat and paused for several seconds. He looked back at Wolff. "He told me that he had been tortured. He had been forced to lie down on a table on the floor. Several men pinned him down and water was poured into his nose and mouth until he couldn't breathe. When he tried to breathe he inhaled the water. He'd put so much water in his stomach that he threw up and sucked the food into his lungs with more water. He said he had never been more scared in his life. He was literally drowning."

"Did he say who had done this to him?"

"He did. He said it was the man who was in charge of the assault squad. An American. An American who spoke Arabic."

"Did you ever confirm who was that American who spoke Arabic and who led the attack squad?"

"Yes. I asked some of the squad members which of them spoke Ara-bic. They said only one did. Their leader. Lieutenant Kent Rathman."

"Do you see Lieutenant Rathman?"

Satterly extended his arm and pointed at Rathman. "That's him, there. At the defense table."

Rat stared at him with violence in his eyes.

Wolff paused and appeared to ponder for a minute. "Just one last thing, Dr. Satterly. Did you ever have an opportunity to confront Lieu-tenant Rathman with this accusation that Mr. Mazmin was making?"

"I did. After Mazmin told me this, I was outraged. I went immediately to the wardroom, where Lieutenant Rathman was eating breakfast after torturing Mr. Mazmin in Sudan. I walked into the wardroom and probably made too much of a scene of it, but I wanted to ask Mr. Rathman what he had done. I confronted him and accused him of torturing Mazmin. I did it in front of the entire wardroom, in front of the captain of the ship." Satterly was clearly pleased with himself.

"What did Mr. Rathman say when you confronted him?"

"He didn't say anything at all. He just stared at me." He glanced at Rat. "Just like he is now."

"Thank you, Dr. Satterly. Thank you for coming all this way. I have no further questions."

Skyles shot up and moved to the podium without any notes. He began firing immediately. "Shall I call you Doctor?"

Satterly was a little confused. "Or Captain. Either one."

"No, no, my question was really about whether doctors of osteopathy are entitled to be called doctors."

Satterly blushed in anger. "Of course they are."

"But you're not a medical doctor, with an M.D., are you?"

"No. They are allopathic doctors; I'm a doctor of osteopathy. I can explain the differences if you'd like."

"You wanted to be an M.D. though. Am I right?"

"That would have been fine, but I am quite happy as I am."

"Do you mean to imply to the jury that you did not apply to regular medical schools?"

"What is the possible relevance of this line of inquiry?" Wolff asked.

The judge was also concerned. "The relevance, Counsel?"

"Mr. Wolff offered Dr. Satterly as an *expert* on the cause of pneumonia and the timing of the terrorist's death. I'm entitled to examine his qualifications."

"Overruled. Continue."

"Did you or did you not apply to regular medical schools from which you would have received an M.D. degree?"

"I did," Satterly said angrily.

"But you didn't *get into* any of those medical schools, did you?"

"No."

"So you didn't even have the chance to finish in the bottom half of a medical school class, did you? You couldn't even get in."

Satterly's face was flushed. "I am not ashamed of my education as a doctor of osteopathic medicine."

Skyles knew he had scored. Satterly was getting defensive. "Your testimony was very convincing that Mr. Mazmin had a very high fever and was near death *every time* he spoke to you." Skyles paused and looked at Satterly hard. "Do you want to change any of that testimony?"

"No."

"Did you meet with Mr. Wolff before your testimony here this morning?"

"Briefly."

"How many times?"

"I don't know, perhaps three."

"Did he tell you that in order for Mazmin's statements to come into evidence he had to be *dying* and aware of the fact he was dying?"

"He mentioned something about it."

"You changed your testimony to portray every statement he made during the entire three days he was aboard the *Belleau Wood* as being near death. Right?"

"No. I did not revise anything. I've told it to you exactly as it was."

"So you were completely accurate when you told us he had a hundred-and-four-degree fever on the first day you saw him and his condition declined from there. Correct?"

"Correct."

Skyles waited, watching Satterly's face to make sure he was quite relaxed and confident; sure he was beating Skyles in their preliminary duel. "Infections that are out of control—like his pneumonia—are accompanied by a high and increasing fever. Correct?"

"Yes."

"And Mazmin's medical condition was deteriorating from the time you first saw him. Correct?"

"That's true." Satterly couldn't figure out what Skyles was getting at. He seemed to be lining his own coffin.

"Fevers often cause delirium and confusion. Correct?"

Satterly now saw where Skyles was heading. "Sometimes."

"And delirium can have people state with perfect clarity things that are untrue or impossible. Correct?"

"That can happen," Satterly said, trying diligently to backtrack on the sand on which he was now standing.

"And that's what happened to Mazmin, isn't it? He was delirious from a high and raging fever, that ultimately led to his death. Correct?"

"No. He was lucid when I spoke with him."

"The whole time? From the time you first saw him with a temperature of a hundred and four, until he died of a raging infection and fever? He was lucid?"

"Yes."

"So a man who died of fever and infection was *completely* lucid the entire last three days of his life while he was, as you have said under oath, dying. Is that your testimony?"

"Yes."

Skyles saw the skeptical faces of the jurors who were beginning not to like Satterly. He knew that juries always give the benefit of the doubt to doctors. They generally admired doctors. But if the doctor begins to look arrogant or dumb a jury will turn on him. Skyles went on to his next line of inquiry. "You don't like Lieutenant Rathman, do you?"

"I don't really know him."

"You don't even like what he stands for, do you? You think he's a cowboy, a Special Forces operator who is given too much freedom of action. Isn't that your opinion?"

"I don't know enough to say."

"You are *outraged* by the idea of an American torturing a terrorist, aren't you?"

"I do find his behavior outrageous. Yes."

"But everything you know about this alleged behavior you learned from a mass murdering terrorist who had a fever of a hundred and four or more. Correct?"

"I don't know if he was a mass murdering terrorist."

"You don't?"

"No."

"You have access to the Internet onboard your ship, don't you?"

"Yes."

"You never typed 'Mazmin' into Google?"

"No, I didn't."

"Really? I mean it's a fairly discrete word."

"Really."

Skyles looked surprised. He actually wanted one of the jurors to go home and look him up on the Internet. The jurors were instructed not to do their own research, not to discover facts on their own, but he thought there might be one who would just take a peek. "So the man you accuse, and that you flew halfway around the world to testify against, you know about only through the mouth of a terrorist, whom you apparently believe uncritically. Is that right?"

"If you want to put it that way," Satterly said.

"Did it never occur to you that perhaps the mass murdering terrorist was *lying* to you? Trying to get the American in trouble with his own people?"

"No. He was frightened. He had clearly been through trauma. He had been tortured."

Skyles put his hands in the worn pockets of his suit pants. "You are out to get Mr. Rathman, aren't you?"

"No. I have no personal stake in this matter."

"You deny it?"

Satterly felt pressed. He didn't know what Skyles had. "I do," he said weakly.

Skyles waited for a moment, until every eye in the courtroom was on him. "Have you ever heard of the ICC, the International Criminal Court?"

"Yes."

"You are a supporter of the ICC, aren't you?"

"I don't think it's a radical idea—people should be held responsible for war crimes, crimes against humanity, genocide."

"But the U.S. never signed the treaty establishing the ICC. In fact opposed it. Right?"

"Yes."

"And you disagreed with that. Didn't you?"

"Objection," Wolff said. "What's the relevance of this?"

"Your Honor, that will be clear in less than a minute."

"Continue," Judge Graham said.

"You disagreed with the U.S.'s position. Didn't you?"

"Yes."

"And when you heard from *Mister* Mazmin what Lieutenant Rathman had supposedly done, at least according to that mass murdering terrorist—"

"Your Honor—" Wolff protested.

"I withdraw the last part of that sentence, Your Honor," Skyles said, anticipating the judge's ruling.

Skyles lowered his voice. "After talking to Mazmin, you sent an e-mail to the ICC and told them about Rathman. Didn't you? You wanted him to be charged with a war crime and tried in an international court, right?"

Everyone in the courtroom waited in a hushed silence for Satterly's reply.

"How do you know about that?" Satterly asked, red-faced.

"Answer the question," Skyles said loudly.

"I have a friend who is involved in the ICC. I didn't have any expectations of him doing anything in particular about it."

Skyles smiled, then the smile faded. "You thought he would want to know because you considered Mr. Rathman's conduct egregious. On the level of a war crime. Right?"

"It was a violation of human rights and a violation of a treaty. The Geneva Convention. I thought they would want to know."

"You told them before you even told any American authorities?"

"Yes."

"The ICC only has jurisdiction if the home country cannot or will not prosecute. Right?"

"Yes."

"And you sent your e-mail before the American system was even aware of a possible charge against Mr. Rathman?"

"Yes. I did," he said proudly, as if he should be commended for his actions.

"Do you still deny you were out to get Mr. Rathman?"

"Of course I do. I wasn't out to get him."

"Sir, you are a supporter and member of Doctors Without Borders, are you not?"

"What relevance—"

"Objection," Wolff said.

"Overruled."

"Your answer?"

"Yes."

"And you financially support the Human Rights Watch. True?"

"Yes."

"And you are a financial supporter of Amnesty International. True?"

"Yes, I believe in all those organizations. Is there something wrong with that?"

"Each of those organizations has condemned the United States and its conduct in the War on Terrorism, have they not?"

"I believe so, but only when we do things we shouldn't."

"And you agree with them, do you not?"

"You'd have to be specific. I'm not sure what in particular you're talking about."

"Okay, let's get specific," Skyles said as he picked up a piece of paper. "When Gerhard Schroeder was reelected as chancellor of Germany he ran on a campaign *opposing* the American position in the War on Terrorism and in particular its plans against Iraq. You agreed with his position, true?"

"I don't remember exactly . . ."

Skyles held up the document, gave a copy to Wolff, and said, "May I approach?"

Wiggins replied, "You may."

He handed it to Satterly. "Do you recognize this, sir?"

"It is a copy of a letter to the editor . . ."

"That you wrote to your hometown newspaper in Burlington, Vermont. Correct?"

"Yes."

"And in it you say, and I quote, '. . . Schroeder's position is right on target, and his Minister of Justice's statement is understandable.'"

"That's what you said, isn't it?"

Satterly looked beaten. "Yes."

Skyles walked back to the lectern and paused for several seconds before continuing. "His Minister of Justice. Understandable, you said. Right?"

"Yes," he muttered.

Skyles asked loudly, "She equated the conduct of the War on Terrorism by the President of the United States as a diversionary tactic, to take people's attention away from domestic problems, much like *Adolf Hitler* had done. True?"

Satterly looked away. "That's what she said."

"No further questions."

Chapter

21

Aboard the *Belleau Wood* Judge Graham spoke loudly over the sound of a Harrier jet starting over their heads on the flight deck. "Commander Watson, you may call your next witness."

Elizabeth looked at her watch, and considered. "Your Honor, based on the lateness of the hour, it seems unwise to start a witness this afternoon that we cannot complete until Monday morning."

"What do you have in mind?"

"Since the confession is to be admitted into evidence, I'd like to read portions of that confession to the court."

Stern stood to object. "Your Honor, the motion to exclude the confession was based on the fact that it was elicited through coercion. There is still no foundation to admit the confession. No one has testified that my client signed it."

"Can you prove that this man signed that confession, Commander?"

"I can, sir. The witness that I would like to bring to the court to do that is on his way from Washington. Which raises another question. He will be flying all night and will be arriving tomorrow. I know the court had planned to take the weekend off, but if possible I would like to have him testify tomorrow during the day so he can get back to Washington. He is extremely busy and needs to be back in Washington by Monday morning."

Judge Graham looked to his left and right, saw general agreement from the members of the court, and said, "I think that will be fine. Any opposition to taking this witness tomorrow? What's his name?"

"Lieutenant Rathman."

"Any opposition?"

Stern and Little shook their heads.

"Very well. Please give us an hour's notice, and the court will convene as necessary tomorrow to receive his testimony."

"Thank you, Your Honor. Now if it please the court, I'd like to read portions of the confession into the record."

"Go ahead," the judge said.

Watson stood back from the lectern and held up the photocopy of the confession. She had the certified translation. "My name is Wahamed Duar. I have been a member of the organization of which I'm now a part for several years. Our objective, my objective, is the downfall of the United States, and the ascendancy of Islam. I have taken many steps to accomplish this. My organization has been responsible for many attacks on many countries, including the United States. We have been responsible for the deaths of at least a hundred Americans, and many Egyptians, Turks, Israelis, English, and Germans. I am proud of what we have done. If given the opportunity I will do more.

"I planned and was responsible for the attack on the American embassy in Cairo. I planned and was responsible for the attack on the British embassy in Tunisia. I planned and was responsible for the attack on Jerusalem last November . . .

"We have executed several attacks against the interests of the United States, and have many more attacks planned and in place. If given the opportunity I will attack the United States again. The United States represents everything that is bad and evil in this world, and I will do anything to bring about its downfall.

"I have also entered into plans with my associates to attack the secular governments of Muslim countries such as Egypt and Turkey. They do not deserve to be leaders of those countries, and their downfall is nearly as important as the downfall of the United States, who supports them and props them up and protects them from the will of the people that they rule so oppressively."

Elizabeth looked up. "That is all I want to read at this moment. In summary, Your Honor, this document is all that is needed to convict Wahamed Duar."

Stern interrupted her. "That assumes, Your Honor, that Wahamed Duar is the man sitting at the defense table. The evidence will show that he is not."

The judge put up his hand. "We will deal with that in due time. I'm confident that Commander Watson intends to prove that your client is the man who signed this document, and is Wahamed Duar. Am I right, Commander?"

"Yes, Your Honor. In fact, the man who will testify about the confession tomorrow will testify about that as well in that regard."

♦ ♦ ♦

In the small courtroom atop the Department of Justice, Wolff stood and spoke. "United States calls Lieutenant Junior Grade Ted Groome."

Rat's heart went to his throat. Groomer could sink him. Rat turned around and looked as the doors opened in the back of the courtroom. Groomer walked in dressed identically to Rat. He wore a tropical white long uniform just like Rat's, with ribbons, SEAL insignia, and a fresh haircut. He looked like someone who could rip the judge's bench up by its roots if he chose to do so.

Groomer walked quickly to the front of the courtroom, turned and raised his hand, and was sworn in.

Wolff regarded him skeptically. He knew that Groomer was a risky witness, but he also knew that if Groomer was honest, his case would be proved. After Groomer identified himself and gave his current assignment, which disclosed that he was TAD, temporary additional duty, to the SAS, Wolff asked him about the raid.

"So after you had jumped out of the C-17 . . ." Wolff steered away from the classified elements of the raid, "you came upon Duar's group. Right?"

"That's right."

"And a firefight ensued."

Groomer took a deep breath. "Well, it wasn't that we just walked in and started shooting. We walked in identifying ourselves as Sudanese

Army—actually Rat did the talking—just so we could get into the room without being shot."

"Rat being a name often used by Lieutenant Rathman?"

"Right."

"Go on."

"Once there, we identified ourselves as Americans and told them not to resist, to put their hands up and no one would be hurt." He stopped. "What in particular do you want to know about?"

Wolff said gratuitously, "I would have been happy to tell you if you had returned my calls or agreed to talk to me about your testimony prior to the trial."

Groomer's eyes narrowed. "In my experience, talking to attorneys you don't know is usually not a good idea."

The jury smiled.

Wolff was not amused. "During the firefight with Duar's men several of them were killed. Correct?"

"Yes."

"Were any Americans injured?"

"One was killed."

"And how many were left at the end?"

"That fellow Mazmin and another guy . . ." Groomer looked up at the judge. "Am I allowed to talk about him?"

"Yes, you are."

Groomer nodded. "A guy from another country and Mazmin. We knew Duar had to be nearby. He was there when we arrived, so he had to be close."

"Shortly after the fight, you saw Mazmin put on the table in that room. Correct?"

"I saw him lying on a table."

"Do you claim to not know how he got on the table?"

"I assumed he was injured."

Wolff stared at Groomer for several seconds. "Do you have any evidence that he was injured?"

"Sure. He was lying on that table, and everybody that wasn't injured was standing up."

"You saw Lieutenant Rathman near him on that table. Correct?"

Groomer hesitated. "Yes, I did."

Wolff relaxed. He could see Groomer's internal debate. "And you saw Rathman pouring water into Mazmin's mouth and nose in an attempt to force him to give out information. Correct?"

"I don't remember that."

Wolff looked up quickly from his notes at Groomer. "You saw Lieutenant Rathman kneeling next to Mazmin. Correct?"

"Yes."

"And he had a cup of water in his hands. Correct?"

"That's right."

Skyles stood. "He's leading the witness, Your Honor."

Wolff replied, "He's an adverse witness, Your Honor."

Judge Wiggins said, "I agree. Continue."

"And Lieutenant Rathman poured water into Mazmin's nose and mouth. Right?"

"I don't remember that."

"Do you deny that Rathman took water from a bucket in cups and poured them into Mazmin's nose and mouth in an attempt to torture him?"

"I just don't know. I saw him giving Mazmin a drink. I figured the guy was injured and needed water. That's all I saw."

"Do you deny that Lieutenant Rathman tortured Mazmin to get information from him?"

"I'm just telling you what I saw. I saw him give Mazmin a drink."

Wolff was growing frustrated. "After he gave Mazmin a drink Rathman suddenly knew where Duar was hiding. Right?"

"I assume so. They were speaking Arabic. I don't speak Arabic."

"Didn't you think it was strange that Rathman suddenly knew where Duar was, whereas before he had no idea?"

"No. I figured Mazmin had told him. I figured he was grateful."

"Grateful?" Wolff choked.

"Sure. He had just killed Nubs," Groomer said angrily. "One of our men. Shot him in the face. Rat was about to return the fire when Mazmin threw down his weapon. Rat didn't shoot. He could have. He could have shot the guy instantly. I don't know how he didn't. I would have. We're talking a matter of one second, maybe two. But Rat held his fire. Lowered his weapon. He was furious. We all were. Nubs had a wife and a little boy. Then Rat gives this guy a drink of water. So yeah, I thought maybe the guy was grateful." Groomer stared into Wolff's eyes.

Wolff tried to back out. "You are a friend of Rathman's. Are you not?"

"Yes."

"You would lie for him, wouldn't you?"

"It would depend. In our position in the CIA currently, and before that in the Navy counterterrorism team Dev Group, we're called on to do a lot of things. It would depend on the circumstances."

"In fact, you just did. You just sat on this witness stand and lied for your friend Kent Rathman, also known as Rat. True?"

Skyles rose slowly. "The question is argumentative and unduly confrontational."

"Sustained."

"No further questions." Wolff returned to his seat, frustrated.

Skyles stood and crossed to the podium with a small smile on his face. "I have no questions, Your Honor."

♦ ♦ ♦

The Director of the CIA had arranged the briefing at twelve-thirty. The entire National Security Council was there. The President was in a foul temper and Sarah St. James felt exposed. She was concerned when she heard that Rat was giving the brief because she had not received a report from him on what he was going to talk about. She would hear it for the first time as he spoke, just like everyone else in the room. She didn't like learning with everyone else. She liked to be ahead of the game.

Rat stood at the head of the table with a screen behind him. He held the computer's infrared remote in his hand. Russell had prepared the briefing slides for him. He had reviewed them on a laptop in the back of the limo from Justice to the White House as Jacobs sat next to him.

Stewart Woods, the Director of Central Intelligence, said, "Mr. President, we have a situation developing, and we see enough things coming together that we think something is about to happen. I'd like to tell you what we know. Rather than pass it through several hands I thought you should hear it from the person who knows the most. Since he is currently working for the Agency, I asked him to brief you directly. Go ahead, Lieutenant."

"Good afternoon, Mr. President. I am Lieutenant Rathman, and today's brief is classified Top Secret—"

Kendrick immediately recognized his name and stared at him coldly. "Aren't you the one on trial?"

"Yes, sir."

"For torturing that terrorist."

Rat winced. "That's the charge, yes, sir. Manslaughter, actually."

Kendrick shook his head and looked at Woods, displeased. "Go on."

"We believe that Wahamed Duar's organization is still operating. We believe—"

"Isn't he in custody on a Navy ship?" Kendrick asked. "Isn't he on trial too?"

"Yes, sir, but others are still operating. And some of them are in the Pankisi gorge region of Georgia. John Johnson of the NSA tracked them there through Internet traffic, and when we went there at the request of Georgia, they told us they believe Duar's people are in the gorge.

"Why would they be there?" Rat brought up the first slide. It was a picture of a Russian RTG. He summarized all he knew, most of which they had heard, from the Pankisi gorge to the *Tbilisi* switching containers and men in Liberia.

Kendrick was deeply concerned. "Do we have a position on the ship?"

"The last position we had was from the radio call to the Liberian International Shipping Company. Since then, nothing. Here is a photograph of the container ship, the M/V *Monrovian Prince*. We have good information on her radar suite, communications suite, and other electronic identifiers. Since that radio call, though, the ship has gone total EMCON. Electronically silent. They have shut down their radars, radios, everything. We have no way of tracking her from our satellites."

President Kendrick was growing frustrated. "Can't any of the photographic satellites track it?"

Stewart Woods shook his head. "Not really, sir, no. That would be sort of like trying to spot the flea on your carpet with a laser pointer in the dark. It can be done, but it's not very likely. We have some other satellite assets that may allow us to find it, but there is an awful lot of shipping crossing the Atlantic, and it's extremely difficult to pick one ship out of the others without an electronic signal."

"Can you pick out the one that doesn't have an electronic signal?"

"That's possible, but also not easy. Believe me, we're working the problem; I'm just telling you that I don't have a great deal of confidence that we can track the ship right now."

"What about the Navy? Have you asked them to help?"

"Yes, sir. Unfortunately there is no Navy ship within eight hundred miles of the last known location. It would take them days to steam to that location, and then try to catch up with the ship, or guess where it is en route. They can try to cut it off, and that's what they're trying to do. They have sent the closest destroyer to try and find it. But it won't be easy."

Sarah St. James asked Rat, "What do you think they are planning?"

"We know they have access to C4. I think it's likely they're going to pull into Jacksonville on schedule and set off the explosives, sending radioactive material all over the city. A quick and cheap dirty bomb. It would take years, if not decades, and billions of dollars to clean up the city. It may or may not kill a lot of people, depending on how much radioactive material they have and how close the people are."

Kendrick was furious at the idea of a ship with terrorists aboard heading toward the United States and United States intelligence and the military being unable to tell him where it was. "This ship is huge. Are you telling me we can't find it?"

"Not easily, sir."

"Stewart, what do you suggest?"

"We need to use every tool at our disposal to find this ship as soon as possible."

"What do we tell Jacksonville? Do we evacuate the city? Do we tell them terrorists are inbound? Do we wait until the day before the ship is scheduled to arrive and see if we've intercepted it? Do we put up a blockade? Howard, what do you think?"

Stuntz had been waiting to be asked. "This is a very serious threat, Mr. President. I would like your permission to sink the ship. I'd like to send out every submarine on the East Coast, sortie every carrier, and inspect every ship that comes within two hundred miles of the United States. If we find the ship, sink it."

"Anybody disagree?" Kendrick asked.

No one spoke. St. James thought, then said, "If Duar's men are aboard that ship, which seems likely, aren't there other, innocent sailors aboard? If we sink the ship, won't they be killed?"

"Tough shit," Stuntz said. "We can't risk the lives of an entire city for a few sailors that are being held hostage."

"I guess I'm wondering if we can do something other than sinking the ship. Disable it, or stop it."

The members of the National Security Council sat silently. They stared at the photograph of the container ship with its massive cranes fore and aft and the details of its construction and performance at the bottom.

Kendrick spoke. "Send the Navy out in full force, Howard. Everything they can send to find this ship. No permission yet to sink it. Find it first, put a couple of warships around it, and we'll decide then what to do about it."

"Will do, sir."

◆　◆　◆

The captain of the *Monrovian Prince* stood on the air-conditioned bridge and looked through his large binoculars at what he thought was a light on the horizon. They hadn't seen another ship in more than two days. He wanted to make sure that they didn't have a collision. Hotary's restriction that they leave the radar off made him feel like a blind man in a dark room hoping not to run into anyone. Although the sun had set three hours before and the moon had not yet risen, the stars were bright enough to illuminate the smooth Atlantic. The swells were minimal and the sea was gloriously flat as the *Prince* glided through the water at twelve knots.

Tayseer Hotary stood just outside the door to the bridge, his presence unknown to the crew. He watched the captain and the other members of the crew on the bridge. He looked behind him at six of his men, who had opened one of their containers and retrieved a case of AK-47 assault rifles. They stood with their backs against the bulkhead, weapons ready. They all gave him nearly imperceptible nods.

Hotary pulled the door open and walked onto the bridge with great confidence. He glanced around at the men there who looked at him with annoyance. He walked to the captain and stood beside him. "See anything?"

The captain did not even put down his binoculars. He immediately recognized Hotary's voice. "I told you I did not want to see you on the bridge ever again."

Hotary waited. "Why would what you say matter to me?"

The captain lowered the glasses angrily. "Because I am the captain of the ship."

"*I* am the captain now."

The captain looked for others on the bridge to be ready to remove Hotary forcefully. "Leave the bridge now."

"I'm afraid I can't do that."

"You will, or I'll have you thrown off the bridge."

One of the sailors who could hear the captain began moving to stand behind Hotary. Hotary knew he was there, but didn't care. "I have done additional calculations. We need to increase our speed from twelve knots to the maximum sustainable speed of the ship."

"That *is* twelve knots."

"No. It is not. It is sixteen knots."

"Going to sixteen knots in the open ocean with this top-heavy load would be too dangerous."

"Not if the ship is handled properly. The ocean is calm. Call the engine room and tell them to increase speed to sixteen knots."

"I will not."

"I was hoping it wouldn't come to this, but I expected it would at some point. Please get on the public address system for the ship and tell your men to assemble in the mess deck. All of them. Including those in engineering, those on watch, every man on the ship. They must assemble in the mess deck in ten minutes. Make the announcement."

"I will not—"

Hotary raised his hand as the captain was finishing his sentence. Hotary's men rushed onto the bridge with their rifles and pointed them at everyone standing there. "You will."

"And if I don't?"

Hotary shrugged. "Then I'll have you shot, and I'll throw your body into the sea."

The captain raged inside but saw no options. He crossed to the back of the bridge and picked up the public address microphone. "All hands to the mess deck in ten minutes. Including those on watch, including those in engineering. All hands to the mess deck in ten minutes." He released the button on the microphone and slammed it back into his receiver.

Hotary spoke to his men in Arabic. He ordered two of them to escort the men from the bridge to the mess deck below. Two other men threw the slings from their rifles over their heads and took control of the ship. Hotary crossed to the navigation table and checked the chart. He saw the course line leading from their current position to Jacksonville, Florida, their supposed destination. He calculated a new heading to a point farther north and turned to the new helmsman. "Set a course of three-zero-five."

His helmsman turned the wheel gently to the right until the large ship started to come around. The helmsman replied to Hotary, "Three-zero-five."

Hotary nodded. "Set sixteen knots." The bridge phone rang. He picked up. It was one of his men on the mess deck. "They're all in a secure room on the second deck. We have locked the room."

"Excellent. Meet us on the deck outside by the forward crane."

"We're on our way."

Hotary and the other men from the bridge hurried down to the crane. The floodlights from the bridge pointed forward and illuminated the crane and the containers stacked up on the deck in front of the bridge. Hotary waited patiently as his men ran from the mess deck up to the crane. Finally they were all there. He searched for the man who was critical to the next step and saw him in the back. "Get into the crane."

The man handed his rifle to the man standing next to him and scrambled up into the cockpit to operate the crane. The large white crane extended into the black sky like a monument. The motor for operating the crane began to hum as the operator familiarized himself with the controls. The crane swiveled and jerked and the cables came slowly to the deck.

Two men climbed on top of the nearest container and hooked the cables to the four corners. The crane operator moved his levers carefully and the cables were drawn tight to just where the container would be lifted off the deck. One of Hotary's men came forward with two backpacks of equipment. Hotary nodded to him and he took out C4 plastic explosive and placed small silver-dollar-sized pieces in four places on either side of the container at its bottom. He hooked up detonators to each of the four spots and retreated behind another container as everyone else sought equivalent shelter. He pressed the electronic trigger and the small explosions cracked in the quiet night, blowing four holes in the container.

Hotary gave the signal to the crane operator, who quickly hauled the container into the dark sky, swung it over the side of the ship and dropped it into the ocean. It hit with a large splash, nearly pitched over, but settled onto its bottom as the ship raced away. Water began to fill the container through the new holes as it disappeared behind the ship.

Two men climbed on top of the next container and quickly hooked up the four cables again. They completed the same process as on the first, only quicker, and it too was dumped into the ocean. They went to the third, and fourth, and every container on the deck in quick succession.

A second team manned the crane aft of the superstructure and dropped containers off the port side of the ship with equal skill. The deck was quickly becoming visible as they went from one container to the next, stacked three high, then two, then none as they moved to the next group of containers. They carefully avoided the three containers that had been loaded last, the ones they had brought aboard the ship.

As the night wore on, they cleared the entire deck except for their three containers. They quickly opened the large hatches that gave them access to the holds below to the main deck. The containers were stacked inside the hold and could be moved to the port or starboard side of the ship by tracks. Several of the men jumped down in the hold to activate the tracks and move containers closer to the hatch so the crane could pull them up. One after another, the containers came up, had holes blasted into their sides, and were dropped into the night sea.

After all the containers had been removed the men lowered their three special containers down into the hold, out of sight, and opened one of them. They handed up electronics, more explosives, and satchels full of other equipment. The man in charge of the electronics hurried to the bridge and climbed on top of it in the blackness behind the lights. He quickly detached the surface search radar antenna, cut the wires long enough to reuse them, and hurled the small antenna over the side. He put a new antenna in its place and wired it quickly to the protruding wires. He hurried down from his perch and searched the bridge for the radar transmitter box. He unplugged it, removed the wires from its back, and attached the new radar transmitter that worked on a frequency very different from the one he had just thrown into the ocean.

The other men on the deck closed the large hatches. The ship now had a clean, unmolested look, devoid of stacked containers. The two loading cranes still stood high against the night sky, illuminated by the floodlights. The crane operator quickly abandoned his post, as the C4 was carefully wrapped around the base of the thick white steel crane. Hotary inspected it and gave his approval. He walked to a safe position and nodded.

The expert detonated the C4. A thunderous explosion severed the crane from its base. It leapt sideways still standing upright momentarily, then teetered. It settled back onto the deck in what appeared to be slow motion then fell toward the side of the ship. It gathered speed as it fell and the sharp-edged bottom gouged the deck as it skidded toward the side. The head of the crane surrendered to gravity and it pitched heavily over the side into the ocean. The splash threw dark ocean water back onto the deck, but the crane was gone.

The same men hurried to the back part of the ship and blew the second crane over the same side of the ship.

Hotary's men gathered wooden two-by-fours that had been brought from their container and constructed a frame around the bases of the two cranes. Only a stub of white steel protruding from the deck showed there had ever been a crane. When the wood was built up to the level of the shattered steel, a gray dingy tarp was pulled over the frame to resemble some covered piece of nautical machinery on the ship's deck.

Hotary looked for one man. "Are you ready? You have the paint?"

"Yes. The seas are calm. It should be no problem."

Hotary said, "Rename it. *Sea Dragon,* Hong Kong. English and Cantonese."

Chapter 22

The CH-53 settled into a hover just above the flight deck of the *Belleau Wood* as the sun broke over the horizon. The South Indian Ocean was tranquil and the gray helicopter blended in well with the overcast morning. Rat had to fight to stay awake. He had been up all night. He did not sleep well aboard airplanes, especially when he was flying to testify in another trial in the middle of his own. He was wearing his khaki uniform with all his ribbons, not just the top row as he usually did. Not only did the SEAL insignia grab people's eyes, but those who knew ribbons could see he had been awarded a Silver Star, an extremely high decoration, rarely given. The write-up for the medal was classified. No one could read it without a clearance and he couldn't talk about it. It was from one of the raids he had conducted while he was with Dev Group. He didn't think about it much, but he knew that people noticed, at least those who knew what the ribbon for a Silver Star looked like, those whose opinion he cared about most.

He rubbed his eyes trying to get the sleep out of his system as the wheels of the CH-53 touched down on the deck and the weight of the heavy helicopter transferred from its rotor blades to its landing gear. Rat wanted nothing other than to head directly to the wardroom and pour the biggest, strongest cup of coffee he could find. Only then would he try to find the prosecutor, a Commander Elizabeth Watson.

As he was ushered into the island by the flight deck crew he removed his flotation vest and cranial helmet and handed them to a sailor standing nearby. He hurried down the ladders without escort to the wardroom and grabbed a large porcelain cup that he took to the coffee urn. He drew a cup of steaming fresh black coffee, blew on it, and drank quickly. He sat at a long wardroom table, the only officer in the wardroom. Two sailors were buffing the tile deck on the other side of the wardroom.

Rat was growing angry. He stared at the cheap painting on the wall and wondered why he should continue to be loyal to a government that wanted to put him in jail. How could he work—even temporarily—for the CIA, brief the President, fly to the Indian Ocean to testify in a trial, and then just go back to Washington, D.C., for his trial like a calf to a veal party? In the rare moments when he was honest with himself about the trial, when he was objective instead of optimistic, he knew they had the evidence to convict him. Satterly's testimony alone was enough. He had to admit the accusations were true. He disagreed strongly that what he had done should be illegal, but he couldn't hide what he had done. He wished he had come back without Duar. Bring Mazmin back, let the CIA "interrogate" him, and let *them* find Duar. Another raid, another day, they would have found Duar. Possibly.

His hands and face felt grimy from the long trip. He gulped the last bit of coffee and picked up a phone hanging on the bulkhead. He punched in Commander Watson's number. She answered.

"Commander Watson. Lieutenant Rathman. I'm aboard, ma'am. I'm in the wardroom."

"I'll be right there," she said quickly and hung up.

He placed the receiver back on the cradle, picked up his cup, and refilled it. Moments later she burst into the wardroom. She crossed over to Rat and extended her hand. "Thank you for coming back all this way. I'm sorry I had to drop that subpoena on you at home. It was really the only way I had."

He nodded his understanding.

"You want to come with me?" she asked. She led him out of the wardroom. He watched her from behind. She was tall and bony. Her hands had protruding blue veins. She looked unhealthily thin. He hooked his thumb over the lip of his coffee cup and carried it with him as he quickly followed Commander Watson down the passageway to her office. She opened the door and directed him to a chair in the small, cramped space. The office was full of books stacked on the desk, papers strewn about, and notebooks lined up on the bookshelf behind her.

"How long do you think this will take?"

"Not very long, really. I don't expect to ask you very many questions and I don't think they'll have much by way of cross. But we'll see. As soon as we're ready I'll call the judge and he will reconvene the court an hour later."

"There's a helicopter to Cape Town at 1130. I'd like to be on it if possible."

"Are we that far south already? Well, we'll just have to see."

She went over the testimony that she expected of him and gave him the general nature of the information she was looking for. She didn't want to give him the actual questions because she didn't want him to appear to be working from a script. After a half hour she was ready. She picked up the phone and called the judge's stateroom. He agreed that he was ready and told her to contact all the other participants to tell them. She called out to her chief, who immediately began calling everyone to the court.

"Do you want to change your uniform or get cleaned up?"

"How much time do we have?"

"One hour."

"I brought my whites. I could change into them if you would like."

"Why not? Go ahead and get cleaned up, change into your whites, and meet me in the admiral's wardroom at 1000. Can you do that?"

"No problem."

"Here's my stateroom key. Make yourself at home."

Rat found her stateroom, shaved and showered, transferred his ribbons and warfare pin to his tropical white uniform, and was ready to go. He walked to the wardroom and stood outside in the passageway. He could hear voices inside, but the sign on the outside said ALL WITNESSES TO REMAIN IN THE PASSAGEWAY.

Time passed, 1000 came and went, and fifteen more minutes, then thirty. He could hear voices being raised and arguments being made.

He had no idea what was at issue in the court, but he saw his time slipping by.

Finally the door swung open and the first-class petty officer said loudly, "Lieutenant Rathman."

Rat walked toward him. The sailor looked at him carefully, confirmed in his mind that this was Lieutenant Rathman, and stepped aside for him to enter the courtroom. Rat walked in and was impressed by the solemn order achieved by the liberal use of green felt on the tables and other visual cues—the scales of justice, the gavel and block, the placement of the counsel tables, and the elevated platform for the tables with the judge and members of the court.

He was ushered to the front of the courtroom to the witness stand and was sworn in. He looked out over the rest of the people in the packed room, officers and enlisted people from the ship, journalists, an artist in the front row, the attorneys, the panel of senior officers who made up the court, and of course, Duar himself. Rat stared at him. Duar avoided his gaze.

After summarizing his background and education, and his work with Dev Group—which he never mentioned by name—he told them he was currently TAD to the CIA. Commander Watson asked him about the Sudan operation. "Were you in charge of the operation?"

"I was in charge of my team. There were several teams flying that evening, only one of which was likely to be close enough to the rendezvous. We didn't know where it was going to be, only about when."

"Did you capture anyone?"

"Two men. A man named Mazmin, and Wahamed Duar, there," he said, pointing.

"Do you recognize the man sitting at the defense table?"

"Yes. That is Wahamed Duar."

"How do you know?"

"We were given a photograph of him before the operation. He matches the photograph."

Elizabeth walked forward and handed him an eight by ten print. "Is this the photograph that you had on the night of the operation?"

He looked and added quickly, "Yes."

"Did you personally bring him back to the ship?"

"Yes I did."

"One last thing," Watson said. "Have you seen this document before?" she asked, handing him a copy of the confession.

"Yes. I saw it in Egypt."

"Did you take this man, Wahamed Duar, to Egypt?"

"Yes. The Egyptian military wanted to ask him some questions about the American Embassy bombing. We complied with their request and I took him to Egypt."

"Did you personally see him sign this document?"

Rat looked at Duar. "No."

"How do you know he signed it?"

"I asked him."

"What did he say?"

"He told me that he had signed it when I showed it to him."

"Does he speak English?"

"You know, I'm not really sure."

"How did you talk to him?"

"In Arabic."

"You speak Arabic?"

"I do."

Watson looked satisfied. "No further questions."

Stern rose to his feet. The journalists were expectant. "Lieutenant Rathman, you had to come here over the weekend in something of a hurry. Correct?"

"I received this subpoena yesterday, and left yesterday afternoon. I flew all night, and arrived here this morning."

"And what were you doing yesterday during the day?"

Watson jumped up immediately. "Objection, irrelevant. Also goes to character evidence that is irrelevant as to this witness. Your Honor, this is what we were talking about. I thought your instruction to Mr. Stern was very clear."

"So did I. What is the relevance of this, Mr. Stern?"

"Goes to bias, Your Honor. Shows how he feels about the defendant and those who allegedly worked with him."

"Why didn't you make this argument when we were in camera?"

"Frankly, Your Honor, I didn't think about it."

"Objection is overruled. You may answer the question, Lieutenant Rathman."

Rat had known he would be asked, but he didn't expect it to be the first question. Everybody who was conscious knew about his trial. It was on the front page of every newspaper in the country. CNN was devoting hours of special broadcasting to it—"Is It Ever Okay to Torture a Terrorist?"—and impaneling law professors to discuss it endlessly. "I was in court in Washington, D.C. I am on trial for manslaughter."

"And?"

"And what?"

"Who is it you are being charged with the death of?"

"Mazmin. The other terrorist that we captured with Duar."

"You did in fact torture Mazmin to death, didn't you?"

Watson jumped to her feet. "As the witness testified, Your Honor, he is on trial. It is inappropriate for counsel to ask a question which calls for the witness to plead the Fifth Amendment. His question should be stricken."

The judge nodded. "Sustained. Mr. Stern, you know better."

"The allegation against you, the charge for which you're being tried, is that you tortured Mr. Mazmin to death. Right?"

"Basically."

Stern changed course. "You took this man," he said, pointing, "to Egypt. Right?"

"That's correct."

"And you were there the whole time he was in the hands of the Egyptians. Right?"

"Sort of. I delivered him to the Egyptians, then went to eat with the rest of my men. Then I brought him back to the ship."

"You observed them torturing him. True?"

Watson tried to stop him. "Your Honor, this exceeds the scope of direct examination."

"Overruled. Answer the question."

Rat was beginning to feel uncomfortable. "No, I didn't."

Josephine studied his face as he answered. She scratched quickly in her notebook.

Stern was surprised. "Why you?"

"Why me?"

"Right. Why you? Of all the people that could have taken this man to Egypt, why did they choose you?"

"Maybe because he knows me," he said, looking at Duar. "And I was familiar with him."

"Or maybe because the government *knew* he was going to be tortured in Egypt, and they knew you didn't have any problem with torture. Think maybe that was it?"

"Objection, Your Honor!" Watson erupted.

"Sustained."

Stern asked as if he couldn't remember, "What is it you're being tried for in Washington?"

Watson interjected, "Asked and answered, Your Honor."

"Sustained."

"What did the Egyptians do to this man?"

"I didn't see it."

"You saw that they had used electrical current on him, right?"

"When I got back to the room they still had him hooked up. I made them take him off the machine."

"You saw him with electrodes attached to his earlobes and scrotum. Right?"

"Yes."

"What else did they do?"

"I'm not sure. They told me—"

"Hearsay, Your Honor," Watson said.

Stern shook his head. "She wanted hearsay earlier, she can't now object."

"Overruled," Graham said.

"What did they tell you?"

"They had wrapped a towel around his head and poured water onto it so he couldn't breathe. He responded well to that, but then they upped the ante."

"They went to electricity."

"Yes."

"And this confession, it was elicited by them electrocuting him."

"I don't know."

"You're aware, aren't you, how unreliable information is when it is elicited by torture?"

"I'm not sure. I don't really have any experience—"

"You've heard, haven't you?"

"Some."

"Men will say anything to make the pain stop. Won't they?"

"I'm not sure. Probably."

He picked up the confession and held it up. "He signed this confession after being tortured, right?"

"Like I said, I don't know. I wasn't there. When I looked at it, it was already written and signed. I don't know when he did it."

"You never saw him sign it, did you?"

"No."

"And it is your belief that this is Wahamed Duar. Right?"

"Yes."

"Please pick up the photograph that Commander Watson showed you."

Rat picked up the picture and looked at it again. He looked up, waiting for the next question.

"It's your belief that the man sitting at this table is Wahamed Duar based entirely on this photograph. Right?"

"Yes."

Stern nodded. "Even though the photograph is black and white, tell me what you notice about the eyes of Wahamed Duar."

Rat looked at it carefully. "They are fairly light, especially for someone from Sudan."

Stern looked at the judge. "Your Honor, I would like for Mr. Rathman to come down from the witness stand and look into the eyes of the defendant."

"And what is the point of that, Mr. Stern?" the judge asked.

"The government is apparently trying to use Lieutenant Rathman to confirm the identity of the defendant. I want to show him he's wrong, and have him so testify."

"Proceed," the judge said.

Stern continued, "Lieutenant Rathman, please come over here with the photograph and look into the eyes of the defendant."

The translator sat next to Duar and spoke in low tones telling him everything that was being said. Duar watched Rat.

Rat stood reluctantly, took the photograph, and crossed over to the defense table. He looked at Duar, then at the photograph, back at Duar, and then at Stern.

"Have you had an opportunity to examine the defendant?"

"Yes."

"You would agree that his eyes are much darker than the eyes of man in the photograph. Correct?"

"That appears to be the case."

"You would also agree that it is impossible to change one's eye color."

"You can do wonders with contact lenses."

Stern nodded. "Assuming there is no funny business with contact lenses here, you would agree that one cannot make one's eyes lighter or darker."

"Generally, yeah."

"You would have to agree with me then, wouldn't you, that the defendant's eyes do not match the eyes of the man in the photograph."

Rat felt cornered. The haunted feeling he had had since standing in the C-17 on the night of the raid had returned with a vengeance. "I would have to agree with that."

Elizabeth was taking notes, trying to hide the panic she was starting to feel.

"It's very possible, isn't it, Lieutenant Rathman, that you captured the wrong man in Sudan?"

"Hard to say. He was there. He fled from the room. He fired at me when we tried to pull him out of a well. So if he isn't Wahamed Duar, he sure acted like him."

Stern nodded, completely unconcerned. "All you can really say is that those things were done by someone. Not necessarily my client."

"No, he's definitely the one who fired at us."

"Did it not occur to you, Lieutenant Rathman, that perhaps there was someone else who was there who looked an awful lot like Wahamed Duar? That maybe that's the entire reason he was there? So in case of attack or capture, *he* would be the one captured, not Duar?"

Rat was stunned. "No, it really didn't."

"Have you not heard stories about how Saddam Hussein had doubles, men who looked just like him who rode around in limos, slept in his palaces, appeared in public, even. Have you heard about that?"

"Yes."

"Yet it didn't occur to you that maybe Duar was doing the same thing, and you were the one who had been tricked?"

Rat didn't answer. He didn't know what to say.

"No further questions."

◆ ◆ ◆

Captain Bill Anderson, the commanding officer of the USS *Ronald Reagan*, reread the message as he stood on the bridge of the aircraft carrier. They had just completed a six-month cruise to the Mediterranean and were headed home. Gibraltar lay just behind them. It had been a good cruise. They had made it all the way through without losing a single person or airplane. But now this. This would cost them at least a week, maybe two.

The message was fairly clear: Intercept the course from Monrovia, Liberia, to Jacksonville, Florida, and find the M/V *Monrovian Prince*, a container ship that had sailed from Monrovia five days before, estimated speed eight knots, maximum possible speed as a fully loaded container ship expected to be twelve knots. Last known position based on a radio intercept was 6° 28' North, 17° 17' West. Expected terrorist activity. Use all possible means to locate the ship. Photographs and electronic signature on their way by back-channel message.

The captain called the navigator, Commander Rich Black, to the bridge. They checked the chart for their current position then asked the chief petty officer quartermaster to mark the last known location of the *Monrovian Prince* and draw the course to Jacksonville. He made two circles around the mark to represent how far the ship could have gone based on known speed and best possible speed. Anderson and the navigator, Commander Rich Black, studied the results.

Anderson said, "We should head toward the closest point to the States. We can continue to DR the ship's position during our transit." He looked up at Black. "Agree?"

"That sea lane has a lot of traffic. It won't be easy to find one ship in there."

"Shouldn't be that tough. We'll have photos. We'll give them to all the aircrew. As soon as we get within five hundred miles we'll get every airplane available to start looking. With a good electronic signature it shouldn't be that tough."

"True enough."

"Give me a course."

The navigator and the quartermaster took less than a minute, then handed him a small printout of the entire Atlantic which showed the projected course and time to reach the *Prince's* most likely path.

Anderson looked at it and walked back to the center of the bridge. "OOD!"

"Yes, Captain?" the lieutenant replied.

"Set a new course of two-five-eight. Twenty-five knots."

"New course two-five-eight, twenty-five knots, aye, sir."

Black stood next to Captain Anderson. "What's this about, anyway?"

Anderson handed him the message.

Black read it as he walked to the port side of the bridge and stood next to Anderson as he climbed into his captain's chair. He looked around to make sure no one was listening. "Terrorist activity? On a container ship?"

Anderson nodded.

"Holy shit."

◆　◆　◆

On Monday morning in the courtroom on top of the Justice building everyone was quiet. Everyone, including the jury, was reacting to the look on Judge Wiggins's face. A large vein that ran down the middle of his forehead was bulging. It went from his hairline to the bridge of his nose and one could almost count the pulse rate. His reading glasses were pushed up too far against his eyebrows again as he stared at Skyles. He looked at the clock once again—9:02—no Rat. Skyles had promised the judge that Rat would be back in time. Or at least that's how the judge remembered it. Not only was Rat not there, he hadn't called or left a message with Skyles or anyone else. Skyles had no idea where he was.

9:03. Still no Rat. The judge sat with his hands folded on the bench. He wasn't going to say a word or do anything until Rat appeared or it was so obvious that he wasn't coming that he could hold Rat in contempt, deem him to be in violation of his bail, and put him in jail.

Skyles tried to avoid eye contact with the judge.

Two more minutes passed, then suddenly there was a commotion in the back of the courtroom. Skyles could hear the rocker switches transmit the code to open the large metal door. Rat rushed in. Although not breathing hard, it was clear he had arrived in a hurry. He was in his khaki uniform and his face had a certain oiliness to it. He walked through the small gate in the wooden fence-like partition that separated the active courtroom from the gallery. The gate swung back and forth as Rat took his seat. He looked at the judge, who had transferred his death glare from Skyles to Rat. Rat stared right back at him.

The judge spoke. "Mr. Rathman. Explain your tardiness."

"I was on the *Belleau Wood* off South Africa. I took a helicopter to Cape Town and caught a commercial flight. The airplane had engine problems and we were diverted to the Ivory Coast, where we sat for twelve hours waiting for a replacement aircraft. I just arrived, as you can probably tell."

Judge Wiggins didn't care what the reason was. "Do I have to remind you of what I told your attorney on Friday?"

Rat hated it when people rode their authority farther than it was meant to carry them. It was common in the military—officers promoted one or two steps beyond where they were competent or who used newly found authority to puff up their opinions of themselves at the expense of others.

"No, I don't believe so." Rat turned to Skyles and whispered, "What's he so pissed about?"

Skyles shook his head. Not now.

Wiggins was visibly unhappy with Rat. He spoke with a restrained anger. "If you are late again, I'll find you in contempt of court. Do you understand that?"

"Yes."

The judge turned his head toward Wolff, who had been enjoying the show. "Call your next witness."

Wolff knew how to take the glare off Rat's face. "The United States calls Mr. Don Jacobs."

The bailiff opened the door and called for Jacobs, who walked in wearing a dark suit. Rat had never seen him in a suit. He had never even seen him in wool pants. He always wore cotton, and his clothes always were disheveled. Jacobs saw Rat looking at him. He tried not to show any particular identification with him or even recognition. Jacobs walked to the witness box and stood outside to take the oath. He was sworn in and adjusted the microphone in front of his mouth as he gave his name. He thought it was silly to have a microphone in a courtroom as cramped as the one in which he found himself. He had not been enthusiastic about testifying.

Christopher Vithoulkas, the general counsel for the CIA, entered the courtroom and sat in the seat that had been roped off for him in the front row. He was there to create a fuss if information that was classified and otherwise not admissible under the Classified Information Protection Act was offered. He was the one who had ensured the passageway and elevators were cleared before his client was called to testify. He had expressed grave concerns in the special hearing at eight that morning about questions that might be posed to Don Jacobs. Judge Wiggins was sympathetic and agreed to minimally intrusive arrangements.

"Good morning, Mr. Jacobs," Wolff said.

"Morning."

"Would you tell us what your current position is?"

"Head of Counterterrorism for the Agency."

"What agency is that?"

Jacobs looked at him, annoyed. "The Central Intelligence Agency."

"To whom do you report? Who is your boss?"

"Mr. Stewart Woods. The Director of the Central Intelligence Agency."

"You understand why Mr. Rathman is on trial, do you not?"

"Of course."

"This charge, this accusation, arose out of an operation in Sudan. You understand that?"

"Yes. When Wahamed Duar was captured."

"Yes, exactly. Lieutenant Rathman, the defendant, was working for you during that operation. Right?"

"He was leading a team that was part of a bigger operation to capture Wahamed Duar."

"Even though he is on active duty with the Navy he is currently on temporary assignment to the CIA, to a Special Operations unit called the SAS. Correct?"

Jacobs looked at Vithoulkas, who nodded. "Yes, basically."

"Mr. Jacobs, the CIA does not endorse torture, does it?"

Jacobs hesitated. Wolff was using him to corner Rat, to block any attempt by Skyles to claim that he had just been doing what he was told. Not effective legally, it was called the Nuremberg defense after the Nazis on trial for war crimes who said, "I was just following orders"; but juries were known to make decisions without the law sometimes. "That's generally true. But it depends on how you define torture."

"How do *you* define torture, Mr. Jacobs? Tell me what is prohibited by the CIA."

Jacobs chose his words carefully. "It would certainly include electrocuting somebody, or pulling out their fingernails, severe beatings with blackjacks, those sorts of things."

"If someone from your shop tortured a man in the field by use of the technique called the water board, that would be prohibited under the CIA regulations today. Correct?"

Skyles wasn't about to let this go by unmolested. "Your Honor, once again, the CIA is not on trial, and Mr. Rathman is not on trial for having violated some unspecified CIA regulation. What the CIA expects or doesn't expect is *completely* irrelevant."

Before the judge could respond Wolff went to his own defense. "Your Honor, we do not know what defense will be taken by the accused. His attorney waived his opening statement, so we must anticipate to some degree his excuses for torturing this man. We don't want to leave it as a possibility that he was only 'following orders,' or was operating within some unwritten CIA expectation."

"You may continue."

"How do you define torture?" Wolff asked.

"Didn't we just go through that?" Jacobs asked.

"Somewhat. Anything you want to add to that definition?"

"Not really. Let me ask you, is sleep deprivation torture?"

"Yes, it is."

"Is aggressive questioning or screaming at the person torture? Is threatening him?"

Wolff didn't usually let witnesses ask him questions, but he wanted to give Jacobs a little room. "Threatening is. The prohibition against torture in international law is against physical *and* moral coercion. It is so defined in the Geneva Convention. Did you know that?"

"Civilians aren't bound by the Geneva Convention," Jacobs said.

"They're bound by the treaty the United States ratified in 1994, the Convention Against Torture, which has the same definition, right?"

"The CIA and the United States are against torture," Jacobs said.

Wolff held his smile. "You are familiar with the water board. Right?"

"Sort of," Jacobs replied.

"The water board is not endorsed by the CIA—it cannot be used by its operatives today. Right?"

"I would assume that to be the case, but I've never seen the water board used. Don't really know how it works."

"You've worked with Lieutenant Rathman for some time now. Right?"

"Yes."

"You know he is inclined to torture people. Right?"

"What?" Jacobs asked, annoyed.

"You remember the attempt by some Algerians to shoot down the Blue Angels at the Paris Air Show?"

"Of course."

"Mr. Rathman was instrumental in stopping that attempt, or at least trying to stop it. Wasn't he?"

"Yes, he was. He did a fantastic job."

Wolff glanced up at Jacobs, clearly showing his disagreement. "He had located a few of the men involved in the attempt before it occurred, right?"

"Yes. He was brilliant. He found them before the attempt."

"Well, the *way* he found most of them was by torturing one particular man. He cut through his nose with a very sharp knife he is known to carry, then cut the man's chest into ribbons—"

Skyles erupted, "Objection!" He considered his options and struggled for some basis for an objection. He just had to interrupt to stop Wolff, to break his rhythm. Anything. He'd come up with the reason later. "Your Honor, based on this inappropriate questioning I move for a mistrial. The prosecutor has knowingly solicited character evidence which is irrelevant and prejudicial in this criminal case. I am stunned that the government felt a need to stoop to such a low tactic, but since their case is so thin, I guess—"

"Your Honor," Wolff replied, "the case of *United States* vs. *Craight* addresses this issue. It holds that this kind of evidence is admissible to show a propensity to do certain distinct acts, certain things that show an inclination. Like an inclination not to wear a seat belt, or an inclination to smoke."

"Not when that's the charge at issue," Skyles protested. "It's like asking for testimony that someone charged with speeding had sped before. It's irrelevant and prejudicial."

"Usually yes," Wolff agreed. "But if he had an inclination to drive with a brick on the gas pedal for some reason, it would be admissible."

"Overruled. You may continue."

"Thank you, Your Honor," Wolff said. "You were aware of what he did to that Frenchman of Arabic descent, were you not?"

"I was aware something happened in Paris. I wasn't there."

"In fact once that operation was completed the French filed a formal protest at the way Mr. Rathman assaulted and tortured that man. Isn't that right?"

"They made their opinion known."

"They filed an official protest in writing. True?"

"Yes."

"So in spite of being aware of Mr. Rathman's propensity to torture people to gather information from them when he, and *only* he, believes it is necessary, you sent him out on additional operations. Right?"

"Absolutely. I have complete faith in Mr. Rathman."

"And you sent him out again because he is effective. Perhaps the most effective counterterrorist operative in the United States Government. Right?"

"I've never known him to fail and have never heard of him failing in any other operation."

"You do not assert that the end justifies the means, do you? That if torture is effective and helps you catch a terrorist, that's okay?"

"No. I would not say that."

Wolff paused and folded his arms in front of him. He waited until all the jurors looked up, to make sure they were now paying attention. "If in fact Mr. Rathman was involved in torturing the man from Sudan who died, then he would have been operating outside of the direction he received from the CIA. Is that right?"

Jacobs wanted to help Rathman, but he couldn't say torture was *within* the direction of the Agency. "That's correct."

"No further questions."

Skyles stood and looked down at the floor for a long quiet moment. "Mr. Jacobs, do you deny that the CIA has been involved in torture in the past?"

"I have no personal knowledge of anything like that."

"Are you not aware of the CIA handbook of 1983?"

Jacobs wasn't biting. "What handbook is that?"

Skyles pulled a copy of it out of his briefcase. He crossed to Jacobs, asking the judge as he did, "May I approach?"

The judge nodded.

"This handbook. Dated 1983, and titled," he read the front page, "*The Human Resource Exploitation Training Manual 1983.*" He handed it to Jacobs. "It not only discusses torture but describes *methods*. Right?"

"That manual was banned by Director Perry in 1996."

"So there aren't *any* copies *anywhere* in Langley." Pause. "Right?"

Jacobs almost smiled. "I wouldn't think so."

"But you don't know, do you?"

"Not really. I don't know. I've never seen it."

"You would have this jury believe that the CIA is pure and pristine and does not torture people even if the greater good of the United States is at stake?"

"That is certainly my policy. I can't speak to what happened before I got there or what happens in other directorates that I don't see."

"Isn't it true, sir, that the CIA requires its operatives to do what it takes to get the job done, but tells them if something goes wrong that they're on their own? And their superiors will deny all knowledge?"

Jacobs bristled. "No. I don't operate that way."

Skyles was surprised. "Have you ever said anything like that to Mr. Rathman?"

He hesitated slightly. "Not that I recall."

"Do you deny saying to him that if things went wrong in Sudan that he was on his own?"

"I don't remember that."

"The United States Government wants results from its operatives, doesn't it?"

"Of course."

"And you encourage them to do what it takes to get the job done."

"Within limitations."

"And if things get political, or don't go perfectly, you back away from them and let them fall on their own, don't you?"

"I don't think that's fair."

"That's what you've done to Lieutenant Rathman, isn't it?"

"No. It isn't."

"No further questions."

Commander Glenn Pugh read the message he had been handed, one of the strangest he had ever received. As the commanding officer of the *Louisiana* (SSBN 743), the latest *Ohio*-class ballistic missile submarine, he received numerous messages every day. Many, like this one, contained orders that dealt with the submarine's mission; but never with instructions like this.

The *Louisiana* was designed to hide in the deepest parts of the ocean and launch intercontinental nuclear ballistic missiles at whatever enemy the United States decided to obliterate. He was *never* sent on a mission to find things, or track other ships, or do anything other than hide. But here was a message ordering him to ignore the operational orders he had received just the day before. Now he was to get under way *immediately* from his home base in King's Bay, Georgia, regardless of the state of his stores, his crew, or anything else. His estimate for getting under way in any orderly fashion was a minimum of twelve hours. Twenty-five percent of his crew was ashore. He didn't have time to recall them. The message was unequivocal, though—get underway *immediately*. He was to head south at maximum possible speed to intercept a course from Monrovia, Liberia, to Jacksonville, Florida, then head outbound toward Africa looking for a container ship called the *Monrovian Prince*. He was to find it and intercept it before it reached Florida.

His intelligence officer had received photographs, descriptions, and electronic signature information of the radars and radios of the ship by classified e-mail. Unfortunately they didn't have an acoustic signature, at least one the Office of Naval Intelligence had confidence in. Pugh thought they had all they needed to find a single container ship. But once they found it, then what? The message was curiously silent. Since secrecy was clearly not critical, he could communicate with Washington when he did find the ship. He had no doubt that he would find it. If it was on the described course, he would find it. He could simply wait off the coast of Jacksonville, perhaps sixty miles, and wait for the ship to come to him. If he was then to sink it, or stop it, or board, whatever he was called upon to do, he would be there and that ship would have no idea he was anywhere nearby, even if it was equipped with the world's most sophisticated sonar equipment, which it undoubtedly was not.

Pugh turned to his Officer of the Deck. "Pass the word to get under way."

The OOD looked to see if his commanding officer was joking. He wasn't. "Under way, sir?"

"Under way."

"Sir, pretty much all the crew from the starboard watch are ashore."

"Under way."

"Aye aye, sir."

◆　◆　◆

Hotary's men continued to work furiously on the *Sea Dragon,* changing the paint, the appearance, and the electronics. They scrambled all over the ship replacing each piece of electronics gear that transmitted anything off the ship, anything that could be identified as unique to the *Monrovian Prince.* Each replacement brought them closer to their new identity, the *Sea Dragon.*

The telephone on the bridge rang. It was engineering. Hotary picked up the receiver. "What is it?"

"The engine is overheating. I don't know if it can handle this speed much longer."

"It will. We must stay at maximum speed."

"We might break down."

Hotary examined the shaft RPM and the speed. He checked their position based on the GPS receiver and quickly recalculated their time to the rendezvous. They had no time to spare even at maximum speed. "We have no choice."

◆　◆　◆

Wolff stood up in the courtroom. "Your Honor, United States calls Richard Velasca."

Skyles turned to Rat and whispered, "Who is this?"

"I told you. Navy SEAL. He's in Dev Group."

Velasca was dressed just like Rat in his whites. He was handsome and tan. His black hair was combed back and gave him a cosmopolitan look. He was generally a carefree person, but he immediately sensed the seriousness of the courtroom. He walked to the front of the room, was sworn in, and took the witness chair.

Wolff asked him his name, his current position in the Navy, and a little bit about his background. He then asked, "Do you know the defendant, Lieutenant Kent Rathman?"

"Yes, I do."

"How do you know him?"

"He was in Dev—my current Navy unit with me until he moved over to the—can I say it?"

"Yes," the judge said, anticipating his concern.

"He was assigned TAD to the CIA. To their SAS group."

"But before that you served on the same counterterrorism team in the Navy?"

"Yes."

"When was the last time you saw Mr. Rathman?"

"A few weeks ago."

"Where were you?"

"At the Little Creek O' Club."

Rat leaned back slightly. "Uh oh," he said to no one in particular. He knew where this was going.

"Did you have a chance to talk to Mr. Rathman on that evening?"

"Sure. There were several of us from Dev Group and a few other SEALs. We were having a few beers."

Wolff leaned on the lectern with his hands on the side. "Did the subject of the raid in Sudan come up?"

"Yes."

"Did Mr. Rathman talk about it at all?"

"Sure. The fact that Duar had been captured was all over the base. It was all over the SEAL community. It was huge. A real coup. Rat—Lieutenant Rathman—is something of a legend in the SEAL community. We wanted to know all about the raid, and he was in town. Frankly, the rest of us still in Dev Group were a little jealous that we weren't in on it."

"What did he say?"

Velasca shrugged. "Basically that several Special Ops teams were airborne that night. They got the call—they were the closest—jumped out of the C-17 with Land Cruisers . . ." he paused as he considered how much to say, ". . . then drove to the rendezvous spot and walked in like they owned the damned place. Sorry. It took the enemy just long enough to figure out who they were that they were able to position themselves for the ensuing firefight. Thankfully only one American was killed; most of Duar's men were killed and he was captured."

"Did he mention how he located Duar?"

Velasca nodded. "He said they got one of Duar's men, I forget his name, but Duar had somehow eluded them, or escaped." Velasca hesitated and glanced quickly at Rat, suddenly feeling the heat of his testimony. He saw Rat staring at him.

"Did he say what he did to this man?"

"He said he had to encourage him to tell them where Duar was. He *knew* Duar was there; the signal for the attack was not to be given unless Duar was present. And the guy who had given the signal was *right there*, he was still alive and standing there. And he said Duar had been right there, right in that room. He didn't know where he had gone."

"What did he do?"

"He said that he had to give the man a long drink of water."

"And then?"

"So someone in the group—there were probably eight of us—said, 'You boarded him?' and Rat nodded and smiled."

A gasp went up from two of the jurors. Rat looked down at the table.

Rat whispered to Skyles, "Isn't this hearsay or something?"

"Yeah. But it's admissible as hell."

Wolff asked, "What did you take that to mean?"

"That he gave the guy the water board."

"Mr. Rathman," he said, turning to look at Rat, "the defendant, said *that* was what he had done to the man in Sudan?"

"He didn't say that exactly, but that was how I took it."

Wolff looked at Skyles. "Your witness."

◆　◆　◆

David Stern had spent hours in the brig aboard the *Belleau Wood* evaluating Duar as a witness, deciding whether to call him. Commander Little said he was a horrible witness and shouldn't be called. That the confession was fatal, and he signed it and admitted he was Wahamed Duar. To call him as a witness would just make it worse. But Stern disagreed. He was sure the Navy had the wrong man, and he wanted their client, whatever his name was, to testify. Duar had listened and agreed with Stern. He would testify.

"Mr. Stern, since the prosecution has rested and we have dealt with your motions, do you have any witnesses?"

"Yes, Your Honor. We would like to call the defendant."

The members of the court were surprised, as was Elizabeth Watson. She had rarely seen a defendant called in a criminal trial. It was extraordinary.

The defendant made his way slowly to the witness chair, was sworn in, and sat down. When asked to state his full name, as the translator gave him the question, he responded, "Mohammed el-Mahdi."

The judge looked at him skeptically, anticipating various games to dodge his guilt.

Stern began, "You said your name is Mohammed el-Mahdi. Yet during this trial you have been repeatedly identified as Wahamed Duar. Which is it?"

"My name is Mohammed el-Mahdi."

"Where are you from?"

"Khartoum, Sudan."

"What is your profession?"

"I drive a taxicab."

"Do you know Wahamed Duar?"

"Yes. We grew up together."

"When was the last time you saw Wahamed Duar?"

"The night I was captured."

"Are you a member of Duar's terrorist organization?"

"He is not a terrorist. And those that work with him are not members of a terrorist organization. They are revolutionaries."

"Why do you think that Duar had you around?"

"Because I look like him. I think he always hoped that if something happened, they might mistake me for him."

Stern looked at the members of the court. They weren't buying it yet, but they were listening. "That could be risky for you. There are many people who want Wahamed Duar dead."

"Yes, some risk. But I would do anything for him. He is a great man," he said with intensity.

"Did he let you in on any of his planning or inside meetings?"

"No. Never. He never told me anything."

"Did he ever tell you what to do if you were captured in his place?"

"Yes. He told me to say anything I wanted. He knew I didn't know anything significant. No one would gain any information about him through me."

"Did he have you dress like him?"

"Yes. I knew that. We didn't really talk about it in the open, but it was obvious. We looked very much alike."

"Except for the eyes."

"Yes. He has very light brown eyes."

"Was Wahamed Duar there the night you were captured?"

"Yes. He was there. He was hiding."

"So the American forces simply missed him. Is that right?"

"Yes."

Stern nodded. "One last thing. This confession that has been admitted into evidence. Did you write that?"

"Yes."

"Where were you?"

"In Egypt."

"Wasn't it after you had been captured by the American forces?"

"Yes."

"How did you get to Egypt?"

"The Americans came and got me off this ship and flew me to Egypt."

"Then you wrote that confession?"

"Yes."

"Is it true? Is what you said in that document accurate?"

"No. None of it."

"Then why did you write it?"

"I had been beaten and had a towel put around my head. They poured water into the towel until I couldn't breathe. I was suffocating. Then I was electrocuted in my ears," he said touching his earlobes, "and then my balls. They tortured me. Almost to death."

"Do you remember that American officer who was here? Who testified?"

"Yes."

"Was he the one who took you off this ship and escorted you to Egypt?"

"Yes."

"Was he there when you were tortured?"

"No."

"Was he was in the room during any of the torture?"

"No."

"Are you Wahamed Duar?"

"No. I am Mohammed el-Mahdi."

"Everything in the so-called confession is untrue?"

"Yes. Completely."

"Why did you sign it?"

"Because I couldn't stand the pain anymore."

Stern nodded his head. "No further questions."

Elizabeth Watson rose slowly. She wasn't sure where to start. She had not anticipated this man testifying, whatever his name really was. She had not prepared a cross-examination, for which she was now kicking herself. "You wear contact lenses, do you not?"

"No."

"There is only one photograph in existence of Wahamed Duar. That photograph was taken of you when you were wearing light brown contact lenses. Correct?"

"No. That is not me in the photograph."

"You admit you were at the meeting when the raid took place. Correct?"

"Yes."

"And you admit that you are part of Duar's organization. Correct?"

"No. I never do anything with him. I just hang around. Once in a while he will ask me to drive him somewhere. But that's all."

"Yet you were friends with him from childhood? And he shows so little faith in you that you're not part of his organization?"

"I'm not very . . . smart. I never got much education. He knows this. I think he really just keeps me around because I look like him. There are a couple of other men who look like him too that he uses for the same purpose."

Watson was horrified. This was getting worse. She felt the burning eyes of the journalists on the back of her head. They were scribbling furiously in their obnoxious little notebooks, ready to transmit to their newspapers and television stations that the United States had captured the wrong man, and Wahamed Duar was still at large. Her name would be in every newspaper in the country for having failed. "If in fact you are Wahamed Duar, it would be very clever for you to have your friend have *his* photograph taken who has lighter eyes, and tell anyone who would listen that he is Wahamed Duar. Wouldn't it?"

"I don't understand."

"Maybe you are Mohammed el-Mahdi and maybe you are Wahamed Duar. You were captured with Duar's organization in the middle of the biggest arms sales meeting in recent memory. Yet you claim complete innocence. Perhaps you're Wahamed Duar and pretending not to be. Isn't that what you're doing?"

"No."

"The photograph we have in evidence is of Mohammed el-Mahdi, isn't it?"

"It looks like Wahamed to me. But it isn't me."

"Maybe you are Duar and the photograph is of Mr. el-Mahdi, your double?"

"No. It is not. I am el-Mahdi."

She thought for a moment, just long enough for those in the gallery to think she had lost her way. "Sir, you were there on the morning of the raid, weren't you?"

"Yes."

"And you were armed, correct?"

"We were attacked and I found a rifle on the floor and picked it up."

"When you were about to be captured you fired at the American forces, trying to kill them, didn't you?"

"I didn't know what was happening. I was afraid."

"No further questions," Elizabeth said, sitting down with a slight smile on her face, a manufactured, disingenuous smile that hid her frustration. She had hoped to place some belief in the minds of the court that this man was in fact Wahamed Duar, who had simply created a clever story to evade conviction. But she doubted the very thing she was trying to sell. It was simply the best she could do.

"Anything further, Mr. Stern?"

"No further questions, Your Honor."

"You may step down, sir," Judge Graham said.

Stern stood. "Your Honor, if it please the court, I would like to renew my motion to exclude the confession. It seems apparent that United States agents were complicit in the confession. If it wasn't solicited by them, they participated by delivering my client to Egypt, then waiting just behind the curtain until the torture was completed. It is complicity of a very dark and troubling kind, Your Honor, and the confession must be excluded to deter American forces from participating in this kind of charade."

"Denied," Judge Graham said with finality.

♦　♦　♦

In Washington Wolff stood up. He was ready to call his next witness. He had just completed Sellers, the one disgruntled member of Rat's team, who had willingly, eagerly, spoken with Wolff on the phone, and had testified gladly. He had nearly skipped into the courtroom, ready to relieve his conscience by telling all, but had suddenly lost some of his enthusiasm when he looked into Rat's face. At the end, all he could say was that Rat had been kneeling by Mazmin, and there was water involved, but he really couldn't see much. Wolff was furious. It wasn't what Sellers had said on the phone. But he too had seen the look Rat had given Sellers.

Skyles turned to Rat. "There are still twelve people on their witness list that they haven't called. A few of them I never even had a chance to contact."

"That just impresses the hell out of me," Rat said, looking at Skyles. "It's my life that's on trial here. Do you understand that I'll be in *prison?* You couldn't even find time to *call* them? What the hell have you been doing?" Rat was seething. The trial was getting to him. He was unable to fight back; he had to rely on Skyles. Why hadn't he followed the advice of his friends and stayed in Dev Group? Don't go to the CIA, they said. It's in Washington, and Washington is poison. Everything is political, and we don't know how to play that game. They don't believe in duty and honor, just power and position. But he hadn't listened. He had been flattered by their interest. It felt like an opportunity to do some things he would never get another chance to do. Now he wanted nothing more than to go back to his regular Navy life, back to Dev Group.

"Don't worry about it," Skyles said.

"The United States requests that the courtroom be cleared," Wolff said.

Judge Wiggins nodded. "All observers and journalists are to clear the courtroom."

The marshals escorted everyone out except the court personnel, the attorneys, and the jury.

Wiggins waited for complete silence, then said to Wolff, "Call your witness."

"The United States calls Achmed Massoud."

Skyles frowned. "This is their big, secret witness."

Rat looked at the back of the courtroom as the man came in. He recognized the man instantly. He tried not to let the jury see his consternation. He said through his clenched teeth, "Oh shit."

Skyles turned quickly to him. "What? Who is he?"

"Acacia. He was there."

"Where?" Skyles said as he saw Acacia enter the room dressed in a khaki-colored Italian suit.

"Sudan."

"Do you have any dirt on him? Anything I can use to cross-examine him?"

Rat thought, then said quickly in a whisper, "When I was—talking—to the guy, Mazmin, Acacia asked me to look away for a few seconds. He wanted to kill him. He was ready to cut him open. Or shoot him. And Achmed's not his real name."

"What is his real name?"

"I don't know. Acacia was a code name. He used all kinds of names."

Acacia's eyes met Rat's as he walked up to the witness chair.

Acacia was sworn in and sat down carefully. His suit was perfect. His shirt matched, and his expensive designer tie gave him a sophisticated cosmopolitan look. He was wearing a Rolex. Rat had known him for two years. He was one of the cleverest operators he had ever met. He always seemed to find his way into the financial side of terrorist organizations, criminal endeavors, or even government corruption, and he always came out ahead of the game. Not only did he roll up the terrorist organization, but he ruined their finances for decades and seemed to somehow make off with some of it. Some of the money probably went to his principals in Jordan, and some of it probably ended up in Switzerland.

Wolff was clearly relishing calling a foreign operative to testify against Rat, to drive the final nail in the coffin. He knew that Acacia had been there, and he knew that Acacia had seen everything. It had been a struggle to get Jordan to force Acacia to come over to the trial. He had been required to go through the State Department and even the CIA to get authorization to identify him.

"Were you present on the night an attack occurred in Sudan by American forces trying to capture Wahamed Duar?"

"Yes, I was."

"Who led that raid for the American forces?"

"Lieutenant Rathman. We knew him as Rat."

"Is he here?"

"Yes, he's sitting right over there," he said, indicating.

"Were you there when the American Special Forces came into the room?"

"Yes."

"Describe for us what happened."

Acacia recounted the events of that night. The jury was riveted. They wanted to listen to Acacia all day. They were dazzled by his suave demeanor and his mystery.

"And after the firefight subdued, Lieutenant Rathman, the defendant," Wolff said, pointing, "grabbed this Mazmin and threw him onto a table. Is that correct?"

"Well, I saw Mazmin on the table."

Rat's heart sank. "Here we go," he muttered to Skyles.

"What did he do?"

Acacia hesitated. He looked at Rat, right in his eyes. For some reason, perhaps wishful thinking, Rat felt reassured. Acacia answered, "He offered him some water."

The jurors laughed. Several of them sat back, thankful for the release in tension. Wolff was not pleased. "By offering him water, as you said, you don't mean to imply that Rathman was trying to satisfy the thirst of the man he had just placed on the table, do you?"

"I don't know what his intentions were. I wasn't watching that closely, and he and I have never spoken about it."

"Did you see him pour water onto his face, in the mouth and nose area of Mazmin, the man who later died?"

Acacia glanced at the jury, then back at Wolff with a starkly serious look. "This Mazmin, this murderer, is part of the most vicious terrorist organization in the world, headed by Wahamed Duar, who was there that night. I *saw* him with my own eyes. These are the men who tried to kill the King of Jordan six months ago. These are the men who murder Americans at every opportunity. They have no sense of justice. I personally wanted to—"

"Did you or did you not see Lieutenant Rathman pour water onto his face?"

Acacia was annoyed. "May I finish?"

Wolff replied, quickly sensing that this witness was getting out of control, "You may continue answering the question, but you may not continue a speech about your opinions regarding—"

Skyles saw his opening. He stood up quickly. "Your Honor, he asked a question, yet now he refuses to let the witness answer it because he doesn't like the answer. That's not justice, that's not—"

The judge turned to Acacia, pressing his glasses up hard into his face. "Answer the question, sir, and you will be given a chance to give your full answer, but it must be responsive to the question."

Acacia nodded. "I personally wanted to kill the man on the table. I had a knife in my clothing, as well as a gun. Lieutenant Rathman restrained me. I walked to the table with the full intention of killing him, but your American officer would not let me do it. He saved the man's life."

Rat tried not to smile.

Wolff wanted to strangle him. "Did you see him pouring water into Mazmin's face?"

Acacia sat there for what seemed like an eternity. Finally he spoke in his quiet way again. "I saw him offering the man a drink, I saw him prevent me from killing him, which I would do today with my bare hands if given the chance, and would do to Wahamed Duar if you allow me to go aboard your ship for thirty minutes, but after I was stopped, I was ashamed, and turned away. I did not see what happened after that."

"You saw Lieutenant Rathman torture him. Didn't you?"

"Leading," Skyles objected.

"Sustained," the judge said.

"Did you see Rathman torture Mazmin?"

"I saw some water, I saw him offer a drink, but if Mazmin needed to be tortured, *I* would have done it, and he would've told me whatever I wanted to know, I promise you. Your Lieutenant Rathman seemed restrained. He seemed unwilling to do what was necessary to truly get this man to talk. I would've been happy to do it."

"But he told Lieutenant Rathman where Duar was, did he not?"

"That is what I understand. Perhaps he was grateful for the drink."

Two jurors laughed out loud and then put their hands over their mouths, ashamed of their lack of control.

Wolff knew he had missed his target by a wide margin. He remembered that phrase before. Another witness had used the same phrase, that Mazmin was grateful for the drink. But who? Someone had gotten to the witnesses and encouraged them not to talk to him, even told them what to say and how to say it. Wolff had been required to call the witnesses cold, without meeting with them first, and they were killing him. Groome, he suddenly thought. The other SEAL. Rat's best friend. "Sir, one last thing. Have you spoken with anyone about your testimony here today?"

"Not really."

"Did you talk to a Lieutenant Ted Groome?"

Acacia looked surprised. "Yes, I did."

"He called you."

"Yes."

"In Jordan?" Wolff asked skeptically.

"No. Here. After I got here to testify at the request of your Department of Justice, an official request through my government in Jordan."

"He called you here?"

"Yes."

"Where?"

"At my hotel."

"How did he know you were coming, or what hotel you would be at?"

"I don't know. Didn't you tell him?"

"No."

"Then I have no idea."

"What did he say?" Wolff regretted the question as soon as he asked it.

Acacia hesitated. "He said he had already testified and that you were trying to hang Lieutenant Rathman, you were twisting the truth and determined to get a conviction because of political pressure. I think that's what he said. Oh, and that the American government was trying to convict a hero."

Wolff wanted to disappear through the floor. He had walked into a trap. "Nothing further," he said.

Skyles fought back a grin. "Sir, did you come here willingly at the request of the U.S. Government?"

"Yes."

"Have you told the truth to the best of your ability?"

"Yes, I have."

"Do you speak Arabic?"

"Yes I do."

"Did you hear Mr. Rathman threaten this Mazmin person in any way?"

"No, I didn't."

"Thank you, sir, no further questions."

Acacia got down from the witness chair slowly and walked out of the courtroom. As he went by Rat, he winked.

Chapter

24

The tribunal members filed back into the wardroom. They had listened with great care to the closing arguments, which dealt almost entirely with the question of identity. Commander Watson was not optimistic. She had felt the case slip through her hands the minute Duar, or el-Mahdi, took the stand.

Stern's heart pounded. He knew if the court believed his client was Wahamed Duar he would be convicted. But Stern was completely convinced that his client was not Duar. The journalists were on his side. They had quickly published the stories about the mistaken identity. They were accusing the United States Government of incompetence for capturing the wrong man, or for letting him slip through their fingers. They were gleefully tying the two trials together, Duar's and Rathman's. They made a once brilliant operation look almost comical. As much fun as it was to write the articles, there was an underlying tone of concern. If Duar wasn't on trial on the *Belleau Wood*, where was he?

The *Washington Post* in particular was enthusiastic about the angle of the defendant being a taxi driver from Khartoum. Literally not one story about Duar, or el-Mahdi, ran in the *Post* without referring to him as a cabdriver. They recounted the extent to which the United States had gone, the efforts put forth with multiple Special Operations teams airborne, multiple jets with in-air refueling, helicopters standing by and innumerable others backing up the operation, all to capture a taxi driver.

Stern loved the image; he loved the fact that people were picking up on the heart of the defense, and that they were assuming to be true what he was trying to prove. They ran the photograph of Duar next to the AP artist's drawing of el-Mahdi. Not only were the eyes different, but on close examination the faces were slightly different as well. Even though the photograph of Duar was of poor quality, similar to a photocopy of a newspaper photograph, it was good enough to tell the difference even allowing for the inherent inaccuracy of the drawing.

Elizabeth Watson sat at the prosecution table next to Stern in her perfect uniform with her ankles crossed and her bony hands folded. Her lips were pressed tightly together, clearly anticipating the not-guilty verdict, ready for the worst. Stern derived great satisfaction from the look on her face. The journalists were anxious for the conclusion. Several of them had satellite phones ready to transmit the result to their principals instantly once they had the news.

Judge Graham looked around the room and waited for quiet. "This court is now in session. I would like to read the verdict of the court." He unfolded a piece of paper. "As to the charge of conspiracy to commit terrorist acts against the United States, we find the defendant . . . not guilty."

The courtroom buzzed as if an electrical switch had been thrown.

"Quiet please," he said, and waited. The noise died down. "As to the charge of murder of American citizens by terrorist act, we find the defendant not guilty." He folded the piece of paper back and handed it to the bailiff.

Stern let out a sigh and smiled. The translator sitting immediately behind him conveyed the result to his client. Stern shook his hand in congratulations. He stood up and faced the judge. "Your Honor, since my client was taken from his country against his will, I request that the United States return him to his country at their expense immediately. I would like that to be part of the court's order."

Graham looked at Stern with a severe expression. "That is a reasonable request, Mr. Stern. But I'm afraid you misperceive the result."

"In what way?" Stern asked.

322 | JAMES W. HUSTON

"While the court certainly had the power to determine whether he was guilty of the charges before it, other powers are left solely to me. I will confirm the tribunal's order regarding the charges against your client. It is the belief of the court that your client is not Wahamed Duar."

"Thank you, sir," Stern said, sitting down.

"But I'm not done," the judge said, raising his hand. He then pointed at the defendant. "According to *his* own testimony, he was part of Duar's organization, even if it was at a low level. He was present at the meeting in Sudan. He was therefore a member of a terrorist group that has the destruction of the United States as its primary goal. Further, he took up arms and fired at American forces in the performance of their duties. As such, he is an enemy combatant as that has been recently defined. I therefore order that he be sent to Guantánamo Bay, Cuba, where he is to be held until the cessation of hostilities."

Stern felt as if he had had his legs cut out from under him. "But, sir, he hasn't been charged with anything other than as Duar!"

"You decided to put him on the stand, Mr. Stern. You asked him questions about his participation in that organization, and he clearly voluntarily testified. That is quite sufficient to prove that he is a member of that organization and took arms against American forces. Either one is good enough. He is an enemy combatant and subject to confinement until the conclusion of hostilities. It's as simple as that. The fact that he has not been charged with anything in that regard makes no difference whatsoever. When a German soldier was captured in World War II, we didn't charge him with something and put him on trial to see if he had actually fired at American forces. He was part of the German Army. That was good enough. He was taken into custody and kept there until the cessation of hostilities. Combatants aren't entitled to a trial, to a defense, to an attorney. They're just captured and kept. Very simple. He is essentially a prisoner of war; but full prisoner of war status has not been granted, as I understand it, because he is not fighting on behalf of a country. You should have thought about it before you called him to the stand. This court is adjourned." The judge slammed down the gavel as

Stern turned to his client and asked for the translator to help explain what had just happened as the MAAs closed on el-Mahdi to take him into custody.

Little muttered, "Then why have a damned tribunal if they can just keep his ass in custody as a combatant?"

Stern looked at him with a pained expression. "Be*cause*, Mr. Little, of the penalty. In case you've forgotten, they were asking for the death penalty, or life in prison."

"Well, too bad for him, huh. Good job getting him off though, I mean from the death penalty and what not."

"Shut up," Stern said, slamming his briefcase and watching the translator's and el-Mahdi's faces.

◆　◆　◆

The USS *Ronald Reagan* had steamed all night. Its airplanes had flown continuously to find the *Monrovian Prince* heading west. They had marked several targets for visual identification at daylight, and had now identified virtually all of them. The list was long. Several of the ships did not need further investigation. They were too small, or the wrong kind of ship entirely—fishing boats or oil tankers. But much to the annoyance of Captain Bill Anderson, they had not located the *Monrovian Prince*. He had sent the air wing's airplanes five hundred miles out in all directions, even back toward Africa; but no sign of the *Prince*. Nothing even close. They were now flying double cycle. Each radar contact was identified and its location marked and transmitted instantly to the remainder of the battle group and to Washington. Like a hungry lion, the *Ronald Reagan* turned further west, plowing through the ocean at thirty knots looking desperately for a container ship from Liberia.

Farther to the west, closer to Florida, the USS *Louisiana,* the Ohio-class ballistic missile submarine, was on the track projected for the *Prince* to take it to Jacksonville. Captain Pugh had crept up on numerous merchant ships, studied their acoustic and electronic signatures, and viewed many through his periscope. But none was the *Monrovian Prince.*

Pugh leaned over the chart table studying the expected track of their target. They should have already seen the ship. He knew there were other submarines that had left base after him that were setting up a barrier in front of Jacksonville to stop the ship when it came near. It left him the freedom to head east at a much higher rate of speed than would be normal. But no *Monrovian Prince.*

"Captain, we have another sonar contact bearing three-six-zero at thirty thousand yards."

Captain Pugh glanced at the chart. This contact would take them well north of the projected route of the *Monrovian Prince,* but he had already viewed all the sonar contacts in the immediate vicinity. He could check this contact out and return to the projected track without losing too much time. He turned to the Officer of the Deck. "Take heading three-six-zero, set twenty knots."

"Aye aye, sir."

The large submarine turned slowly from east to north and began its pursuit of the newest sonar contact.

♦ ♦ ♦

Judge Royce Wiggins spoke to Skyles, "Mr. Skyles, do you plan on calling any witnesses for the defense?"

Skyles rose slowly. "Yes, Your Honor. The defense would like to call Andrea Ash."

The gallery, which had been readmitted, turned as one to look at her. The marshal went into the hallway and called her name. She walked into the courtroom and lit it up. Her shimmering white uniform and bright look brought energy to the entire procedure. It was something she had encountered for so long she barely noticed. But this felt different. She didn't know what the signals were that people were giving off. She had been unable to watch the trial because of the judge's rule excluding witnesses until they had testified. She had waited for Rat at the end of each day though. She had been warned by Skyles not to because it would put her testimony in jeopardy. The jury would assume that she was testifying because of her relationship with Rat. She said she would take that risk. Rat didn't seem to mind.

Her shoulder boards were different from Rat's only in that she wore the medical insignia that Satterly had worn instead of Rat's five-pointed star.

Skyles asked, "Do you know Dr. Satterly?"

"I work with him aboard the *Belleau Wood.*"

"Do you know him well?"

"I haven't been aboard that long, but I see him frequently throughout the day."

Wolff wasn't going to let Skyles have much room. "Objection, Your Honor. What is the possible relevance of any of this testimony?"

"Mr. Skyles?"

"It is to show the *bias* of the witness on whom Mr. Wolff has relied so heavily in his otherwise nonexistent case. If Dr. Satterly's testimony is—"

"That's enough, Mr. Skyles. Overruled," Wiggins said to Wolff, annoyed by Skyles's editorializing.

Skyles looked at Andrea. "Have you ever heard Dr. Satterly say anything that made you believe he was out to get Lieutenant Rathman?"

"He used those very words. One time he said to me that he was going to get Lieutenant Rathman if it was the last thing he did."

"What did you take that to mean?"

"He seemed to take the death of that terrorist personally. He was really offended by the fact that he died. He blamed his death on Lieutenant Rathman. He wanted him to be punished."

"Did he say these things to you?"

"Several times."

"Did he ever call Lieutenant Rathman any names in your presence, anything critical?"

"Well, he called him a murderer. He said he was a murdering barbarian, and that he was cold and amoral."

"Do you know Lieutenant Rathman?"

"Yes, I do."

"How?"

"When I was the flight surgeon for the Blue Angels he was assigned to the team to defend one of the pilots from an attempt to assassinate him, to shoot down the team. I met him in California and got to know him."

"Did you form a personal relationship with him?"

"Yes."

"Have you maintained that personal relationship with him?"

"Yes, we continue to date."

"Are you the kind of person who would lie or make things up to protect him?"

"No. I wouldn't do that."

Skyles paused. "You sure?"

"Yes. Quite."

Skyles nodded, letting her testimony sink in with the jury. "Did Dr. Satterly do anything else that made you think he was out to get Lieutenant Rathman?"

"He told me he'd done a tour with NATO in Belgium. He loved his tour of duty there, and made friends with one of the European lawyers assigned to NATO headquarters. I don't recall his name—I'm not sure he told me. He stayed in contact with him. He e-mails him maybe once a month."

Skyles waited, letting the tension build. He then asked, "Why does that matter?"

"That European lawyer is now assigned to the International Criminal Court in Holland—the court set up to try international war criminals. As soon as the terrorist died on board the *Belleau Wood,* Dr. Satterly e-mailed his friend and told him the ICC should put Lieutenant Rathman on trial. As a war criminal."

Skyles looked at each of the jurors. He wanted them to smell the conspiracy that lurked behind the curtain somewhere. A conspiracy so deep he couldn't get to it, but he knew it was there, and he knew the jury would smell it if he let them. People loved to believe in government conspiracies. All it would take was one juror to think something was wrong with this trial, something they couldn't see, some reasonable doubt, and he would have a hung jury. Good enough. But if enough bought it, Rathman would walk. "Did he tell you he had e-mailed this European attorney?"

"No."

"How do you know he did?"

"I brought a copy of it with me," she said, holding up a piece of paper.

Wolff was stunned. He stood.

"Did he give it to you?" Skyles continued quickly.

"No."

"How did you get it?"

"I asked to borrow his computer when he was gone because mine didn't have the right Ethernet card to work on the ship and I couldn't do e-mail yet. When I turned on his computer I found this e-mail saved to the hard drive and printed it."

Skyles glanced at Wolff, who was turning scarlet.

"What is the name of this European attorney? The one Dr. Satterly e-mailed?"

She looked at the "To" block of the e-mail. "Didier Picque."

"The very attorney mentioned in the *Washington Post* this morning as the one who allegedly told the Secretary of Defense that if Lieutenant Rathman wasn't prosecuted *here* in *this* court, they would drag him to The Hague and try him as a war criminal?"

Wolff erupted, "Objection! Hearsay, argumentative, four-oh-three, Your Honor! This is outrageous!"

"I withdraw the question." Skyles glanced at the jury, then turned to Wolff. "Your witness."

♦ ♦ ♦

Captain Pugh held the *Louisiana* at periscope depth. He had been watching this latest target on sonar for miles. It had been consistently heading northwest. It looked like just another routine merchant contact, but he had to check it out. He glanced down at the photograph of the *Monrovian Prince* they had received from Washington again, then at the clock. The sun had broken the horizon and he was up sun of the target. "Up periscope," he commanded. The cylinder hissed as it quickly moved up past him and brought the eyepiece to his level.

As the periscope broke the surface of the ocean he looked toward the ship clearly illuminated on the horizon. No telltale cranes, no containers stacked on deck.

Pugh turned to the Officer of the Deck. "Put me a thousand yards astern of her. Let's get her name and call it in."

The lieutenant complied, turning quickly to port and increasing speed. Minutes later the *Louisiana* was astern of the ship and Pugh raised the periscope again. He wanted to get a photograph to transmit to Washington with the others he had already sent. The periscope broke the surface. He twisted the handle and digitally zoomed in on the stern of the ship. He read it aloud, "*Sea Dragon*. Hong Kong." He squeezed the trigger, capturing the image with the high-resolution digital camera. "Down periscope!" He looked at his lieutenant, the one in charge of electronic warfare. "How's her radar?"

The lieutenant had been expecting the question. "Matches the *Sea Dragon*."

Pugh nodded as the periscope retreated into the deck at his feet. "No cranes, no containers, wrong name, wrong city, wrong direction, heading for the wrong port, wrong speed, you name it. Send the name and location off with the others. Set a course for our next contact."

"Aye aye, sir."

◆   ◆   ◆

"Would this be a good time to take a break, Your Honor?" Wolff asked, desperate for some time to think, maybe make a few phone calls.

"No," Wiggins replied. "It would not."

"Very well," Wolff nodded, as if that was what he expected, trying not to show his frustration and anger.

He strode slowly to the lectern and looked at Andrea Ash, one of the prettiest women he had ever seen. He could tell the jury loved her. She had come across as capable, bright, energetic, honest, and she had even elicited sympathy for coming to the defense of her boyfriend, a fact that was usually fatal to an ordinary witness's testimony.

He also didn't know what else her little briefcase contained other than the e-mail to Didier Picque. Wolff had sent one of his associates to get Dr. Satterly back to the courtroom to testify in rebuttal and help them attack her, but he hadn't yet arrived.

"Good morning, Lieutenant Ash. Or should I call you doctor?"

"Either one," she replied.

"Lieutenant Rathman, Rat as we've learned he is called, is your boyfriend. Isn't that right?"

"Yes."

Wolff didn't know enough facts so he was going to have to take some chances. "You live together, don't you?"

"No. We don't even live in the same state. And right now I'm stationed aboard the *Belleau Wood*, which was in the IO but now is in the South Atlantic."

"You don't like Dr. Satterly very much, do you?"

She shrugged almost imperceptibly. "He's okay."

"Do you think it's okay to read other people's mail?"

"I'm not sure what you mean."

"Well, when you were using Dr. Satterly's computer, his laptop, you came across this e-mail that you've shown us here. And probably others, right?"

"Sure."

"Did it ever occur to you that his e-mails were none of your business?"

"Yes."

"Yet you read them anyway?"

"They were about Rat. I was interested."

"But they weren't addressed to you, were they? . . . So you were reading someone else's mail, or e-mail."

"More or less, I guess."

"You think that's okay?"

"I don't know. It's probably not the best thing."

"He wouldn't have approved, would he?"

"Speculation," Skyles said.

"Sustained."

"But you never asked Dr. Satterly for permission to do that, did you?"

"No."

Wolff nodded. "Haven't I seen you sitting outside this courtroom for days?"

"Off and on."

"You've been here for days, you saw Dr. Satterly come and testify . . . and you never took the opportunity to ask him if he would mind you reading, then printing, and showing to the world, a private e-mail that you found on his computer. Right?"

"Yes, that's true."

"And what you have come here to say, as I understand it—and correct me if I'm wrong—is that Captain Satterly expressed his concern and anger to a friend of his, a Belgian lawyer, about the torture and death of a man he had treated as his patient." He waited. "Correct?"

"Basically."

"No further questions."

◆　◆　◆

The entire National Security Council and a few others met in the situation room at the White House. The tension was clear on President Kendrick's face. He had heard enough of how hard it was to find "one ship." All the others in the room felt the same thing. The new information they were hearing was deeply troubling. Kendrick looked at Stewart Woods. "So where are we?"

Woods looked at Admiral Billy Robinson, the Chief of Naval Operations. The admiral knew that was the only reason he was there: to answer the question that he had no answer to. "Frankly, sir, we don't know. We can't find any trace of it. We have been scouring the seas all along the East Coast both north and south of its path, and haven't seen any sign of it at all. We've increased the circle to all possible locations at maximum possible speed in any direction. I've also checked with Navy intelligence and the NSA, and we have no satellite interception of its electronic signature. It seems to have vanished."

"Is that what you believe has happened, Admiral?"

"Of course not, Mr. President. That ship is out there, unless it sank, which I doubt. The question now is why are we missing it? Ever since Secretary Stuntz told us to go look, I sent out every ship and airplane available on the East Coast. I've sortied a destroyer or frigate every four hours from Norfolk, I sent out every airplane from Oceana; we sent all of our maritime patrol aircraft all over the western Atlantic; we even have our ballistic missile submarines looking for the ship. We have the *Reagan* returning from the Mediterranean checking the course from the east side, and still nothing. So why are we missing the ship? Two possibilities: One, the ship is not headed for the East Coast of United States at all. Initially we were concentrating on Jacksonville as that is the ship's destination. That obviously assumes the ship is going to its *listed* destination—a dangerous assumption. Perhaps it is instead headed for New Orleans, or Tampa, or New York. The other possibility is that the ship has disguised itself. That's not easy to do without serious structural change. The *Monrovian Prince* had two large cranes fore and aft, which don't move. Those are hard to disguise. It also is filled with containers. Those are not easy to disguise either. They could change the name, but the appearance is much harder. Likewise changing the electronics aboard is not impossible, but not easy. But if someone was dedicated to changing the appearance, and they are more clever than we have given them credit for, then they could be out there right now, looking like another ship, and we may have already seen her."

"What do you propose to do to find the ship, Admiral? Because if you don't find it, we could be in for a catastrophe."

"Sir, I think we need to put a blockade into effect. I think we need to station Navy ships and Coast Guard cutters at every major port on the East Coast and stop every ship. Some we can let go immediately because they are clearly not our ship, those that are three hundred feet long, or are bulk cargo carriers, etc. But if it is anywhere close to our target ship in size, then we board and make sure we have what we think we have."

"How long would it take to put the ships in place to do that?"

"I'd say about forty-eight hours at a minimum. Probably seventy-two to be effective. I'm also not sure we have enough ships to do it. There are an awful lot of ways to approach every port."

"We may not have forty-eight hours," St. James said. "We've all been assuming that the ship was only going to travel at ten knots. But if the ship has picked up speed, it may be here tomorrow. Mr. President, I think we need to put in place assets to attack the ship and sink it. We need to put airplanes on runways with air-to-surface missiles and prepare some SEAL teams to board if that's what's necessary. We need to be ready to strike. I don't think we're going to stop it in the ocean. We're missing something."

Stuntz looked at St. James and then at Kendrick. He hated agreeing with her, but he had no choice. "I agree, Mr. President. But we will need to know our rules of engagement. If we identify the ship, are we cleared to sink her?"

President Kendrick looked at Woods. "How sure are we that Wahamed Duar is aboard that ship?"

"Fairly sure, Mr. President. Not positive, but fairly sure."

"Sure enough to kill several innocent civilian employees of a Liberian shipping company? Because if we sink the ship, it's not just terrorists who will die, it's the innocent sailors aboard the ship."

Woods considered before speaking. "Sir, if it was up to me, I would wait until the situation developed before making a decision on what we're going to do. I say let's see how this plays out. You can certainly give the order to sink it anytime you want but if you give an open order to sink it now, and new information is developed later . . ."

President Kendrick closed his eyes momentarily. When he opened them he looked at Admiral Robinson. "Find that ship. Find it now. Stop every ship on the East Coast that is anywhere close to the right size. If that ship gets anywhere near the United States, I will hold you personally responsible."

"Yes, sir," the admiral replied. "There was one odd thing I might mention. It may mean something, and it may not. We had two sightings today of the same ship. One by one of our Boomers—Captain Pugh reported sighting the *Sea Dragon* out of Hong Kong at first light, and a couple of hours later it was spotted by one of our P-3s. Both ships had the correct electronic signature, same radar, and the like. If you take the position of the sub sighting, and DR it ahead—advance it based on the known course and speed—you don't end up at the second sighting. Not even at flank speed. Based on our calculations, the sightings equate to a difference of about thirty nautical miles. Sometimes our airplanes aren't that good at marking the latitude and longitude that accurately, but with GPS it just isn't that hard. So it may be that there are two identical *Sea Dragons* out there. Which I find very strange indeed."

"What are you going to do about it?"

"We've got destroyers on the way right now. I just hope they can reach them before dark."

◆　◆　◆

Judge Wiggins brought the courtroom to order and asked Wolff, "Any rebuttal witnesses?"

"Just one, Your Honor. We'd like to recall Captain Satterly." Wolff knew that most, if not all, of his case now turned on the testimony of Dr. Satterly. He'd given the medical evidence of the cause of death and its link to torture. He was the one who had spoken with Mazmin, who brought his "dying declarations" to the jury. If his credibility was lost, the entire case might fail.

Satterly came into the courtroom triumphantly and took the witness stand. The bailiff reminded him he was still under oath. He nodded and looked at Andrea, who was sitting at the back of the courtroom watching him carefully.

"Good afternoon, Captain. Thank you for your willingness to return to this trial."

"Glad to help," he said.

"I just have a few questions for you, then we can let you get back to your patients. Sitting on the table in front of you is an e-mail that was brought here after it was taken from your computer by Ms. Ash. Have you seen it before?"

"I've seen it, although I've never seen it printed out before."

"Did you give Ms. Ash permission to access this e-mail, or any other for that matter, on your computer?"

"I did not."

"Is it authentic? Did you write it to Didier Picque?"

"It is, and I did."

"Are you ashamed of it?"

"Not at all. I was very disturbed by what Lieutenant Rathman did. I think torture and murder, or manslaughter, should always be investigated wherever they occur. And when it is done by Americans, we owe it to ourselves not to let this type of thing become ordinary, or accepted. I will do what I can to not let that happen."

The jury was warming to him. Several had uncrossed their arms.

"Did you have anything to do with what Didier Picque may or may not have done about Mr. Rathman at the International Criminal Court?"

"Not at all. I have never even spoken to him about it. If he responded to this e-mail, I don't remember it being a very significant response."

"Do you have a bias against Mr. Rathman? Are you out to get him?"

"No, sir. I have nothing against him personally. I do confess to a bias though against cruelty and torture."

"No further questions," Wolff said. He looked at Andrea, and sat down with his back to her.

Skyles rose slowly, gathering his thoughts. "Good afternoon, Doctor."

"Good afternoon," he replied.

"You have no bias against Lieutenant Rathman, right?"

"Correct."

"You're just biased against torture, and things like that. Right?"

"Right."

"What about justice? Are you biased in favor of justice, and truth, and fairness?"

"Yes, of course."

"And yet you ran into the wardroom, interrupted the captain of the *Belleau Wood,* accused Lieutenant Rathman of criminal conduct, all based on the statements of a terrorist and mass murderer. Right?"

"I wouldn't put it like that."

"You never spoke to *anyone* other than a terrorist about what happened in Sudan, did you?"

"I've talked to many people—"

"You haven't talked to *anyone* who was there, other than a terrorist. True?"

"I don't know that he was a terrorist."

"Oh, you don't?"

"No, I don't."

"You're prepared to give him a *huge* benefit of the doubt, but not an officer from your own service? You'll take a terrorist at his word, but you don't even *ask* Lieutenant Rathman what happened?"

"I didn't need to ask him. I had physical evidence."

"The only so-called physical evidence you had was vomit in the terrorist's lungs. True?"

"Essentially, yes."

"And the *only* possible cause of that is torture. Is that your testimony?"

"There are other possible causes, but none of them apply here."

"There *are* other possible causes, aren't there?"

"Yes."

"And you never asked Lieutenant Rathman what happened, did you?"

"No."

"You never gave him a chance to explain, did you?"

"No."

"You just put him on report to the ICC right away, like a schoolboy running to the teacher?"

"I sent the e-mail."

Skyles walked back to his place at the counsel table and stood behind his chair, right next to Rat. "Not only did you send an e-mail to Didier Picque, but you sent e-mails to others about the incident, didn't you?"

Satterly looked concerned. "I'm not sure what you mean."

"Simple question. You sent e-mails to other people, other organizations with which you identify, about what you thought happened in Sudan. True?"

"I don't remember."

Skyles slowly reached down and lifted his briefcase to the table. He opened it and removed several pieces of paper. He looked at the first one. "On the same day as your e-mail to Mr. Picque, you sent an e-mail to the Human Rights Watch. True?"

"Perhaps."

Skyles went to the next page. "And to Amnesty International. Right?"

"Maybe."

"And to Doctors Without Borders. True?"

"Probably."

Skyles glanced at the others. "In fact there were several others to whom you sent such correspondence, weren't there?"

"Yes."

"This was a *crusade* for you, wasn't it?"

"Are those more e-mails from my computer?" Satterly asked, straining to see what Skyles was holding.

"Could they be?" Skyles asked.

"I don't know."

"Why not? Did you send such e-mails?"

"I'm not sure."

"You answered 'yes' to my question about other such e-mails. Were you telling the truth?"

"I think so."

"You think you were telling the truth?"

"I'm sorry, I'm confused. Are those from my computer?"

Skyles ignored him. "In fact, sir, you identify more with the terrorists than you do with the American Special Operations forces trying to catch and punish them, don't you?"

"No."

"You don't?"

"No."

"You believe they have been mistreated and not given the protections they deserve under the American justice traditions. True?"

"Yes."

"And you were prepared to take steps to ensure that your concept of justice was achieved for these terrorists, true?"

"Not really. It's not my role."

"You deny it?"

"Deny what?"

"That you were personally involved in attempting to achieve what you think is justice for terrorists in the custody of the United States."

"I am in favor of justice, sure."

"No. That you were *personally* involved, active, engaged, in pursuing justice, pursuing and defending their rights, on behalf of terrorists."

Satterly stared at Skyles for several seconds. The silence alone spoke to the jury. "I'm not sure what you're getting at," he said finally.

"You are aware that Wahamed Duar was on trial aboard the *Belleau Wood*?"

"I know the person that was *thought* to be Duar was on trial, but that it turned out they got the wrong man," Satterly said with deep satisfaction.

"You wanted Duar to receive the best possible defense, the best possible lawyer, didn't you?"

"Sure he should get a defense. And it looks like his defense was successful, doesn't it?"

Skyles brushed aside his attempt to turn it to his favor. He lowered his voice. "You *paid* for Duar's attorney, didn't you?"

The courtroom was completely still. Everyone stared at Satterly.

"What do you mean?"

"Do you deny it?"

"Deny what?"

"That you paid Mr. David Stern of the ACLU to defend Wahamed Duar, or who everyone thought was Wahamed Duar, in his tribunal aboard the *Belleau Wood*?" Skyles removed an e-mail from the bottom of the stack he had been holding.

Satterly was speechless. "Is there anything wrong with that?"

"Move to strike," Skyles said.

"Sustained," Wiggins said, listening to every syllable, every nuance of Satterly's testimony.

"Did you help pay for the defense of the man accused of murdering hundreds of Americans and dedicated to murdering more?"

"I helped a little."

He walked to Satterly without asking permission from the judge. But no one was going to stop him now. He had a certain momentum that no judge would interrupt unless he clearly abused it. "I'd like to show you an e-mail you sent to a person by the name of Deborah Craig. Do you recall this?" he said, showing him the e-mail. "You tell her in this e-mail that you had just sent a check for a thousand dollars to support the effort to provide Duar with a capable attorney. True?"

"Did she steal that one too?" he said, pointing at Andrea.

"Is what I said about the e-mail true?" Skyles demanded.

"There was a fund-raising effort, by a group, I forget who, and I responded. It seemed right to me. People should have an attorney, not just a military attorney, when held on a ship and charged."

"And it goes on to confirm that you support not telling that lawyer who was really paying him. True?"

"Yes."

"And the man who is to contact that lawyer, David Stern, was paid by you and others. Correct?"

"It wasn't my idea, but yes. He deserved—"

"Stern never knew that the man who had retained him had no such authority from Duar, and that the money came from you, did he?"

"Probably not."

"In fact, you had that man *lie* to Stern to achieve your sense of justice, didn't you?"

"I wanted to be sure—"

"When your sense of *justice* is in play, the truth is a casualty, isn't it?"

"No, that's not fair," Satterly protested.

Skyles sat, waited for a few seconds, then said, "I have nothing further, Your Honor."

fter the recess Wolff began his closing argument. As he got deeper into how Rat was an unwashed criminal, a runaway Special-Operations-homicidal-maniac, a mean-spirited killer, Rat's thoughts drifted to the rental car parked two blocks away with a bag in the trunk. It was a gym bag no one knew about. Not Andrea, not Don Jacobs, not the Navy, not even Groomer, or Robby. The black Adidas bag contained several different passports with different names from countries like St. Kitts, and Costa Rica, several law enforcement badges including the FBI and the Coast Guard, and cash. Lots of cash. About as much as he had. If this went badly, if he was convicted, he would leave the country somehow and never look back. No one knew he had even rented a car. He had rented it under one of his other identities, and knew they would never track it until he was long gone.

He was trying to decide where he should go. The list was short and represented the convergence of two primary criteria: he had to be able to get by either in English or Arabic, and the country couldn't have an extradition treaty with the United States so he couldn't be brought back to the States for sentencing. He wasn't sure about the treaties, but figured he could find out the answer fairly easily.

Rat turned in his chair and looked at Andrea sitting in the back of the courtroom. She was staring at Wolff with a look of barely restrained hatred. Rat loved the look on her face and the faith in him that it represented. He didn't know if she now believed he had been falsely accused, or had thought about it long enough to no longer care whether he had done that of which he was accused.

Finally Wolff was done and it was Skyles's turn. Rat didn't want to listen to him either. He was sick of the process. Duar was still out there heading toward the United States, and he couldn't do anything about it except sit and listen to this ridiculous process. Rat suddenly noticed the judge was staring at him. He began paying attention to what Skyles was saying.

". . . the usual way the government proceeds. Ready, fire, aim. They decide the result they want, or who they want to *get,* and force things to come together to achieve it. But maybe once in a while it's appropriate to ask why. Why is Lieutenant Rathman on the hot seat? Why has he been charged? Are they trying to make an example of him? For what? A murdering terrorist died under low-level interrogation. So what? Why can't we all admit that we're actually *happy* about that?"

"Your Honor, this is totally inappropriate as a closing—"

"Confine yourself to the evidence, Mr. Skyles."

"Yes, sir." Skyles picked up right where he left off. "Somewhere behind the screens in this case, some Wizard of Oz is moving the levers, manipulating people and witnesses to put Lieutenant Rathman away for reasons you and I will never know. You can feel it, can't you?" He scanned the faces of the jurors who were listening intently, but with some skepticism.

"We're all pawns in a much larger game. We don't know who is pulling the levers, nor do we know what those levers are attached to. What we do know, because you've seen him testify before you, is that someone is out to get Lieutenant Rathman. And he was called as the *star* witness by the government. Did they not know about the facts that ultimately came out or did they just not care? Are we just part of some *simulation* of justice here, where they throw a bunch of nonsense in front of you, and hope you're not smart enough to figure out that it's completely inadequate? Maybe they think you'll be so impressed with the setting and the somberness of the procedure, that you'll overlook the fact that there is *no evidence* sufficient to convict Lieutenant Rathman." He put his hands in his pockets and shook his head. "Don't buy it. Don't convict a man of a crime without evidence. Don't take Lieutenant Rathman's life away from him. We need him out there, we need him operating on our behalf fighting these terrorists. You heard everyone. He's the best operative the United States has. Who here wants to disarm him?"

Skyles waited, looked at the jury again with a challenge, returned to his seat and sat down. The judge sat in his leather chair and picked up the jury instructions in front of him. He pushed on his reading glasses. "Ladies and gentlemen of the jury, it is now time for me to read the jury instructions that you'll use as a guide in arriving at your verdict. After I read the instructions, you'll be dismissed to the jury room to begin your deliberations. All I want you to do today is to elect a foreperson since it is already four o'clock on Friday afternoon. After electing a foreperson you'll be in adjournment until Monday morning at nine when you'll return to this building to begin your deliberations on the verdict. Now please pay close attention as I read the instructions to you."

◆   ◆   ◆

The destroyers didn't get there before sunset. Not even close. They based their intercept calculation on the heading the two *Sea Dragons* were holding when they were last sighted. But Hotary's *Sea Dragon* had changed course immediately after the Navy P-3 had disappeared. Now in the darkness, Hotary had ordered his men to darken ship. No lights were to show outside of the ship at all. The bridge was so dark the faces of the men on the bridge were lit only by the glow of the instruments. Hotary knew moonrise wasn't until two in the morning. It gave him plenty of time. The hours passed uneventfully as the *Sea Dragon* headed almost due north off the coast of Virginia searching for its prey.

To the merchant traffic along the East Coast the *Sea Dragon* was just another cargo ship slipping through the dark Atlantic on a dark night with its surface-search radar on, a radar common to half the merchant vessels on the ocean, making eight knots. Hotary knew that the real *Sea Dragon* was within fifty miles of them and hoped the confusion between them would hold just long enough for the next step.

Hotary walked over to the radar repeater where his assistant was studying the blips. "You see it yet?"

The man pointed to one of the blips on the screen with his pudgy finger. "This should be it."

Hotary studied the blip and quickly measured the distance. "Only five nautical miles." He glanced at the RPM indicator. "Increase speed to sixteen knots. Take heading to intercept the ship."

The man nodded at him and confirmed the order. The ship turned slightly to the northeast and began closing on the radar blip. Their target was traveling at ten knots. The *Sea Dragon* closed on it steadily from a constant bearing.

On the bridge of the other ship they noticed the radar contact approaching them from the southwest, closing with each minute at a steady pace. They grew concerned as the dark ship bore down on them. Their own ship was larger and not very maneuverable. The deck officer called the captain to the bridge. "Contact approaching from the southwest. Two miles away. It is overtaking us, and is on a collision bearing. Speed is sixteen knots." The captain looked at the radar repeater and then at the deck officer who was looking through his binoculars. "See anything?"

"No, sir. Nothing."

"Reduce speed to three knots. Try to raise her on the radio."

The change was transmitted to the engine room and the ship began to slow—if a collision course was in place, changing any part of the collision geometry would avoid the collision. Slowing was the easiest.

And it was exactly what Hotary had anticipated. He turned the *Sea Dragon* slightly more to the east, repairing the collision course, maintaining sixteen knots. The radio crackled as he heard in a heavy Japanese accent, "Ship heading northeast off Virginia at thirty-two degrees North, seventy-four degrees West; this is the *Galli Maru*. State your intentions."

As they approached one mile, Hotary said to the other men on the bridge, "Get everyone ready."

Everyone left the bridge except Hotary, his second, and the helmsman. He could now see their objective, a huge ship with white writing on its side. Forward of the superstructure it was mostly flat, like an oil tanker. In large white block letters on the black hull were "L N G," widely spaced and as big as buildings. Liquefied Natural Gas, natural gas cooled to such a temperature that it was rendered liquid in form, one hundred twenty-five thousand cubic meters of explosive gas.

Hotary could not help but smile. Everything depended on this ship being on course and on time, and there it was, like clockwork. The liquefied natural gas ship was exactly where it was supposed to be, exactly when it was supposed to be there.

The *Sea Dragon* continued to bear down on the *Galli Maru*, now within several hundred yards but still invisible. The concern on the bridge of the *Galli Maru* had grown to a panic. The radio calls were growing more insistent. They had slowed to three knots and yet the ship from the dark continued to come. It was as if the invisible ship was *trying* to collide with them. The captain grabbed his binoculars and studied the darkness. He couldn't see anything. Not even the reflection of a bow wave. The captain spoke to his first officer without looking at him. "Has this ship changed course at all?"

"Slight modification about fifteen minutes ago. Before that we weren't tracking her closely."

"Maybe it's disabled. The entire crew may have been overcome," the captain said. "They may have lost power and only the engine is running. They don't have any lights and they can't respond to us on the radio. Turn on all our lights. Floods, everything. Light us up. Hold course, but slow down. If she's unmanned, I don't want her ramming into us."

Hotary watched the *Galli Maru* through his binoculars. He saw the floodlights come on. His job had just been made easier. The captain of the Japanese LNG ship was confused. He hadn't even considered a malignant explanation. People rarely did. It was what Hotary relied on.

As they closed to two hundred yards and looked as if they were going to pass by the *Galli Maru* on its port side, Hotary nodded to the helmsman, who turned the wheel sharply to the right and drove the *Sea Dragon* directly toward the LNG ship side to side.

The *Sea Dragon* was now illuminated by the floodlights of its target as they were only fifty yards apart. The *Galli Maru*'s main deck was ten feet below that of the *Sea Dragon*. Hotary braced himself as the ships closed at a surprisingly rapid rate. The Japanese captain was running outside to the flying bridge then back inside. He was acutely aware of the near inevitability of a collision and what could happen to his cargo if his hull was pierced.

The helmsman turned the wheel to the left just as they were about to touch and Hotary threw the engine of the large cargo ship into reverse to slow quickly to the *Galli Maru*'s speed. The two ships scraped together side to side with a sickening, metallic crunch. Hotary ran from the bridge down to the deck and gave the signal to the four men waiting there with large shotgun-like firearms. They aimed them high and fired. Titanium grappling hooks attached to half-inch-thick steel cables flew from the *Sea Dragon* over to the deck of the *Galli Maru*. The hooks jerked and hopped across the deck looking for anything hard to grab. Three set, then the fourth, hooking on railings, ladders. As soon as the cables were taut, the four men secured them to hard fittings on the *Sea Dragon*.

Hotary looked over and saw the Japanese captain staring in disbelief. He was confused and furious. The captain disappeared inside the bridge of the *Galli Maru*. Hotary had hoped to get over there before they got back on the radio. One of his men yelled from the bridge, "He's transmitting on emergency frequency that he's an LNG ship being boarded by pirates."

Hotary turned to three men standing on the bow. He raised his hand to them, the signal he had hoped not to have to give. They raised the three rocket-propelled grenade launchers, the RPG-7s, and fired into the antennae on top of the *Galli Maru*'s bridge. They knew to avoid the radar antenna if at all possible. They fired almost simultaneously at the radio antenna nicely lit up in the *Galli Maru*'s attempt to be conspicuous.

The rocket motors sent the warheads racing across and slaughtered the antennae over the bridge. The explosions amid the blend of metals, aluminum, steel, titanium, and other composites sent sparks and a multicolored fireworks display high into the dark night. The radio transmission stopped, but they had gotten off enough to complicate Hotary's plan. He had expected it but had hoped to be quick enough to avoid it.

Hotary ran for one of the cables holding the two ships together. He threw on the backpack that had been handed to him and threw the AK-47 strap over his head. His men handed him a stainless-steel device with two handles designed to accept a steel cable. He slipped it over the cable, and jumped off the deck of the *Sea Dragon*. He slid down the cable onto the deck of the *Galli Maru*. Three other men jumped onto the remaining cables while five more stood on the deck of the *Sea Dragon*, rifles drawn, waiting for the sure opposition.

Hotary heard a commotion as men emerged from several hatches aboard the LNG ship. The captain was one of the first down to the deck and began screaming at Hotary in Japanese. He looked up at the burning wreckage in the superstructure of the ship, and back at Hotary. He just couldn't believe this was happening on the high seas off the coast of the United States.

The captain yelled for his men to grab weapons out of the arms locker. They scrambled back up the ladders as the men on the *Sea Dragon* opened fire on them. Their AK-47s barked loudly as sailors from the *Galli Maru* fell. The captain ducked back into the bridge, tried the radio, then a backup radio, both of which were disabled.

Hotary jumped over the railing in one easy motion. He pulled his assault rifle over his head and ran toward the bridge. He raced up one ladder, then the next. The other men who had crossed with him were right behind him. He burst onto the bridge. The captain turned to him with fury and screamed at him in Japanese.

Hotary put up his hand. "Speak English," he insisted.

"Get off my ship!" the captain demanded.

"I'm not here to hurt you. But this is my ship," Hotary said. He noticed movement on the bridge and fired at the corner. A man screamed and dropped a shotgun then fell to the deck with his arm bleeding profusely. Hotary walked to the man and shot him in the back where he lay. He went silent.

The captain cried out. "Not here to hurt us?! You cannot do this! You are murdering my crew!"

"If you want any of your crew to live you will tell them to do *exactly* as they are told! If they try to stop us, they will be killed," Hotary yelled.

The captain looked more closely at Hotary. "Who are you?"

"It doesn't matter."

The captain stared. "I have watched news from satellite. You look like the man that was on trial on U.S. Navy ship. But it wasn't him." He suddenly realized who he was dealing with. He gasped, "You are Wahamed Duar!"

"You will tell your crew to do exactly as they are told."

The captain nodded slowly, terrified of what he was involved in, now knowing who had possession of his LNG ship.

On the main deck below, three men ran from a lower hatch carrying twelve-gauge shotguns. They aimed at men crossing over on the cables but were quickly cut down by Duar's men, who were waiting for them.

Duar pointed to the helm and yelled at one of his men to take over. He yelled to the others to scour the ship and find the rest of the crew. They ran from the bridge and headed down one of the internal ladders. They knew the layout of the ship as well as they knew that of the *Sea Dragon*; they had studied a diagram of the entire ship for weeks. Duar pulled out a set of steel handcuffs and turned back to the captain. "Give me your hands."

"No," the captain said.

Duar hit him in the face with the barrel of his gun in a slashing movement. The gunsight cut the captain's face and blood ran down his cheek. "Give me your hands!"

The captain offered his hands.

"Behind you," Duar insisted.

The captain turned and Duar handcuffed him behind his back. "Sit down," Duar ordered. The captain sat on the deck of the bridge and stared at Duar and his men with palpable fear.

Only six of Duar's men were left aboard the *Sea Dragon*, three to handle the ship, and three to empty the contents of the special containers, bring them to the deck of the *Sea Dragon*, and transfer them to the *Galli Maru*. They hurriedly transferred the explosives, radioactive cores, and weapons across from the *Sea Dragon*. When all the equipment had been transferred, Duar grabbed the captain. "On your feet," he said.

The captain stood awkwardly and Duar pulled him to the ladder. He handed him over to one of his men, who dragged him down the ladder and hooked him to the two-handled device. A line was tied to the end and he was pulled up and over to the *Sea Dragon.*

Duar checked his watch, gave the signal, and the three men left on the *Sea Dragon* released the cables and turned away from the *Galli Maru.* They headed due east. The *Galli Maru* turned west for the Chesapeake Bay.

◆　◆　◆

"Captain Pugh?"

The submarine captain turned to the first-class petty officer, who was carrying a sheet of paper. "What?"

"Here's the text of that transmission on the international distress frequency. It's not far from here at all."

Pugh frowned and grabbed the paper. He read it aloud, "This is *Galli Maru,* at thirty-two North and seventy-eight West. We are LNG ship boarded by pirates." He looked up at the first-class petty officer and then at the Officer of the Deck. "You think he means *being* boarded by pirates?"

"Yes, sir. He had a heavy accent."

"Boarded by pirates? An LNG ship? Are you *shitting* me?" He looked at the chart. "Where are they?"

The petty officer leaned over with a pen and pointed to the location. "Right about here, sir."

"Thirty miles or so from here," Pugh observed. "How long ago was this transmission?"

"About five minutes."

"Do we have anything on the ship itself?"

"We're not sure, sir. Last time we did a radar scan there were about thirty ships in the area. They're sort of lining up to go into the Chesapeake. Hard to tell which one it was."

"How strong a signal was their mayday call?"

"Not very, really."

"Get a message off to the Coast Guard. Retransmit that mayday call in case they missed it. Tell them we're on the way. They need to get a cutter or helicopter out there right away. Send it to Washington and Norfolk as well." Pugh paused and thought. "Why the hell would pirates want to take an LNG ship? They think they're going to break it up into little pieces of natural gas and sell it on the black market? It's not like you can unload one of those ships just anywhere."

Lieutenant Commander Terry Foss, the Officer of the Deck, a clever officer that Captain Pugh found annoying but incredibly insightful, asked, "Did you see that message that came in a little bit ago?"

"Which one?" Pugh asked.

"They think the ship we're looking for, the one that sailed from Africa, has Wahamed Duar himself aboard."

Pugh looked at him. He didn't remember seeing such a message. He might have missed it if it started talking in depth about terrorism. Not a lot of terrorists in submarines. "So you're thinking maybe this is his work."

Foss nodded.

"This LNG ship is ahead of us. And if the 'pirates' are led by Duar, that means the ship he is on went right by us."

"Yes, sir."

"How?"

"Don't know. But if we get there right away, maybe we'll see."

"Get us to that LNG ship, *now*." To the petty officer, "Tell the comm officer I want to get a message off to Washington right away. Tell them we're near an LNG ship which we believe may have been attacked by the ship they're looking for. Tell them we're requesting instructions on what to do when we get there. Are we cleared to sink her? Go, go! Get that message off!"

◆　◆　◆

Sarah St. James could feel the acid in her stomach. Things were starting to happen too fast. They had had no information for weeks, and now it was pouring in from all sources, mostly in agreement, but some in conflict. Wahamed Duar had been acquitted, although it wasn't Wahamed Duar. He was probably on a ship that no one could find heading for United States. The entire United States Navy, Coast Guard, NSA, and Air Force could not locate one lousy ship. And now a liquefied natural gas ship, which had the explosive power of a small nuclear device, was being taken by "pirates." This had been heard by the Coast Guard, and the Navy, and was confirmed by a submarine, which was thirty nautical miles away.

The Office of Navy Intelligence, ONI, and the Director of Central Intelligence both believed that Wahamed Duar was the one taking the LNG ship.

Sarah St. James thought they were probably right. The President was so concerned he had called yet another emergency meeting of the National Security Council. He was livid. The situation room felt unusually cold. Someone had turned the air conditioning down to bring the room temperature into the high sixties, probably expecting a lot of heat to be generated in the meeting.

President Kendrick dispensed with the niceties. He turned to Woods. "It's your belief that Wahamed Duar was aboard the ship that we couldn't find, and that he has now somehow taken a liquefied natural gas ship off the coast of Virginia. That about sum it up?"

"Yes, sir. I can't explain how he got by the pickets, but he did. And he is now probably on board that LNG ship."

President Kendrick said, "I don't know much about explosives, but I'm prepared to guess that the large ship full of liquefied natural gas is extremely volatile and if it went up it would be a very bad thing."

Woods looked at Robinson, the Chief of Naval Operations, for an answer. The admiral replied, "It would be very difficult to get it to explode instead of just burn, but if done right, it would be the equivalent of setting off a small nuclear device."

St. James added, "And if Rat is right, then the ship probably also has a bunch of radioactive cores aboard, which would make this into a very large very dirty bomb that could take out an entire city. Is that about right?"

Robinson replied, "I don't know if take out an entire city is really accurate. The explosion would certainly take out an area of about four or five city blocks, and the radiation would contaminate everything for a long way. It would take an unbelievable amount of money and a very long time to clean up whatever city this hit."

Kendrick looked at each person individually. "Where is he going?"

Robinson answered, "We don't have a heading since the attack. Who knows now what he'll do. Pretty clear his whole Africa ship thing was just to get him to the *Galli Maru*."

St. James said, "He took the ship off the coast of Virginia for a reason. He would know that if he takes it a long way from his destination, we'll find him and get him one way or the other before he has time to do what he has come here to do. What's really close to him now? Nothing really. Maybe Virginia Beach, but that's not a very sexy target. I think he's headed into the Chesapeake. To come right here, to Washington. Or maybe Baltimore, even Philadelphia."

Kendrick looked horrified. "Here?" He looked at Robinson. "Could he get that big a ship to Washington?"

Admiral Robinson hesitated. "I'm not sure, sir. There are a lot of bridges and it narrows considerably. I'm also not sure what the *Galli Maru* draws, or how high the Potomac is right now. But it is theoretically possible."

"They'll never get into the bay," Stuntz said confidently.

Robinson hesitated, then said, "How would you suggest we stop him?"

Stuntz was surprised by the question and who had asked it. "Why wouldn't we be able to stop it?"

Robinson replied, "The *Louisiana* is trailing him at periscope depth. Captain Pugh. Very capable. He's starting thirty miles away though, from the South. If Ms. St. James is right, and Duar turns the LNG ship west to the Chesapeake, it's going to be hard for the submarine to catch him, depending on the speeds. And the faster the *Louisiana* goes, the harder it is to hear the sonar contacts around her. We've sortied every destroyer that could get its engine going and had at least a skeleton crew. Anything that could sail is away from Norfolk, not sitting there waiting to be called.

"The good thing is the LNG ship, if headed for the Chesapeake, has to go to the mouth of the bay. We can wait for them, or set up a picket line, if we can get the ships lined up in time. We're going to be very hard-pressed to get more than two additional ships to sea before sunrise. Based on my quick calculations, if the *Galli Maru* makes twenty knots—which I'm told it can—it will be across the Chesapeake Bay

Bridge-Tunnel and into the bay before dawn. That means we have to find the ship at night. I think we will find it, I'm sure we will find it. But it won't be simple, and stopping it is a different matter entirely."

"Different?" Kendrick asked.

"Will you give us permission to sink it right now if we identify it?"

Kendrick shook his head. "We have to assume they're holding the entire crew of the LNG ship hostage. Until we have no other option, we can't kill a bunch of innocent people."

Robinson disagreed. "I sure as hell would, sir, if you don't mind. If we don't, this LNG ship with radioactive material will just steam into the Chesapeake Bay. Just like shooting down an airliner full of innocent people that is about to fly into a building."

Stuntz had been shaking his head. "How sure are we of what exactly has happened? We *think* we know that Duar is aboard a ship that we can't find because some FBI agent claims to have seen someone who looked like him in Liberia. Of course we now know there's at least one other person who looks like Duar—we just put him on trial on a Navy ship. How do we know this isn't just *another* look-alike? And we *believe* the LNG ship has been boarded by 'pirates' based on a weak radio transmission that has not been confirmed. Fair enough that the only LNG ship in the area is now not responding to the radio. *Something* has happened. But we couldn't even find the ship that Duar was supposedly on, and now we're assuming that he is not only on a ship from Africa with radioactive material—which was never confirmed—but that he has somehow boarded this LNG ship at night, transferred radioactive material, and is now in charge of the ship. We're so sure of that we're prepared to sink it? I don't think so."

Kendrick snapped at Stuntz. "What would you do, Mr. Secretary?"

"I'd find the ship, send out some Special Forces in helicopters, and board it."

St. James responded. "I'd send airplanes with antisurface missiles, or get the submarine up there, and sink it now."

Stuntz frowned. "And cause a nuclear-size explosion full of radioactivity fifty miles off the coast of Virginia? If the wind is from the east you'll radiate the entire Eastern seaboard!"

352 | JAMES W. HUSTON

"Not if we do it now, while he's a hundred miles out. We *have* to take the chance. To let it get any closer simply means we're increasing the risk of something worse happening. He's taking this ship somewhere, near something, and setting it off. If he gets near the Chesapeake, he could set it off at any time. If he gets to a city it's just gravy. I say get the submarine or an airplane to sink it."

President Kendrick looked at Admiral Robinson. "Could the submarine sink the LNG ship?"

"Yes, of course. Assuming we can identify it clearly. He has Mark 48 torpedoes, which would sink it easily. But he would have to catch up with it first."

Stewart Woods cleared his throat. "Would that set off the gas? Would it blow the ship up and spread the radiation?"

"That torpedo is intended to open a ship up like a can opener. I've got to assume that all the natural gas would go. I kind of doubt it would blow up, but it would burn until the ship went down. It would go down pretty quick, especially if he put four fish into her side."

"Would that put the submarine at risk from the explosion or radiation?"

"Not really. I wouldn't be concerned about the submarine, but with twenty-four nuclear-tipped ICBMs of its own, we'd have to be sure first. I'd want to talk to some people."

"I think our course is pretty clear, Mr. President," Stuntz said.

Kendrick looked at Stuntz with impatience. "And what might that be?"

"The first thing we have to do is find the ship. I think we've established here that it could be at the mouth of the Chesapeake before daylight. That means we have to identify it at night. Our ships and airplanes are doing their best to accomplish that, and with a few Coast Guard ships out there, we ought to be able to check every ship coming into the Chesapeake. Let's make this hard for him if he decides to come into the bay. We ought to get every tug that's available to be ready to drive him onto a sandbar if he shows up. Then I still think we can stop the ship without blowing it up or killing a bunch of Japanese hostages. We either run it aground, or send our Special Forces, or both."

St. James reacted. "We can't *do* it like that. If we run this thing aground in the mouth of the Chesapeake, he'll set it off and radiate the entire southern Chesapeake Bay for years to come. It might even cause the Chesapeake Bay Bridge-Tunnel to cave in, and it could radiate all of Norfolk. We can't take that risk. We have to get to him before he gets into the mouth of the bay."

Kendrick sat down and leaned back in his chair. He put two fingers to his mouth and considered his options. "If we sent in Special Forces, who would it be?" he asked Stuntz.

Stuntz glanced at Admiral Robinson for confirmation and answered Kendrick. "I think it would be Dev Group. They're very close. They're based in Little Creek, right at the tip of Virginia at the mouth of the Chesapeake."

The admiral nodded.

St. James jumped in. "We should use Lieutenant Rathman."

Stuntz nearly choked. "Why in the hell would we want to use him? Isn't he still in trial as a criminal defendant?"

"He was assigned to Dev Group before he went to the CIA. And he's not a criminal. He knows more about Wahamed Duar than anyone. He's the one who tracked them into Georgia, into the Pankisi gorge, he's the one who figured out that it was probably Duar who took the radioactive cores from the Russian power generators, he's the one who tried to stop the ship through the Dardanelles. He briefed us. And yet all this time we've been prosecuting him—don't get me started on that again."

"Where is that prosecution now?" President Kendrick asked.

"The jury is out." St. James replied with a touch of spite.

"So we're going to ask this guy to save the East Coast at the same time we're asking a jury to put him in prison?" Kendrick asked.

"Yes, sir," St. James said.

Kendrick was skeptical. "Does anyone agree that it should be Rathman either with his CIA people or with Dev Group?"

"Hell no," Stuntz said. "That guy is a criminal. He's probably going to be convicted. Is that the guy that we want leading this operation? Why would anyone think we don't have other men who can do as good a job as Rathman?"

"Because he is the best, and everybody knows it. Ask Admiral Robinson. Ask Stewart," she added. "Who would they send?"

Stuntz asked Robinson, "How long would it take Dev Group to get ready?"

Robinson replied, "They're always on standby. They're all on beepers and can be ready to go in minutes. I'm quite sure that the officers currently assigned to Dev Group can do a fine job."

"There you are," Stuntz said triumphantly. "Let's get them activated. Get them ready to go. Soon as we locate the ship, they can hit it. The farther out, the better."

President Kendrick looked at St. James, then responded. "It should be Dev Group. And I think Rathman should lead it. He knows this Duar character. He knows how he thinks, and he's the one who dropped down on him in Sudan. And he's the one who *failed* to get him last time. Let him fix it. Let him finish the job." He turned to the admiral. "How should they do it?"

"We'll activate them right away. Somebody needs to get ahold of Rathman. We'll need to get a jet to fly him down to Little Creek immediately. I want him and the others from Dev Group on a helicopter ready to go right now. As soon as we locate the ship, we can vector them in. Going at night will actually be to our advantage."

Chapter

26

O ne of Duar's men, who had cut his hair so short that he looked almost bald, held a large handgun to the head of the Japanese captain. They stood in the radio room of the *Sea Dragon*, heading east as fast as the ship would go. The *Galli Maru*, the LNG ship, was twenty miles behind them heading west at the same speed.

He pointed to the transmitter button and nodded. The Japanese radioman looked at his captain with the gun against his head and pressed the button. He spoke as he had been instructed, in a loud whisper. "This is Ichiro Tanaka, radioman of the *Galli Maru*. We have been boarded by terrorists, and are being taken out to sea. They have killed two of the crew and threaten the rest of us. I heard them telling our captain that they are to rendezvous with another ship somewhere to the east, tonight. Our current position is latitude thirty-two degrees fifty minutes North, longitude seventy-four degrees twelve minutes West. I do not think I will be able to transmit—"

Duar's man pulled Tanaka's hand off the transmitter. "Good." He put the handgun to Tanaka's chest. Tanaka looked up at him in disbelief. He had done exactly as he had been asked. The handgun looked large and menacing and he could feel the coldness of the steel through his shirt. Duar's man pressed the gun hard against his chest. He hesitated. "Maybe we will need you on the radio again. Come with me."

♦ ♦ ♦

Rat found himself drifting off on his comfortable couch. He knew it was rude, and he knew that Andrea would be angry, but he couldn't help it. The trial had been more exhausting than he had expected. The idea that a few jurors stood between him and a decade in prison—or fleeing the country—was enough to cause him to lose sleep, lose confidence in himself, and question everything. He had his arm around Andrea, who seemed to be pondering the meaning of life. They hadn't spoken in fifteen minutes.

They had spoken about the trial at length and about the possible outcomes. He had told her of his tentative plan to be out of the country when the verdict came in. She reminded him that Skyles had told him he had to be there when they read the verdict. So if he was convicted they could put him in confinement immediately. They didn't give criminal defendants out on bail a chance to call in and find out what their verdict was so they could run for it before going to prison. He had not wanted to remember that and tried to think of some way to have an escape route if he was convicted. Nothing had come to him yet.

But Andrea went on. She thought he should have more confidence in the jury. He told her he had no confidence in the jury or the legal system. The whole thing felt rigged. He didn't want any part of any of it. He had soured on the government at the highest level.

Rat knew he wouldn't get much sleep again, but he needed to start trying. He started to sit up when he heard a knock on the door.

His body was immediately flushed with adrenaline. Nobody ever knocked on his door after midnight other than Andrea.

Andrea was as surprised as he was. She stood slowly as he jumped over the coffee table and rushed to his peephole. She began to say something but he put up his hand for her to be quiet. He looked through the lens and saw a man in a Navy uniform. "Who is it?"

"Lieutenant Peter Cole. CNO's office."

Rat opened the door. "What's up?"

"May I come in?"

Rat looked at him carefully. "What's this about?"

Cole looked at Andrea and evaluated how much he could say. "There's an op on. You're the lead."

Rat frowned. "Why didn't the Agency page me?"

"It's not an agency op. It's Dev Group."

"When?"

"Right now. I'm to escort you to Andrews. There's a C-9 waiting. They're to fly you to NAS Norfolk. Dev Group will be waiting for you there."

"I'm coming with you," Andrea said.

Lieutenant Cole shook his head. "I'm instructed only to get Lieutenant Rathman."

Rat shook his head. "The C-9 is huge. It could carry everybody I know. She can come."

"No, sir. She can't. Just you, and the others on your team who are going."

Rat nodded. "Then let's go."

The lieutenant reached inside his coat and handed a cell phone to Rat. "The CO of Dev Group wants to talk to you on the way. He already has a plan, but wants to discuss it with you."

"Thanks," Rat said, taking the phone. "What's the target?"

"Your good friend Wahamed Duar. They think they've found him. He's taken an LNG ship."

"Holy shit," Rat said. "Where?"

"Off Virginia."

Rat's anger grew; he dialed the number from memory as they walked quickly out toward the black government sedan. A driver was holding the door for them. Rat stopped before getting in. He asked Cole, "What about getting Groomer and Robby? And Banger?"

"Yes, sir. All three."

"Let's pick them up."

"They're being picked up separately, sir."

"Let's go," he said.

◆　◆　◆

The Navy C-9 taxied to the end of the runway in the darkness at Andrews Air Force Base, turned onto the runway, and kept rolling as the pilot went to full power. As the four passengers settled in on the large passenger jet, empty except for Rat, Robby, Banger, Groomer, and the flight crew, the C-9 rotated and climbed rapidly into the sky. Rat pulled out the cell phone he had been given and pressed the redial button.

Rat put the phone to his ear and listened to the ring. A petty officer, a member of the air crew dressed in a blue jumpsuit, caught Rat's eye and told him to turn off the cell phone. He couldn't use it on the airplane—it was a violation of FAA regulations. Rat frowned and ignored him as the Dev Group CO answered the phone.

"Commander Frickey."

Ted Frickey, Tick as he was known, was widely respected in the Special Operations world. He had been a Navy SEAL for fifteen years and had been on innumerable operations that the Special Operations community—and few others—knew about. He had taken over as the Commanding Officer of Dev Group when Rat was there, before Rat left to go to the SAS. Rat liked him immensely. He had a dry sense of humor and loved to kid people with a total deadpan look on his face. Rat liked the way Frickey's mind worked. He thought out an operation with extreme thoroughness. Rat modeled his own operation planning after Ted Frickey's.

"Skipper, Rat."

"Rat. Good to hear from you. Where are you?"

"Just took off from Andrews."

"What's your ETA to Norfolk?"

He glanced at his digital watch, which illuminated with a flick of his wrist. "Fifty-four minutes from now. They're authorized to burn as much gas as it takes to get me there at their maximum speed."

"What big shot do you know high up in the government who thinks you're special? We could do this without you. They must know you're just an average SEAL."

"Wasn't my idea. And whatever friends I thought I had in the government must not be big enough shots to keep me from getting tried for manslaughter."

"You'd probably rather stay in Washington and sweat some jury's decision than go out and kick some terrorist's ass."

"You got me there."

"Listen. Here's the plan, but I want your input. Intel just reported that we intercepted a Japanese radio operator transmitting that their hijackers were taking them east at twenty knots. He gave his name, and his voice has been authenticated by the Japanese shipping company. Needless to say the ship owners have been sweating bullets ever since we notified them. The radio operator was cut off before he could finish his transmission. We got a good location on them though, and have the ship on radar. He said they're heading east to rendezvous with another ship. There are lots of ships out there, and we have no idea which ship they're going to rendezvous with. It does take some of the pressure off though, 'cause they're not heading toward the Chesapeake."

Rat frowned. It seemed completely inconsistent with what he had expected Duar to do. Duar must know that they would be on to him by now. They would locate his ship and try to stop him. It seemed extremely strange for him to head east into the Atlantic where he was no danger to anyone. And very much out of character to let some radioman have access to a radio, even for one minute, to disclose their location. "What's the plan?"

"We're going to take the ship down. There has been a lot of consideration of just sinking the ship, or blowing it out of the water, but they think there are at least fifteen or twenty Japanese crew still on board who would be killed. Somebody from our side told the Japanese shipping company about the plan to sink it and they told the Japanese government, which immediately accused the United States of not caring about Japanese lives. They of course reminded us of the fishing vessel off the coast of Hawaii that was sunk by a U.S. submarine in an accident a couple of years ago—remember that?"

"Sure."

"You knew we'd hear about that again. Anyway, they said if we think that their protests about the sinking of their fishing boat were loud, we haven't heard anything if this liquefied natural gas ship is sunk and Japanese sailors are killed in the process. It would be hundreds of millions of dollars in losses, and lives that should have been saved just because we were too lazy to come up with a better way to do it."

"Great."

"Anyway, Washington wants us to take the ship down, with the objective of saving the Japanese sailors and not losing the cargo."

"Oh sure. No problem."

"We've got your gear ready. Soon as you get to Norfolk there'll be a Pave Low helo waiting. They'll fly you straight to here and the rest of the team will load up. I picked all men that you know. You and the helicopter crew will be prepped with night vision, weapons ready to go, and you'll fly right out to the ship. We've got a good position on her heading east, and you should get out there in less than an hour."

"Sir, did they tell you Groomer, Banger, and Robby are coming with me?"

"Yeah. No problem. We'll be ready for them too."

"Good."

"Rat, I heard all about the op in Sudan. Too bad you snagged his double. Don't miss him this time. Bring him back alive if you can—I know a lot of people who want to ask him some questions."

"I'd like to ask him a few questions myself, but I'd probably get charged with something if I did."

"Get your ass down here. We've got to get out there *right now*."

♦ ♦ ♦

Duar and his men bent over the diagram of the *Galli Maru*. He thought he knew where to place the radioactive cores, but wanted to be sure. If he put them inside the hull, the radioactivity might not spread during the explosion. If he put them too high, for example, in the superstructure, the cylinders might not be breached in the explosion and the core containers would just be thrown a great distance for no purpose. He concluded they had to be on the main deck, outside.

Two men on the corner of the bridge illuminated the diagram of the *Galli Maru* with a small flashlight. In addition to the bridge lights, Duar had extinguished the running lights, the floodlights, the interior lights, which might shine through portholes in the crew quarters, and anything else that would allow them to be seen by another ship. He had also turned off the radar, the radio, and anything else that might send out a recognizable electronic signal. He relied only on the ship's passive GPS system to establish their position; he had even brought his own sophisticated GPS receiver to double-check that of the ship. He was confident of their position to within ten meters.

Duar joined the two men hovering over the diagram and reviewed the explosive placement again. He marked on the charts the proper placement for the incendiary bombs to be located underneath the tanks holding the liquefied natural gas. The bombs would go off and burn magnesium at astonishingly high temperatures, but wouldn't explode. They would heat the tanks holding the liquefied gas until the pressure inside the tanks was intolerable. The safety valves would be disabled and the pressure would continue to build until the explosive devices were triggered, rupturing the tanks and sparking the gas. It would cause the very thing all the LNG ship owners said couldn't happen—a BLEVE—Boiling Liquid Expanding Vapor Explosion. It was the worst thing that could happen to liquefied natural gas, and would produce an explosion bigger than any other man-made nonnuclear explosion in the history of the world.

"How long do we have?" one man asked Duar tentatively.

The light from the flashlight reflected off the sweat on the man's forehead. "As much time as we need. But I want this done in an hour. Sunrise is in six hours. It will all be over by then."

Several men nodded and headed down to retrieve the explosive devices from the main deck. Duar spoke to four others. "Over the side. Paint out the 'LNG,' change the name . . . you know what to do."

◆　◆　◆

Tick was waiting at the bottom of the rolling passenger stairway when Rat and the others descended from the C-9. He shook Rat's hand. "Welcome to Virginia, big shot."

"Tick, great to see you, sir. Make sure you call me a big shot when you come to visit me in prison."

"Come on. Helo's waiting over there. Hey, Groomer, Banger, Robby."

"Sir," they said in unison.

They walked under the turning blades of the large CH-53, stepped into the helicopter, and strapped themselves into their seats. The helicopter climbed into the dark sky and headed toward Little Creek Amphibious Base. They were there in less than ten minutes. The CH-53 Pave Low settled onto the helo pad next to the Dev Group building. They ran inside, right by the watch desk. The petty officer jumped up and stood at attention for the commanding officer of Dev Group.

Rat and the others followed Tick into the operations area. The rest of the team that had been selected by Tick was waiting, as were several other members of Dev Group who just wanted to be part of whatever was happening. Those who were going with him were cleaning their weapons and checking their gear. Their faces were all business. They had intense anxious looks, only partially hidden by the dark camouflage they wore on their faces. Their dark clothing had a flat luster to it to ensure it reflected no light.

Tick spoke. "Guys, Rat's here. He decided to grace us with his presence."

The men looked up and greeted him, but smiles were few. Rat acknowledged their greeting. He knew them from his recent time at Dev Group. Those he didn't know, the ones who wouldn't be going with him, he quickly evaluated with his experienced eye.

"Your gear is right over there," Tick said.

"What's the latest position on the ship?" Rat asked as he walked across the room.

Tick nodded. "Ever since we got that transmission from the Japanese radioman, we've fixed the position and tracked the ship. We have a P-3C airborne with antiship missiles aboard. Right now they're about twenty miles away from the ship and tracking it on radar. It continues to head east at its maximum speed. They're going to be moving in closer to use their ISAR radar and IR sensors to get a positive ID, but so far the ship is continuing east for a rendezvous that the radioman described."

Rat looked at the chart, then looked at Tick. "How would that radioman know that?"

"He said he overheard them saying they were heading east for a rendezvous."

Rat frowned "You have a recording?"

Tick gave a signal to a petty officer, who had a small recording device. He turned it on. Rat listened to the recording of the Japanese radioman, his whisper, the abrupt termination of the transmission.

Tick asked Rat, "What do you think?"

Rat shook his head. "Something's wrong." He stared at the chart, then at his commanding officer. "Duar isn't that stupid. The Japanese radioman overheard him? In what, English? Japanese? I don't think so. Either he wanted to be overheard, or the radioman is making this up—probably because he's got a gun to his head. In either case it's because that's what we're supposed to think."

"Then what is Duar doing?"

"Don't know. We know where the LNG ship is, right?"

Tick nodded.

"So maybe it's all a head fake and the real threat is still aboard that other ship. What's it called?"

"The *Sea Dragon.*"

"Maybe the whole LNG thing is just to throw us off. It's what we've got, but the Coast Guard or someone had better be watching for anything else that looks suspicious. They jamming the mouth of the Chesapeake?"

"Every ship that can float is heading out. Norfolk Naval Base is like a firehouse. Thank God for turbines instead of steam. They're getting under way pretty fast. They've even got fighters up from Oceana and the Air Force is flying out of Langley. We're checking and ID'ing every ship out there. But it's not that easy in the pitch darkness."

Rat folded his arms. "The P-3 hasn't ID'd the LNG ship yet. Right?"

"Not positively."

"Nobody has."

Tick pondered. "I guess that's right. Except the Japanese radioman's call—"

"Which was probably staged—"

"So what are you saying? If we disregard that transmission, where are we?"

"How do we know the LNG ship isn't still heading for the Chesapeake? How do we know the radioman isn't on the *Sea Dragon*?"

"I guess we don't."

"He's trying to draw us out to the east, it's so we leave the gate open."

Tick nodded. "Could be."

Rat put on his helmet and checked his machine pistol. "I say we take up a position over the entrance to the bay, and be ready when someone IDs this ship. Then we hit it. If it turns out to be the ship out to the east, we can go get it later. The farther east it goes, the less of a threat it is to us."

Tick nodded, and looked at the faces of the other men. They all agreed with Rat, especially Groomer, who was nodding vigorously and bouncing up and down on the balls of his feet. "I agree. Go get 'em."

♦　♦　♦

The helicopter lifted off noisily and headed out over the dark Chesapeak. The Air Force pilots stayed low and fast. The Pave Low's GPS system and its three-dimensional image screen showed them flying east over the entrance to the Chesapeake Bay. They raced into the Atlantic Ocean fifty feet above the waves. The twelve Navy SEALs sat in the back of the helicopter in silence. They had gone over the plan before leaving. There was nothing more to be said. They had all rehearsed similar operations numerous times and knew what to do. They had reviewed the diagrams of the ship that had been sent to them by the Japanese shipping company, and knew how to take the ship down. Rat had given assignments to each of the members of his team, but emphasized he would be the first one on the ship and the last one off.

Rat unstrapped and walked up to the flight deck where the pilots sat and looked out of the front of the helicopter. "You have your ISAR radar on?"

"Yeah."

"Anything yet?"

The copilot glanced at him. "We're checking them all out. Nothing yet." He concentrated the radar energy on the next ship.

Rat nodded. "Doesn't look like a tanker. The one we're looking for doesn't look like a regular LNG ship. Doesn't have those big tits—

those big balloon-looking things sticking up out of the deck. It's mostly flat, like a tanker. You have an IR with a zoom or a low-light TV?"

"Sure."

"Approach the ship from the stern. Stop about two miles out, and let's take a look at this thing."

The helicopter slowed to sixty knots as the copilot zoomed the infrared lens in on one of the ships ahead of them. "Nope. Not it."

Rat was anxious. "Keep looking. Let me know as soon as you see anything. They got other planes out here looking?"

"Not over fifty," the copilot said as he looked at Rat through his night-vision goggles. "I just hope we don't run into one of them."

"Nobody watching the air picture?" Rat asked concerned.

"Yeah, there's an E-2 up from Norfolk. We're good," he said, smiling.

Rat went back to the belly of the helicopter and sat down. "Shit," he muttered, wondering how they would find the *Galli Maru* in the dark, in time to stop it.

Chapter

27

Captain Pugh looked through his periscope. It was very difficult to see in the dark, but running lights were clearly visible. What perplexed him was that the ship they had on their sonar had no running lights. The entrance to the Chesapeake Bay was just over the horizon twenty-five nautical miles away.

"All ahead one-third. Port ten degrees."

The enormous submarine maneuvered closer to the ship.

Pugh reached for the squawk box. "Sonar, Bridge."

"Sonar, aye."

"You sure this ship is still the one we picked up at the rendezvous?"

The third-class petty officer hesitated. "Yes, sir. Nine out of ten that's our boy. There were a lot of ships around and the sonar picture got a little confused, but at least nine out of ten, sir. We heard them scrape together, and you said to stick with the one that went west."

Pugh frowned. He liked ten out of ten. He moved his ship to a course paralleling the dark ship to his starboard. It had decreased its speed to twelve knots; he found that curious. It had been racing westward at twenty knots and had suddenly slowed. He saw it as an attempt to disguise its maneuvers, to look like a normal oil tanker. But he had a digital photo that Washington had transmitted to him of the *Galli Maru*. He had studied it. The L N G on the side of the ship would be impossible to hide and impossible for him to miss if he got close enough. It was a very distinctive ship, at least in the daylight. But the periscope had night-vision capability.

They waited silently seventy feet below the surface. The *Galli Maru* passed by. Pugh studied it in the periscope. He strained to see the outline of the dark form and the huge white letters on the side. He zoomed in. No lettering. Nothing. Just a dark hull. He looked carefully. No LNG at all. He was sure. But everything else about the ship looked right. Right size, right superstructure, it looked just like the *Galli Maru*. But why no letters? Nothing a little paint wouldn't take care of. Son of a bitch. And why else would a ship turn off all its lights? He thought again of the Japanese radioman's transmission that the LNG ship was heading east. No it wasn't. He had it right here in his sights.

He yelled over his shoulder. "Get off a flash message. We have the *Galli Maru* twenty-five miles off the coast. Give them the position, heading, and speed, and tell them we'll trail her. If they want us to sink it we'd better do it now. And get the weapons officer up here."

◆   ◆   ◆

The crew chief motioned for Rat, who was sitting back down with his men in the belly of the Pave Low helicopter. He hurried to the flight deck and put the headset on to talk to the pilot. "What's up?"

"Sub found the LNG ship. It's heading for the Chesapeake, about five miles from here."

Rat's heart raced. "What's its position?"

The copilot pointed to the navigation system. They had a radar contact that was being shown on the screen. It matched the latitude and longitude that had been given to them, and showed a speed vector indicating the heading and speed the sub had relayed.

"He'll be inside the Chesapeake before we can stop it."

The pilot nodded. "That's the way I figure it too."

Rat thought about his options. "We'd be better off with rubber bullets. We'll probably set this whole ship off and we'll go up in a vapor cloud."

◆   ◆   ◆

The USS *Winston S. Churchill* (DDG 81), an *Arleigh Burke*–class destroyer, saw the *Galli Maru*. Captain Lee Palmer confirmed the identity with his binoculars. "That's her. Flank speed."

The four GE turbine engines on the *Churchill* responded instantly, sending one hundred thousand horsepower to the two screws. The *Churchill* lurched forward leaving a huge rooster tail behind it as it accelerated to its maximum speed.

There were numerous ships around the *Galli Maru* but none seemed to appreciate the danger they were in. The *Galli Maru* was about to enter the Chesapeake Bay at ten knots, now with its running lights on, looking every bit like the tanker it was trying to imitate. But Palmer had received the *Louisiana*'s message. They knew the LNG had been painted out on the side of the ship and it was trying to pose as a tanker heading toward Washington, Philadelphia, or Baltimore, or somewhere else inside the bay.

Palmer had no idea how he might stop the ship without causing a catastrophe in the process. If he fired on it, the whole thing could go up, spreading radioactive material. Even if he stopped the ship by sinking it, it might still blow up before it went down, and would certainly create an environmental disaster probably resulting in the closing of the entire bay. His orders were simple—stop the ship. No one had told him *how* he might do that.

The *Churchill* raced toward the LNG ship at thirty-five knots. Palmer considered shooting out the bridge with his five-inch gun. But he didn't have sufficient confidence in his ship's gunnery to hit *only* the bridge, only the superstructure, and not the rest of the ship. He also did not know how explosives might be set or rigged in the ship and wasn't prepared to take the risk that the shell hitting the superstructure might trigger more than he had bargained for. But he had to try something.

He turned to the Officer of the Deck. "Fire a warning shot across her bow. Be careful not to hit her or any of the other ships out there."

Moments later the five-inch gun barked, sending a tracer round across the bow of the *Galli Maru* from three miles away. Palmer watched the ship for any reaction. The *Churchill* was clearly visible, clearly antagonistic, and clearly intending to do whatever it could to stop the ship, but nothing changed on the Japanese ship, which was ten times larger than the destroyer. No movement, no change of course, and no apparent concern. The ships continued to close.

◆ ◆ ◆

A faint pink line highlighted the horizon as the helicopter hurried toward the *Galli Maru*. There were ships everywhere. Rat peered through the windscreen toward the bay and watched the tracer round from the *Churchill*. Rat saw another muzzle flash from the *Churchill*. Then another. They were getting close. He waited to see any impact of the shells on the *Galli Maru* but was confident the captain of the destroyer that was firing was trying not to hit the target. Rat looked one last time out the windscreen of the helicopter, and went back down to his men. "Get ready!" he said angrily, realizing the ship was already inside the bay. Whatever submarine was following wasn't going to sink it in the bay. It would cause the very thing they had been trying to avoid. The politicians were probably unwilling to sacrifice the Japanese crew. *If they had been an American crew . . .* he thought to himself.

They unstrapped, stood up, and hooked the fast rope lines to the hard points on the deck of the helicopter. It was still dark, but not dark enough to need night-vision devices. They wore helmets, gloves, Kevlar vests under their uniforms, and carried their weapons on straps around their shoulders anchored to their chests.

The helicopter banked sharply to come in from the stern of the ship. The *Galli Maru* accelerated to twenty knots as it passed over the Chesapeake Bay Bridge-Tunnel. The LNG ship was now surrounded by the *Churchill* and numerous Coast Guard boats dashing around it angrily, unsure how to stop a huge ship with so much momentum. Even if the *Churchill's* commanding officer drove his ship into the bow of the tanker, it would only result in the sinking of his ship and could cause the LNG ship to explode.

Rat stood on the flight deck between the pilots.

"Where you want it?" the pilot yelled.

Like the oil tankers it resembled, the *Galli Maru* had a long flat deck from the superstructure to the bow, impeded only by some piping. It would be the easiest place to land on the ship, but would also be the most vulnerable to gunfire from the terrorists. "On top of the superstructure. We'll take our chances with the wires."

The pilot nodded his agreement. "You got it." Rat joined the other SEALs who were standing, waiting.

Suddenly they were over the superstructure of the ship. The helicopter's nose went up at a dramatic angle as the huge rotor blades stopped the forward movement of the helicopter. The nose came back down and the helicopter hovered over the white superstructure of the Japanese LNG ship.

Chief Petty Officer Wilkinson, the senior enlisted man of the team, kicked the two fast ropes out the door. Rat jumped out on one of them, grabbing the rope with his gloved hands. He slid down the rope unchecked until he neared the deck on top of the superstructure. He squeezed hard, slowing his descent, and stepped onto the ship. He pulled the rope away from the antenna to make sure no one got tangled in the electronics gear sitting on top of the ship. The other rope, six feet away from the first, lay on several wires. Groomer descended too quickly and his left leg jammed into the steel deck after it had been turned by a wire. He could feel the ligaments snap as he sprained his ankle badly. He cursed as the pain shot up his leg. He got to his feet quickly though, looked over, and limped away from his landing point to pull the rope from the wires so Robby and the others would have a clear field. The rest of the SEALs threw themselves out of the helicopter onto the ropes and down to the deck in quick succession. In less than thirty seconds they all stood on the top of the ship with their weapons ready.

Rat jogged toward the edge of the deck. He took his MP5N in his hands and covered the ladder where he expected someone to come up after them any second. As soon as the last SEALs touched the deck, the Pave Low helicopter pulled up and away from the ship. The Air Force crewmen pulled in the fast-ropes as the helicopter dropped down to the water level and raced away from the ship.

He was surprised they hadn't yet met with resistance from Duar's men aboard the ship. He gave hand signals for the SEALs to man the perimeter of the deck around the top of the superstructure. All the members of the team responded on their radios.

"Groomer, how's the ankle?"

"Hammered it pretty good. I'll be okay though."

"Can you walk?"

"Yeah."

Rat spoke to them as a group as he began walking toward the ladder that would take them down to the rest of the ship. "We have authorization to shoot to kill. Watch out for any hostages—they're all Japanese. If anybody's holding a hostage and you can get a shot, take it. We're not playing 'Let's Make a Deal.' We've got to get the ship away from Norfolk or Washington or wherever they're going. We've got to move." Rat glanced up at the lights of the city of Norfolk only a few miles ahead and to the left. He noticed the ship was continuing west, not turning northeast to run up the Chesapeake. It was headed for Hampton Roads, just across the water from Norfolk. But why? He realized the ship could turn quickly southwest and head for the Norfolk Naval Base, the largest naval base in the world.

Rat heard a helicopter and looked up. An SH-60 raced toward the *Galli Maru* from the port side. The side door was open and a sniper rifle protruded. Tick had told him he would try to get a sniper team airborne to support him. Rat switched the radio on his belt to encrypted UHF. "Team Two, you up?"

"Two's up. Rat, that you?"

"Yeah. You see anything?"

"Lot of activity on the bridge. They're scrambling around in there. I expect they'll be coming out any second."

"You got a good line on them?"

"I do on this side."

"We're going into the bridge. Anybody you see that isn't Japanese, you're cleared to hit."

"Roger that."

"Stay on this freq."

"Wilco."

Rat switched back to the intercommunication for his team. They were all waiting for his order. They were kneeling with their weapons facing outboard all around the top of the superstructure. The black stack loomed ominously behind him as exhaust poured out of it. Norfolk was two miles away to their left.

"Let's go," Rat said as he trotted forward, followed immediately by a grimacing Groomer, Robby, Banger, and the others. Banger carried his M-25 sniper rifle. They reached the corner of the superstructure with twenty-five knots of wind in their faces. The ship had increased speed. The bridge had a flying bridge extension which was just below them to their left. Rat stole a quick glance at it and saw that no one was on the flying bridge. The door from the flying bridge to the bridge was closed. Rat nodded to Groomer and Robby, who quickly ran their thick belaying ropes around hard points on the top of the superstructure. They expertly looped them through their harnesses around their waists and prepared to belay down the side of the ship. Six other SEALs stood directly behind them. Rat gave Groomer and Robby a quick nod and they went over the side of the superstructure and walked down the vertical white steel to the level of the bridge. They held their MP5Ns in one hand and the belaying rope in the other to arrest their descent, covering the flying bridge area.

Rat reattached his weapon to his chest, threw a rope around the base of an antenna, checked it for strength, and walked over the side of the superstructure down to the flying bridge. Three other SEALs joined him on the small flying bridge, covered by Groomer and Robby, who were still hanging over the side of the superstructure, their weapons leveled at the door to the bridge.

The *Galli Maru* raced through the dark gray water throwing up a vigorous bow wave. The Coast Guard boats and Navy ships stayed near and around the ship, not sure what to do, whether to get in the way and cause a collision, or fire at the rudder and try to disable the ship. At least for now they had been told to stay close but do nothing. Every officer now knew why as dozens of sets of binoculars were trained on Rat and his men.

The city of Norfolk was on the left of the ship. Cars were stopping on the road to Norfolk to watch what was now live on the news as the "developing situation." A Norfolk traffic helicopter had abandoned its coverage of a car fire when it saw the Pave Low helicopter race up and drop men off on a civilian ship. The news helicopter had taken up a station one mile from the *Galli Maru* and was transmitting the live image of Rat and the other SEALs to Norfolk. The live feed had been offered to CNN, which had immediately snapped it up and was now showing it live nationwide.

Rat looked carefully inside, staying low. "Four on the bridge. No hostages," he transmitted to the team. He switched on his radio. "Team two, take the helicopter and your sniper to the front of the ship. See if you can get a shot in through the windows to the bridge. We're going in in ten—"

Suddenly the glass in the door between the bridge and the flying bridge where Rat stood shattered from the hail of bullets that came from the bridge, a steady stream of automatic fire. "Stay covered!" Rat yelled as he pressed his back against the white steel. He could feel bullets slamming into the other side of the steel. "Two, can you see inside?"

"We've got them," he said. The helicopter accelerated ahead, turned to the right, and flew sideways in front of the ship. A SEAL sniper sat on the deck of the helicopter with his rifle pointed out the side door. His high-powered scope took him through the front windows of the ship's bridge. He fired once, the window shattered, and one of the automatic rifles inside the bridge fell silent. Then a second. There was a pause in the shooting. Rat raced for the door, threw it open, and charged into the bridge screaming in Arabic for everyone to surrender and lay down their weapons. Groomer and Robby flew around the superstructure and hung in the air in front of the windows of the bridge. Duar's two remaining men on the bridge were surprised by the sudden entry. They raised their weapons to fire but were too slow. The SEALs fired in short bursts. Each trigger pull by each SEAL sent three bullets into the chest of one of the men on the bridge. Only one of the men was able to return fire and his bullets went into the overhead. In seconds they were both dead. Blood ran toward the back of the bridge as the ship continued its twenty-knot pace and maintained its course without a helmsman.

Rat's breathing increased and his eyes darted around the bridge as he looked for an explanation. Something was wrong.

"Cover the wings," Rat said. He ran to the engine order telegraph and moved it to reverse one-third. Nothing happened. Rat went to the helm. He turned the wheel of the ship to the right, ordering a sharp starboard turn of the huge ship. The wheel spun in his hand. It was completely disconnected from the rudder; the ship began to turn the other way, southwest, parallel to downtown Norfolk and directly toward the Norfolk Naval Base on its own, as if on a rail.

Rat glanced up to look out the window, past the bow of the ship. The sun had risen above the horizon and the chop in the Chesapeake had picked up. White spray hissed down the sides of the ship. Directly ahead of the ship, easily visible and not far away, was pier twelve of the Norfolk Naval base—one of the carrier piers. And moored at pier twelve was the USS *Eisenhower,* a nuclear-powered *Nimitz*-class aircraft carrier of 98,000 tons.

"Holy shit," Rat exclaimed. He switched his transmitters to the UHF radio. "Team Two, get on the guard frequency, whatever it takes. Notify Norfolk Naval base that this ship is inbound and I'm not sure we can stop it. Tell them to evacuate everybody, get every ship underway that they can move. I don't care how many crewmen are aboard. I don't care if they rip the lines off the pier and tear up their stanchions. Get every ship out of the Navy base *now!*"

Rat headed off the bridge carefully, watching for booby traps and men. He hurried down the passageway behind the bridge. "They must be controlling the ship from after steering."

Groomer asked, "Should we evacuate Norfolk?"

"No time. It would just jam up the roads and cause a panic. We've got to find Duar and stop this ship. Everybody remember the layout of the ship?"

They nodded.

"To the mess deck."

With Robby and Groomer, they covered each other as they went through one door after another, then down ladders to the heart of the ship. The other SEALs moved quickly behind them, covering every edge and ensuring no one was coming at them from side passageways or from behind them. They worked their way expertly down to the main deck, where the crew lived and ate.

Rat knew Duar was waiting for him. He put up his hand. "Groomer, Robby, you remember where after steering is?"

"Third deck, at the stern."

"Take two other men with you, get into after steering, and stop this ship. We've got like three minutes."

"On our way." Groomer pointed to two of the SEALs in the back of the group and motioned for them to come with him and Robby. They ran down the passageway, took the first ladder, slid down it quickly, and hurried toward the stern and after steering, the emergency bridge buried deep in the ship from which the ship could be operated if the bridge became disabled. Most ships operated from after steering during drills at least once a month. Some ships did not have a specific after steering compartment, but they all had some means of operating the rudder and engine far away from the bridge.

"The rest of you come with me," Rat said.

They turned the corner and entered the mess deck and were greeted by a hailstorm of bullets. The noise of several automatic weapons was deafening. Duar's men had been waiting with their guns trained on the entrances to the mess hall. Rat felt a bullet graze his right arm and the man behind him fell as a bullet hit him full in the neck. His MP5N clattered to the deck as he fell and cried out in pain. Blood spread on the deck from the arterial bleeding.

Rat ducked back behind the steel bulkhead until the shooting died down. The other SEALs waited with him. He spoke to them over their radios, then attacked. They dashed into the room firing and spread out. They aimed with precision, hitting with each shot. Bullets flew between the two sides fifteen feet apart ricocheting off the steel flooring, bulkheads, and into the insulated overhead as men fell on both sides. Two SEALs lay on the deck, and four of Duar's men. He saw one man jump and run out of the mess hall through a hatch in the back. Rat recognized him instantly. It was Duar. The SEALs increased their fire. They were accustomed to it and practiced shooting every day. They could hit a playing card with a five-round grouping of bullets from twenty-five yards every time. Their fire was deadly. Duar's two remaining men fell, and the deafening echoing banging of automatic weapons died down. The pungent smell of gunpowder was everywhere. Rat jumped over two dead men and ran after Duar.

He threw open a door, jumped back from the entrance, waited one second, then ran through the door. He saw Duar at the end of the long passageway just about to turn and head inboard. "You're not going anywhere!" Rat yelled in Arabic. He stopped and fired at Duar's legs, remembering Tick's order to take him alive. Two bullets tore into Duar's calf. He fell to the deck screaming. Rat stopped firing and ran to where Duar lay. He spoke to him loudly in Arabic, "How do we stop the ship?"

Duar looked at him, but did not respond.

"Where is the transmitter to detonate the explosives?"

Duar looked at him with contempt, satisfaction.

"Where is it?" Rat insisted, as he reached back with his fist in a tight ball as if he was about to punch Duar.

"You can do nothing," Duar hissed.

Rat let his fist fly and punched Duar in the ear. His head snapped to the side. "Where is it?"

"You will never stop this ship!" Duar said triumphantly.

Rat felt the white anger returning. He felt it consuming his being. He wanted to choke Duar to death and watch the life drain from his eyes. He tossed his weapon to Banger.

"Where are the Japanese crewmen?" he asked as he pulled a pair of needle nose pliers out of his vest.

Duar didn't respond.

"You're going to lead us to them."

Still nothing.

The situation was dire. Rat looked at his watch. He could feel the deck of the ship vibrating from the maximum speed it was making. He knew he had little chance of getting the Japanese hostages off the ship. He also knew he had little chance of preventing the explosion. All he could do was minimize the damage. "I'm going to ask you this once, and only once. Where are the radioactive cores?"

Duar grimaced, but acted confused, as if he didn't know what Rat was talking about.

Rat had taken the pliers out to squeeze the knuckles of Duar's fingers one by one, to shatter them into so much bone dust and watch him go pale in pain and fear, to feel what he had done to so many others. If Duar stayed on the ship and died in the explosion no one would know what had happened . . .

Rat took a thin steel cable and plastic tie handcuffs out of his vest. He bound Duar's hands together behind his back, and ran the steel cable through the handcuffs. He threaded the cable through the handle on the hatch, and held the ends together, as if he was about to crimp them together, forever tying Duar to the ship.

"Where are they?" Rat demanded through gritted teeth. He moved the pliers to Duar's middle finger and began to squeeze. "Where?"

Duar said nothing.

Rat looked at Duar's bleeding leg. He changed his mind "You might bleed to death. You need to get that bullet out. Let me help you."

Rat took the pliers and stuck the pointed ends into the oozing wound on Duar's calf. Duar screamed out as Rat opened the mouth of the pliers and probed for the bullet. "Let me see if I can find . . . that . . . bullet for you . . ."

"Stop!" Duar cried. "Stop!"

"I know this hurts, but it's for your own good," Rat replied. "I had some corpsman training. I saw a video where they took a bullet out of a guy. I think I can do it. Where are those *cores*?" he yelled as he drove the points of the needle nose pliers deeper into Duar's leg, probing, grabbing.

"Ohhhggaaggh," Duar said as sweat ran down his face. "Main deck," he gasped. "Both sides."

"Let's go," Rat said. "On your feet!"

"I can't walk!"

"Banger, drag this asshole topside. If he gives you any shit just smash him in the face."

"Pleasure," Banger said as he pulled Duar to his feet and began dragging him down the passageway.

Rat put the steel cable and the pliers back into his vest, grabbed his weapon, and ran to the ladder leading to the deck. Rat spoke into his microphone, "Groomer, what you got?"

Rat heard the reply immediately in his headphones. "We're in after steering. Nobody here. The engine controls and the helm are frozen. I think they got underneath the deck plates and locked the cables. We were going to get under the deck, but the whole place is rigged with C4. If we touch anything, we're all going to go up. We're willing . . ."

"You think that would stop the ship?"

"Can't tell—it's possible . . ." Groomer said, understanding the implications.

"Forget it. The radioactive cores are up on the deck. If this ship goes up we can't let it send radioactivity with it. You start aft, we'll start forward. Find them and chuck them over the side. Divers can get them later, but we can't let them go up with the ship."

"We're on our way."

Rat dashed up one ladder after another, breathing heavily. The other SEALs were right behind him. Banger dragged Duar, who was crying out from pain. He begged Banger to stop. Banger threw him over his shoulder like a sack of grain and carried him up the ladders, not caring that his bleeding leg was smacking against the railings and bulkheads.

As Rat broke into the daylight he switched his transmitter to UHF. "Kujo, you up?" he asked, speaking directly to the Pave Low pilot.

"Kujo's up. That you, Rat?"

Rat looked at the *Eisenhower*. It was less than a thousand yards away. "We need to get out of here. Prepare for SPIE Rig extraction."

"Same place we dropped you off?"

"Affirmative."

Rat dashed forward to the bow of the ship. On his way he looked for anything out of place. He quickly spotted the sinister metal containers, the radioactive cores. They were taped to the deck with ordinary duct tape. He ran past several of them as he went forward, pointing them out to the SEALs behind him. They broke up and kneeled near each one individually. Rat ran to the bow, pulled out his switchblade, pressed the blade into service, and cut the tape on the core closest to the bow. He quickly tossed it over the side and watched it splash into the sea as the *Galli Maru* raced toward the nuclear-powered *Eisenhower* at twenty knots. The carrier looked huge in front of them, its flight deck much higher than the deck on which Rat stood.

Rat turned to run back to the next container on the port side. He stopped. The ship was turning—no, he quickly realized—the *Eisen-*

hower was backing away from pier twelve. A huge rooster tail kicked up behind the carrier as the four enormous propellers dug into the dark water and pulled the massive ship away. He could hear the taut mooring lines snap as the *Eisenhower* broke free. He could see faces of sailors peering over the side of the flight deck as they watched the *Galli Maru* in morbid fascination. Rat looked back and saw the other SEALs throwing their radioactive cylinders over the side. "How many? How many cylinders?"

Each SEAL who had thrown a cylinder over raised his hand. He looked back at the pier, then back at the second cylinder he had been heading for. He ran to it, cut it free, and tossed it as far as he could. He looked up at the carrier. They were going to hit the *Eisenhower*. "Emergency extraction! Everybody to the insertion point!"

The SEALs cut at the cylinders and threw them. They looked madly for more but didn't see any.

"Go!" Rat yelled.

They ran down the deck and up the ladders to the superstructure. The Pave Low hovered over the superstructure as the crew chief kicked the SPIE Rig (Special Purpose Insertion/Extraction) onto the deck. The SEALs rushed to the two large ropes with attachment points and hooked their harnesses up. Using two ropes simultaneously from the same helicopter was only done in an emergency. But everyone involved realized they had to get off on the first extraction—there wouldn't be a second. Banger was on his knees next to a visibly suffering and weakened Duar. Rat crossed to them and looked at Duar with fury. "You're going up with this ship," Rat said to Duar in Arabic as he quickly pulled the cable back out of his vest. He glanced up to make sure the rest of his men were hooked up to the SPIE Rig, ready to go. He looked ahead at the *Eisenhower* as they approached the pier. He ran his cable under Duar's arms. His hands were still bound behind him. As Rat reached down for an anchor point, he suddenly thought better of it. He ran the cable through his harness, grabbed Duar, and picked him up.

The *Eisenhower* was now moving at three or four knots, and was backing quickly away from the pier. They had two hundred yards before impact. He yelled at Banger, "Get hooked up!"

Banger ran to the aft most SPIE rope. Rat was right behind him. He dropped Duar onto the deck, hooked his harness up, and gave the helicopter a thumbs-up. "Let's go! Let's go!"

The helicopter pulled up gently. The SEALs hung underneath, and Duar hung precariously underneath Rat by the steel cable which ran through Rat's harness and under Duar's arms. The pilot pulled up quickly on the collective, increased altitude, and pulled into a hard right climbing turn. The *Eisenhower* had averted immediate disaster by getting out of the way in time to avoid the collision. The *Galli Maru* missed it by fifty feet. The *Eisenhower* continued to back into the bay in full reverse. The news helicopter was torn between filming the *Eisenhower* and the helicopter lifting the SEALs off the deck.

As they spun in the air, Rat watched the liquefied natural gas ship hit the pier in slow motion. The ship stopped dead in its tracks and the enormous pier shuddered under the force. The stern of the *Galli Maru* came out of the water—Rat could see the screws turning in the air, trying to drive the death ship forward. For a moment Rat thought that perhaps Duar had not rigged the ship to explode and they could go back and get the Japanese crew off. But just as the thought formed in his mind, all hell broke loose. The sides split and the top of the ship opened like a soup can with a stick of dynamite inside. Before Rat could hear anything, he saw the shock wave, the concussion spreading out from the ship. The water was driven back from the explosion; the pier was obliterated and threw splinters of wood and pieces of concrete into the sky. The *Eisenhower*, only two hundred feet away now from the explosion, was thrown back, and its bow caved in.

He could see the force spreading over the ground toward the Norfolk Naval Base and the city of Norfolk in a second. The shock wave spread far faster than its sound. It slammed into the helicopter. He felt as if he had been dropped into the top of a hurricane.

They were battered around and banged into each other as the helicopter fought to stay airborne. It pitched over and headed toward the water as the turbulent air ripped the lift out of the helicopter's blades. The SEALs bounced up against the bottom of the helicopter and down again as the unstable air thrashed them around the sky. Rat looked down and saw the cable cutting into the underarms of Duar. One of his shoulders looked like it had been ripped out of its socket.

The pilot fought to maintain control as the helicopter plummeted. The SEALs were jerked back down as the helicopter regained some lift. The pilot had the collective in the full up position demanding maximum lift from the blades and the jet engines. The engines whined as the blades beat the air down trying to keep the heavy helicopter from crashing into the water. The news helicopter, which had filmed everything including the explosion, was thrown upside down and smashed into the bay.

There was nothing left of the *Galli Maru*. It had vanished, a victim of the BLEVE, the Boiling Liquid Expanding Vapor Explosion Rat and the others had dreaded. As the force of the explosion reached the city of Norfolk, Rat watched the glass from the distant windows being blown out of taller buildings. Cars were thrown over on their sides. At the Navy base, the ships that had been unable to get under way were being hurled around and smashed into the piers to which they were moored. The water in the Chesapeake looked like it was in the middle of a storm.

The shock wave passed the helicopter. The Pave Low climbed and pulled away to the northeast. As they hung freely in the air, Rat looked at the massive destruction beneath him, the ships and boats fighting the chaotic water, and the Navy ships struggling to free themselves from their piers.

Rat was angry that they had not been able to stop the ship. They simply hadn't had enough time. How many had died? How many people had had their lives ruined?

He reached inside his vest and pulled out his pliers. He looked down at Duar dangling below him. Duar was either unconscious, or was staring at the water, dreading his future. Rat slipped cable into the wire-cutting teeth of the pliers, and started to squeeze. He found his anger building again, taking over. The last thing the United States needed was a circus trial with the world's most wanted terrorist. The tribunal had turned into a fiasco, and since Duar had been captured on U.S. territory, they might not get another tribunal. He'd probably end up in federal court, where Rat himself was returning. It would be obscene.

He squeezed harder on the pliers, yearning to cut Duar loose, to watch him fall to the bay a thousand feet below. Wait, he thought. He pulled his pliers back. He switched his transmitter to UHF. "Kujo, you up?" he said to the pilot fifty feet away.

"Go ahead, Rat."

"We lost two men on the ship. All the hostages and terrorists were on board when it went up," he said transmitting in the clear, so anyone listening would be sure Duar was dead. "At least we think the hostages were. We never saw them."

Kujo paused. "You didn't get any of them off?"

"Nope. Just us. Ten of us."

The other SEALs looked at Rat, confused. Then they got it. They nodded and smiled.

"Why don't you take us to Langley?"

"Wilco," Kujo said.

"And maybe you can call my bosses so they can meet us there."

"Roger that. Understood." He understood completely. Rat's bosses were the CIA. He wanted his friends from the Agency to meet him at Langley to quietly take Duar off their hands.

♦ ♦ ♦

Those in the situation room in the White House sat back, partly out of relief, and partly out of anger. The ship had made it into the Chesapeake and had plowed into the carrier pier at Norfolk Naval Base. Several ships had been damaged, a few badly, but thankfully none had been sunk. The *Eisenhower*, apparently part of the target along with the city of Norfolk, a city of 350,000, not to mention Hampton Roads, Newport News, Virginia Beach, and the Chesapeake Bay, had been damaged but not seriously.

President Kendrick stared at the map and the images on CNN that continued to be repeated up to the moment when the news helicopter pitched over into the bay. "Not good at all," he finally said. "Any indication of radiation?" he asked of no one in particular.

Stuntz replied, "No, sir. The nuclear officers on the *Eisenhower* have been checking carefully. They have very sensitive instruments in case of their own nuclear problem. They're not detecting any radiation at all."

Kendrick nodded. "Could have been a hell of a lot worse. How many people killed?"

St. James looked at a message she had been handed. "Very preliminary, sir, but it looks like twenty-three so far, not counting the Japanese crew. Looks to me like Lieutenant Rathman did a fabulous job, considering."

Stuntz replied, "He didn't stop the ship, he didn't get the Japanese hostages off, he didn't divert the ship, he allowed it to blow up inside of one of our major cities and the largest Navy base in the world."

"Considering we gave him about four hours' notice I think he did admirably. In fact," she said, looking at the President, "I think we owe it to him to stop the trial. I can't even imagine what the *Washington Post* would do with the story of a Navy counterterrorism hero convicted for manslaughter of a terrorist, the very one who worked for the man who just blew up Norfolk Naval Base. How do you think that will sound?"

"Who cares how it sounds? We can't just stop a trial."

"Why not?" She turned to the Attorney General. "Can't we just ask the U.S. Attorney to dismiss the charges?"

The Attorney General shook his head. "If we do that without some new evidence it would look like we were just pandering."

"Mr. President? What do you think?" she asked, watching Kendrick's expression.

"The trial will take care of itself. Now if you'll excuse me, like you, I've been up all night. I'm going to go prepare a statement to the press, catch about twenty minutes of sleep, and go tell everyone how great we are."

Chapter
28

The courtroom was jammed with reporters and spectators. They had started lining up the night before. The press was in a frenzy with coverage of the explosion near Norfolk, and when they realized the man who had averted the disaster was the same one on trial they were beside themselves. Full-page coverage, photographs, special articles on Special Forces, diagrams of SPIE Rigs, continuing coverage of the Navy divers who were searching the bay for the Russian radioactive cores, and pictures taken from the exhaustive coverage of the media helicopter were everywhere. The print journalists had fought for the passes to the front two rows of the gallery for Monday morning, when the jury was expected to come back with a verdict on Lieutenant Kent Rathman.

The jury didn't let them down. After one hour of deliberation on Monday morning they announced to the bailiff that they had reached a verdict.

Judge Royce Wiggins brought the courtroom to order and the jury was called in. Rat and the others stood. He had a dressing on his forearm where the bullet had grazed him aboard the *Galli Maru*. He wanted to be outside the building, even outside D.C. when the verdict came in, so he could get his athletic bag and head to the airport if necessary. But Skyles told him he had to be there. He'd have to wait and be released on bail during the appeal. But Skyles told him that was unlikely. He was trapped.

The clerk stated, "Please be seated. This court is now in session."

The judge looked at the jury. "Have you reached a verdict?"

A frail elderly woman in the front row stood up. "We have, Your Honor."

The bailiff collected the verdict from her and handed it to the clerk, who handed it to the judge. With a completely unexpressive face, the judge looked at the verdict to make sure it was in order, refolded it, and handed it to the clerk. "Please read the verdict," he said to the clerk.

"In the case of *United States versus Kent Rathman,* for the charge of manslaughter, we the jury find the defendant . . . not guilty."

The gallery erupted.

Wiggins frowned and banged his gavel. "This court is adjourned," he said.

Skyles turned with a big grin on his face and shook Rat's hand. "I told you. I told you we'd get you off!"

The relief washed over Rat as he nodded at Skyles. "Can I go?"

"You sure can. You're a free man."

"I'll be in touch," Rat said as he walked out of the courtroom without looking back or acknowledging the calls of the journalists. As he pushed through the enormous steel door to the hallway, he looked for Andrea and saw her immediately. She ran to him with her eyes full of questions and doubts. "What happened?"

"Not guilty."

"Thank God," she said, taking a deep breath. "I'm so glad. I'm glad the jury did the right thing."

They walked quickly to the elevator as several sailors from Dev Group blocked the path of anyone who was considering following them. They stepped into the elevator and the doors closed. Rat looked at her. "You think maybe the article in the Sunday newspaper may have been a factor? Rat this, and Rat that. Big hero, saved Norfolk from radiation, risked his life, the whole thing."

"What are you saying?"

"Our names don't get put in newspapers, Andrea. Somebody planted the story. Somebody who wanted the jury to read it."

"Who would do that? Who would have the power to do that?"

"I don't know. Wish I did." He held the elevator door for her and they stepped out into the lobby then walked out into the Washington sunshine.

She said, "The article said Duar was killed in a gun battle on the ship so you left him on board." She thought about what Duar had done. "I'm not sad to see him dead. What a horrible person."

Rat walked along silently.

She read something in his silence. "He is dead, isn't he?"

"No, I secretly dragged him off the ship and pulled him out on the SPIE Rig with us. Just us SEALs and our good friend Wahamed Duar. In fact I carried him off myself. Rigged a special steel cable so he could come with us. He's probably all showered and clean now, smoking a cigarette somewhere."

She laughed. "I'm still glad he's dead."

Rat put his arm around her. They walked for half a block, away from the buzz that was forming behind them at the courthouse, and stopped on the curb. He looked at her. "I need some time off."

She nodded, not sure what he meant.

"What do you say we go to the Virgin Islands? You have a scuba certificate?"

"No. But I've always wanted to."

"I'll teach you."

"I'd like that," she replied as he stepped into the street to hail a cab.

ACKNOWLEDGMENTS

I received tremendous assistance from several people in the preparation of this book. I'd like to thank my good friend Robert Conrad, the United States Attorney for Charlotte, North Carolina, for his help and guidance. Likewise, John Wallace, the Special Assistant to the Attorney General, helped me through the maze of international human rights law and the Geneva Convention. His experience in military law and prosecuting U.S. forces was invaluable.

I would also like to thank my good friend Don Chartrand, whose insight and advice was, as always, invaluable.